Other Books By Daniel Peterson

Short novels
King of Shards
Free Body Diagram

The SUNWARD ROAD

by

Daniel Peterson

Fourth Edition (printed 2013)

This book can be purchased, rated or reviewed at www.lulu.com .

Edited telepathically by Mary Foster.

ISBN: 978-0-9854957-2-5

To my patient Wife.

The SUNWARD ROAD

PROLOGUE

Human colonization had been spreading through the Milky Way galaxy for ten thousand years and Homo sapiens still occupied a ball of space only about one hundred light years across. A disappointingly small percentage of the approximately five hundred "G" type stars in this volume possessed habitable planets. Most colonists could see Sol in their night sky and knew it to be the home sun. But one planet, settled five millennia ago, had no night. The revolution of this planet around its star and the rotation on its axis had the same period. One face of the planet saw the sun perpetually--the other side, never. This left the descendants of the colonists, limited to occupying the sunny side, in the peculiar position of having no first-hand knowledge of other stars. In time, the static nature of this world lulled the people into forgetting their origin and losing the technology of   a   space-faring   species.

PART I

Chapter 1

The peak of the ice-covered mountain exploded and shot steam five kilometers into the dark, frigid air. Sunlight from beyond the horizon lit the dense mist of the cloud's roiling top a brilliant white. Nothing lived in this twilight land that lay beyond the snow barbarian's domain.

Chapter 2

Tane loved hunting though he wasn't old enough to be accepted as a hunter. His twenty fifth tooth hadn't erupted, and he was expected to be performing odious tasks like rendering animal fat for fuel and food.

He thought there was only one good thing about having no father: freedom. Getting around his mother was easy. The men of the village, Kendee, had enough to do controlling their own sons and just surviving. Living came hard in this sparse, snowbound land. Naturally, when he sneaked off to hunt big-foot rabbits, nobody growled much if he brought back an animal or two. His mother would complain about respect for her and his duty at home, but rabbit stew calmed her.

He had carved his own throwing club from the dried jaw of a cow taken long ago in a raid on the herders to sunward. He never practiced throwing at stationary targets, assuming that if he intended to hunt rabbits he should hunt rabbits. He learned early that it takes a long time and lots of digging to find the valuable weapon if thrown into fresh, powder snow (it turned unpredictably after entering and always went further than expected). Crusted, old snow made the best stop. His hunting was dismal for a long, long time, but eventually the throw became habit. Now he was as skilled as any man but not allowed the chance to prove it.

Tane crawled quietly out of the snow-covered stick hut before his mother awoke. He wandered toward the rendering pot to placate a couple of watching hunters. Kendee was large for a snow village but it was no trick to be out of it and gone before anybody could collar him.

He was thin, leaner even than the other scrawny village boys. He possessed a pug nose, to his mother's delight but not his-- apparently his maternal grandmother had passed this to him--and a natural mischief sparkled his gray-green eyes. His hair was the standard white. As he matured it would darken to light brown, then fade again to gray when or if, in this harsh land, he grew old. Small freckles sparsely banded the bridge of his nose and upper cheeks.

"I'll get to the pot later," he mumbled, weaving between quiet huts. "We need meat."

He loved the hunting and everything about hunting. He liked the quiet squeak of snow underfoot, the patterns of shadow cast by slender needle-leaf bushes, the ghostly vapor of his breath, the squinting search for the tell-tale dark spot of a rabbit's eye against a background of white fur and snow. He enjoyed the stark beauty of his world. His solitary stalk gave him a feeling of freedom and power. He was alone in the world and on the prowl for food, as wily and dangerous as any carnivore that trod the snow.

The harsh world he occupied seemed perfectly ordinary to him, so his imagination furnished a more adventuresome place. He pretended he was the last survivor of world plague, living by his wits and ability. He would search for companions, taking his living where he found it, but, oh, the loneliness. He affected a limp and tried to squeeze out a tear. Somewhere, he felt, others must have survived the catastrophe and be living near death, awaiting a salvation named Tane.

He broke from his fantasy, stopped to admire a soaring bird, and a rabbit burst from cover, dashing away antisun. He drew his arm back for the cast but froze as the rabbit leaped a drift and bounded unharmed into the shade beyond. Tane stood, arm back and staring at the white, hoary head rising in the great distance.

This was not an ordinary cloud. It stood alone in the sky, growing straight up out of the land. Real clouds always came from sunward or sunright and passed into the shadowland. Its resemblance to a white-headed giant sent a shiver through Tane, and he remembered those stories.

"The prophecy," he whispered and, whirling, sprinted home.

* * *

Fog hid the slow lava. The molten rock flowed across hard ice, carving small valleys and shaking with steam explosions. The eruption ended, the flow stopped five kilometers from the source, just surrounding a knob of compacted ice and snow. The heat from the rock melted the base of the knob to a slender neck supporting an ill-shaped head. The head, eventually too heavy for the narrowing neck to support, rolled off its perch and crashed to the stone. It broke into large pieces that melted away in rivulets. From one block dark patches emerged that, when finally exposed, did not melt. When the ice was gone a lumpy bundle wrapped in brown fur lay exposed, drying and gently warming.

The hand that shakily reached out to push back the edge of the fur cape was large and calloused, with scarred knuckles. The face that gazed out of the opening suited the hand. It was large, angular, bearded, and marked with its own scars. Piercing black eyes scanned the rubble of ice and stone. The jaw was prominent even beneath the black beard, and when the tongue pushed out to moisten narrow lips his square, spade-like teeth flashed. Gaps in the teeth from old battles, won or lost, punctuated his jaws. The brows bushed and the cheek bones were sharp. Sprigs of raven hair peeked from a domed fur cap.

He lay looking out through the thinning fog, bewildered at the twilight ice-scape and the mist towering above him. He grimaced as he slowly, painfully, carefully straightened his body.

His mind struggled to capture a coherent thought from mental turmoil. When he was able to raise himself and stand without weaving, the sight of water sluicing over the steaming rock brought his thirst to the fore. He tottered to the edge of the lava field and knelt to drink from a temporary brook.

He stood to his height of nearly two meters, closed his fur cape more tightly, looked again at the desolate land and croaked, "I am Eskander. My name is Eskander." He paused. "But who is Eskander, and where is he?"

Eskander worked to purge his mind of the inner turmoil and the outward distractions, willing himself to think. He knew his name. He felt the familiarity of his core self, but he remembered nothing of what made him that, nor what brought him here, wherever here was. "I am Eskander," he repeated, and shook his head slowly as if to rearrange the thoughts inside.

He felt around in his cape until he found a water bag. He poured out the remnants, rinsed and refilled it in the stream. For a long time he looked around, puzzled, and drank from his bag.

A complete survey under his cape discovered chest armor, fur clothing, a double-edged sword, an ornamental dagger and, best, a kilogram bag of a mixture of fat, cracked grains and jerked meat. The fur cap covered a practical bronze helmet filigreed in delicate silver.

"And I'll die here," he said, "If I don't move."

He filled his water bag again, corked it tightly and stowed it under the cape. The reddish, lighter sky to sunward beckoned.

His first long step carried him across the brook to thaw slicked ice. He slipped and nearly fell into the stream. "If I believed in omens..." he murmured, and touched his chest over his heart with his right fingertips. The second step took him to dry, hard ice, and for three more weak strides his damp boot soles crackled.

* * *

Tane found the people already in an uproar. A crowd gathered at the shaman's hut. Hunters straggled in from the field. Tane ran to his mother's hut but didn't find her there. He ran to the chief's lodge and met another crowd, including his mother, jostling along with the chief toward the shaman's.

Grimm, the chief, was a big man by his people's terms. Though only slightly taller than average, he was much broader than most other men. His face, when not irate as now, appeared avuncular with a bulbous nose and laughing eyes. Not brilliant, he still possessed a practical wisdom, an ability to charm and a talent for governing. These lay submerged for the moment in his also natural impatience.

Gossipers, fools, and whiners, he thought. He glanced over at the cloud poking its head above the horizon. Not that it isn't worrisome, but can't they just shut up and wait till I know something?

He shouted over their questions, "It's stupid. Stupid! How can you say this cloud is the sign of the prophecy? It takes too much imagination to see a Frost Giant in a cloud that looks like a cow, or a rabbit, or," he looked over his shoulder, "a fat woman. Speaking of fat women," he added as he raised his arms and pivoted around, "don't you all have something else to do?"

"We want to know what the shaman has to say about this," Saper, one of Kendee's best hunters, shouted.

Tane's mother, Lentie, typically quiet and meek, surprised them by blurting, "I just had a dream about the Frost Giant. He spoke in a voice like groaning ice and said ..."

"Superstition!" yelled the chief. "Let's see what a man of wisdom says before we start rumors. Are you a prophet?"

Lentie was the matured, feminine version of Tane's forming features. She owned the pug nose, though not to his degree, and even at her age still showed a dapple of freckles across it. The gray eyes, when unguarded, still whispered mischief, but said out loud, *sorrow* and *pain* and *duty*. Her hair had never darkened and so remained an almost pearlescent white. The heavy furs hid a compact and shapely, flesh-and-blood woman.

"Let her talk," Saper said and the crowd grumbled their agreement.

The chief stopped. "Well, Lentie, let's have it. What did the Frost Giant say? You're using too much salt in your rabbit stew? You're not scraping all the tallow off your hides? Anything so practical?"

Lentie cast her eyes down and froze. A very round woman approached him from behind and hit the chief in the kidney hard enough to make him gasp. She said, "Grimm, you be nice to her!"

The chief, recognizing his wife Darla's snarl, and fist, turned back with a shrug to Lentie and said more calmly, "All right, I'm sorry. What is it?"

"Well," she said, glancing at Darla for support. The chief's wife smiled so she continued. "He said, 'Hot bronze will break cold ice. Love your son.'"

The chief paused and his face first went slack with thought, then tightened in anger. "Huf love us," he shouted. "What does that mean?"

"Let's ask the man of wisdom!" Lentie yelled back, red faced, then turned and struggled away through the crowd.

"Gargh!" the chief growled, continuing toward the shaman's. The crowd flowed with him.

"That was great, Mother," Tane said as he popped up next to Lentie.

"And where have you been, lazy?" She snapped.

"I was at the pots."

"Don't lie to me. I went there. Buna saw you leave. And don't give me that rabbit stew talk! I don't see any rabbit."

"But we need the meat, Mother! So I was hunting and I saw

the Giant's head."

Lentie stopped and glared at him, softened her face, stroked his cheek and said, "I wish your father was alive." They turned together to follow the crowd.

At the shaman's hut the villagers made a continuous rumbling, discussing the cloud, the prophecy and their frustration with an unresponsive magician. They hushed and parted as the chief approached.

"What's the shaman say?" he asked Plint.

"Nothing. When he heard about the giant's head, he came out, stared at it, then ducked back into his hut. He's ignoring us."

The chief bent near the hut door. "Ryne, it's me, Grimm. Let me in."

The hide curtains swayed as the ties were undone. Gnarled fingers slipped through to pull one aside. They beckoned the chief in. Grimm ducked through the door but, before anyone else could enter, the shaman pulled the covers tight.

Ryne's hut had never appealed to Grimm. In any other home the dark corners left unlit by the lamp were cozy nooks. These were sinister. The tools of a shaman's trade are grisly and disgusting. The magician had arranged some foul items around the lamp and the heat made them exude almost visible fumes. The reek of the shaman's occupation, coupled with the typically unclean smells of bachelorhood, could stun if not kill. It was hard to imagine how anyone could stomach eating a meal here, and no wonder the women shunned Ryne. Grimm suspected that such a life was why the shaman's flesh looked as thin and stringy as a strip of jerky.

Because Grimm considered the shaman his closest friend, he never hinted at his feelings about the man's home. He also did not let on that frequently his friend baffled him. The condition of the hut meant a colossal indifference to others' opinions, yet the shaman's stock-in-trade was an understanding of not just the god's and spirits, but also of human nature. It did not make sense.

Grimm watched the lean, nervous man retie the door flaps

and made an effort to ignore his own nose.

"Ryne," the chief said, "How are you?"

"Well. But very busy."

"I would leave you to your work, but we have to talk. The People are worried."

"Let them worry, let them wait." Ryne shuffled close to the lamp. The yellow light carved ghastly shadows in his narrow, lined face. He turned to Grimm. "Maybe they could learn some respect. They yammer out there like dogs on a rabbit trail."

"They get scared and forget the amenities. But they do respect you, and your powers. That's why they're here."

"No, it's just like you said, they're scared. If they are content, they never come. It's only when fear barks at their heels, then they come to the shaman. Of course," he shrugged, "where else would they go?"

"You're the only one that can explain this cloud or Frost Giant or whatever it is." Grimm paused. "So, what is it?"

"That's another reason I make them wait."

He mumbled the next and Grimm asked, "What?"

"I'm just not sure!" Ryne spat in irritation. "I'm not sure what is rising out of the dark land! And you can't face the people with doubts or they lose faith. True Power comes from only four sources--the ancestors, the animal spirits, human faith, and Huf. Our god, Huf, and the spirits are more potent than human faith, but faith can alter the balance. Very complicated and uncertain."

"So," Grimm asked, "what *can* you tell me?"

"Not much. I drew an augury," he gestured toward the mess around the lamp, "that says Huf is active. I haven't had time to take Passage Beyond to ask the spirits. So, for now, all I have is the prophecy itself. And it is not specific.

"As you know, it says: 'When the Frost Giant is seen in Kendee the Bronze Man will come from beyond the sun to lead the People of Snow to conquest under high sun.'

Ryne paused with a frown and idly patted the back of his

right hand in the palm of his left. "That isn't much," he said. "What does a frost giant look like? That cloud looks a little like a bearded head, but is it a frost giant? We believe the phrase 'beyond the sun' means the shadow world to antisun, but considering the man is bronze, a sun color, maybe he comes from behind the sun. Anyway, the word is 'man' not 'god', and a man can't live in either place!"

Ryne delved into his lecture and paced the little room, picking up a long bone to gesture. He had not seen Grimm flinch at the reference to bronze.

"With what we know," the shaman continued, "and since magic is not exact, we should tell them the cloud is nothing. Which is probable. I'll journey Beyond to ask the spirits, but they don't always cooperate. We must rely on the third power: faith. If you and I agree, the village will believe us, and that's what counts."

Grimm cleared his throat. Ryne stopped pacing.

"Yes?" he said.

"Nothing. Well, maybe one more thing."

"What?"

"Lentie had a dream."

"Ah," Ryne sighed meaningfully. He nodded his head, scowled, and pawed his thin beard in thought.

"So?" Grimm prompted.

"Lentie's great-grandmother and my great-grandmother were the same person."

"Oh?"

"My great-grandmother was a seer."

"Oh."

"Yes." Ryne nodded. "What was the dream?"

The chief stared thoughtfully into a corner. His eyes focused on a crawling maggot so he faced Ryne. "The Frost Giant appeared and said something about bronze."

"What about bronze?"

"I don't remember. I was angry."

Ryne considered. "Maybe she got the bronze from the prophecy. Or it could be real foresight. I have to know what the Giant said."

"She's outside. Ask her."

"No. Let's think. How do we manage this?" He pursed his lips and gazed at the lamp flame. "That 'conquest' part of the prophecy sounds good, but *war*, by Huf! Wars are such a waste!"

He turned about. He shifted from foot to foot. He rubbed his right eyebrow with a forefinger. "If we say the cloud is the Frost Giant and no Bronze Man shows up, we'll be run out of Kendee. If we say it's fairy tales and a bronze man does come it's the same. Oldsters who hear Lentie's dream will remember great-grandma. Fool's tongues will grow speculation on rumor, and it will get out of hand."

He laced his fingers behind his back to resume pacing. The chief patiently watched the shaman at work. Ryne stopped and faced Grimm.

"This is serious, but it calls for a simple strategy. We'll hear Lentie's dream and vouch for it, then give them the line about Huf testing our worth. The prophecy is on the brink of coming true but won't unless everybody starts praying and leading a spiritual life. I wager the chief and the shaman are due some holy gratuities. Everybody will feel better whether the bronze man appears or not."

Grimm said grudgingly, "It'll work. But I'm still nervous about a war. What do you really think is happening?"

"Like I said, I have to hear Lentie's dream, but I doubt there's anything to it. Huf is a comfortable god. We're born, and age, and die, but the world doesn't change. Believing the Snow People will go to war would be like expecting to see the sun wander off across the sky."

Outside, Tane had tried to work his way to the front of the mob, but they were tightly packed and not yielding. He returned to his mother on the fringe.

Lentie smiled at her son and rested her hand on his shoulder. He was more than a handful without a husband. He was a good boy, wanted to be a good son, but he was excitable. It wasn't easy for him to stay out of trouble. Now she knew that whatever was happening she would not be able to keep Tane out of it, especially with the warning of her dream. All she could do was hope that Huf and the spirits would protect him.

Tane and his mother knew when the chief and shaman left the hut by the shouted questions followed by a wave of silence. Then Lentie stiffened and goosebumps crawled up her arms as the chief called, "Is Lentie still here?"

She considered whether it was best to run or stay and hope they didn't see her. The decision was made when Tane jogged her elbow and said, "Go on, Mother."

Beside them a man raised his arm to get the chief's attention. "She's here," he called.

"Send her up," Grimm said.

The people shifted to make way ahead of Lentie and Tane, who tugged her forward by the hand, and closed again behind them. Among the watchers Lentie's stricken look raised smiles, some of amusement, some of empathy.

At the hut, the chief and the shaman stood facing the people. Closest to them were the highest ranking villagers, respected hunters and the members of the elder council. Lentie became more distressed in their presence. The chief's wife, Darla, put her chunky arm around Lentie's shoulder and reassured her. "Don't worry, dear. You're fine. I'm with you."

Grimm smiled, leaned close and murmured, "I'm sorry about before, Lentie." He raised his voice. "The shaman told me that he and you are cousins. That the grandmother you share was a seer. He thinks maybe the dream you had will help explain things."

Lentie smiled and Darla gave her shoulder a squeeze.

Ryne said, "Could you tell me your dream?"

"Well," she hesitated, "there wasn't much."

"Fine. Tell us what there was."

"The Frost Giant..."

"What did he look like?"

Lentie became pensive, then said, "He was as tall as three men and naked." She blushed. "But he was covered in long white hair from head to toe. Every hair was jagged with hoarfrost. His nose was flat and wide, and pink. His eyes were silver and sparkled like an icicle."

"Ah," Ryne said.

She looked at him and he nodded encouragement.

"I was gathering sticks antisun from the village. It was all so clear and real. It was cold and the sky was pink with low clouds. I heard a crackling, and squeaking snow. When I looked up the frost giant stepped onto a ridge about ten meters away. He stopped and looked at me. Sparkling frost drifted off his hair. He was so white it was like he had light inside him. In fact he lit the shadows and bleached some of the pink out of the clouds. My knees wouldn't hold me and I fell. I covered my head. I expected him to grab me, but he just stood there."

Ryne frowned.

"When nothing happened I raised my head. He saw me look up and pointed behind him at a copper glow on the horizon. Then his mouth cracked open and said, 'Hot bronze will break cold ice. Love your son.' I hid my head and closed my eyes so tight that I saw blue lights. Then I woke up in my sleeping furs. The lamp was out and the hut was cold, but I was sweating. That's all."

For five heartbeats there was silence, then a woman said, "Huf protect us," and touched her heart.

A sudden babble covered what Ryne said to the chief. What the chief heard was, "Grimm, it sounds real." Grimm looked into the shaman's eyes and felt fear. He had an overlying vision of his people fighting and dying under an alien sun while a horrible, choking dust blew into the sky, turning it a sickly gray. The fear showed on his face. Ryne nodded.

"Quiet," the chief shouted, and raised his arm. The noise dropped. When everyone was looking forward he said, "Let's hear what Ryne says."

Eyes shifted to the shaman. He lifted his head, paused, cleared his throat and said, "Lentie's dream seems genuine..."

Somebody in back yelled, "Speak up!"

Ryne raised his voice, "I said, Lentie's dream is genuine. And it answers one of the questions about the prophecy. The frost giant pointed back to the land without sun, to a copper glow. That glow means the bronze man, and he comes from antisun. What 'Hot bronze will break cold ice' means, I'm not sure, but I don't like the sound of it. 'Love your son' is obviously directed at Lentie. I fear for the boy.

"We know the prophecy promises conquest, but I cast an augury which says we have to be worthy. We must be righteous. We must love Huf. We must live a clean life, and provide more goods as sacrifice to Huf. The augury says if this isn't done the prophecy will not come in our time."

Foss, head elder, asked "If we do this, when will the prophecy begin to bear out?"

The shaman glanced at the cloud dominating the antisun sky. "Soon," he said, and thought to himself, I fear.

"Now, everybody get on with your business. You won't hurry it by standing here. Go home.

"And thank you, Lentie. You've helped."

The crowd dispersed. Some people started forward to talk with Ryne, but he said to the chief, "Grimm, come into my hut."

Grimm looked at the hut, carefully keeping a neutral face. "Actually," he said, "I was thinking of asking you to share a drink in my hut. Maybe have dinner so we can talk."

Ryne nodded acceptance. Before the stragglers could surround them they left in conversation.

Lentie and Tane, the boy glowing with pride, strolled home.

"Isn't this great, Mother? Just think, a Bronze Man, and war! We'll be rich. I could have a bronze throwing club and you could have metal pots."

"Don't be silly, Tane. You're a boy and I'm a woman. If there's a war we won't see it. We'll be right here doing what we always do except life will be harder because the men will be gone. One thing will be different, though, you'll be a hunter. We'll need all the hunters we can get."

"That's right! Isn't this great?"

She did not remind him of her dream or Ryne's comment: 'I fear for the boy'. Fatherless and willful, Tane would be even harder to control in the coming upheaval.

As they neared their hut Boda, a hunter who had been too far afield to be at the meeting, caught up with them. Tane frowned. Boda was nice enough, though not a good hunter which lost him Tane's esteem. He had become a suitor to Lentie after her husband died. Tane particularly objected to this, since he did not need help providing for his mother. Boda was also ugly. His teeth came in crooked and he was wall-eyed. The unusual breadth of his face made it appear short and frog-like, though no one in Kendee had seen a frog to make this comparison. Behind his back they called him Gwatch, which was their name for an owl that lived in the snow lands. Obviously the man was wooing a widow with a son because the younger, unattached females shunned him. As for Lentie, she liked him well enough, but felt he suffered by comparison with Tane's father who had been the catch of the village when they wed, and a good hunter. Despite her doubts about Boda she knew the realities of trying to live husbandless and couldn't bring herself to push him away hoping for a better match. She did not encourage his advances but did not reject them. If Tane knew how his own behavior drove his mother closer to marrying Boda, he might have been a calmer boy.

To Boda, Lentie was not just a convenient suit. He was ugly and a poor hunter, but he was not stupid. Other bachelors saw the responsibility of raising another man's son when they thought of courting Lentie. They saw a woman without dowry. And who was to say that it wasn't marriage to Lentie that had been the death of her first husband? Of course they all knew it was a freak accident (he'd slipped, broken his spear, fallen and impaled himself on the splintered shaft), but what if she's a jinx? Boda had heard all that. When he looked at Lentie he saw a pretty woman barely marked by raising a rowdy boy alone, a woman of proved strength and character. He'd seen men take a beautiful, young wife with great hopes only to find she couldn't bear healthy children, or wouldn't work to make a suitable wife and mother. He was also aware of how both Lentie and Tane felt about him. He liked Tane despite the resentment, and respected the boy's energy. He was sure that adopting him would be an interesting challenge. Also he felt that Lentie's resistance would vanish if he persisted. If she married him only as a provider and a father for her son, eventually she would learn to love him as he already loved her.

He approached them smiling and held out a weasel to Lentie. Lentie's thanks was more than worth Tane's remark, "I see you were *lucky*. And only a weasel." Weasel meat was tough and bitter, but they had a delicate pelt and were not easy to get.

"How many weasels have you killed?" Boda asked.

"Hundreds, maybe thousands."

Boda laughed.

Tane frowned harder.

Boda gestured at the white cloud, "Has the shaman been told about that?"

"Come in the hut," she said, "I'll tell you what happened."

Chapter 3

Eskander had time to wonder and time to begin remembering. He had a whole life time, that is from the moment he awakened till the instant he expected to keel over from starvation and freeze to death.

When he had walked away from the lava flow toward the hazy sky-glow, his mind remained blank. For the first three kilometers he was occupied with the pain in his legs as he worked out the stiffness, and with keeping his footing. The pain eased, his stride lengthened, and he began to see images. His mind's eye saw buildings stirring with the people that run a nation. It saw markets massed with bargainers elbowing their way among awning covered stalls. It saw thousands of armored men marching over dusty plains, dwarfed by their war machines. And it saw faces.

"Who are you?" he asked.

The faces remained unnamed, but he felt sharp emotions with each one. The woman with long, black hair and exotic eyes brought desire and anger. The short, wiry old man with gray stubble and sparkling eye brought warm humor and respect. He was immobilized when he remembered the man with the black eyes and square jaw. That face lingered while hate welled up. He clenched his fists, willing these memories to expand, but nothing came.

"I know you, bastard." he said to the last. "I'll remember."

Eskander shook his head, relaxed and continued walking. It would come eventually. It would all come. Meanwhile, if he didn't keep moving, there would be no point in remembering.

He left the foothills of the torn mountain behind and started across a wide plain. The surface was a landscape of miniature, wind eroded ice peaks linked by drift ridges. The easiest walking lay between the drifts, but occasionally he had to force a path through one. The thin, frozen crust would almost support him then collapse, making every step a costly one.

Distance in the wasteland was marked only by the slowly brightening sky and his need to drink or eat. He pulled out his meager supplies each time he stopped and ate the least required. He also pulled out his memories, trying to give them substance.

His boots crunched. They and his puffing breaths were the only sounds. Their solitary rhythms magnified the impact of the surrounding emptiness.

"Too far," he muttered. "Too cold. I'll never make it."

"But look at the bright side. Nobody can hear me talking to myself." He smiled. He looked around the horizon and yelled, "Right?" The shout died in the snow without echo.

When he could no longer resist sleep he lay down in the lee of an ice spire and withdrew into his cape. As sense faded, the faces and scenes returned, and he dreamed tortured dreams of the square faced man.

He woke when a wind pushed the cold in. He shivered, reached into his cape and pulled out the supplies. When he'd taken as much as he felt he could afford, he tucked the remnant back and rose, stretching. He relieved his bladder. The urine cut a groove in the ice spire, steaming as it ran to threaten his boots. He spread his feet wider. Eskander smiled. He recalled drinking himself sick with Blute and being challenged to a pissing contest. The crusty, old fart must have had the bladder of a horse. How else could he arc it three meters standing flat footed? They'd had some rowdy good times. The lined, grinning face floated in Eskander's mind, and then he remembered Blute's death.

* * *

Blute's age had been his worst enemy on their trek. He was the oldest of the party and shouldn't have been there. Before they left the sun Eskander took him aside.

"Blute, you can't go. This base has to be organized. If the snowmen jump the camp, we won't have food to get home."

"Skander, if I don't go along and watch your back, you won't live three sleeps out there." He glanced at the soldiers rolling their packs. "And that's certain. We might not lose this camp if I go, but if I stay you'll be too dead to need it."

"You worry too much."

"Soldiers who don't worry die quick. You suppose I worried too much at Rendize?"

Eskander didn't like using his friend's age against him. He knew Blute felt his manhood slipping away. He'd always been a man of power and ability beyond his size. That was his pride, his foundation for existence.

"Blute, you're worn out getting this far. From now on it'll be harder. There isn't a man I'd rather have with me whether I'm fighting or looking for the bottom of a beer keg. If you die from frostbite who'll help me fight and drink?"

"You trying to deny me the right to die as I want? How many times have we said to each other 'It's a good time to die' and waded in together? Well, now is a good time to die." He set his stance and crossed his arms.

Eskander looked at his feisty friend. Finally he shook his head and laughed. "By Huf, it is a good time to die. Roll your pack."

Blute grinned, punched the big man's arm, hard, and squatted to assemble his things.

So they marched together, watching each other's backs and sleeping alternately. The sun crept further below the horizon with each leg of the trek. Twilight deepened. The further they went into dark wilderness the more nervous Blute became. The worry and difficulty started to show in his lined face, red eyes, and dragging step. Eskander also became more concerned. He kept a running tally on the food, since it would gauge the turn-around point. If they could make it to the limit his obligation would have been filled and he could turn back. He just hoped Blute would make the round trip, not only for Blute's sake; without someone to share the watch Eskander would likely be murdered.

Eskander called rests more frequently. The soldiers began grumbling and once Captain Loat came to him.

"General," he said, "we're only making about five kilometers per kilogram of food and we're running low. The king wouldn't like our progress."

"Loat, go eat your balls, you never use them. Let me worry about the king."

The captain reddened but didn't say anything. He stomped off. At the next meal, Eskander noticed that he had put the men on stricter rations.

Eight sleeps later, when Eskander checked the supplies, even Loat agreed they must turn back. The captain gazed at the black horizon, disappointed. Five sleeps back a mysterious pinprick of light had appeared there and climbed in the sky with each march since. It had encouraged them all. Even Eskander had been intrigued. Now all hope that they could reach it died. Loat ordered the men to shoulder their packs and turn back sunward.

Blute grew wearier, but as they slowly drew nearer to their base camp Eskander believed the tough old bird would keep going long enough. He suspected that Blute would walk for two kilometers after he'd died. Mentioning it to the old man got a smile. Blute asked, "Did I ever tell you about the dead man who's penis haunted a convent?"

"Only about a hundred times."

"Then one more won't hurt..." and he told it again.

The company stalled while traversing a glacial slope on the sunward face of the mountain. A crevasse had opened across the path since their ascent.

Everything happened so fast. Eskander walked forward to survey the barrier. Loat was approaching him across the snow and, as Eskander moved left to get a better view, the lip of the crevasse broke under him. The fall was not long, maybe four meters, but he was dazed. Snow collapsed above, partly burying him. He looked up to see Blute peering over the edge. As Blute was shouting that he'd get a rope, Loat appeared at his side, looked down on Eskander, and reached into his cape. Eskander tried to yell a warning as the dagger came out and drove up under Blute's armor. Loat pulled the dagger and shoved Blute over the edge. More snow buried Eskander, shutting off the view of his falling friend's surprised expression. The last he sensed was the impact of Blute nearby, followed by tonnes of ice and snow.

* * *

Eskander felt a twist of guilt. He had walked away without considering that his friend must have been near. He tried to assuage the guilt by insisting Blute could not have survived the stabbing and burial. Besides, how could he have found Blute even if he'd remembered before leaving. And what about the lava flow? These thoughts were pushed off by realizing that Blute would be dead now anyway, even if Eskander went back and found him. It was a good time to die.

He looked antisun. "Goodbye, Blute." He raised his palm, sighed and turned back sunward.

* * *

Crumbs lined his food pouch. He turned it inside out and stripped the fat off with his fingers, finishing by licking off all but a remnant of taste. Throwing the empty pouch aside, he removed the water bag from under his cloak and stuffed snow through the narrow neck as tightly as he could. It would melt to supply fresh water. The last ridge he had crossed after bidding farewell to Blute put him high enough to finally feel direct sunlight. It had lifted his mood enough to offset the pointed depression of eating his last meal.

"Light of my life," he chuckled, grinning sunward. "Maybe."

A ribbon of pink clouds angled ahead. He thought of courtier's clothes with colored stripes and streamers. His memory opened and he saw Tissa, the dark haired beauty. They were sitting together in a corner of the palace ballroom, isolated by lovers' rights, talking intently while party-goers laughed nearby.

* * *

Tissa was nobility, and Eskander had courted her from the day he became a colonel. At that time he was one officer among many, undistinguished, unable to get the attention of a woman who set her sights on royalty. Her father had already sent feelers to a neighboring king about his third son's marital expectations. Then came the war with Rendize, where Eskander distinguished himself enough to come home a general, and Tissa began to notice the tall, homely man. She still intended to wed royalty, but she enjoyed the attentions of a popular hero whom all her friends considered a catch.

For a long time Eskander's suit was encouraged without progressing. Frustration was settling in hard when, unknown to him, a friend of Tissa's mentioned how the general walked more like a king than a soldier. The casual remark became inspiration as the ambitious woman realized there was more than one route to the throne. History overflowed with tales of kings who had not been born to the crown but took it with power, the help of fate, and perhaps of a strong woman. She was such a woman.

The royal banquet wove around them while Eskander studied Tissa. She seemed unreservedly happy, something rare. Huf had been generous to Tissa. She was justly considered one of the great beauties of Prater. The almond eyes and high cheeks lent an exotic cast and the small ears and mildly pointed chin added a hint of the elfin to her features. The party and the prospect of becoming a queen had her glowing.

She had begun discussing their plans, but he was nervous.

"Tissa, we can't talk here."

"Why not? Nobody can hear what we say over the party noise. They think we're romancing. And people could never believe anyone would plot insurrection at a royal dance."

Eskander glanced around and said, "But if we find a secluded spot they'll still think it's romance and I'll feel safer."

Tissa laughed. "Sometimes your upbringing shows. As long as we're in plain view we have privacy, but if we took one step outside the hall the court gossips would tear each other apart to see what we're doing. They're innocent enough, we all love gossip, but it would be disaster."

He liked it when she laughed; it made her magical. Too bad she couldn't laugh less at him and more with him. He said, "I'd rather be romancing anyway. Forget plans now."

"But, Love, you know that without the plotting there'd be no romance. If I were a peasant girl and you a farmer it would be different. I'd marry you now. But this is for a kingdom!

"The child prince will soon be engaged to his cousin, Atida, which, even if I were much younger, puts me out of the running. Prince Wold of Selta is receptive to my father's queries on my behalf, but he's very boring—a fault I could stand if he was higher than third in succession. Unless Queen Ettra dies and Fotane marries me, you're my best hope. I have the ancestry, you have an army and the people. I love you, but you have to be a king."

And worse, he *wanted* to be king. After she had carefully suggested the idea, and he'd considered the possibility, it struck him as right. Eskander, King; it sounded good. He also had to admit that a revolt without her would fail, and she was queenly material.

His loyalty to the king was purely pragmatic. He had never liked the man. Nor did he believe a king ruled by divine will. If Huf existed, it wasn't likely he took interest in who was tormenting the people. In fact, if Eskander could steal the crown it was as good a sign of godly favor as being born king.

Eskander's rise had begun when his father, a small landowner, scraped together enough money to buy his son an officer's rank. Beyond that his ability and luck, like making friends with Blute, had shot him up the ranks. Now he was one, dangerous step from the throne and found he wanted it.

"I want to be king," he said. "And to live through this party. But you're right about the privacy. What do you have in mind?"

* * *

The plan was set. When Ettra went into labor Eskander joined his troops and spoke to his trusted officers. The celebration would not begin for a sleep after the birth, so Blute and he returned to town for a small party of their own.

Much later Eskander's aide found him and Blute, drunk and dripping blood in a ditch outside the Tin Biscuit tavern, from which they had just been violently ejected. Blute was shouting, "Where's them whores? Where's them whores? Damn! That one is even too ugly for me."

Eskander focused as best he could, "Blute, you ass, that's Captain Jengo. But you're right, he's too ugly even for you.

"Come on, Jengo, me and Blute are lookin' for whores. You come too. Got any money?"

"No sir. I mean, yes, sir. But the king needs his officers to attend him. His wife and new son have both died."

* * *

After the funeral of Ettra and the child the king again summoned Eskander. The general noticed with surprise that Tissa was seated among the king's female relatives. Something was wrong.

"My, lord," he said, bowing. When he rose and looked in the square face and black, staring eyes of Fotane he knew something was very wrong.

"Eskander," the king said. He smiled but the smile didn't reach his eyes. "Your talents are well known. I want to reward you for your ability and loyalty. As of now, you are promoted to Commander General and will be leaving immediately with your enlarged unit to retrieve lands on my sunright border."

"Thank you, lord." Eskander said, confused and momentarily lost. He had begun to expect torture and death, but he was being rewarded.

"I leave the details to you. You may withdraw."

His unit, three times larger, marched sunright five sleeps later. In that time he was unable to persuade Tissa to meet with him.

They were only two sleeps out when a king's messenger caught them and recalled the general. His army moved on.

This royal audience was peculiar. Foreign men described a city far to antisun where glistening gems studded the buildings, and roofs were sheathed in gold. When this farce was done, the king called Eskander.

"General. I see you're as intrigued as I."

Eskander restrained a snort and forced a smile.

The king continued, "I have prepared a company of men to find this city. I couldn't think of a man more able than you to direct the mission. The glory you attain will make you remembered forever.

"Retire, rest and then prepare to go."

Eskander left, depressed.

He did not use his time to rest. Blute and he talked over their options and sent Jengo to gauge the sentiments of other army units. Those that were sympathetic he visited himself. The final tally left them without a position; no one would risk supporting him. The only hope left was to go exploring, and try getting back alive.

He sent message after message asking to see Tissa. At last, just before he was to go, she agreed.

They met in her new apartments in the royal palace.

"Am I speaking to the future queen?"

"I knew you'd understand," she answered.

"I don't understand. What about us?"

"You know the throne comes first with me."

"But I was almost there. You'd have been my queen."

"Yes," she said, "But that was a gamble. This is safe."

"But not for me."

"Oh, yes. Even for you. You know you should be dead now. But because of me you aren't. When I went to Fotane I secured a claim on the throne by telling him about the threat from you. I think he really believes it was your idea, but he's not stupid. He figured I had known about the treason before the queen died, but he also knows that while I sit by him I'll be his most ardent supporter. It turns out that he already fancied me. And, as you have always known, my resources are considerable. He was willing to listen when I told him you should be isolated from your soldiers but not killed. Martyring a popular hero would be more dangerous than having you alive. So you'll go on a long mission and be forgotten. Even if you come back, you'll be harmless."

"So you invented this gold city."

Tissa laughed. By Huf, she was still beautiful. "Believe it or not, that's real. Those foreigners showed up just before you left and conveniently became part of the plan."

Eskander snarled, "Thanks for my life, bitch. Goodbye." He strode toward the door.

She bristled, then relaxed and smiled. "'Bye, love," she called. "Bring back some diamonds for your queen."

He hurried to his company. When they were ready to leave he looked for his aide. A Captain Loat came to him and explained how poor Jengo had been attacked by robbers and killed. Loat would be his new aide. He was stunned by the news, but more stunned when Blute took him aside. "Skander," he said, "do you know these men?"

The general looked around. "Most of them are palace guard."

"That's right. And all killers."

"I expected the king to have his own men here."

"Sure," Blute agreed, "but that's not the worst."

"And what's the worst?"

"When we left our command, the two new battalions disarmed our unit and murdered our officers."

"What!"

"That's right. Makes a person wonder who those robbers were that did Jengo."

Eskander turned toward the palace and raised his fist in an ancient, obscene gesture.

The men around him chuckled.

* * *

Now, trudging through a white wasteland accompanied by the ghosts of Blute and his loyal officers, he understood the dark well of hatred that he'd found in himself and he ached for revenge. He wondered if Tissa had been aware of the whole plan, including his own murder. It wouldn't surprise him. He remembered her remark, "Even if you come back..."

"Well, I'll get back, and royal heads will fall if it takes me the rest of my life. Even if it kills me."

The purpose that Eskander gained from the savor of revenge gave him new drive. For four sleeps his anger overcame weakness, but no human spirit can sustain a dying body indefinitely. He refused to allow himself to sleep, fearing that he couldn't rise. He rested when he must, leaning against ice outcrops. The cold affected him more, numbing his toes, then his feet until he felt he walked on blocks of wood. His thoughts became hazy speculations about who was left to mourn his imminent death. The passing of his father, not long before his mission to the sunless land, left nobody likely to miss him. There was an uncle perhaps, who had left the region of Prater while Eskander was still a child, never to be seen since, and maybe some of his father's former servants, and two estranged sisters who had never forgiven him for remarks he'd made about their worthless husbands during a fit of roaring drunkenness, but he was already dead to them. The wandering thoughts touched back upon his enemies and he caught himself chanting with each shuffling step, "Kill them. Kill them. Kill them..."

Finally, he gave up dreams of beheading Fotane and began counting his steps. "I'll keep track," he muttered. Around twelve kilometers he lost count and contented himself with knowing when another kilometer had passed.

He walked and counted on his fingers until he forgot which finger was to go out next. Then he ignored the fingers and just counted steps to ten and began again, over and over.

Eskander had no idea how far he had been doing it when he realized he was no longer counting his own steps, but footprints ahead of him in the snow. He staggered to a stop. His eyes followed the track to some stick huts. With the new focus he heard voices and smelled stale humanity. He spared a smile and stumbled on.

Chapter 4

Escape for Tane became difficult. Lentie slept lighter since the Frost Giant, and he could not get out quietly enough. This wake-period he found himself with a crew of women and children stripping the fat from a bear. The animal had been feeding on scrub berries, giving the fat a bitter smell. The bear was old, nearly toothless, obviously had been near starving, and would not produce much grease. It hardly seemed worth the effort.

Worse, there had been great luck hunting, so several more carcasses awaited processing. His mother and the village elders would make his life even more miserable if he was caught trying to sneak away now.

He backed off to breathe, then attacked the bear again with his scraper.

Tane was soon slime up to his elbows. His mood became as sour as the bear's fat. When he heard some kids laugh he jumped up and looked around fiercely, but it hadn't been directed at him.

He considered sending a prayer to Huf and half began to look for a choice piece of meat to sacrifice to the god but he was saved from that sudden religious turn by a shout. Those around him jumped, then started toward the sound. Tane ran.

The crowd had solidified by the time he arrived. He danced on the outskirts, jumping to see over and trying to wedge his way in. An opening spread briefly. He was into it, elbowing and stamping. The arches he bruised jerked aside and hands grabbed his shoulders. He twisted and forced forward, slipping from angered adults.

The last wall broke and he stumbled to within centimeters of the face of a horrible specter.

Tane shied back against the crowd. His movement caught the gaze of the monstrosity, which peered dully at him before lapsing to disinterest.

It was a man. He was supported by two hunters and making no effort to move. Even bent the fellow was huge. Upright he would be twenty centimeters taller than the biggest villager. His nose and cheeks peeled from frostbite. Under the beard the flesh clung thinly over bone. The eyes were red, squinting and dead.

Grimm, bellowing, shoved his way through the mob and froze, as startled by the stranger as Tane.

"What we got?" he asked, when his composure returned.

"He just dragged in," a hunter said.

"Big devil. Who is he?"

"Hasn't said anything."

Reluctantly Grimm asked, "Did he come from antisun?"

"Yes."

Grimm studied him. Was he the bronze man? His skin was almost a bronze color when compared to the pink villagers. But he was obviously just a man, for all his size and foreign appearance. His condition proved that he wasn't built of metal.

"Who are you?" Grimm asked. The man didn't look up. Grimm waved his hand in the man's view. When the eyes came up he asked again, "Who are you?"

The eyes unfocused and fell.

"He's in no shape to stand around here. Who'll take him in?"

Nobody volunteered.

"You have the biggest hut, Grimm," Foss said.

"And the least room," Grimm replied. "Well?"

Tane stuttered, "W-w-we have room. There's just two of us."

"Would your mother think so?"

"Sure."

"Where's she at?"

"I don't know. Probably home."

"All right," Grimm said, "let's take him to Lentie's. Somehow it fits."

The bearers nudged the man and started forward. He dragged, then moved his feet, joining the slow dance through the village. The murmur of the crowd drew Lentie out of her hut as they approached. Behind her, Boda came out. Tane scowled at the ugly hunter.

"Lentie," Grimm said, "we got a stranger here that needs help. Tane says you have room. Can you put him up?"

"We barely have enough to feed ourselves."

"The village will feed him. And you, if you'll take care of him." He scanned the people. "Right?"

General agreement mumbled back. One voice said, "Sure, if he's the bronze man."

Lentie didn't need the hint to suspect the man's identity. She examined him. If he's our prophesied conqueror, she thought, wouldn't the gods have taken better care of him? I would have expected him to come on a gold sled pulled by wolves at least, maybe bears--but on foot, frozen, ratty and almost dead?

"We don't know that he is," Grimm said. "Which reminds me; where's the Shaman? Somebody get him." Three boys dashed off.

Lentie said, "I'm really busy."

"I'll help, Mother." Tane said. "Let's take him. Please."

"You'll be hunting and dreaming, not helping."

"I swear. I'll do it all."

Boda spoke, "I'll help."

"We don't need you," Tane said.

"Tane," his mother said, "be quiet."

She looked at Boda and at the stranger. "Bring him in."

They shuffled the man through the cramped door while Boda held the curtains. He followed and helped lay the stranger down. "We'll need more furs," he shouted back out the door.

Grimm designated three women. "More furs."

The assisting hunters left. Lentie and Tane crouched in and looked at the already sleeping man.

"Well," Lentie said. She knelt to tug at the big fur cape. Boda joined her, loosening the ties and spreading the cloak. When it was pulled aside, a gold-red gleam showed at the neck of the heavy coat. Boda leaned closer, spread the coat and felt underneath. He rapped with his knuckles. He grabbed the lamp, spilling grease, and pulled it close for light.

"Bronze," he said. "Bronze!" he shouted to the watchers outside. "He's wearing bronze."

Grimm groaned, "I hate this."

He shouted, "Where's Ryne?" just as the nervous Shaman walked up.

"So the Bronze Man came," Ryne said. He smiled ironically. "We have been a holy and righteous people."

He nudged Grimm. "What does he say?"

"He's too weak to talk."

"So, he's a man after all."

"Seems like."

"I look forward to hearing his story."

* * *

The chief regularly checked the stranger's progress. He went through the man's possessions, admiring the craftsmanship. All the metal made him envious. He was especially fond of the helmet they discovered under the fur cap, even tried it on.

They slept two times awaiting the man's waking. When he finally roused he said nothing but gestured for something to drink. They gave him water. He looked around in evident discomfort till Lentie gave him a hide bag and Tane mimed pissing into it. The man tried to rise. Lentie left the hut. Boda came in and helped Tane shift the fellow to manage urination.

Lentie returned. Tane went to fetch the chief while she made a meal, and Boda tried to question the guest.

"Who are you?" he asked.

The fellow looked at him but didn't answer.

"Where are you from?"

No response.

Boda said to Lentie, "I don't know if he's deaf, mute, too weak to speak, doesn't understand."

"I think he just needs time to feel better."

Lentie was feeding him when the chief arrived.

"How's he doing?"

"He's weak," Boda said. "Hasn't answered us yet."

Grimm waited while the man ate. He didn't eat much, and when he stopped Grimm spoke.

"Welcome to our village. I am Grimm, the chief. Who are you?"

The stranger gazed blandly at the group.

Grimm tried again. "You're safe here. You can trust us. Where did you come from?" But as he spoke the man's eyes sagged shut in sleep.

The wake-up ritual repeated. Eskander was sitting up in the furs, feeding himself. The chief asked again and Eskander guessed the meaning from the context even if the words meant nothing.

"*I am Eskander.*"

"What?" Grimm asked.

The big man pointed at himself. "Eskander."

Grimm said, "Eskander?"

Eskander nodded, lifted thick brows and pointed at each of the group.

Grimm introduced them, "Boda. Lentie. Tane. Grimm."

Eskander repeated their names and nodded.

The chief realized the futility of more talk. He grunted to his feet and tugged Tane outside the hut. "Tane, your job is to teach this Eskander to speak. Can you stay with it until he learns?"

"Sure. It'll be fun."

"Maybe. Just do it anyway."

Grimm left to arrange more food for the stranger's increasing appetite.

* * *

Eskander was relieved when the boy began tutoring him. He would have suggested it soon himself. The initial lessons were straight-forward: names of objects. When Tane exhausted these and started action words the classes became pretty comical. Eskander laughed hard when the boy began demonstrating abstract words like happy, fear, or friend.

The language was familiar. Many words were the same in his tongue but sounded funny in the snowman accent. Because of the familiarity he was understandable in the new language before five sleeps, but conversations remained halting and frustrating.

He ate more, felt better and left the furs for bodily functions. Tane dug a latrine pit behind the hut. Eskander knew his health was back when, returning to the hut once, he noticed Lentie's lingering, warm, musty smell, and felt his pulse pick up. It was time to get outside, exercise, and investigate.

Tane watched Eskander dress, pause over his weapons and then set them aside. The boy asked, "What are you doing?"

"Going out." He leaned on Tane and urged him through the door.

Tane let him guide them. Eskander slowly steered to the extreme sunward side of the village. He turned them left to begin the circuit. They encountered people along the way who smiled but said nothing. Everyone had been continuously apprised of Eskander's progress by one or another of his caretakers and they all felt proprietorial about him.

They stopped to rest. Eskander looked at the sparse landscape, the pitiful homes, and the boy. He shook his head. It was a marvel they could live. Civilization lay fifteen hundred kilometers sunward, where people had time left after feeding themselves to pause for beauty and contemplation of higher ideals. Even given the time, where could these poor people turn for beauty? Frigid desert lay all around. He did not know that if he had shared these thoughts with Tane the boy would have pitied his blindness. He could only see cold death as far as the eye reached. For him there was no music when snow squealed underfoot, nor when the wind hummed through needle brush. There was art in neither a wind carved drift, nor in the sparkling teeth of hoarfrost.

"Tane, what is this called?" He waved at the village.

"Kendee."

"Does the word mean something?"

Tane puzzled. "No," he said, "it's just home. It's Kendee."

"What do you do here?"

Tane smiled. "I *garble*. Do you like to *garble*?"

"What is *garble*?"

Tane mimed some familiar activities.

"Yes," Eskander said, "I like to hunt. What do you hunt?"

"Mostly bigfoot rabbits. When you're better we can hunt together."

"I'd like that."

They strolled around to the beginning. It had all looked depressingly unvaried to Eskander.

He fell immediately asleep after a meal.

The pair became a common sight. Eskander soon walked without support but never left without the boy. He liked Tane's company and his innocent enthusiasm, something Eskander himself could only muster, without the innocence, by imagining various tortures for his nemeses back in Prater. They went further afield. Tane anxiously showed his giant friend the world as he saw it, but Eskander failed to understand that beauty can be wherever you want to find it.

Once, as they climbed a ridge, Tane pointed back at the village. Cloud cover stretched away toward, but did not obscure, the brilliant sun, reflecting a golden light down on the snow-covered stick hovels.

Eskander made a startled exclamation, then began laughing. He laughed harder. Tane stepped back, chuckling a bit uncertainly. When Eskander didn't stop, Tane touched his arm and said, "Are you all right?"

The man bent double, holding his belly, and fell to his knees in the snow. He removed a mitten and wiped tears from his face. Tane grabbed him. "What is it?" he yelled. "What's wrong?"

Eskander gasped, pointing. Tane squinted down fearfully, but all he saw was the village—huts covered with golden snow, icicles bouncing jeweled rainbow sparks from stick ends.

"I...I've...found it," Eskander coughed. "Now...I can return...with honor."

* * *

Darla lost her patience. She stopped stitching the boot and asked, "What do *you* think we should do?"

Grimm paced and growled.

"Well?" Darla said.

Grimm tripped on a bundled fur. "Murder Huf!" he swore, kicking the fur against the far wall. "Can't you keep this place clean?"

Calmly, through gritted teeth, Darla said, "Grimm, if you yell at me one more time, I'll cure your snoring by cutting your big nose off."

He stopped, then blustered, "You...But..." He deflated. "Hah! I can't sleep anyway."

"I know. You have to relax! If the prophecy's real there's nothing you can do. If it isn't, it'll work itself out."

"No, we can make our own future. What worries me is not the prophecy. It's the people making it happen whether it's real or not."

"If it's what people want, let them have it."

"But they don't know! They talk about wealth. Nobody remembers the dying part of war. Me, I see it different. I see us drowning in our own blood. Even if we win, what do we have? Grief. Mourning. No treasure is worth it. This life here is hard, but we manage. We live well. We're happy. Why can't everybody see that?"

"Ask Ryne," Darla said. "Or try listening to me once. People take everything for granted. It's natural to want a better life. You want our girls to live better than us."

"Sure. But I want to live to see it."

"Nobody really believes in their own death."

"What about you, Darla? What do you want?"

She thought. "I want two bronze pots, and a servant to use them. But not enough to lose you."

"That's good news. How do I stop it?"

"Talk to Ryne. See if he's on your side."

"Ryne? Of course he is!"

"I don't know. He's been saying the signs are good for war."

Grimm nearly ripped the curtains down bolting out the door.

"Goodbye, husband," Darla muttered. "Food's almost ready."

* * *

Here was a man Tane could admire. He was a giant beside the village men, a general commanding eighteen thousand, telling stories that raised the boy's hair. What must it be like to conquer cities, destroy kingdoms?

Information flowed both ways. Tane was told not to talk about the prophecy, and to his knowledge he didn't, but Eskander understood that Kendee believed him to be important.

The general's health returned to full vigor. He had remembered his revenge as soon as sense had returned, and those thoughts were accompanied by a roil of schemes. Among his fanciful plans, he considered Kendee. If Kendee believed him to be a figure of importance, maybe that was a lever to engage them as a tool of revenge. He added up the numbers.

There were fewer than four hundred fighting men in the village, but there were other tribes to sunright and sunleft. Tane knew five personally, and had heard of twenty more. Two tribes, one smaller than Kendee, the other larger, lay to sunleft between it and the sea. Kendee traded with them exchanging tool stone for ivory. Grimm's people also formed a link in the sea trade with the villages to sunright. Rarely, snow tribes joined to raid the sunward herders, an event that had occurred only once in Tane's lifetime.

Eskander's estimate gave a potential force of ten thousand soldiers, and a seasoned commander could do a lot with that many hardened men.

And the snowmen were hard. They were the bronze sword, hardened by blows from the hammer of their harsh land. Eskander had never seen untrained men so ready for war.

Meanwhile Tane made plans, too. Wouldn't this man make a great father? Granted, he was ugly, but if his mother tolerated old Gwatch then ugliness wasn't a problem.

Tane hadn't seen Eskander hunt, but weren't men the most dangerous game?

The boy invited him hunting. They hiked to antisun.

Tane carried his throwing club and Eskander had fashioned a sling for hurling stones. An unanticipated problem after he'd made the sling was finding the ammunition. Eventually he discovered rounded pebbles exposed by fast flowing water under thin ice at the edge of a small stream. Tane thought the sling was ridiculously inaccurate, though the damage it did wherever the missile landed pleased him. He tried a few disappointing shots.

"Did you hunt when you were a kid?" Tane asked.

"Some. Mostly I fed pigs, herded sheep and helped grow corn."

"You were a farmer?"

"My father was. He owned land and had a few tenants. We ate well and gained a little wealth, but I never really wanted to farm."

"What'd you want to do?"

Eskander hesitated. "I wanted to be a musician."

"No!" Tane laughed.

"It's true."

"Can you sing?"

"I thought I could. I made a fiddle. My father called me rebellious. I'd sit around, dream-eyed, and saw that fiddle and sing stupid ballads I'd written. I've learned since that you can't write a ballad without living first. I feel foolish thinking about it."

"How did you get to be a soldier?"

"My father's solution to his dreaming boy. He wasn't going to have a sissy for a son. Too embarrassing. If I wouldn't learn farming, by Huf, I'd be a soldier. He spent a year's receipts to buy me an officer's rank. Nearly broke him."

Tane asked, "Do you have a wife?"

"Almost."

"Almost?"

Eskander told about Tissa and Fotane, leaving out his own role as usurper.

"So...what do you think of my mother?"

Ah, Eskander thought, here's trouble. "She's nice," he said. The truth was he found it hard to live in the same hut and not have her. She was a pretty little woman. She could be distracting. He'd already considered her as a bed partner, but he doubted it was what Tane had in mind. Taking a wife and son did not enter Eskander's plans.

"She likes you a lot," Tane said.

"I'm glad. Everybody likes to be liked. I like you."

Tane grinned. "That's great."

Boda had more insight to Eskander's feelings about Lentie and of course it made him jealous. The stranger didn't need any more nursing, yet he slept at Lentie's. Boda feared what might be going on, but couldn't broach it to anyone. Lentie would deny it, true or not. Eskander would boast, true or not. And how do you ask a child, especially one who hates you, if his mother has been playing hide-the-sausage?

Grimm was not in his hut when Boda looked for him. Darla said he'd gone to the shaman's.

The two met midway. Boda had trouble attracting Grimm's attention, finally hopping along sideways at pace to match Grimm, repeating the chief's name several times. The chief still retained his fury over a disappointing encounter with Ryne, and felt willing to take it out on somebody else.

"Look out, Gwatch!"

Boda stopped then and bristled. "Grimm, I have to talk," he shouted.

The chief pulled up and rounded on him. "All right! What!"

"The stranger, that is, the Bronze Man is healthy. He doesn't need nursing. Lentie's done her share. Her hut is crowded. Shouldn't we move Eskander out?"

"Out where? There are no empty huts."

"We should build him one. My friends and I could do it."

"And who will hunt while you build? You're a bachelor. You don't have a wife to build for you. Kendee needs you out hunting, not doing women's work."

Boda thought, then said, "But don't we dishonor the Bronze Man?"

Grimm exploded, "Dishonor! Bronze Man! Should we support every beggar that stumbles in here? That armor doesn't make him a bronze man any more than this hairy coat makes me a bear. Let him prove his worth!"

"But I thought..."

"No you didn't," the chief said. "Nobody around here thinks."

"So..."

"Forget it! No hut. He stays where he's at."

Grimm ended the talk by walking away. An angry, puzzled Boda ground his teeth. He left the village to avenge himself on an unwary animal.

Walking aimlessly, he crossed a low ridge and saw two figures below going toward Kendee. It was Eskander and Tane, each carrying several rabbits. So, his big rival could hunt too. It was all the more reason to avoid them. Boda could practically hear Tane's taunts.

This, Boda thought, ends my chance with Lentie. I can't compete with that man.

* * *

The invitation to Eskander was a dilemma for Grimm. Grimm didn't want to validate the prophecy by according him respect, nor did he want to snub a dangerous figure. He might even have to treat him well, on the face of it anyway, for his own purpose; if he could enlist Eskander to squelch the prophecy it would be like setting the bear to eat himself. Hating it, he finally offered the Bronze Man dinner in the manner reserved for village rulers.

Darla and Grimm met Eskander at Lentie's. They leisurely escorted him to their home. With protestations of humility, they asked if he would honor their hovel. Grimm entered first as tradition required, holding the curtains aside with both hands. Eskander was seated on the deepest furs. Darla prepared food.

Grimm passed the man a skin of bitter gni, a drink of fermented scrub berries. He gulped at his own.

They drank and talked. They discussed trivia, told their histories, got to know each other. They ate and talked. Kingdoms rose and fell in their words. They drank. Laughter spiced the air.

By Huf, each thought, I like this man.

Silence sat momentarily between them. They reclined, full of good food and humor, lit orange by the lamps. Both gazed into flames.

Grimm's satisfied smile faded. Without looking up, he said, "I need your help."

"I'll do what I can."

"Your arrival was prophesied twenty-three generations ago."

Eskander snorted. "You're joking."

"I'm not."

Grimm told him the prophecy, and Eskander found room in his practical soul to marvel. He had never been a believer in gods, spirits or mysticism. A man made his own fate. Opportunity appeared or did not. You did what you could or had to, but you did not count on supernatural help, nor fear supernatural retribution. Yet, here was a man who'd known of his arrival since childhood, and a people who'd known of Eskander's unborn war before he was born.

Eskander said, "And you want me to lead your men."

"No!" Grimm barked. "I want you to go back where you came from!"

"I don't understand."

"Look," Grimm said, "I like you, and that surprises me. But the best thing for Kendee is if you disappear. Everybody's hungry for war. You make them think Huf is behind them. But you and I know the only winners of war are those who stay out: the kings, the merchants, the weapon makers."

Eskander replied, "I'm a soldier. I've seen enough men die to know the worst of war. But sometimes not fighting costs more. The kingdom I defended is the greatest civilization in the world. It would be a crime to let barbarians destroy it."

"Barbarians like us?" Grimm asked quietly.

Eskander blinked at this unexpected consideration. "I hadn't thought of that," he admitted. "Living here makes it hard to see you as the barbarian."

He also hadn't seriously considered that if he led them it

would eventually be against his kingdom, against his comrades. Could he do that for personal revenge? Was it possible to attack his nemesis without destroying what was precious? And there were the snow people. Could he justify using them in a war that he could not allow them to win?

"What'll happen if I disappear?" Eskander asked.

"In time they'll forget you were here."

"What about you?"

"Me too," Grimm chuckled.

"Very funny. What will happen to you if they find out you chased me off?"

"They might want a new chief. But if you leave, Ryne will come around. With him on my side, I'm safe."

They reverted to small talk then and finally parted on good terms. Grimm and Darla ushered him to the entry of Lentie's hut and wished him good rest. Grimm felt the Bronze Man would leave Kendee, though Eskander made no promises. Eskander kept his thoughts to himself. Grimm had not learned that Eskander had his own reasons for war.

Eskander spent time talking with villagers about the prophecy and he particularly wanted to speak with Boda. During his recovery he'd been impressed by the man's intelligence but he could never catch him.

Eskander returned to his lodging to find Lentie cooking. He asked if she had seen Boda.

"No. He hasn't been here in a while."

"Has anybody seen him?"

"He's been in his hut, and out hunting with friends. But I think he's avoiding me. I guess I hurt his feelings."

"I don't see how. If he can take Tane's insults he can stand anything."

She shot him a glare. "Some injuries hurt less than others. He's a good man with a good heart. Why do you want him?"

"To talk about the prophecy."

"Oh, that," she shook her head.

"You're skeptical."

"Grimm's a big wind bag, but for once I agree with him. This prophecy... 'Hot bronze will break cold ice.' I don't like it."

"What's that? Hot bronze, cold ice?"

"Didn't Tane tell you my dream?"

"No."

She related it and he thought, more mysticism.

He watched her eyes shine as she told it. Again he noticed her odor permeating the hut. Even when she was gone, it stayed, an undertone to grease fire and cooking. With the awareness, he felt himself twitch.

Her story ended. She sat staring at him till the silence became too long, his gaze too intense. She resumed cooking.

Eskander reached out, caressing her pale hair. The contrast of his dark, scarred hand near her smooth, white face intrigued him.

"Please, don't," she said, pulling away.

He leaned closer, caressing her cheek.

She froze. Her light face went even whiter. Eskander stroked her cheek gently. He moved closer to her. His hand cupped a breast through soft fur. He pulled the clothing aside. The pink nipple crinkled at the invasion of cold air. Eskander smiled, tweaked the nipple. His gaze rose from breast to face just as a small, feminine hand, swung from way back, connected hard with his cheek. His head spun.

Eskander caught her hand, swinging a second blow, and grabbed her by the throat with his other. He glared and she glared back. Neither said a word. When his temper eased he gave a little shove and she fell back onto her sleeping furs.

Lentie covered her breast. "Get out," she said.

He stayed just long enough to claim it as his own choice, then stood and ducked out of the hut. Outside he rubbed his cheek. What a wallop, he thought. This cold country makes frigid women.

Eskander wandered from the village to think. His pride suffered at the rejection. It wasn't the sort of story he'd like to have spread around. He considered going back and forcing her, but figured that wouldn't be politic.

He barely noticed a hunter approaching until he stopped in Eskander's way.

"Oh, Boda," Eskander said, "I've been looking for you."

"And I'm looking for you." Boda blurted out. "I've decided not to give up. If I have to, I'll fight you for Lentie. But she's going to be mine."

Another time might have been different, but now Eskander said, "You can have the frigid bitch!"

Boda's jaw dropped. Without thought, he slammed a fist into Eskander's face, and the big man staggered back.

"Has everyone gone crazy?" he said, putting fingers to the twice abused cheek. Then his anger blazed and he leaped on Boda, driving him into the snow. He flailed at him. Boda curled into a ball, taking the blows on arms, legs and back. The thick furs absorbed most of the punishment, but he would be too stiff to hunt for some time. When Eskander's arms wearied, he stood and backed off, puffing.

"Damn you savages," he gasped, and strode away cursing.

Boda rolled onto his back to stare at the sky. Long after the Bronze Man left he lay in the snow, aching, wondering. His whole world had turned over since the Frost Giant appeared. Life, never great before, had become worse. Boda thought everyone believed Eskander was their savior, but Grimm straightened him out on that. The possibility of losing Lentie had struck him hard even though he never really had her. His sudden determination to win her seemed right but went sour; something had got under Eskander's skin. He'd really intended his challenge as a gallant bluff, never expecting to have to fight. Now he hurt everywhere.

He groaned. He sat up painfully. Wait a bit, he thought. Eskander said something. '...the frigid bitch.' So, he did try something, but she rejected him!

Boda laughed. He felt terrible. He struggled up and shuffled toward Kendee.

After a cooling-off period and some searching, Eskander found Boda in the village. Boda watched warily as the big man approached and was not entirely assured by Eskander's bruised smile.

"Boda," Eskander said as he strode up, hands spread in appeal, "I apologize for that little misunderstanding. I should have made it clear that Lentie, desirable as she is, has no hold on me, nor I on her. I've been a grateful guest in her home, but that's as far as it goes. She's yours. And she's said things, you know, about you. She's fond of you."

"Really?" he asked doubtfully.

"Really. And I'm really sorry."

Boda studied him. "All right, forget it then." He smiled, grimacing a little when he stretched his cut lip.

"Good. Thank you," Eskander said. "Say, would you have room in your bachelor's hut for another man?"

Boda smiled wider and a bead of blood dewed his lip. "I think we can squeeze you in. Need help moving?"

Eskander thought of facing Lentie. "Please."

They entered Lentie's hut together and, on seeing their battered condition, she jumped to a conclusion near the truth. The fresh damage to their faces made her blush. She greeted both warmly, and showed regret that Eskander had decided to leave. He detected relief in her glance at Boda, and Boda beamed.

The doorway curtains parted and Tane joined the scene. "What's going on?" he asked when he saw the awkwardly posed adults.

Eskander broke the growing silence. "I'm moving in with the bachelors. I have a campaign to plan and it'll be easier there."

"I'll go, too."

"No, Tane. You stay. Help your mother."

Tane glared at them all. Tears glazed his eyes. He ducked out the door and ran.

"He'll be all right," Eskander said. "Kids are tough."

Boda helped carry the bedroll, armor and weapons to his hut. By careful reorganization and much loss of privacy they squeezed out a sleeping spot for Eskander.

"Bodie?" Eskander said when they had stepped back out into sunlight.

"Yes?"

"You're not a fool, but in case you didn't think of it, now is a good time to talk to Lentie."

"You think so?" Boda asked.

"Sure. Besides, it's crowded in there." He gestured at the hut.

The snowman tipped his head to one side querulously for a heartbeat, then smiled, nodded and left.

* * *

"Lentie?"

"Yes," she whispered. Louder she said, "Yes, Boda. Please come in."

He rustled through the hides. "Hello," he said.

"Welcome home," she said.

* * *

Much later Boda returned and asked if Eskander would return the favor in helping him move his things. He did gladly.

When they had deposited Boda's simple goods at Lentie's, Eskander said, "I wish you the best. May you have many strong children."

"Thank you Eskander," Lentie said. "And speaking of children, Tane worships you. Could you find him and talk to him?"

"Isn't it better coming from you?"

"He never listens to me. You know that."

"I'll do what I can," he smiled and, nodding to each, left the hut.

He walked away satisfied. He had corrected his blunder. He'd regained the friendship of two people who'd done much for him lately, while helping join a pair likely to have been destined for each other. Now, except for placating Tane, he could concentrate on managing his return to Prater.

Eskander knew that Tane would probably be hunting, and where, so he collected his sling and stones, to set off directly antisun.

As he searched for the boy, Eskander considered his situation. He lived among an honest people, by their kind charity, who coincidentally held a prophecy which suited them perfectly to his use as a personal tool of war. This was the kind of convergence that made a religious skeptic like him question not only his disbelief, but also puzzle about what greater purpose Almighty Huf could have for Eskander beyond just granting him his petty worldly goal of revenge. Was it likely that Huf had a grudge against king Fotane? Or did he so love (or hate) the snow people that He would throw them across the world on a path of destruction? Or, and this seemed most likely, was there an unknown purpose to which these humanly grand endeavors were nothing by comparison?

With his inward turn and his continuing indifference the world still failed to charm him, though he walked through a magic land in shades of blue, white and gray. To sunright a blizzard was blowing in. The distant falling snow strung out in long sweeps like bristles of a worn straw broom. A breeze drifted the powder snow at his feet in rivulets of glittering crystals and ran it off low ridges like herded bos panicked off a cliff. He looked only for Tane.

Tane steamed. Adults are so stupid. Kids don't matter to them. He might as well keep right on walking. It wasn't as if they'd miss him. And if they did, it'd serve them right. Why not? He could hunt as well as a man; he wouldn't go hungry. The world sunward promised adventure and a chance to get away from the awful contradictions of grownups. Do this, they say. Do that. Who cares what you want? You're just a kid! Act like us--act your age--grow up--give it time! For Hufsake, can't they make up their minds?

He was so distracted that he flushed two rabbits without caring. By the third he'd calmed enough to try a throw but not enough to hit it. The fourth he missed too, but before the rabbit vanished, the air sizzled and the animal tumbled, spewing blood.

Tane gaped. Then he glanced right. The familiar giant, Eskander, stood there on a rise, casually swinging his sling, watching Tane.

The boy gathered his throwing club, ran away fifteen meters and stopped, turning again to look at the big man. It would be futile trying to escape. He walked to the carcass, picked it up and carried it to meet Eskander.

"Not a bad shot," he grumbled.

"Thanks."

They stood watching the approaching sweep of snowfall without really noticing.

"Shall we get more?" the man asked.

"Maybe. I could use it to travel."

"Going someplace?"

"Sunward. I'm tired of snow."

"Me, too. Can I come?"

"You wouldn't," Tane stated. "You have plans to make."

"True. I would rather go with an army. If you wait, you'll travel with an army."

"Mother says only the men will go."

"Who's the general, me or your mother?"

Tane stood firm. "I can't wait. I'm going."

Neither moved. Snow flakes whirled around them. Eskander, finally concerned, looked up at the sky. "Looks like a bad time to travel. Maybe we should go home before we get lost."

Tane looked at him oddly. A shadow smile flickered across the boy's face. "No," he said, "I'm leaving." Tane strode away with the wind whipping flakes against his right cheek.

Eskander caught up. "Look," he said. "This is no time for childish pride."

Tane stopped. "You...you grownup!" he shouted.

"All right, I'm sorry. But can you see the wisdom of getting home before the blizzard really hits?"

"But if I'm not going home, what do I care?"

"That does it. Come on." He grabbed Tane's arm and started toward the village. In two hundred meters visibility was gone. He blundered them into drifts, crossed ridges, got them totally nowhere.

"See what you've done?" Eskander grumbled. "Now we'll have to wait out the storm. One rabbit to eat for who knows how long. No shelter." He studied the area. "Let's dig a cave in that drift."

"Why?"

"Because I'd rather not die yet."

"Why don't we just go home?" Tane said with a hint of something which puzzled Eskander.

"Because," Eskander gestured around at the thickening snowfall, "we're lost."

"*We* aren't lost. Because it takes both of us to be *we*. And only *you* are lost."

Eskander grunted, "You can find the village?"

"Easy. We're antisun of the village, right?"

"Sure," Eskander said, now patient again. "But there's no sun."

"There's wind."

"Tane!"

"The storm came from sunright. The storms always come from sunright. The wind always blows from sunright during a storm."

"You mean," Eskander looked around, "if we walk with the wind on our right, we'll find Kendee?"

Tane grinned. "Who's the general?"

Eskander laughed. "You are, Sir!" he said. "Shall we go home, Sir?"

"Why not?"

They pulled fur flaps over their right cheeks and went home. On the way Eskander explained the new situation at Tane's hut. He thought at first that the wind had covered his words, but he'd been heard. Tane shrugged. "I thought it'd happen before long."

It would have been worse, but Tane was reveling in his superior snow-craft. And he was remembering Eskander's promise of going sunward with an army.

* * *

The elder council consisted of four members: three men, and one woman. The occasional tie vote was Grimm's opportunity to swing council decisions. Fortunately the interpretation of council orders was his. Ryne, as religious leader, and Grimm were the effective rulers. Whatever they did, if it stayed in the rough bounds of council order, was not questioned. Good government resulted.

But Grimm worried now. Ryne did not take a stand and if the council decided to follow the prophecy they would soon begin war upon the sunward lands. There had never been a doubt that it would come to a council vote since, according to ancient rules, dissent between the chief and the villagers required it.

Grimm, of course, considered the whole council a batch of idiots. It was not wise to voice that opinion, and Grimm was *not* an idiot. Only Darla heard much.

* * *

The shaman, after studying every spiritual avenue of information available to him, interviewed Eskander. He was curious about events that had made the Bronze Man a tool of prophecy.

Ryne considered Eskander's puzzling story. The general's party had passed through a snow village, but Ryne had heard nothing about a group of foreign men. Eskander claimed those villagers had spoken a different tongue more similar to his own while to Ryne's knowledge the furthest villages spoke identically to Kendee. Even the herders, three hundred fifty kilometers sunward, with whom they had little contact, were easily understandable.

Ryne sent out messages to neighboring villages asking about Eskander's company. Even if they had bypassed all settlements on their return, some evidence of their presence should have been noticed.

* * *

Eskander knew enough about politics as surrogate warfare to assess the combatants, both potential allies and enemies, before engagement. He sought out and interviewed all of the village council. From the men he garnered expected, tacit support, but he underestimated Resta. Her weakness, for making the most outrageous, unthinking statements, made him believe she was stupid. However, restraint and intelligence are not necessarily related.

He found her directing food division near the pots. She saw him coming.

"Girls!" she said, "Look, fresh meat."

He smiled. "Lady Resta, I'm not *that* fresh."

She patted her gray hair and managed the best curtsy her fat, aging legs would allow. "Lady! He calls me Lady! You *are* fresh. And, by the size of you, packing plenty of meat. Here," she said, picking up a bear ham, "I'll trade you this for a peek in your satchel."

The watching women laughed. Eskander was mildly embarrassed by the unabashed attention, but he decided to bluff it through. "For you, my lady, it'd be free. But maybe we should find some privacy first."

"You're funny," she laughed, and hit him with the ham.

"Ow! That hurt. By Huf, if I had a hundred soldiers like you swinging hams, I could rule the world."

"If you had a hundred soldiers like me," she patted her belly, "all the bears in the world couldn't keep us in weapons."

"If we won, we'd have all the food we wanted," Eskander pointed out.

"And who says we'd win?"

"The prophecy. And me. I've won my share of campaigns. And I've lost a few. I know what it takes to win."

"There aren't enough of us," she pointed out.

"There are other villages. Ten thousand fighters live within two hundred kilometers of Kendee."

"Ten thousand can't conquer a world."

"Not alone. But alliances can be made," he said.

"Who would join an attacking army?"

"The enemies of those you attack."

"You've got it all figured, haven't you?"

Eskander smiled. "Yes, I do."

"No you don't. How many of us will die?"

"Sacrifices have to be made."

"We sacrifice to Huf, not war. And we don't sacrifice men; they're too valuable."

Eskander realized that his research had fallen short. He was learning that Resta was not the buffoon she acted. He tried again. "You lose men all the time to this small, deadly piece of the world you have. Are you saying even the loss of one life, that will be lost here anyway, is not worth the rest of the world?"

"But it wouldn't be one."

He said, "If it was just one, would it be worth it?"

She looked at him suspiciously and thought briefly, then said, "If, like you said, that death would happen anyway, yes; that's acceptable."

"What if two died?" he asked.

"We could likely stand that."

"How about three?"

"I," she said with disgust, "will not stand here and bargain away the lives of the village one by one."

"Of course not, but it demonstrates my point."

"Which is...?"

"You are willing to accept a level of risk. Where you set that level is just juggling numbers. In war the goal is to win with minimal losses. We reduce deaths with training and strategy. The rest is up to Huf."

"Yes, you're really a general, aren't you? You can juggle numbers and not feel anything more than losing pieces in a board game. But each of those pieces is a face and a name to *me*. When one of us dies, we don't just close ranks and march on. We stop everything. We honor the one gone to Huf, and thank him for all he's given us. We don't take death so lightly as you. We can't afford to. There aren't that many of us."

Eskander shook his head. "You get me wrong. I don't take death lightly. The best man in the world was murdered for trying to save me. Should that death go unavenged?"

Resta raised her eyebrows. "Avenged? Is this a personal feud?"

He had said too much. He glanced at the small audience of women, frowned, looked down at the pile of bloody meat and scratched his beard. Now should he lie, tell it all, or just shut up? Resta was probably too bright to swallow a lie. Telling the whole story would cast him badly. Shutting up was too late, and left too much to her imagination.

"Not entirely," he said, "but yes. I want to kill the man that killed Blute, or had him killed. But I also want Kendee let out of this cold prison. I like you. If I also fight for revenge it means that my heart will be in the battle."

"My heart is Kendee. It doesn't have to be in the battle. It won't be if we stay here."

"You'll vote against the prophecy?"

"Prophecy doesn't need my vote. I vote against death."

Eskander paused, looking at her. "You are a surprising woman, Lady Resta."

She laughed again. "That's nothing. Come to my hut and you'll get a real surprise."

"Yes," he chuckled. "But I'm afraid it'll be more than I can handle. I respectfully decline."

The bemused man turned to go and the fat woman goosed him. He jumped, glanced back, and walked off shaking his head and smiling, hearing Resta's laughter.

* * *

The chief had been putting off calling the council meeting, hoping Eskander would leave on his own. Obviously, though, Grimm had misread the man. He tried once more to persuade the general to disappear. The general claimed to be a victim of fate and prophecy. He said he'd leave if the vote rejected war. Grimm wondered if Ryne and the general had been drinking the same water, or whether he had some unknown motive keeping him in the village. Grimm considered whether the Bronze Man was hoping to make a renewed claim for Lentie, but had detected no interest by the man there since Boda moved in, and he'd made no overtures to the few other available village women.

Grimm had been informally polling villagers and council. It looked bad. He wished Ryne would see sense. The two of them could stop this idiocy.

Unable to delay the inevitable, he called the meeting. But the council vote, three to one, was a foregone result. The people *must* have their prophecy.

Chapter 5

The grand purpose of Kendee had always been mere survival. What little time they could spare went to simple diversions. That changed. Where people had used their leisure for dancing and story telling, now they spent it in war preparation. They had always preserved extra food for hard times. Now meals were rationed, and every uneaten scrap was smoked, dried, or cooked and sealed in boiled lard.

Eskander established three rotating teams of hunters who shifted tasks every sleep. When one group hunted, another made weapons and the third trained.

He kept track of the most promising soldiers among the trainees. He would send the best to train the other tribes. The distance between the tribes was optimal for what food the land provided, so to bring them into one group for training would mean starvation. Ideally they would each complete preparation by a set time and gather to march sunward.

The snow villages lay along a staggered line where the sun stood close to the horizon. Eskander worried about the difficulty of organizing an army that must remain spread over two hundred kilometers. Timing the march would be crucial to avoid consuming their food too soon. Obviously the furthest villages must march toward the rendezvous earliest, allowing them less time to train and gather materials. Therefore, the other tribes must supply some of the food and weapons. Training would have to be continued on the march even if it meant traveling much slower.

About this Boda asked Eskander, "Why don't we just train longer here?"

"Because you can't keep a soldier's edge just training. If we over-train here, waiting for the others to peak, our people will become jaded and complacent. They might even decide to quit."

Boda didn't say it, but he thought quitting was a good idea. He and Lentie had talked a lot about the war. He hadn't considered it much before, but now she had him thinking. She was smart, and persuasive, and they had been married recently enough that her charms were a big influence. Her fears had become his fears. He wasn't a bachelor anymore; now he had something beyond himself and the village to live for. His reluctance hadn't shown much. After all, they were going whether he wanted or not.

And there was a certain irony. Eskander noticed that Boda, the poorest hunter, learned the war trade quickly. The general accelerated his training and began tutoring him in tactics and strategy. Boda was against war as a practice, but the theory and principles excited him. He couldn't help but absorb it.

Grimm had been foul tempered since the village meeting. He practiced fighting reluctantly and didn't seem to have a flair for it, though his physical strength made him a dangerous man. Eskander tried showing the chief the rudiments of tactics, hoping his leadership could transfer to the battlefield. It became obvious that the chief's abilities lay in politics and administration. Eskander, to save Grimm's honor and corral him into the effort, accorded him the rank of colonel, charging him with organizing the coercion of other villages. Given something to do, and reminded of his promise to not shirk, Grimm grudgingly did it.

The chief sent emissaries to the twenty-five known tribes. They were to detail the magnificent prophecy coming true for the snow people and offer each tribe a part of the glory. He worded the messages sent to the tribes as persuasively as he could and coached the emissaries in answers to questions other chiefs were likely to ask.

Surprisingly, it was his idea to organize a raid on the herders. That would give them more food quickly, and maybe a chance to practice the new war skills.

"I like your idea, Grimm", Eskander said. He and Boda were supervising training. "How long would it take to get there and back?"

"Twelve sleeps to go, sixteen to bring back the cattle."

"We should have answers from most of the tribes by then. What do you think, Bodie?"

He thought a bit. "Would it be better to wait and collect the cattle later as we march through?"

"Why?" Grimm asked.

"Well, the men that go on the raid will be missing training. The cattle we bring back will have to be butchered because we can't feed them, and we'll have to carry the meat. But picked up on the way they can graze as they walk."

Grimm lifted an eyebrow at Eskander.

The general said, "Makes sense. Do these herders have horses?"

"Yes," Grimm said.

"Hmm. Ever see a cavalry charge?"

"No," both replied.

"It worries me. These hunters," he gestured at the sparring warriors, "could be the best infantry in the world. But without cavalry we'll be limited. We'd have to leave the open field to anybody mounted, just fight in rough terrain where horses can't maneuver. But the war prizes won't be in rough country."

"We can't fight horses?" Boda asked.

"There are tactics for it that we'll teach the men, but you can't hold a field long. And you'd never beat them."

"So what do we do?" Boda asked.

"We use Grimm's idea. But we don't take cattle, because you're right about picking them up on the way. We get horses and grain to feed them."

Grimm said, "You can't turn snowmen into horse soldiers."

"I came up through the ranks of the infantry. The cavalry bragged on their horsemanship, and looked down on us. But when I began commanding combined units I found there's no more to it than any other skill. You learn by doing. And you get good with practice."

"You're the general."

"Don't worry, Grimm. I know the limitations. I don't expect them to beat professionals. For one thing, the horses we'll get can't match the monsters bred for war. Ours will be faster but won't have the weight or strength. Our cavalry will just harry them, never fight head-to-head. We'll fight infantry and pull the enemy cavalry off our own foot soldiers."

"When do we raid?"

"Now. Bodie," Eskander said, "take fifty of the men we've marked as trainers. Start sunward as soon as you're ready. We can't send much for carrying grain. You should be able to find whatever you need there. Get as many animals as you can. They'll be easier to herd if your men can ride. It may be tough to learn on the trail, but if the herders get organized you'll have the incentive. Good luck."

"I have to tell Lentie."

"Tell the men first," Grimm said. "They have wives too."

"All right. See you in twenty-eight or so sleeps."

Grimm and Eskander watched Boda pick out his men and send them to their huts. When he had run off toward his own home, Grimm spoke. "Can he do it?"

Eskander tipped his helmet back and scratched his head. "I think he's born for this. If he doesn't get too brave, he'll do it. The first three battles are the worst. If he lives that long he'll be a good commander."

"If...?"

"There are no guarantees for any of us."

"Wasn't that Resta's argument?"

Eskander didn't answer. He turned back to the troops. They had stopped at the interruption and were discussing the implications. "Back to work," the general shouted. "You'll get your turn."

Lentie was biting her tongue, torn between duty to her village and anger at the situation. It wasn't her place to order her husband, but a woman is required to keep her man from doing stupid things. Going on a raid this soon without the general's direct guidance was stupid.

"Tane," she said, "go for a walk."

"Aww..."

"Now."

The boy left.

Boda kept his eyes on his packing. He was already getting a feel for Lentie's moods.

She opened a slit in the closure, watching Tane till he disappeared. Turning to her husband she said, "Why you?"

"Why me what?" he said, still looking down.

"Why are you leading this raid instead of the so-called general?"

"He has to train the men."

"You could do that."

"I don't know enough."

"But you know enough to lead them sunward?"

"It's just a raid, for Hufsake."

"And nobody ever gets hurt on raids? I think you're enjoying this!"

Boda sighed. "Look. All my life I've been Gwatch, the lousy hunter. I don't like this war, but it's the first time I've been best at anything. If I back out, the village will think worse of me than ever. You agreed that we have to help the village even if we hate what they do. This is how I can help. Already, both of us have greater status than just twenty five sleeps ago, when you were a poor widow and I was a rotten hunter. Since we have to support the village anyway, why not do it where we gain the most?"

"Or lose everything."

He did something he'd heard from other men, and now understood. "Women," Boda sighed.

"Men!" Lentie spat and stamped out of the hut.

Boda shook his head and finished assembling his gear. He could hear men gathering outside. He wished he and Lentie had parted on better terms. She was right, of course. But so was he. Before becoming a husband he never knew that two people could have completely opposing views and still both be right. Life certainly had become more complex.

One of the warriors shouted, "Are you in there, Boda?"

He pushed aside the curtains and dragged his pack out. "Is everybody here?"

They all looked around and mumbled.

"All right," Boda said, "five ranks, here." He gestured.

Men chuckled, but they shuffled into position. Eskander had anticipated this behavior, telling Boda that at first the men would feel foolish or think it was a joke. Later, even though they would never stop complaining, when they found the training saving their lives they would take pride in the military discipline. Boda hoped so; he could foresee problems in controlling them. His only authority lay in being chosen for the job by the general.

When they were formed he had the first rank count off. Ten full columns meant fifty warriors. Everyone was there.

"Let's practice what we've learned, men. You five in the right column, take advance position. Go." They trotted off sunward. "When we clear the village you five on the left, take the rear. Face right." He rolled his eyes at the ragged compliance. "Campaign march, now, let's go." The company moved out.

Now and then during the first march, Boda could see his advance and rear guards silhouetted on the horizon. If they were visible to him they could be seen by an enemy. He'd have to speak to them.

They made twenty five kilometers before the first sleep, not bad for a late start. Several men grumbled when Boda set up the perimeter guard. "Who's going to bother us this close to Kendee?" Saper asked.

"Nobody," Boda said. "But we have to try this soldiering now, before we really need it. Figuring it all out in the middle of the herders will be too late."

They still grumbled, but they did as he said. He had each guard-change wake him to see that everything was correct. Once he woke on his own and made the rounds. All the guards were in position and alert.

This time, he thought, they'll do it because it's new. When they get bored I'll have trouble.

The ninth march dropped them over a snow-capped ridge into a broad, forested valley. They left the snow as they descended. An old river meandered through slow curves that cut away at tree foundations, leaving them in various states of collapse. The green canopy of the mature wood inhibited underbrush. Walking was easy on the mossy, needle-strewn valley floor. Progress slowed only at deadfalls and wide stream bends. They avoided most of the latter by keeping to one side of the valley, occasionally climbing a ridge to pass. The water was too cold to want to ford despite the convenient shallows, and the snowmen associated immersion with death. None ever learned to swim.

Boda felt nervous about the limited visibility. An enemy could lurk behind every tree. He continually sent out men in short, looping patrols to supplement the usual guard. A pair of men would move out to the side, then forward until they contacted a member of the advance party, then back to report. After thirty kilometers like this and sighting only occasional squirrels, Boda relaxed and stopped the spot patrols. He knew they were still several sleeps from the herders.

Still, he didn't allow fires when they stopped, and the men grumbled louder. To occupy them, he had them establish a cache for their warmer clothing and some of the food.

Boda was sleeping less than the men due to his guard checks. This compounded the existing jumpiness, which in turn made it more difficult to sleep. He tossed in his furs when he lay down, then would rise to roam the camp and the guard posts. During one of these fitful rambles, as he'd feared would eventually happen, he caught a man asleep on duty. He kicked him awake and as the man rolled over, scrabbling for his spear, Boda saw that it was Saper, one of the loudest complainers.

"Let's get back to camp," Boda said.

Saper, wary for a moment, relaxed and fell in beside his captain. "Get's boring out here," he said.

Boda was quiet.

"That warm sun, you know," Saper said. "It makes a man's mind wander, makes his eyes squint. I bet it almost seemed like I was sleeping, didn't it?"

"Yes."

"That's right. Almost as if I was sleeping."

The short walk to camp didn't give Boda the time he wanted to think this out. The test had come. If he didn't handle it right, he'd never be able to command men again. Eskander's backing wouldn't help him if the troops weren't willing. The snowmen were used to the discipline required to survive the harsh wilderness, but their society was based as much on cooperation as on authority enforced from above.

Plint lay awake in his furs and saw the pair returning. He sat up. Boda motioned him over.

"Plint, get the men up and send Rinn out on guard at sun-sunright."

Saper had thought that Boda was going to move them out earlier than usual. Now, with a guard replacing him while the men were aroused, he suspected worse.

He turned to the captain. "Boda," he said, "what are you doing?"

"Plint," Boda said, "you and you three men," he pointed, "take Saper's weapons."

"Now, wait, Boda..." Saper started.

The four men looked puzzled. Boda stared at them, but didn't speak. Plint eased toward Saper, and the other three followed. Saper started backing away so two moved out to flank him.

"Drop your things, Saper," Boda said.

"Listen, Boda. You said yourself how it was easy to think a man was sleeping when he wasn't. I was just dazed with the heat and light."

Saper's stalkers realized the significance of that. They glanced nervously at each other. They all knew the penalty for sleeping on guard. They also knew that Saper, a master spear-man, knew. Their approach stopped. Plint said, "Boda?"

"He was asleep. I had to kick him to wake him up."

"But this isn't the battlefield. What's the fuss?"

"Since our customs aren't military customs, I'll explain, but this is part of the problem too.

"On the hunt, we all help because we all gain. We don't leave one man to bait a bear alone because next time it might be one of us. We cooperate knowing what everybody has to do so we can all eat. As hunters we're experienced. As soldiers we aren't. What we have is a little training--very little. The training says a commander doesn't have time to explain decisions. He must be obeyed immediately, without question. If you stop to form a committee at every order, you die before the vote."

Plint said, "But there's time." He gestured at the peaceful surrounding forest.

"Do we stop to discuss the hunt?"

"Of course not."

"Why?" Boda asked.

"Like you said, we all know what we're doing. Why stop?"

"We work by habit, you mean?"

"I guess so."

"What habits guide soldiers?" Boda asked.

Plint thought. He glanced at the other men. He shrugged. "So, I don't know."

"Because we're hunters, not soldiers. As soldiers, what we're doing now is getting those habits so we *will* know what to do without talk. Do you think hunting is more dangerous than war? Will we have time to stand around like old women and gossip the enemy to death?"

Plint was quiet. Saper saw things going badly and took up the argument. "But there *is* time now!"

Boda looked at him. "How do we form the habits that will keep us alive later if we don't practice them now?"

"We'll do what we have to when the time comes."

"Instantly? Without confusion?"

"Yes!" Saper shouted. The volume didn't help convince the others. He saw it on their faces.

"I'll spear the first one that touches me," he hissed.

They didn't back off, but they didn't move forward.

Boda said, "What's the rule concerning sleeping on guard, Plint?"

"Arrest by whoever finds him, to hold for judgment by the highest ranking commander on the scene."

"What's the penalty?"

"For the first offense, with no damage caused, flogging."

"Do you think that's fair?"

Plint hesitated. "No."

"What is Saper's job on a hunt?"

"You know that."

"Yes," Boda said. "He's a spear caster."

"He's one of the best spear casters we have," Plint replied.

"What about you?"

Plint puffed his chest. "I *am* the best!"

Boda smiled. Saper glowered.

"Has Saper ever left you to the bear when you missed a throw?"

"I don't miss."

"I've seen different, Plint."

"Well...of course he never did. He spears the bear."

"What if he ran and left you to the bear?"

Plint chewed on the idea for a bit.

"Well, he'd be stripped of weapons and furs and driven from Kendee."

"And he would die, because nobody will take in an exiled man," Boda finished. "Do you really think that's fair?"

Plint studied the ground. He furrowed his brow. A pained look crossed his face, and he said to Saper, "Drop your stuff."

Saper edged toward a gap in the ring, but they raised their spears and closed up.

"Come on, a flogging's better than death. You knew the penalty, now take it like a man."

"But a whipping! It's...humiliating. I'll die first!"

Boda said, "You're more practical than that. Think about it."

Saper looked defiance at Boda, then searched the faces of the gathered, silent company. He sagged. The weapons dropped from his hands.

The guards picked them up and surrounded him but didn't touch him. Plint asked, "Now what?"

Boda said, "The men will draw lots to pick a man for the whip."

The result of the lottery made Saper wither. Chance had picked Frendel, a thick armed hunter with a barrel chest. He was known for his ability to throw a spear farther, however less accurately, than anyone else in Kendee.

Saper was stripped to the waist and tied to a tree. Frendel stood, embarrassed, the knotted leather thongs dangling in his right hand. He glanced at Boda who nodded and said, "Don't shirk."

Frendel reluctantly turned to Saper, half raising the whip. Saper cringed. Frendel stopped and asked Boda, "How many?"
"One."

* * *

The company's spirit plummeted. The next two marches passed in near silence. There wasn't the usual joshing and boasting. Saper in particular had become very quiet. He no longer complained at all and responded to orders quickly and precisely. Boda worried.

They were breaking camp for the thirteenth march out of Kendee. A guard ran into the camp, hushing the men and looking for the captain.

"What is it?" Boda asked as the man approached.

"Herd of bos," he puffed, "with three drivers coming down to water on the other side of the river. A kilometer off."

"Show me."

The guard guided him along the river to a ridge ending as a stream-cut bank. They climbed the slope and crept over the brow through concealing ferns. There were about forty cattle. The three herders were young boys.

The muddied ground had been stirred up by hooves for generations, so no grass grew on the river bow where the cattle watered. The boys allowed habit to do their herding for them. The cattle knew the routine. They swayed past the boys already seated on the green grass left back from the stream. The wide horns swung in half-hearted jockeying for a position in the water.

Boda marveled that they were not blinded by their mates' sharp headgear.

He looked beyond them. They had come down a path following a dry gully, and there was no sign of adult herders. Why should there be? The bos hardly seemed to need anybody at all to control them.

At this point he decided the best plan to be patience. The snowmen would keep out of sight until the herd left, then send scouts after them. Boda left the guard to keep watch and returned to camp.

He gestured Plint over. "Have the men pack up quietly. Be ready to go."

"What're we going to do?"

"The scouts will find out what's up that gully. If there are horses, we'll scout better and plan a raid. If there aren't, we'll stay with the river to the next settlement."

Plint circulated through the warriors.

Boda rolled his sleeping furs and checked his weapons. His stomach wanted to crawl up past his lungs. Is this what it would always be like as captain? Do the other men feel so tense? He looked them over. The spirit that Eskander said made a company survive was not there. A few banded into groups to talk quietly. Most sat absorbed in their own thoughts--not happy ones by the expressions. Saper sat on his furs, back to a tree, at the extreme edge of camp. Boda walked over and squatted beside him to stare in the same direction. He busied himself stripping grass stems, finally chomping on one before he spoke.

"I always admired your hunting skill." He paused, but Saper was quiet. "The men look up to you, too. You know, they could all die on this raid. They need to work together. If you come up with something to bind them, I'd appreciate it."

"I've always done my duty to the *village*, ...Sir."

"That's all I'm asking."

Boda pushed his palms down on his knees, coming upright with a grunt. My god, he thought, when did I start grunting? Could this job age me so fast? He returned to his kit, glancing back once to see Saper still studying a distant, invisible horizon. Boda sighed. I'm failing, he thought.

When the messenger came to say the herd was leaving, Boda gathered the men and headed downstream searching for an easy ford. Half a kilometer below the watering hole they found a large deadfall lying part way across the river. Where it stopped there were stepping stones to cross dry. The tree butt lay half submerged in the deep, slow pool on the outside of the river bend. Its broken top had shattered among the stones, which gave way to sand toward the other shore. The sand became a wide, dry beach with a small rush-grown pool on the downstream edge.

Boda sent his men single file over the bridge. When half had passed, he stepped onto the root mass. Saper followed him. The rest took their turn as space was made.

Boda was gingerly stepping among branch stubs over water a meter deep when the butt of Saper's spear snaked out between his ankles. He flailed for balance but just had time to shout "Whaa..!" before his mouth filled with water.

He came up gasping from chill and need for air. His terror of drowning became fury when his feet found bottom in the shallows. He waded ashore as fast as the water-logged furs would let him, looked back at Saper, coughed a river spray, opened his mouth for some scorching curses, and noticed that all his men were roaring laughter. Boda blushed, closed his wide mouth, then said, "Damn you, Saper."

They all gathered around him, still laughing. "You should have seen your face!" "You thought you were drowned!" "By Huf, it was a great dive." "You looked like a gwatch diving on a rabbit!" "Why didn't you tell us you wanted a bath?"

He quickly stripped the wet clothes. They got another good laugh at his pale goose flesh before they handed him some dry furs.

Gruffly, he sent his scouts to catch the cattle.

When his clothes had been hung in the sun to dry, and the men were calming, he looked at them as he had before. Now the spark was back. They chatted in groups, they laughed, and Plint mimed his plunge. He smiled and looked for Saper. Saper was staring back with a smirk. Boda chuckled and gave him a nod.

From then the men called him Captain Gwatch, and, though he snarled about it, he was secretly pleased. He never spoke to Saper again about the impromptu swim.

* * *

The watch Eskander had set blew his horn three calls, then ran toward the approaching horse herd.

The villagers dropped what they held and hurried sunward. Eskander looked up from the hide on which he'd been laying out map sketches, stretched his back and rubbed his knotted neck.

He had begun worrying about Boda's men. They were four sleeps overdue. Three horn blasts meant success, and a success now would be happy variety.

Eskander fell in with Grimm and Ryne going to meet the raiders. Grimm had been insufferably happy for the last two sleeps and, with the return of the fifty valuable hunters, his smile was etched in place. The politics had Ryne trying to reconcile his relationship with the chief, and his auguries lately were less favorable to the war. Eskander felt a headache coming.

"They're back," Grimm said.

"I heard," Eskander replied.

"With horses."

"Yes."

Grimm laughed. "We'll eat well," he said.

Eskander grunted.

Then a wail arose at the edge of Kendee. "We lost somebody," Ryne said. They quickened their steps.

Men were relieving the raiders of responsibility for the herd. Wives were clinging to returned husbands. Families gathered by their men, but the jubilation was embarrassed and restrained, leaving wide circles around the three groups wailing their grief.

Eskander sought Boda. A tug at his cloak turned him. Tane gestured and said, "Over here." Eskander followed him.

Neither Boda nor Lentie had close kin, so they stood, an island of two, lost in each other, eyes closed, clinging.

Eskander looked away patiently. Tane said, "Ick!"

Lentie looked up at the general. The happy tears in her eyes didn't soften the glare she gave him. Boda levered himself half out of her embrace and, smiling, faced his commander. "One hundred ninety two horses, Sir," he said.

"How much grain?"

"About three thousand kilos."

"Amazing. You did well."

"The men did well."

Eskander looked at the mourners. "Who did you lose?"

Boda's face fell. "Rans, Jaben and Plint," he murmured.

"Your first heroes."

Lentie blurted, "You heartless bastard!"

Boda looked at her, surprised. Eskander's expression didn't change. "Lentie...," Boda started. She pulled free of him and ran into the village.

"I'm sorry, Eskander. She doesn't understand."

"Of course," Eskander said, watching her disappear among the huts. He knew what she did and didn't understand. He'd become inured to the losses of war, but he remembered the way it was at first, and the fresh memory of Blute made him sympathetic. He also knew that a good cause made the loss tolerable but not forgivable. In time Lentie would turn a tearless face to the dead. He would push harder to continue the fight, to win it, so those dead would stay heroes instead of becoming fools.

Eskander also knew another thing which Lentie knew and Boda didn't. Boda would have to be caught up on the news.

Grimm strode up and welcomed Boda home. "We'll eat well," he repeated, nodding toward the horses. Boda looked mildly puzzled at the remark.

Eskander said, "Go on and tell him, Grimm. You'll bust a gut if you don't."

Grimm beamed. "The answers have come back from most of the villages."

"And...," Boda prompted.

"They all told us to go to hell!"

Chapter 6

Kendee sent the spirits of the dead Beyond to the ancestors and Huf. Elder Trake began a collection for the widows and orphans. Grimm, in a magnanimous mood, gave them two horses each. Plint's wife was already well off, and, with such wealth, her prospects for another husband would be good when her mourning passed.

Eskander chafed at the delay and regretted the loss of the horses, but he respected decorum; heroes deserved honors. He went back to taking long walks and hunting with Tane. On three occasions, with Lentie's permission, he took Tane on excursions of several sleeps each. When they returned from these, he spent the next entire wake period shuffling through sheaves of sketches. He carefully transferred the information to one large map.

Village life returned to normal after twelve sleeps, normal for the time pre-Eskander. Nobody reported for training. Eskander located Boda.

"Let's round up the troops, Bodie."

"Why? The war's over."

"What makes you say that?"

"The other villages..." Boda trailed off at Eskander's patient smile.

"What did you expect?"

"You knew they wouldn't join us?"

"Bodie, look how hard it was for Kendee, even with a prophecy."

"But if you knew, then what was the point?"

"No, Boda, I didn't know. Ryne might have. I only guessed. But the point is that we had to train and work so hard that nobody else would suspect the other villages might need persuasion."

"What do you mean, 'persuasion'?" Boda asked, knowing the answer.

"They'll have to be drafted."

"Force?"

Eskander shrugged.

Boda made another connection. "That's why you've been drawing maps."

"Yes."

"But Kendee doesn't want to go on with it."

"They forgot the possibilities. We'll remind them."

Boda shook his head. "No, sir. I can't push my people into war. I've seen it now."

"Look, do you want Plint's death to be for nothing?"

"It wasn't for nothing. We have more meat in the village now than anybody can remember."

"Just another hunt, eh?"

"Raid."

"Yes," Eskander said. "Not a war, just a raid. Men lost for a taste when you could have the whole meal."

Boda didn't answer. He looked up at the general. He wanted to say that an appeal to greed would not move his people to war, but he'd already seen that it would. He wished he could say this with power and conviction, make it be true, but that was more in Ryne's field. And he remembered what Lentie had said, that Eskander would not push so hard only to make Kendee richer. He didn't belong to Kendee. His heart was in another place--a heart that was determined to drag Kendee to that place through war. Boda wondered if Eskander could be killed.

"You will destroy us," Boda said.

Slowly Eskander replied, "It is not my prophecy."

"It is now. You've taken it from us. You'll use Kendee for your own reasons and not give a damn what happens."

Boda walked away.

Eskander called after him. "I'm no saint, but I'm not a demon. Give it a chance. I won't let the deaths be for nothing. Go with me. Help me."

Captain Gwatch paused, looked over his shoulder, shook his head and left.

* * *

The time to mourn the dead passed. Now the celebration of new wealth could take place. They butchered a horse despite Eskander's resistance. Huge fire pits were assembled, fueled and lit, and spitted horse quarters began sizzling over flames.

They assembled the village supply of gni and divided it into individual drinking skins. The people struck up drums and blew flutes and horns. The timid held back, waiting for the gni to take effect, but the rest began dancing and soon had to strip off furs. People laughed openly for the first time since the raiders had returned.

The third wake period following the party several men appeared at the training ground. They talked about hunting for a while, then left. The next period there were more, and a few tussled in mock battle. The raiders told untried trainees their personal stories of the raid, acting them out in exaggerated boast.

Boda, passing by, dropped his jaw at the sight. He was not aware what celebrating the raid had done to the village outlook. It had put distance between the living and the lost. What remained was a herd of horses while the heroes, gone from sight, were forgotten.

Saper saw him. He shouted, "Captain Gwatch, show us how you flew off the log." Saper dived into the snow and men laughed.

Following the next breakfast, Eskander stood on the training field while his soldiers gathered. Boda appeared at his side.

Eskander put his hand on Gwatch's shoulder and said, "Thank you. Let's line them up, Captain."

It was three sleeps before Lentie would speak to Boda again, but by then the momentum was beyond stopping.

Grimm became surly again.

* * *

The two villages sunleft of Kendee had their backs to the sea, with Kendee between them and the rest of the snow people. Eskander felt they would be the lesser threat at his back, so the army turned sunright.

Scouts kept them apprised of the schedule of Rentoon, the first village. The map Eskander had made allowed them to work their way undetected almost to the hut walls.

There was no struggle to mention, since most of Rentoon was asleep when the attack began. Orders had been given to work quietly to maintain surprise for as long as possible. In less than half a sleep, the whole population had been subdued and disarmed. Five of the Rentoons were injured and two Kendeans, but there were no deaths on either side.

As agreed earlier, Grimm spoke to the chief and elders of Rentoon while Eskander remained aloof but present.

"There he stands," Grimm said, gesturing to Eskander, "proof of the prophecy. Here we all stand. Do you grant that Huf is with us? How else could this happen?"

"We don't grant anything," Jado, Rentoon's chief, responded. "Except your treachery. Why?"

"You wouldn't join us."

"So? Is joining you to die in war and being killed by you in our sleep any different? We're dead either way."

"Nobody died."

"What if we refuse your 'offer'?"

"You won't refuse. Look." Grimm waved and his men led twenty horses into view. Jado's eyes widened. His elders gasped and whispered among themselves.

"What's this?" Jado asked.

"This is one tenth of the wealth from a small raid. You see, we want to share an opportunity with you. If fifty men can do that, what could a thousand do, or ten thousand? The prophecy calls all of the snow people."

Jado scratched his chin. "I must talk with my elders."

"Of course."

They withdrew for a spirited whispering contest. It appeared that attempts were made to gesture "loudly" in hope of dominating the discussion. From what could be overheard, the content concerned division of prospective wealth more than it did the possibility of refusing to join. Jado finally resorted to shouting out loud to halt the talk.

He returned to Grimm. "We will join your prophecy..."

"And your prophecy."

"Whatever. After we agree on shares."

Again Eskander chafed. The negotiation took four sleeps and included a preliminary gift of six horses. During the talks, scouts spied on the next village. It disturbed Eskander to find they were fortifying. The word was out. Now each sleep wasted in talk increased the number of those who would die in the coming attack. The general pointed this out to Grimm who passed the news along to the Rentoons. They, unaccustomed to war but wise to the ways of bargaining, insisted on a larger share to make up for these deaths, and delayed the attack another sleep.

Fear of too much delay drove Eskander to suggest Grimm give them whatever they wanted. Grimm gave in on the last compromise and the bolstered army marched sunright.

The second village was called Sprill. The army surprised the fully armed and ready inhabitants when it marched past them far to sunward. Eskander hoped to overtake the spreading news and catch the third village, Lolo, complacent in their distance beyond Sprill.

Lolo had made a small beginning at fortification but there was little progress and no guards watched the perimeter. If some outlying hunters had not met the army Lolo would have fallen as quickly as Rentoon. Too many hunters were afield. Sleep or work distracted those at home. Nobody was organized.

Still, resistance in places proved fierce. Five men and one woman died before surrender.

Boda visited his wounded, housed in a commandeered Lolo hut.

"Plist, how's the leg?" He asked.

"Sore, but is was a straight thrust. I doubt I'll even limp."

"Good. You fought well."

"Oran," he said, "That eye looks terrible."

"Just bloody and puffed up. I'm more worried about my hamstring. Cut half through. Ryne says it'll heal, but I don't know."

"Ryne is a good shaman. You'll be fine."

He said a few words to each and left. Their suffering tore at him. Was this loss really worth whatever they might eventually gain? Despite the promises of prophecy and greed and Eskander, it was most probable that nothing in the world could be worth this. Grimm had said so before the whole village, and they hadn't listened to him. There was nothing Boda could do now to stop the waste and pain. The best he could hope for would be a reduction to it. He fretted over the losses on both sides and pondered ways to avoid more bloodshed.

Eskander sat on his overturned helmet in front of the fire, warming his hands. He looked tired. The battle was never thick where he fought--the enemy avoided the bronze giant--but he had done his share. He slept less than the men too, something Boda now appreciated.

"General."

"What, Bodie?"

"You need rest."

Eskander chuckled. "Tell me something new."

"Everybody else is weary, too, but I think we should move on right now."

Eskander raised his bushy brows. "What?"

"If we keep moving, the next village won't have as much time to prepare. Maybe we can catch them completely unaware. Maybe nobody will get hurt."

"Oh. Now I see. I thought you'd gone crazy. Good idea, but you're missing something. How do we get control here before we go? How do we rest the men?"

"Split the army. You and Grimm stay here with half to negotiate and rest. I take the others on forced march to capture Eteel. It'll be hard, but we can do it. By the time it's taken, your men will be fit to pass to the next village and capture it. Then we rest and pass you. If we can keep on that way, we'll have them all with the least loss."

"I have doubts, but it beats waiting for them to get ready for us. One change. I'm going with you. Grimm will stick to what he does best. Get the men up."

But even at that pace, word traveled faster. No women or children were in Eteel. Most of the fighting men were gone, and those present did what they could to slow the army without meeting it head on. When Grimm caught up, the fighting was still going on well to sunright of Eteel, heading slowly to the next village.

Eskander stopped pressing the advance to send flankers out on both sides. The three prongs overcame the light resistance, but the general was unhappy with the capture of a small force.

He became uneasy. The territory where they fought now was strange to his army while the defenders knew it well. If he couldn't meet them and defeat them soon, his men would tire and grow hungry despite Boda's village hopping idea. He sent for reinforcements from the villages they'd already taken and urged his own forces forward faster, maintaining the three prong formation. The trident crushed the defenders whenever they were overtaken, but keeping contact with his flanking troops was very difficult in the unknown terrain. Twice, enemy troops squeezed through between the prongs and attacked the central force from the side and rear. These maneuvers were ineffective but annoying.

Six sleeps later they stood forty kilometers further along but had accomplished nothing. The reinforcements arrived, but he pushed on with the whole force, giving no chance for the tired to rest.

The central party marched thinly strung across a long slope rising to sunward. They moved quickly. Resistance had stopped for nearly half a sleep. Communication with the left prong had been lost.

"Boda!" Eskander called suddenly, "stop the advance."

Boda blew his horn, watched the rank halt, approached the general and asked, "What is it?"

"It's been too long since we heard from the left flank. Send three men to scout that sunward ridge."

"We won't lose the initiative if we stop?"

"It hasn't got us anywhere so far."

They watched the scouts trudge uphill. The remaining troops rested where they had stopped. A small breeze blew at their backs from the chill, dark lands. Nobody had much to say that hadn't been said a dozen times, so quiet dominated the field. The scouts topped the hill and stopped.

They whirled and ran. A thick flight of spears leaped over the brow and dropped among them. All three fell to the snow, prickling with spears.

Uncountable warriors broke screaming over the ridge. Eskander's men nearest the attackers retreated down slope, running, disordered.

Eskander cursed and yelled, "Cover your backs, you idiots! Stay together! Don't leave anybody!

"Boda, take sunright, close them up and watch for a flank attack. Saper, you take our back. Climb that hill and hold the top as a retreat, but scout it first."

When his running men arrived he brought them to order and began the move toward Saper's position. He waved Boda into motion. They marched briskly until the enemy closed to range, then they formed a spear bristling front and continued backing. The third line stuck the butts of their spears into the snow, readied bows and nocked arrows. They paused, then loosed. A few of the attackers fell. Eskander's men, obviously rattled, hurriedly nocked again.

"Easy," he shouted. "Set your aim. The more you get now, the better it'll be later."

Eskander glanced along his line. His men looked, to him, as hardy as a stand of reeds. He had given his soldiers four things the enemy lacked, bows, shields, organization, and horses, but the enemy had numbers—a shocking bunch of numbers. "Cavalry, to the left flank. Attack their side."

The thirty horsemen swung from behind him and swept left. The horses maneuvered with difficulty, breaking through the snow crust on which men could run.

The archers loosed another flight, more effective this time at closer range. The enemy right flank saw the horses coming and curved back away from them to form a front. The cavalry dipped their lances and made a floundering charge.

"Damn snow," Eskander muttered. This was the first trial of his freshly trained horse soldiers. He'd anticipated problems with new men but even veterans, thrown into this Huf-forsaken ice nightmare, would have fared poorly.

He glanced up at Saper's group, still well below the hilltop. Above him, on the sunward slope of the valley, the two infantries crashed.

He wished the men had been better trained. They were holding, but having trouble keeping the line straight and closed up. The natural impulse was to fight individually and the passion of battle fed that desire. Some of his poorer soldiers were lured out of line and fell immediately. He yelled commands to hold positions, but the noise of weapons on shields, and the screams, and the pounding blood in every man's ears covered his voice.

He moved closer to the front line to shout encouragement and caught a spear on his shield. He snatched it up and hurled it through a man.

The enemy stood twelve deep, his troops only four. If the training didn't hold them in a solid line, they wouldn't have a chance. It was only the limiting of the contact to fronts of equal length that gave them any hope.

Grimm worked his way up to Eskander. A horse screamed and they watched it fall under a wave of warriors. The cavalrymen hadn't had the momentum to crash through the line, failed to regroup and were soon the isolated centers of enemy mobs. Within sixty heartbeats all the horses were riderless. Six of the animals lay dead or dying.

"What happened?" Grimm shouted in Eskander's ear.

"An alliance!"

"What?"

"The rest of the villages, they formed an alliance."

Grimm paled. "Then we're finished."

Eskander gave him a death's head grin. "Not yet. Fight, coward."

"Bastard," Grimm said, and advanced.

Eskander laughed, moving forward with him.

Saper topped the hill. Coming up the other side were a straggle of warriors that he recognized as remnants of their triad's right prong. Another large force harried them along. The hill provided a good panorama of the whole battle scene. As Saper surveyed the dismal prospect, a third large force rounded the base of the hill in the trampled snow of his own army's path.

His strength left him. He sat down hard in the snow and put his head in his hands. His troop looked away embarrassed as he rocked and moaned. "My family," he said. "What will happen to my family?"

A horrified groan built among troops to Eskander's left. He turned to see another force, equal to the one he faced, approaching the flank. "Shit," he said.

"Form a square!" he bellowed. "A square!" He grabbed two men and sent them along the line. When he knew the ends had received the message he waved them around.

The retreat continued as the square formed. They had reached the bottom of the shallow valley and the ends worked up the hill toward Saper as they closed. The fresh enemy warriors engaged the sunleft side of the square before it was solid, but Eskander's training held and the line stayed, wavered but stayed.

The general looked up the hill. He could see the ends of a line to right and left that Saper had formed around the other side of the peak. Good, he thought, the square will meld with that crescent and we'll hold the high ground. He busied himself with closer matters. When he glanced up later, the back of Saper's line was visible on the hilltop. He watched with sinking heart as the line backed over the ridge and the hilltop battle became plainly visible.

Boda's corner held firm, but the corner at sun-sunleft lost contact with the line strung up the hill. Eskander ran toward the gap. A roaring hoard broke through. He gathered men from the rear of the near line and strung them along to encompass the infection, but the damage was done. Above him the line began to fragment, and, when Saper's troop backed down to join the square, chaos erupted. The sunleft line crumbled into individual combats. The enemy attacked the backs of their lines from inside the square.

Boda took time for a breath and to look around. So, he thought, it ends.

Despite Eskander's height and gleaming helmet, he couldn't spot him in the meleè. He pondered, what's the bastard going to do now? How will he get us out of this? He must still be over there.

Without word from Eskander there was no other choice, so Boda reformed his men locally into a smaller square. It began moving back sunleft in an attempt to gather loose warriors and regroup with Eskander, Grimm and Saper.

The understanding that they were finished gripped Eskander. Now, even if he could reform the square and hold off the enemy indefinitely, he would never break free. They were far from their own land. The enemy had short supply lines while his were already cut. He looked across the valley at the point of engagement. Men had dropped their packs when the battle started. Most of the supplies lay there, among the bodies and the wounded. His concentration dulled the battle sounds as he surveyed the scene. There were quiet, crumpled fur bundles, writhing fur, screaming fur. He couldn't stifle a laugh at the sudden ludicrous image of thousands of animals parading naked, having given up their clothing to these men. Blood spread everywhere. It lay in dark scarlet splotches fading to pale yellow where the stir of battle had thinned it with snow.

Screaming warriors interrupted his revery. He threw up his shield deflecting a spear. Frustration, anger and desperation seized him. Time dilated. His attackers' motions slowed. His shield side-slipped and the point of his sword took a man's heart. His boot crushed a knee. The sword pommel smashed a face. A spear slid by him and he directed it into an enemy spine.

He advanced half aware. The snowmen saw the death he made and gave way. It was a small corner of the battle. They knew they could do better elsewhere.

Eskander's near men tried rallying to him but found themselves blocked by the re-closing enemy wall. Boda's square still struggled at an unreachable distance.

Then he had nobody to kill. The battle stood behind him and only trampled snow ahead. He swung around and a man whose eye he caught ran away. The general peered at the swaying mass of warring bodies and could see no remnant of the square. A small bubble in the middle of the brawl could have been Boda's small square. He wasn't even sure that during his small berserk he hadn't killed some of his own people.

A riderless horse stood five paces to his left, eating from a spilled grain sack. He took those five paces, scooped up the reins with the sack, swung onto the horse, and heeled its ribs.

He didn't analyze what he was doing. He didn't try to justify it. The sounds dwindled behind as he rode away. Once an arrow whizzed by.

Eskander read the story in the snow. "They marched along our trail here," he muttered.

The sounds faded. "They waited here until the noise of the first assault."

By now, though he couldn't know it, his warriors were throwing their arms down and asking for mercy.

When the battle was beyond hearing he mused, "That's where they found our trail after circling behind us."

He stopped once there to look back. He saw nobody.

"It's just us two, now," he said. He patted the horse's neck and urged it on.

PART 2

Chapter 1

They turned sunward at the first opportunity.

It was a good horse. Eskander imagined it becoming fond of him. Occasionally he stepped down and led the animal to let it rest and to stretch his own muscles.

"You know, horse," he said after their first sleep, "we're stuck together, so we might as well be friends."

The one-sidedness of the conversation did not disturb Eskander, whose monologues in the twilight land had been extensive. For three sleeps he touched on the weather, the sparseness of game, the inadequacy of the horse's rump for strong starts, and reminiscences of past glories, military, pugilistic and sexual.

"Sorry," he said after a particularly explicit exploit in the last category. "You, as a gelding, don't want to hear that."

After the fifth sleep, he finally broached the subject he'd been skirting so long.

"So, what could I have done if I'd stayed?" He glared at the horse. "The war was lost. You saw how many they had. All the training in the world won't help one against six.

"It wasn't my prophecy! They wanted it or they wouldn't have come. It wasn't my fault.

"I couldn't have helped by dying there. And Blute still hasn't been avenged. I can't let failed snowman prophecy keep me from that. I'll find another way to get at Fotane."

For five more sleeps, Eskander returned frequently to his defense against the accusatory horse, which said nothing but looked at him sidelong like a judge from his lofty bench. When Eskander wasn't arguing his case, he worked on new plans for revenge.

He passed from the ice to wet, to dry, to green over green. Hardy, cold-bound struggling shrubs gave way to large sheltering trees.

At twelve sleeps, he became detached as he traveled. Peculiar, embarrassing memories forced themselves on him. Some were awful enough to make him shudder, and no mental diversion could block these torments. Then he became depressed. After the next sleep, he was feverish, dizzy and uncertain of his actions. Most peculiar, when he turned his head, the world hesitated before it turned in his sight. That wake period he stayed on the horse the whole time and was swaying by the time he stopped near a small stream. His appetite failed and he rolled shivering into his sleeping fur.

"I must have got some bad water," he moaned, and vomited.

He sat up, aware that he must have been sleeping and, because of the residual dread, having bad nightmares. Eskander shook his head and winced at the pain it caused. The fever, though reduced, still gripped him. He was too dizzy to stand.

He lay back down. His heart, racing from the fever the dream and the effort of rising, finally calmed. He slept again without dreams.

Chapter 2

A cold rain settled over Eskander for three sleeps while he sweat off the last of the chills and fever. The crude shelter he'd thrown together in small fits of labor leaked, but he relied on his furs to shed what the cut boughs could not. Occasionally he felt the misery and wet would be too much for him, that he would relapse and die, but he didn't. Several attempts to make a fire failed until he foraged far enough and found dry, sheltered wood that would catch at the end of the long effort of bringing glowing tinder to a real flame. He had made the mistake of trying hopeful shortcuts to a fire, each of which failed. The eventual success cheered him. He stopped imagining his corpse rotted and spread around the forest by scavengers.

He missed Tane and the others. "I hope they make it."

Eskander finally hobbled the horse, then gave it some grain. "You're a loyal animal," he told it. "I'll name you Blute, for my loyal friend."

When the weather broke he laid his furs in the sun and, after they dried, gathered his armor and wrapped it in them. The sword went into the center of the roll with the grip hidden by a flap but accessible. He folded the flaps of his hat under to fit snugly without the helmet. The warm air cheered him, so he sang as he tied the bundle across the horse's shoulders.

As he swung up on the horse he said, "Blute, isn't it strange that a man always feels best after a fever or a hangover?"

No outward sign of his occupation remained as he rode sunward. He felt and looked like a new man.

* * *

Eight sleeps later Eskander saw the first evidence of people. A fish weir spanned a stream near his crossing. Until then he was not aware how secure he had been feeling; even in the wilderness the greatest carnivore ignores a human unless molested or unable to hunt usual game. He became uneasy.

He remembered his careless entry to Kendee. It amused him now, but what choice had he had then? Only other people could have saved him.

The fish trap was empty or he would have helped himself. Unless it was a poor stream the person who'd set it must not be far away. Eskander pointed the horse up the side of the valley seeking a high point. Before he reached the ridge a drifting smoke column caught his eye and, lonely without more than the horse's conversation, despite his uncertainty, he turned toward it.

How does one approach a stranger? If there were many people he could be in danger. If there was only one Eskander might inadvertently scare him away.

He stopped about three hundred meters from the smoke source and tied Blute to a tree. He debated which weapons to carry, finally deciding the dagger would have to do. It was less to carry if he had to run and less obviously threatening. He was confident that unless the strangers had bows and shot him on sight he could either talk himself into their grace or, met with animosity, approach closely enough to make the dagger a bargaining point. Even faced with a sword he doubted he would be in much danger. Anybody out here was unlikely to have had training in the fine points of close combat.

* * *

"What's your name?" she asked.

He felt compelled to answer with sincerity if not truth whatever she might ask, considering how sinister the cross-bow looked from this end. He wondered where it had been hidden until she swung it to point at his chest. He regretted the distance between him and the good armor rolled in fur on his horse, though the bolt from the bow could pierce it easily.

"Eskander."

"What the hell's an Eskander?" She asked scornfully.

She was not beautiful, nor pretty, nor cute, nor the least attractive to him, especially in this circumstance. She wore her hair like a man. Except for the voice pitch and obvious shape of hips under her furs he would have continued the assumption that she was a man. They were man's clothes, man's tools, and man's manners, but without the familiarity of male empathy, even antagonistic male empathy.

"A wanderer."

"Does that pay well?" she sneered.

"Not in these parts."

At this flippant remark she shouted, "Asshole! Sprout feathers!"

Eskander dove. The cross bow twanged, the fletching stung his neck as the quarrel passed, and he tumbled toward a thick tree.

She ran behind another tree and started pulling back the four bowstrings. Eskander scrambled for footing on the dead leaves and decided that running would be safer than trying to reach the woman before her bow was ready. He'd made about ten long strides when a bolt sprayed bark off a tree he had just dodged. He got in another ten meter dash to an unfortunately slender tree and paused awaiting the next quarrel. It didn't come. Eskander looked ahead. The next tree was twenty meters away and even smaller than the one where he leaned. "Shit," he muttered.

All she had to do was approach him directly with the bow ready, step around the tree and take him. "Shit," he said again.

"Hey," he shouted, "What do you want?"

She didn't answer.

"I haven't done anything to you," he called.

Silence held for a while and then, too close, "Nothing yet, asshole, and nothing ever if I get a shot."

"Listen, I'm really just passing through. I saw your smoke and wanted some company. You don't want company, that's fine, I'll leave. You don't have to kill me."

"Maybe I want to," she chuckled.

His neck stung badly and when he carefully raised a hand to it he felt a fat welt oozing clear fluid. That had been a close shot. She was far enough away that the tree hid her from him, but he was larger and wondered if it offered him the same shield. "What do you want?" he asked again.

"Shut up, I'm thinking."

This was the most encouraging thing he'd heard since they met. At least she had stopped stalking.

"You're a wanderer, eh? By your accent, you've wandered a long way. What business could you have around here?"

"I.."

"Shut up!" She didn't talk again for some time and Eskander feared she was sidling up to the tree, but when she spoke again she hadn't moved.

"Two things bring foreigners this close to snow barbarians: the law, or a stupid adventure. Either way you might be worth something. If you're a criminal there could be a reward. You look like a criminal. But if you're hunting adventure you must be well backed. Reward or ransom, I like it."

"May I suggest a third possibility?" Eskander asked.

"You don't sound much like a criminal. Ransom it is. That's fine; rewards are set but with an ear or a finger ransom can be negotiated. Step out slowly."

An ear or finger? He shook his head. "How do you expect to ransom a nobody?"

"Oh, that's up to you. You'll help me or die."

Eskander sighed. He stepped carefully from hiding with his hands held out from his body, expecting death.

She didn't shoot him but her grin was not reassuring. "Did you come on foot?" she asked.

He considered the armor and what she would think of it. He thought of the horse left tethered to die of thirst. Perhaps Blute could break free when he became desperate for water. If the woman saw the armor she would be convinced that Eskander could be ransomed, perhaps for more than her first estimate. If he could convince her that he was worthless she would let him go. Or she would kill him. Hmm. Maybe the woman could be deluded longer into thinking he was worth keeping alive for ransom if she saw the armor and, besides, he didn't want his loyal Blute to suffer.

"I have a horse over there." He nodded toward Blute's hiding place.

"Let's fetch it."

She made him stand back from the horse while she poked through the bundle. Her grin broadened when she saw the sword and armor.

He studied her now that they were not moving. He'd been right. She was not pretty, but she was not ugly. He had expected her to be ugly. He had hoped she was ugly. But she was handsome in a female way--not masculine but too square for a woman.

"Where are your people?" Eskander asked.

She glared at him. Apparently that was none of his business.

After rummaging through all of his things the woman pulled a long braided leather cord from her pouch and tied a slip knot in the end. She said, as she laid the loop on the ground and fed slack, "When I tell you, pick up the loop, turn your back and put your wrists in it."

When she'd backed five meters from the knot she stopped and said, "Now." The bow always pointed at him.

Eskander had a sudden thought that the real curse of his existence was women--not all women of course, just the smart ones. Tissa had exiled and nearly killed him, Resta almost defeated his plans for Kendee, and even shy Lentie had just about subverted his most valuable soldier. How he longed for a pretty but vacant whore.

He obeyed her commands. As soon as the cord was around his wrists she pulled the loop tight and, with quick flicks, sent twisted waves down the cord that snugged his wrists in two half-hitches. Eskander was learning to hate her. He had hoped for some incompetence somewhere, something that would let him get close enough to take control, but it didn't look like it would happen soon, if ever.

She briefly trussed him to a tree and searched his person intimately. Her eye gleamed at the ornamental dagger.

Only after she had moved him to a tree at her camp did she become a little more loquacious.

"Are you comfortable?"

"Do you care?"

"Sure. Don't want to harm the goods. Unless I have to." She grinned that scary grin. "And I wouldn't misbehave if I was you. Just the horse and armor would feed me a good many sleeps. You be too much trouble and I'll settle for them."

She pulled the dagger out when she sat down, and admired it. "This I'll keep," she said.

She tucked the dagger in her furs, leaned back and gazed into the fire. Eskander saw no choice but to wait her out.

He discovered where the crossbow had been hidden. Whenever she stood she hung it from a shoulder strap that held it angled across her back. Her hips were wide enough to conceal the short quad of bows and the stock lay behind her right shoulder.

For two sleeps neither said a word as they traveled sunward, she riding the horse, he walking short, hobbled steps and burdened by the woman's large backpack.

He fortunately had grown beyond bodily embarrassment, because she would not allow him to pass waste until she must, when she would tie him to a tree, hide from his sight awhile and then return to give him enough leash to perform his necessities. Years of close military living had eradicated any vestiges of his shyness. The knowledge that women are only human eased his difficulty being human around them. But nothing had prepared him completely for the unrelenting glare of this bitch.

After the second waking, as he squatted, he finally asked, "Would you at least look the other way?"

She laughed but turned aside.

They went another fifteen kilometers before stopping to eat. During the meal he gave up on silence. "What's your name?" he asked.

"Natta."

"Natta, how do you think you'll hold me and still arrange for ransom?"

"I know some people."

"What people? Where are we going?"

"Why does such a big man have such a small tool?" she asked.

That shut him up for another sleep.

"Where are you from?" he asked when he had again tired of the silence.

"Rotosch."

"Never heard of it."

"Nobody ever heard of it. One of the reasons I'm not there any more."

"What are the other reasons?" he asked.

She just swung up on the horse and prodded Eskander along.

They passed herders that march who, when they saw the pair, bustled their animals into a group and stood with weapons threatening. Word of the raid had gotten around.

"You're not a herder?" Eskander asked Natta.

"I'm a hunter."

"Why were you so far antisun?"

"You ask too many questions."

They went quietly for fifty heartbeats, then Natta said, "The furs are better."

"What?"

"The further antisun you go the better the animal furs."

"So you don't live there either."

"No," she said, "only animals, barbarians and the likes of you can stand the place. I go there for as many sleeps as it takes to fill my pack with dried hides, then come home."

Eskander considered his good luck to still be sweating in his own hide.

"Home?"

"We're almost there," Natta said. "You saw the way the herders acted. We make them nervous."

I can understand that, he thought. So the snowman raid wasn't all the herders had to fear.

Risking a compliment he said, "If the women are all like you, Natta, the men must be fearsome indeed."

The wad of spit that hit Eskander on the cheek was well aimed but lacked mass, probably through haste in acquiring it.

He lunged, trussed as he was, at Natta and the horse. "Bitch!" he yelled and tried to bite her leg with a good enough grip to drag her down and stomp her. She kneed him in the jaw, put her foot in his chest and shoved. He tripped in his hobbles, falling hard.

"What was that for?" he yelled.

"Shut up!"

They stared at each other until Eskander's breathing had settled, then she gestured him to rise and proceed. Hesitantly he obeyed, rolling over under the pack with difficulty and struggling up.

Five kilometers further along they crested a ridge which gave view to a village of six dozen or so huts swaddled in smoke from two cooking fires and a smithy. Irregularly divided garden patches made continuous open ground all about the village. People moved among the huts and gardens.

Eskander asked, "What is the name of your village?"

"We call it Free. For reasons you will soon see."

Stranger and stranger, he said to himself, when they entered Free. It took him several heartbeats to grasp what made it strange, and he took a grip of himself to stifle an outburst as everything about his captor suddenly became clear.

"How many men are in the village?" he asked Natta.

"One," she said, "standing in your boots."

"I thought Amazons were a myth."

For only the second time since they'd met, Natta laughed out loud. She laughed until Eskander blushed and then she said, "What a fool! Your friends will be too embarrassed to pay your ransom after that remark."

The Free women stared as Eskander shuffled to the village heart. Like Kendee, Free had a central meeting area. A well worn hollowed log hung there by cords from a wood tripod. Natta dismounted, took up the club and beat the log three booming strokes. Soon women crowded the square, gawking at Eskander and speculating among themselves.

"I think," Natta called over the chatter, "I think we have valuable goods here." By then they were quiet. "This thing has money. We can ransom him."

"Natta," a gray haired woman in front said, "you are impetuous. Give us a heartbeat to organize the sisters and we'll do this by the rules. First, will someone please take the horse out of the square?

"Thank you, now everybody sit ... except you," she said to Eskander. Then, "Natta?"

Natta said, "I request a public meeting for the good of Free."

The older woman looked over the crowd and said, "No one objects. Go on."

Natta stood, described the encounter with Eskander and proposed that Free send agents to discover his worth so he could be ransomed.

Eskander watched the women. Some looked at him with curiosity, some with fear, and many with hatred. He hoped that he could escape before they discovered nobody would pay for his rescue.

"Does anyone wish to speak?" the gray woman asked.

Three stood.

"Pluseet, say your piece." The other two sat.

"We tried this twice before and never came out ahead. The second time we had him whittled down to a stub and nobody cared. What makes this different?"

"Look," Natta said and pulled out the dagger. "No bum carries something like this unless he stole it. And what about this?" She rolled Eskander's bundle out on the ground, tumbling the armor into the grass.

They murmured appreciatively over the ornate metal.

"Shall we try again, Sisters?" the gray one asked. "All in favor..." Nearly every hand shot up. "Opposed?" No one raised her hand. "The usual abstentions. Natta's proposal passes."

He saw no present alternative to cooperation, so he told them he was an officer in the Prater army. They should contact Colonel Antu.

Eskander hoped that, barring escape, Antu, one of the officers Eskander had approached for help after Jengo's murder, thought well enough of him to buy his freedom. If the colonel was discrete Eskander would take the king's head before Fotane discovered that his nemesis still lived and had returned to Prater. He did not tell his captors about his quarrel with the king, fearing their thoughts would turn to reward as an option to failed ransom. They might divulge his whereabouts accidentally to the wrong people anyway, but he had to accept that risk.

As the meeting broke up and Eskander was being led off toward a shack a slim woman skipped up to Natta. The two embraced and Natta kissed her hard on the mouth. Eskander's jaw dropped and he cursed himself as an idiot at the sudden understanding of how things really stood in Free.

* * *

He had feared suffering terrible boredom awaiting Antu's response but Free wasn't going to keep him for nothing. They put him to work in the gardens, or cutting wood, or helping with heavy work. Since they could guard him in shifts his sleeps were far apart and his weariness grew with each waking. And they were not generous with food.

The bronze smith intrigued him. Given the occupation he expected her to be one of the more burly Free women, but she bordered on dainty. Her name was Ree and she was one of the handful who neither feared nor hated him. Most of the villagers either ignored or avoided him, but she gabbed with Eskander whenever he helped her.

"My father is a smith," she replied to his first query. "He used to let me hang around his smithy. I'm the only one here who knows the trade, so I do it despite being small. I make up for my size by using helpful tools." She gestured around the smithy. Eskander admired the system of winches, pulleys, beams and levers with which she moved the material and equipment of her job. Where the smiths he knew relied on muscular arms and a big hammer to forge hot metal, she used a foot powered trip hammer. Not only did it use her stronger leg muscles to advantage, it also left both hands free to position the bronze. A tall stack produced sufficient draft in the charcoal fired forge to work metal. For smelting, her furnace bellows was run by a wind mill on the roof, or by Eskander if the wind didn't blow.

The hobbles slowed Eskander and a guard kept watch always. Fifteen sleeps of this drudgery prompted him to ask Ree, "Do I have to wear these forever?" gesturing at his ankles.

"Keep pumping the bellows. You were brought by Natta?"

"Yes."

"Did she frighten you?" Ree asked.

"More than any man I ever met."

"Let me tell you a story.

"In the small, backward village of Rotosch the priests of Huf rule. It is a very a rigid sect. Life in Rotosch is bound tightly by traditions and the laws of Huf as interpreted by the priests. Anybody 'unconformed', as they call it, faces increasingly harsh penalties until they come into conformity, or die in the process. How well do you think Natta fit in there?"

Eskander grunted.

Ree continued, "Her hurts and humiliations are hers to tell or not. She deserves privacy. But I will say that she bears scars on her body and her soul that would even gag you, soldier boy. The marvel is that she doesn't kill every man she meets. She escaped from Rotosch and found Free through rumor and luck, same as the rest of us. She healed some of her mind wounds and learned to love her friend, Irba. But she'll never trust a man again. Most of the women here have similar stories. Think you'll get out of your hobbles?"

"When I'm three sleeps dead."

"If then."

Eskander worked the bellows a while. "How will you contact Antu? It's a big city."

Ree laughed. "Easier than you think. Men have absolutely no control over themselves concerning sex. Judell, Fweela, and Ona are very beautiful. They are also consummate, or should I say inconsummate, prick teasers. It's a game they played for fun and profit before finding Free. They'll make friends with soldiers and find out anything the poor boys know."

"Sounds dangerous."

"For the men. The women work as a team and have no scruples about using the push-daggers they carry."

Eskander grunted and the bellows wheezed, then the bellows grunted and Eskander wheezed.

"Women are my bane," he said.

"All men say that. Help me with this pour."

They donned long cuffed, thick gloves. He handed her the skim. They fitted rods through eyes on the hanging pot and poured carefully. Shining, molten bronze raced down paths into the mold. Steam shot out of vents and risers. When the metal came up they stopped and watched the surface crystallize.

"That was smooth," she said. "You have a fair hand for this. You should apprentice to me and learn a useful trade."

"I'm good at what I do now, thanks."

"Hostage is a rotten career."

"I meant soldiering."

She laughed. "Sure, but is killing people a *useful* trade?"

"I suppose your three beautiful investigators, not to mention Natta, find it useful enough."

"But they only kill men who, generally, deserve worse."

"No compassion?" Eskander asked.

"Gone by my second rape."

Eskander thought of unwilling women he had used as war spoils and finally wondered what their lives had become.

"That why you're living in Free?"

"Mostly."

"I'm sorry," he said.

"It wasn't your fault. As individuals men are usually tolerable. It's in groups the beast comes out. Like dogs they need the pack to stiffen their backbone. Or their frontbone."

He was less all right than she thought, but he did not correct her. This moral dilemma was the same he had faced in planning to use the Snow People to vanquish Fotane. Initially they were just barbarians to throw away when finished, but, on personal acquaintance, they became humans and friends. Women to him had always been objects of desire, chattel or tools. His present, unusual position among women who managed every aspect of village society without even one male, was educating him. Not that his ways would change. Generations of culture do not alter with a few sleeps, even in one man. But he would use this new outlook in future dealings. He would shed his bane.

A personal concern reduced his sleep even more. Immersion in a purely female society should have overwhelmed him with desire but awakening his "frontbone" in solo endeavor failed. He also had little privacy for the practice. Several sleeps passed as the condition only worsened until he feared it would become a permanent disability, providing he survived. The hard work, starvation, lack of sleep, and the unaccustomed role had emasculated him.

* * *

Eskander shuffled along the vegetable row, an oak hoe in hand, weeding. He took pleasure in this one chore, a surprise to him considering the lengths to which he had gone escaping a farm life. It was peaceful, calming and productive. His worries left him alone in the garden.

Voices raised in the village. Eskander's guard looked toward Free and when the drum boomed she stepped in its direction. This brought her closer to the prisoner.

Eskander hopped quickly at her, raising his hoe. The crossbow pivoted to aim at his chest and his guard glared him back. He smiled, shrugged, and tossed the hoe down. She gestured and they walked into Free.

Three men and two strange women stood near the drum surrounded by Free citizens. The strangers were uneasy but not cowed. The women of Free watched them closely but did not point weapons directly at them.

They're emissaries, Eskander thought. I wonder if this has to do with my ransom.

When everyone near had gathered, the gray-haired village mistress, Swan, spoke.

"Who are you, and why are you here?"

One of the men touched a female companion's arm, urging her forward. She said nervously, "We're herders from antisun of your village. You are fearless fighters, and we need your help."

"The world doesn't want us. We help only ourselves now," Swan said. "Go away."

The man interjected, "But you're in danger too!"

Hundreds of hostile eyes pinned his lip shut and he stepped back. The strange woman said, "He's right. The Snowmen won't stop if we lose, and you'll be next."

Eskander barked, "What!".

Swan glanced at him. To the strangers she said, "Tell me more."

"Thousands of barbarians are marching sunward from the snow land. Herders have been fleeing ahead of them with all their animals and goods. Our pastures are beaten down by the refugees, the Snowmen are a handful of sleeps away, and our backs are up against you and the farmers. If we overrun the land sunward we'll be pinched between the farmers defending their fields and the barbarians taking our pastures. We have no choice. If you and the farmers don't help us, we're doomed."

Swan said to Eskander, "You're not a snowman."

"No."

"But you know about them."

Eskander shrugged.

"Tell me," she said.

"They have a prophecy. I thought it was wishful thinking. I assumed their civil war would destroy them or send them back to the villages, but obviously the alliance lives, guided by the prophecy." He laughed. "They were to be led by a 'bronze man', which they took me to be, and now here they come, following me."

Swan asked, "What did the prophecy say? Will they destroy us?"

"It spoke of conquest under high sun."

She glanced at the sun. "How high?"

"I don't know."

"Who's conquest?"

"The snowmen said it meant they would prevail over their enemies but, now that you ask, I see it might mean the Snowmen would fail."

"So," Swan said, "they could be stopped antisun of here, or crush us and be destroyed sunward, or they really could conquer the world. Typical prophecy. You think they'll be stopped antisun?"

Eskander looked at the herders. "No," he said.

"Why not?" one of the men asked.

"Because you're not ready and they are."

"If Free and the farmers help us we can muster more fighters."

"You'd need four times their army," Eskander said.

"That's crazy. How can they be that dangerous?"

"Because I trained them," Eskander stated.

Exclamations stirred the watchers. When it calmed Swan said, "Then you know how to stop them."

"With what? You and these? And maybe some farmers if you scare them into fighting? Those barbarians fight every day just to live. If Boda survived the civil war and commands them now even the Prater army might not stop them."

"But you know more than your pupil. There are things he didn't learn, and what he did learn you know how to counter."

"But he has a trained army. I don't."

Swan thought for several heartbeats. "We have nowhere to run. Our village grows only because sisters who come looking can find us. If we move they'll be lost and we risk extinction."

"What about the children to keep the village alive?" Eskander asked.

"They arrive with pregnant newcomers. Nobody here chooses to mate. We'd love daughters but laying with a man is repugnant."

"Move out of the path, wait until they pass and return to your village."

"If we move we fight. People call us 'abomination' and won't take us in or even let us live. Fighting to defend our home is better than fighting to be allowed to run away. At least here the neighbors fear us." She looked at the herders who all nodded heartily. Swan smiled. "They know how the sisters fight. You disparage our strength, but look into the eyes around you."

Eskander didn't need to. He'd seen the concentrated hate and fear. He remembered the old saying about the size of the fight in the dog. These bitches had huge fight in them.

He said, "How many?"

"Three hundred thirty fighters."

"The Snowmen have ten thousand."

Swan asked the herders, "You can muster more?"

Their spokeswoman looked at the men. The head man said, "Eight thousand of us and six thousand farmers if we can persuade them."

Eskander asked, "Why don't you move sunleft or sunright until the barbarians pass?"

"And if they don't pass, but settle our land? The pastures sunleft and sunright won't carry the extra burden. We know it and the herders on them know it. We face the same dilemma as Free. The war will come to us or we'll take it with us, but we can't run from it."

"Mistress Swan," Eskander asked, "would your women fight alongside men, accept orders from a man?"

Swan shouted, "Vote sisters. You heard it all. How many would fight by men with this fellow's orders?"

No one put up a hand. "It seems, man," Swan said, "that you have a point.

"Sisters," she called. "Who would fight beside men under *my* orders?"

Three quarters of the village raised an arm.

"Well, hostage," Swan said, "you are now my military adviser. And you won't outlive me if your suggestions are worthless.

"You herders," she continued, "tell your people we follow in one sleep. Will the farmers join?"

The herdswoman answered, "Our emissaries are there. We'll know in two sleeps."

Chapter 3

This herder tent stood surrounded by hundreds more, was the largest, and now held the combined leadership of the forces about to face the snowmen.

Eskander had convinced Swan that hobbles on the military adviser would undermine their confidence and that his armor could bolster it. For the moment he appeared majestically free, if somewhat sallow through exhaustion and poor diet at the hands of his captors. He felt he rattled inside his chest armor like a clapper in a bell.

"It's very shiny armor," Joot was saying, "But does it prove his ability as a leader, or his loyalty to us? Who is he, anyway?"

"He's a general of Prater," Swan said.

"Who told you that? Him?" Joot gestured at Eskander. "And for that matter, who are you?"

Shazer stepped between Joot and the pair of Swan's women raising their bows.

"She," Shazer said, "is an ally. We're here to stop the Snowmen, not fight each other."

"I just want some kind of assurance about this man," Joot said. "Why should we listen to him?"

"He isn't carrying a letter of introduction. What would convince you, Joot?"

"What battles has he fought?"

Eskander said, "I became a general in our war with Rendize."

"There," Joot cried. "Caught in a lie already!"

Shazer looked puzzled at Eskander. "General," he said, "news doesn't reach us quickly, but the last we heard Rendize had been a peaceful subject state to Prater for three generations. Have they revolted?"

"Your news must be very slow. Their revolt was a man's age ago. They were a free state when they attacked our sunright border two weenings back."

"Hah!" Joot snorted.

"Our news is never that old," Shazer said, his suspicion aroused. "What proof can you give that you are who you say?"

Eskander, angering, glared around. "You're confused. I didn't ask for this. I've been coerced. Find another man if you don't accept me."

"Well, Swan," Shazer said, "you suggested him."

She looked at Eskander with disgust. "Our agents haven't returned from Prater. I can't vouch for him. He knows that he'll die if he betrays us, but if none of you trust that..." she shrugged. "Do you have anybody else with military training?"

"I have a test," Joot said.

"What?" Shazer asked.

"Let him prove himself by combat."

"By Huf!" Eskander exclaimed. "Send me back to the gardens and get on with your damned war."

Swan said, "You'll have time for gardening later. Now you will do as we say." She looked at Joot. "You will fight him?"

"Ah," Joot hesitated. "I'm not young anymore. Never did anything but herd. I wouldn't be much of a test."

"We'll find someone, Swan," Shazer said.

* * *

Eskander stood with a staff in hand facing a cheerful looking man just shorter than himself, but wider by a hand.

"Shall I kill him," Eskander asked, "or just cripple him?"

The man stopped smiling.

Shazer said, "He's a good man, General. We'll need him. Now begin."

His opponent feinted and Eskander countered, then caught an upswung blow from the other's staff butt with his own. He slipped the man's staff out and up, continued the arc begun with the top of his staff and cracked the fellow on the side of the skull. He dropped like a stone.

Eskander turned and walked back into the tent.

* * *

"We don't have time to become an army that will beat them," Eskander told the gathering. "All we can hope is to hurt them enough to turn them back.

"First, and most critically, we pick the battlefield. I'll give the requirements to our scouts. They'll select several sites. We hope to lure the snowmen to one of them.

"Next, there are simple things that will help, that the snowmen don't know. They have horses and can use them, but we won't fight as they expect. Our horsemen can't learn field maneuvers and lance techniques in two sleeps, so they will be mobile archers and attack enemy horsemen in lightning strikes and withdrawals. This occupies the snowmen away from our soldiers."

Joot said, "Anybody can use a club. We'll ride in and knock them off their horses."

"No," Eskander said. "You'd never get close enough. Their lances will kill you before you touch them."

"It's worth a try."

"Why repeat a mistake already made by dead men? Nobody fights horseback with clubs because it doesn't work."

"I've seen horse soldiers with long swords," Joot replied. "What's the difference?"

"Those are only for fighting after a front is broken, when the horseman has no room to charge with his lance. That's a situation we can't allow. If it does happen our mounted archers have to break free and use their bows."

Joot sulked but said nothing.

Eskander went on, "To defend our infantry from their cavalry a rank of pikemen will be added behind the spearmen and in front of the archers. As the horse soldiers attack, the pikemen step ahead of the spears. Group your pikemen in teams of three that coordinate defense against a single horse. Other teams must not encroach but guard only their own front. Kill the horse if possible, the rider then is just a poorly armed foot soldier.

"Never break ranks. If they draw you out singly, you die. Remember, to beat them all we have to do is stop their advance long enough that they grow tired and hungry. We won't push the attack until they retire to rest. They must not be allowed to rest. You have to push them until they're too weary to stand."

"Where will the Amazons fight?" Shazer asked.

Swan opened her mouth but thought better of it and looked at Eskander.

He said, "They are the headquarters guard."

"Yes," Shazer said, "I see they guard you well enough." He smiled.

Eskander ignored him as he had been ignoring the two Free archers watching his back.

"Tend your soldiers," he said. "We move after next sleep."

* * *

The Snowmen knew they were there. Eskander had selected a site with a long ridge that passed well behind his lines for a defensible communication and supply path. The slope to the valley floor was smooth enough to retreat easily while providing an advantage for down hill charges. A difficult, rocky hill sat on the far side of the valley with archers and rock throwers to keep the snowmen from attaining high ground. The enemy could not pass without suffering a sweeping attack from above, nor attack in return without working up hill. Even if they reached the sunward end of the valley it narrowed there so archers on both ridges could drop arrows into them.

A misting rain fell from very low clouds, pausing intermittently to give hope of relief but then continuing.

Eskander's scouts followed barbarian parties that investigated paths around his flanks. When they found no safe route for a large force the whole Snowman army marched straight into the mouth of the valley.

"Well?" Swan said to Eskander.

"We'll wait to see if they attack up the hill. If they do we wait till they come two thirds up and are tiring, then meet them. If they proceed down-valley we can't let them start into the neck. We'll attack the flank to turn them up hill against us before the last enter the valley. We can't cut off their retreat or we'll think we've slapped a bear on the nose. They'll retreat with a place to go, or kill us without one."

"You're a cheery fellow," Swan muttered.

He gestured with his chin. "Here they come."

The barbarians turned their backs to the archers on the far ridge and climbed slowly up Eskander's hill.

"They're conserving strength," he said. "Bugle ours down now."

The horns blew. Herders and farmers rose to their feet, lifted weapons lashed together hurriedly in the last three sleeps, and stepped off down the hill. They carried spears made of staffs with knives lashed to the end, or merely sharpened stakes. Farmers favored pitch-forks. The pikes were green poles with whittled points, and the bows were fewer than the general needed. Eskander discouraged axes. They are as dangerous to friends as enemies and have no defense against a man with a spear or sword. Still, many carried axes and Eskander put them behind the archers to take down enemies that broke through the ranks.

"Foolishness," he mumbled.

"What?" Swan said.

"This is crazy. Look at those Snowmen. Their weapons. Look at the tight, straight rank. They've come a long way since I knew them. They're battle hardened. Over there. See that ugly man with the frog-face? That's Boda, born tactician.

"See our supposed warriors? Boda could take a nap through this one. His men don't need him to commit massacre here."

"We knew it would be hard."

"Mistress Swan. Hard would be a relief. This is impossible."

"Shut up. My Sisters can hear you."

"Bugle the archers, Swan."

The horn blew. A massed flight of arrows plunged into the advancing troops. A handful of men dropped but the rest continued, many with arrows sticking from shields. Three more flights rose and fell before answering fire from the barbarians. Too many of Eskander's shieldless herders crumpled.

The lines clashed. Astonishment grew in Eskander as his men held, did not break ranks and, with the fury of rats defending the nest, began forcing the intruders down hill.

His people dropped like mowed wheat, but men always stepped in to fill the rank. Some picked up downed barbarian spears and fought harder.

Boda signaled retreat. Eskander saw the poised horsemen ready to pass through Boda's ranks to assault the herders as they followed to flatter ground.

"Call them back, Swan! Call them now or they'll be minced!"

The snowmen backed in orderly fashion and the herders moved down on top of them. The horn sounded retreat and those that heard it looked puzzled at each other. Those who missed it in the fever of battle kept moving, so the rest went with them. They were winning! They wouldn't stop now.

Eskander shouted, "Call them, Swan! Call them!" The horn blared out desperately.

"When our people turn send the mounted archers between the lines at their horsemen."

Barbarian cavalry plunged out through openings in Boda's infantry and smashed into the herders. The pikemen held most of them but the line broke in three places as horses rode the men down. Boda had learned the lessons of war. His cavalry regrouped immediately and crashed back through the enemy ranks into the safety of their own lines.

Horseback herders rumbled forward as the panicky foot soldiers finally responded to the horn and started a confused retreat up hill, dragging what survivors they could. The barbarian lines opened again and the cavalry rode out to meet Eskander's mounted archers. They pounded straight at them then stopped in skids as the archers split around them and released a hail of arrows. This time they were surprised and lost several riders before retreating to the haven of their infantry.

Eskander recalled his horses.

* * *

Clouds grazed the hilltop, briefly cutting off the view from the valley floor. Among the Snowmen the seriously wounded were passed behind the lines and helped away.

Grimm gave comfort where he could and thanks where he could not. Most of these men were strangers. The alliance had become the prophecy and now he feared for all of his race.

"Boda," Grimm said approaching the commander, "I have a bad feeling about this."

Boda smiled. "But you always have a bad feeling about everything."

"They're well organized."

"Yes, Grimm, but inexperienced and badly equipped. They gave me a couple of surprises but they can't win."

Grimm said, "They shouldn't have done this well."

The clouds broke momentarily, allowing sun to strike the hill and beam a flash from something there.

Boda pointed to the top of the ridge. "That's their headquarters. What do you see?"

The flash of sun on shined bronze pulled Grimm's eye. He shouted, "Pluck me naked! That bastard Eskander! Boda, how do you expect to beat him?"

"Like I said, he has poor soldiers. Besides," Boda said, "he's been beat before."

Grimm did not add that Boda was beaten in that same battle. The transformation Grimm had seen made it hard for him to believe Boda was the same poor bachelor hunter he'd known only seventy sleeps ago.

Grimm, caught up in the chaos of the last battle of the snowman civil war, did not know precisely when the Bronze Man had abandoned them. Boda's square had been unbreakable, finally picking up Grimm and bursting out of the enemy body, escaping while the foe took control of the surrendering warriors. War was done, but the winning tribes succumbed to the lure of loot just as his people had. Grimm wished he had never seen those beautiful, poisonous horses. The allied tribes came to the small band of Grimm's remaining fighters, inviting them to return. Boda's feats at the final battle had demonstrated that he should command the new alliance. The prophecy lived.

Boda had brought them a long way and grown in others' esteem, and in self confidence. But he served at the request of the people and still felt personally uncomfortable with the war. At the same time he harbored resentment for the Bronze General. Grimm hoped Boda's judgment would hold while facing the man he blamed for the war. What would he do if he captured Eskander, Grimm wondered.

* * *

Swan asked Eskander, "What now?"

"Now they'll attack again but they won't pull back until they push us off the ridge."

"You're saying we didn't stop them?"

"Boda was testing. Granted, if we'd shown less resistance he wouldn't have stopped. I hope he was as surprised by our troops as I was."

"So what do we do?" she asked.

"When they start, we start. Meet them as low on the hill as possible. Force them to fight all the way up. Boda knows now that his cavalry is weak against our pikes. He won't use them again unless he can break our line permanently.

"Keep our pikemen close to fill the front as men fall but don't let them delay the spearmen as they back up the hill. Watch our flanks. Split our horses in two and set them to repel a flank attack.

"Did we design a signal to call the men on that ridge," he pointed across the valley, "in case we need them to attack Boda's rear?"

"No."

"Shit. Oh well, it would be a desperate act anyway."

The snowman horns called and their army marched.

"Send them down, Swan," Eskander prompted.

When she'd signed to the signal corps and the horns had blown, Eskander asked her, "Do the herders have a song?"

"What do you mean?"

"A song that's special to them. Traditional, powerful, moving. They need inspiration."

"I've heard one called 'God Bos'," Swan answered.

"Ask their leaders to start it."

Swan walked to the men and explained what Eskander wanted. They looked at him quizzically but faced out over their descending men and began to sing.

"God Bos, god Equus, god Caprus,
Feed us, carry us, clothe us.
From the sun grown grass
And the rain fed rivers,
Through your flesh, you are the givers.
Without you, we would pass.
Help us, save us, love us,
God Caprus, god Equus, god Bos."

The nearest soldiers joined before the end of the first verse and the sound of it swelled in a wave along the marching line as each man picked it up. Their steps fell into time with the solemn tune and the echo boomed back from the opposing ridge. Eskander saw the men over there stand beside their barriers and, late by a heartbeat, heard the answering voices in song.

He felt the emotion in his own dispassionate breast. This will do, he thought, but it won't do enough.

The armies met half way down the hill and men began to fall. At first the momentum of the herders carried them and the snowmen twenty meters further down, but the song faltered and the push stopped. Very slowly the grim snowmen forced the herders back up-slope. Eskander's men dropped at an alarming rate but did not turn. Rain fell again to slick the already treacherous hill.

Swan paced back and forth, occasionally looking at Eskander, waiting for the next suggestion, but none came. Eskander watched the battle.

The initial fighting roar dimmed as the warriors grew tired. Clashes were shorter and the advance slower. However slowly, the herders still retreated.

Boda's horses swept left and attacked Eskander's flank. The mounted herdsmen gave ground, rode in circles about the enemy lancers and showered them with arrows. A party of archers broke from the circle and attacked the barbarian cavalry with swinging clubs.

"That idiot Joot!" Eskander grunted.

The lancers quickly unhorsed the clubbers. No more herders attempted close battle. Their arrows flew thicker and Boda's horses withdrew.

A quarter of a sleep gone and the fighting boiled just below the brow of the hill. Swan finally turned to Eskander.

"What do we do?" she asked.

He studied the approaching struggle then looked at Swan and said, "We've done it all. There's nothing left but to run or die."

"The Sisters don't do either easily, General."

"Give me my sword, Swan."

She stared into his eyes and, for the first time since they'd met, she smiled at him. "I should kill you," she said.

He shrugged.

"Get the general's sword, Sisters. It's time to fight."

The warrior women walked to the ranks and worked their way to the front with Eskander among them. The tired herders parted to allow them through and when the snowmen appeared before them the women shrieked their anger and plunged forward.

Eskander had once seen a lynx cornered by two hunting dogs. It turned five directions at once, leaving bloody streaks on both hounds as it spun, all the while screaming and spitting hellishly at its tormentors. That's how these women fought.

The snowmen, as horrified by the idea of facing women as at the damage the shrill harpies caused, stopped their advance. Eskander laughed aloud at the looks on their faces and taunted them, "Not afraid of spoons and cooking pots are you?"

The snowman line bowed back where the Free women struck. Both ends stopped moving and, to maintain a straight line, backed down the hill. The momentum shifted to the herders and they hit again with renewed vigor.

When the fronts re-stabilized lower on the hill, Eskander took time out to look for Boda. He did not want to meet him, nor Grimm. Unfortunately, he saw a knot of snowmen working their way toward his position and in that knot both Grimm and Boda walked. Eskander saw that he was their goal.

He began edging himself away from them, fighting as he went, but had not gone ten meters when an arrow pierced his left arm just above the elbow. Blood gushed out around the shaft and down his forearm. His hand went numb though it maintained a good grip, or as good as slippery blood allowed. Shortly, clotting glued his hand to the knife and he wondered if he could ever release it.

The fighting raged hotter around him. He weakened with blood loss and decided to stop running from Boda and die where he stood. I wish those women had fed me better, he thought. This scratch wouldn't have slowed me down.

But it was more than a scratch. The continued motion worked the arrow in his arm and kept up the deadly blood flow. Dizzied, he weaved as he swung his sword. His ears rang and darkness gathered at the corners of his vision.

As his sight became circled in dark, Eskander stood in one spot and warped his sword back and forth to keep the enemy at bay. Light left his eyes completely and the ringing in his ears overcame the noise of battle. The last of his sense was slipping from him but he determined to fight till he fell.

A multitude tackled him from behind, pinned his arms and tumbled him to the slick ground. Rude hands pried his weapons away and dragged him off along the hillside. He thought, now they will show me off before killing me slowly.

The arrow in his arm caught the soil. He cursed, grabbing it with his good hand. The pain sharpened his mind and his vision briefly. He looked around to see if Boda was among his captors, and he saw the Free women dragging him to safety.

"Imagine that," he groaned, and gave up to darkness.

* * *

"I spent half my life recovering from injuries, disease, wounds and drunkenness. It's getting damned boring."

"Shut up, Eskander," Ree said. "You might not recover this time."

"If I'm strong enough to breathe I'm strong enough to talk. What happened?"

"They brought you back."

Eskander raised his pale face and looked down on his injured arm. Bloody bandages wrapped the elbow but obviously the flow had stopped. He wiggled his fingers. Needle pricks stung the hand; the feeling would return. His head fell back.

"We didn't win," he stated.

"No. Our army is retreating. They're holding the snowmen as best they can to give the rest of us time to go."

"Go where?"

"We'll join the other refugees going sunward."

"I thought the Free women would rather die than run."

"But the herders and farmers won't stand with us. It's hard to hold the sisters in a fight to defend somebody else's pasture and crops."

He asked, "Won't they stop and defend the village?"

"Some want to, but the village is just buildings. It's the women that make the community. Swan will be disappointed but we rule by majority vote. We'll leave."

"You'll miss your smithy."

"I'll make another."

Eskander closed his eyes. "Did many women die?"

"No," Ree said, "the snowmen respect us."

"Good," he replied and faded into sleep.

Ree smiled. She returned to her packing.

Chapter 4

The cart rattled along the crude trail. Mud churned by thousands of passing feet clung to the wheels and the rocks hidden in it jounced the cart. At the greater lurches Eskander groaned from the pain in his arm. It was swollen and mottled blue-black. He feared gangrene had set in. Ree assured him that there were no signs of sepsis, only bruising. It was her cart. A nanny goat pulled it. The more valuable of Ree's smithing tools poked through the blankets on which Eskander lay, vying with his arm at causing him agonies. Ree helped the cart along when potholes and stones made the goat give up pulling. Free women struggled around them, carrying burdens or urging pack animals. A few other carts also bounced along with the caravan, some occupied by elderly Free women.

Eskander asked to be allowed to walk but both Ree and he knew he couldn't walk far, and would only slow the already creeping train. It took little resistance from her to keep him in the cart. The third time he asked she just ignored him.

At the first sleep stop, a frustratingly few kilometers along, they set up camp among trees, surrounded by others who'd arrived earlier. They minimized noise out of courtesy, hoping the neighbors would do the same when they left.

Eskander felt as if they were living in a flowing city, a river of humanity that changed as it poured across the country. For the moment they were an eddy bypassed by the main current of herders and farmers. After sleep they would be swept into the channel again and onward to the human sea of Prater.

Prater; it was the focus of his dreams, thoughts and plans. He hadn't asked Ree yet if he was still a hostage. His condition kept him where he lay, free or bound, so there wasn't a rush to define his status. If he kept his arm and his life he figured escape from the refugee stream would be simple. The regimen of the Free women was broken and they had greater worries than losing a hostage of unknown value. And if recovery was slow, or he lost the arm, they were carrying him where he wanted to go anyway.

Four sleeps gave him the strength to walk briefly with the cart and the smith's tools gave him the incentive. The swelling in his arm retreated and the color dimmed. The holes left by the arrow stopped weeping and scabbed over. Eskander praised Ree's medical skill.

"Thanks for saving the arm," he told her.

"You'd have healed without me."

"Maybe, but I'm glad I didn't have to find out. Certainly, I'd be dead if your sisters left me on the battlefield."

She avoided the opportunity to explain his rescue. He noted the omission and suspected his ransom value had been the motive.

Fatigue came quickly, forcing him back to the torturous bed.

They had made seven kilometers beyond the fifth sleep site when Swan and the exhausted war party caught up to them. The snowmen had stopped pursuit so the women broke off resistance and hurried on to join the fleeing Free villagers. Eskander asked Swan why the snowmen had stopped when they had the initiative, but she did not know.

Eskander had speculations that he kept to himself. He feared that the Snowmen held up the advance to await followers. Those followers were most likely the families of the warriors, providing a situation both bolstering and dangerous to the snowmen. The women and children could free warriors from the jobs of finding food and caring for wounded and they would boost the morale of the fighting men just by proximity. Proximity also made for jeopardy, which is why Eskander had originally planned to have them tag along. Threat to their families would be great incentive to fight against any odds. Therein also lay the danger to the snow people; if they were defeated and their families taken they ceased existence as a group.

Faster travelers overtook them regularly, from whom they begged news of the barbarian progress but, for six more sleeps, the snowmen had not contacted anyone. On the seventh sleep a horseback hunter informed them that the army was again marching, though at a slower pace than the fleeing refugees. The relief this news provided was tempered by an uncertain future waiting in Prater. Some of the Free women had come from Prater. They had been prominent among those protesting abandonment of the village, and spoke out now for seeking an alternate destination. There would be little sympathy for them anywhere but, they felt, less would be found in Prater.

Eskander volunteered no opinions either way since he, too, felt ambivalent about the entry to Prater. The city he considered home held great attraction for him, and the urge remained to see Fotane's blinking head roll from his body into the dust. But, in the obverse, he was unprepared. His strength grew at each sleep yet he was far from whole. Even considering the twenty or so sleeps until Prater he would not be the man he had been. Oddly, if he'd not been recently wounded and had not suffered the grinding hunger, the long travel, the sickness, and the disorientation of awakening from the snow, he still thought he was no longer the man he'd been before in Prater. His experience among the snow people and the Free women could have altered him. Or was it Blute's absence? Eskander had relied heavily on the old man. Or was he just growing old himself? The last time he'd trimmed his beard he had found gray hairs among the black. Was he as willing to say "It's a good time to die", and step into the thickest fight? He wondered. How had Blute managed it at his age? He imagined Fotane's severed head yearning for its twitching body in the last moments before his horror faded in death. No, the vision just didn't bring him the satisfaction that it had.

Eskander's legs remained un-hobbled despite his growing strength, for which he was grateful. The trip would have been unbearable walking short steps or forced to ride all the way in the torture cart. He became complacent about his status, forgetting for now that he could still be a captive, until two women came to him.

"Fweela is back. Swan wants to see you."

"What did they find?" he asked.

"Swan will tell you."

* * *

"You don't exist," Swan said.

"What?"

"There is no trace of you in Prater."

"You mean Antu denied he knew me?"

"I mean," she said, "that Antu doesn't exist, and you do not exist. The three Sisters," she nodded toward them, "found no hint that what you told us is true."

"Liar," Fweela spat at him.

Swan studied his astonishment.

"But..." he started, and stopped in confusion. Then his face cleared and he smiled. "Ah, this is the bargaining phase. How much did Antu offer?"

The women glanced around among themselves. Swan said, "No. There is no Antu. There is no General Eskander of Prater. Yet you stand here, surprised by the news. Genuinely surprised as far as I can tell. There's a mystery here, but we have other worries. You're worthless to us."

They're serious, Eskander realized. What does this mean? Then, fixing on her words, he looked at Swan. "And what happens to people worthless to you?"

"Usually we kill them."

"Usually?" he asked.

"You obviously believe what you told us, but we can't ransom you. We know that you're a practiced military commander. When the war went sour you fought well. We appreciate that.

Consider us even. From here on, though, we can't support you. You have to leave."

These women were always unpredictable, but he had to ask, "With the things I brought?"

"The armor and sword, but Natta won't give up the dagger, and the horse is too valuable to my sisters in this hateful exodus. You're well enough to walk and your long legs are faster than the cart you rode. Leave quickly."

"What's the hurry?"

Swan hesitated, uncertain whether to discuss it. "Your fate is---a cause of dissension."

"How so?"

"Some hate you, but some of the women...," she paused again (and Eskander said to himself, "Fancy me.") "...consider you a sort of pet," she finished.

Eskander's look of surprise made Swan and her sisters burst into laughter.

"Pull yourself together, Eskander. Admit we're beyond your grasp. Stop trying to bend us to fit your view."

He chuckled with them. "I thought I'd learned everything a man needs to know. But you and the snow people surprised me. Now I'm---confused. I wonder if *everything* I thought I knew was a dream. How can I credit your agents? How can my history be false?"

"That's for you to solve, Eskander. I hope we never meet again. But if we do, tell me what you find out. Now get away from my people."

He tried to think of some pithy farewell, but decided it served no purpose. He smiled and raised his palm to them, then left to retrieve his goods.

* * *

"Goodbye, Ree. I wish you well."

"So long, Eskander. Give yourself some credit; you're not as bad as you think."

"I don't think bad of myself, Ree."

"Whatever. Don't take life so serious."

"With the Snowmen on our tails we'll all be taking life more serious."

"Go away, Eskander. Go with happiness or despair or whatever consoles you, but go."

He smiled at her, hefted his gear and strode off down the mucky track.

Three turns in the road put the Free women out of sight forever.

* * *

Ah, the ambiguity of freedom, Eskander thought. Here I am, free to do what I want, not hobbled, not tied, not guarded. Free to go wherever. And free to starve.

He traveled for three sleeps begging what scraps he could from other refugees. Few had much they would or could spare. A discarded gourd became his water jug, so he suffered less between streams and springs, for people were even more reluctant to share water that they had carried for kilometers. Hunting was not a consideration. Even if the refugees had not driven the game away, his sword was inadequate to take a fleet animal. Given time he could fashion a spear, or even a bow and arrows--time during which he would grow too hungry to hunt. He did cut pieces from his cape to make a sling, but found no game on which to use it. Off the road once during a piss stop he discovered a snared rabbit. Furtively, with a scouting eye, he removed the rabbit, pocketed the wire snare and quickly left.

Eskander shared the stolen rabbit with a small family he met. He feared that irony would make them the same people who had set the snare, but they were not.

After sleep and a breakfast of water and scent-of-rabbit he joined the human flow but went at a greater pace than the more encumbered parties. Like him before, the people he passed asked for news of the snowmen, and he told them what he could without hinting at his special knowledge, or speculating about what was to come.

That march caught him up to a large company made of a rich landowner with his family, servants, and tenants. Eskander was being shooed away from the cooking pot when the landlord caught sight of him looming over the cook.

"You," the landlord called. Eskander looked up. "Yes, you. Come here."

Eskander warily approached, a hand inside his duffel on the sword pommel, aware that he was surrounded by this man's people. "What?" he asked.

The landlord was distinguished easily from his followers by his marvelous girth and fine clothes. He affected large, gray mutton chops that completely hid his ears, and any distinguishing facial features lay buried under fat. His teeth were perfect. He looked Eskander up and down twice, his multiple chins stretching and swelling.

"By Huf, you're a long and rocky furrow. What's your name?"

"Eskander."

"Eskander, I'm Dovane of Kade, son of Pord. Do you know anything of weapons and their use?"

"Some."

"How would you like to take service guarding my caravan? Been losing goods to the scavengers. Need a good scare-crow like you. Even if you don't know broadhead from fletching, your look should keep them off."

"What would it pay?"

"A share of the food and a gold eagle when we reach Prater."

"Two gold eagles now, and another when we reach Prater".

"No time to dicker, man. One now and one at Prater."

"Done," Eskander said, and joined the train.

So much for freedom, he thought.

He traipsed along with Dovane to the big tent where he received initial payment, then wandered back to the pots for an authorized meal. Eskander's lean body was beyond lean now and into skeletal. A scare-crow is exactly what he felt suited to be, and, when the cook turned away, he dipped deeply in the pot for the meat and fat to replace that gone from his own frame. His belly protruded like a pregnant woman's when he left the kitchen area.

After that he barely managed to stay awake through his watch while the train slept. As soon as they had pulled up stakes, rolled and loaded the tents, and then embarked, he collapsed in the back of a not quite full cart.

Chapter 5

Dovane's party was allowed beyond the inner city walls only because they carried resources exceeding the immediate needs of their group. The people who lived directly outside the walls in a suburban sprawl had been the first to enter and now poorer refugees, refused entry, filled the abandoned houses, barns and shacks. A growing tent metropolis spread beyond these, crushing unharvested crops in the field.

Eskander wondered what protection the squatters thought was afforded by living outside the walls of Prater. He also believed the state of panic exceeded the threat. Admittedly, the snow people had the capacity to cause severe damage, but they were still far away and might never come near Prater. Even if they did attack the stronghold of Prater they knew nothing of siege tactics. He heard rumors detailing the impossible numbers of the invaders, and their proximity. He knew these both to be false, but now he understood the uproar. He did not dispute the rumors since it would be fruitless and unappreciated.

Immediately through the gates, Eskander approached Dovane for his pay.

"Eskander," Dovane said, looking around at the elbowing crowd, "this place has more thieves in a fifty meter circle than all we encountered on the road. Stay, and I'll pay a gold eagle every twenty sleeps."

"Sorry, Dovane. I have other business."

"But I need guards. You need a living. You can do your business and still watch my caravan."

Eskander shook his head. "The money I have should last long enough."

Dovane frowned, thought of persuading him further, but gave up at Eskander's look. He dug in his purse and handed over the gold. "If you change your mind, you're welcome back."

"Thanks, Dovane. Good-bye."

Dovane shrugged, a gesture that resonated for some time around his vast body, and turned away as Eskander made his return to Prater.

Eskander pushed his way down the boulevard looking for familiar sites. He knew this city, and yet it was not as he remembered; familiar buildings stood among strange ones, multiple structures stood where he thought one had, and single units covered ground that should have been occupied by many. A few businesses occupied the same sites he recalled, but most did not.

Eskander remembered the investigation the Free women had prosecuted and the unbelievable results. Until now he had put it off to some misunderstanding or failure on their part, but this city was not his Prater. Even so, it took an excessive strength of will to finally accept that whatever was wrong had to be a fault of his memory rather than the world. Looking around he could finally accept that Fweela's search found no trace of him here, because he could find little trace of here in his memory.

The crowds remained thick on the boulevard. Eskander turned down a more familiar side street, looking for an inn. The throng diminished, but he still dodged heavy traffic. The first inn he entered was packed with people shouting for service and rooms.

The fifth inn later provided as little hope as the first. He turned his path toward the squalid Finders section of Prater, so called because whatever one sought he could find there. The Lance and Foil, Blute's old haunt, occupied a crumbling corner in this sector if it existed in this strange world, but he would avoid that for fear of being recognized.

The decay grew and the crowds thinned. No one here dressed well—to do so invited robbery. People moved furtively. None met the gaze of others.

Beggars made their difficult way to or from the holes here where they slept. Begging locally was profitless, so they must commute to and from the moneyed areas, where they were roused if they tried to sleep. The refugee panic bode ill for them; as resources become scarce during siege the helpless and hapless are the first to starve.

Eskander stood for a time, staring up at the board swinging over the inn doorway, trying to interpret the flaking painting. He decided it depicted a rutting pig and a voluptuous woman in a situation compromising to both.

The owner of the Boar and Whore welcomed Eskander with an obsequious leer and asked what he would have the privilege of providing for such an honorable person as the master so obviously was.

"Your best room," Eskander said, vacillating between dread and hope.

"All our rooms are the best, sir. Probably why they're all full."

"Then a mug of beer at that table." He pointed at the only one unoccupied. A beer and rest would give him the strength to continue searching.

The innkeeper's eyes blinked at the sight of Eskander's gold coin, and, as he made change, he glanced through a side doorway and gestured subtly with his head. Eskander watched the man's reaction, then strolled through the crowd to the table and sat with his beer.

He was nearly finished when a woman approached with two more mugs and sat down. She pushed one mug across to him and took a slurp from the one she held. She wiped the foam from her lip with the back of her hand. "Mind if I sit here?" she asked.

Eskander looked her over, reached across, took the mug from her hand and replaced it with the one she'd set by him.

"Suspicious, ain't we," she said and drank from the new mug.

She was of the race from Mikkeny, a nation of islands standing just off the coast a thousand kilometers up sunward from Prater. An interesting people, they claimed to have once ruled a majority of the world, and, indeed, their warriors were coveted as mercenaries. Their seafaring abilities were unexcelled. They produced sculpture and architecture unlike that found anywhere else. Rumors spoke of buildings on the main island so ancient that even the Mikkenys didn't know what they had been. Now the island nation was vassal to Prater.

Generally speaking, a person's skin color darkened as the land they lived in lay further sunward. As Eskander's color was darker than the snow people, so were the jungle people and desert people further sunward darker than Eskander. This woman also was a tone darker than Eskander. She had the narrow nose, typical of her race, that did not indent at the bridge but swept in a straight line from the brow. It was a long, prominent nose, an exotic nose. He liked it. Her close eyes were mahogany. He assumed her hair had likely been black, or a dark brown, but she had altered it to a streaked bronze. Her face was sleek. A few minor pit scars caught shadows low on both cheeks from, he guessed, pubescent pimples or a pox. She was slender, with breasts that certainly had not been a model for the sign outside the door. He doubted her ability to bear children easily but suspected that she could run very fast. Momentarily he imagined trying to catch her in an open field, or even a closed room. It's been too long, he thought. Her hair was tied back in a tail. The clothes she wore kept her covered but he doubted that they kept her warm.

"At my age," he said, "there are two types of men, suspicious and dead. I'm not dead."

"Don't worry. Dead customers make poor repeat business. I just want you happy, so you'll come back with more gold."

"I admire your honesty. What's your name?"

"Atna. What's yours?"

"You don't need to know."

"Well, Sir You-don't-need-to-know, what can I call you for short?"

Eskander smiled. She did impertinence well. He said, "In my youth I knew a girl named Virginia. We called her Virgin for short but not for long. Call me Sky."

"As in 'blue as the...'?"

"Yes. I hope you never become as blue as Sky."

"Not me. I'm built happy from the ground up, with a special dose of ecstasy in my crotch. I like to share that part."

"Don't you mean, sell that part?"

"No," Atna said, "I sell a cheap copy of love. The ecstasy is for sharing."

He laughed. "Who's paying for these beers?"

"Didn't you order them?"

"In retrospect I do," he said, still chuckling. "Innkeeper," he shouted, "two more beers."

Atna got up, took the mugs to the bar, refilled them and returned.

"Thanks," Eskander said.

Atna asked, "Where are you from? You talk funny."

"But, I'm from...," and then it struck him. He did talk funny. She talked funny to him, but everybody in Prater spoke just as she. The people in Prater did not speak the language with which he grew up. They spoke differently enough from even the herders that words here were new to him, one more proof that his Prater lay far away. "Can you understand me?" he asked her in the language of his youth.

"What?"

"I'm from--a different world, I guess," he said, puzzled. "I thought I was from Prater, but this is Prater. And I'm not from here." What had happened to him, to the world? Was it one or both? He could mis-remember a place, but how could he mis-remember a language? The old words meant something to him. They were not gibberish.

"Are you all right?" Atna asked. "You look pale."

He gulped his beer and sat silent for a time with concentration lining his face. Atna didn't push him. She sipped her own drink.

"Let me ask you something," he finally said.

"Sure."

"Has the king had a child by Tissa yet?"

Atna laughed. "I hope he hasn't. The queen would go mad with jealousy."

"Tissa isn't queen?"

"What? You are from far off. Monsal is queen."

"When did Fotane remarry?" Eskander asked reluctantly.

"Who the hell is Fotane?"

"Fotane is the king!"

"Sky, one of us is really out of touch. The last I heard, which was just after I woke, Klinden is still king, and has been for a dog's age."

He threw the remaining beer down his gullet.

"Innkeeper!" Eskander called, "Two more!"

"Just one more, Sky. I can't keep up with you."

"They're both for me, Atna. I need them."

"Come on, sweetie. Slow down, or later will be less fun."

"Later?"

"In my room."

"Oh. But I need those beers. And who said there'd be a later?"

"I should leave?" she asked with feigned hurt.

He looked at her. He thought of his long dry period, so dry that, for a time, he couldn't wake Donniker at all. He considered the potential embarrassment of failing with Atna, but then Donniker twitched and began asserting itself. "No. Don't leave," he sighed.

* * *

Eskander woke before Atna because of his beer bloated bladder. When he stood he swayed, and when he returned to bed he couldn't sleep. She stirred but settled again and snored pipe-like through her slim nose. Eskander had paid her for a full sleep period. Atna would get her rest and allow him his before ejecting him.

But he couldn't sleep. His temperature was elevated metabolizing the alcohol, so he sweat in the bed covers. His mind reeled from both the beer and the revelation of how different this world really was from that he had known.

His old wounds eventually began aching, the sure sign that laying abed now was fruitless. He shook Atna till she fluttered her eyes and looked at him. She smiled, reached out and pulled him to her. "Good rising, Sky."

Eskander started to reply, but she pulled her head back from his shoulder and kissed him. "And good rising before, too," she said. "Both times."

"It had been a long, lean time. Sorry I was so eager."

She kissed him again and stroked his flaccid member. He didn't protest, but said, "That's not why I woke you."

"Who cares?"

He felt Donniker swell, so he caressed her thigh and said, "Who cares."

This time they dallied and lingered.

* * *

Even more sweaty now, Eskander let the glow die and his breathing return to normal before he said, "I should have woke you for that. But I really wanted to ask if I could rent this bed from you. All the other beds in Prater are overflowing."

"Rent my bed?"

"I can't find a room. I need a place to sleep and keep my things while I look around."

"I don't rent rooms. You know what I rent."

"A fine piece of property, too." He patted her belly. "Please, I have nowhere else."

Atna considered.

"You'd have to pay the going rate," she said.

"Of course."

"You couldn't be here during business. Only when I'm sleeping."

"That's fine."

"No other privileges," she smirked and gave Donniker a squeeze.

"No problem."

She laughed. "You say no problem now, but give it a sleep or two."

Now Eskander mulled. "Occasional privileges?"

"We'll see," she said.

"I'm paying the going rate."

"Property values are up. Rent is dear."

"And so are you, wench. Do I get the room?"

"All right. Pay me now for the next sleep."

* * *

Eskander had intended to shave his beard by way of a disguise. Nobody he knew had ever seen him without it, but there was nobody here who knew him. The beard stayed.

He walked everywhere. Everything he saw bolstered his first impression of a different Prater, though, among a handful of immortal structures, the palace gates looked the same. After two wake periods on these rambles he decided that walking the streets would not answer the question he posed.

Four public knowledge reserves existed that could hold records useful to him. The royal archive, despite his new anonymity, would be difficult for him to enter, even if his nerve would hold up. He could not present a believable new persona with his poor resources that would get him access there.

Scrivener Hall housed the finance and trade records of the city. Properly read, these could say much to an experienced man. Unfortunately, he was not experienced and unlikely to persuade a member of the clannish city scribes to help him.

The university guarded knowledge as if it was a treasure, and that treasure suited only for the initiates of their own self-esteemed profession. Younger sons of nobility don't inherit. The military and university were the two most popular alternatives to begging from elder brother. Based on his past experience with the nobility among his fellow officers, he feared the treasures held by the university were heavily laden by the deep tarnish of misinformation, distortion, and lies.

The priests of Huf kept records of the secular world only as it impinged on the functioning of the church. Eskander figured that royalty, by its very existence, must be a subject of great concern to the church. The records were filled with inspirational thought so, far from being sequestered, were open to public scrutiny, intended as another guide toward salvation.

The illiteracy of the populace at large required a full time church librarian and several readers. Contrasting intentions between a priest librarian and a lay homeowner hoping to, say, resolve an old property dispute, frequently took searches far afield. The priest sought passages most enlightening to the petitioner's soul, while the layman hoped to discover mundane proof against his intrusive neighbor. The organization of material made searches even more difficult, since information was filed by subject in categories sorted by relative importance to the church philosophy. A property boundary may be mentioned as an aside in a list of miraculous appearances of frogs, and the entry could lay beside a similar incident occurring seventy generations earlier. Chronology, to an eternally minded church, was a poor base for organization.

"What sort of inspiration are you looking for?" the wizened little priest asked Eskander.

"I said information, not inspiration."

"Oh, but information here is by Huf's grace and is, therefore, inspirational to mortals."

"You're right, of course," Eskander conceded, hoping to shorten the sermon. "I'm looking for a history of the royal family."

The priest snorted. "Little of use to be found there," he said, shaking his head.

"Is that a comment on the piety found in the palace?"

"Oh, they're pious enough in their way, but that way is not necessarily beneficial to the salvation of a soul."

Eskander said, "You speak incautiously. Aren't you afraid that I could be a spy?"

The priest chuckled and looked Eskander up and down. "Even if I feared them, you are no spy. But as I said, a history of royalty can hardly be called valuable."

Eskander shrugged. "Surely, the value of the rare gem is greater than the common river stone."

"Depends on whether you plan to build a bauble for your vanity, or a foundation for your house."

"You've had this conversation before, little priest," Eskander smiled.

"Many seek here for the mundane and push aside the miraculous to find it."

"Will you help me search or not?"

"Huf's purpose for me is to help you search. My dream is that you may find what Huf wants you to."

Eskander nodded. "That'll have to do. Where do we start?"

"I recall an interesting passage concerning royalty, taxes, and the church over here. Something about rendering unto Prater, or some-such. Come with me."

Eskander followed the shuffling old man deeper into the stacks of dusty tomes.

When Eskander's bones ached and the librarian's voice became reduced to a barely audible whisper, he gave up and returned to the Boar and Whore. He drank two beers and ate a weak soup with bread and cheese, waiting for Atna to finish her work shift.

She finally collected two mugs filled with beer and sat by him.

"How'd it go?" she asked.

"I've learned a lot about things I don't want to know. But nothing I was looking for. Did you know that His Glory Soondi, five generations back, was the royal heir before giving it up for the church and eventually becoming Huf's number one priest?"

"No. Fascinating," she yawned pointedly.

"Right."

"Giving up?"

"Not yet. Ready for bed, Atna?"

"No. You go ahead. I'm done with work but want to see some friends."

"All right. See you later." He stood and went into the back.

Later he woke to gentle strokings and squeezings.

"I thought there were no privileges," he said.

Atna smiled. "This is *my* privilege. Part of the rent payment."

"Greedy."

"Why do you call it Donniker?" she asked, fondling him.

Eskander shrugged. "Blute, an old friend, used the word. I picked it up from him."

* * *

Over the next twelve sleeps Eskander fell into a rhythm of eating, researching, sleeping, and sex with Atna, a life almost homey if he could forget the financial basis of their relationship. He had slipped briefly out of remembering that basis on the fourth sleep and realized that Atna was intruding upon his emotions, and growing in importance each sleep. He knew better than to become attached to a prostitute but easily found arguments against such bias. She sold the emotional lies for a living, as she had said, so he held no confusion about the possibility that her supposed affection was anything but acting.

"Such persistence will be rewarded," Joit, the priest-librarian, said when Eskander arrived after the twelfth sleep.

"Don't scare me, Little Father. I've heard the word 'reward' used for hanging criminals."

"Has anybody mentioned your sour attitude?"

"Very recently. I live with it." Eskander smiled. "Where into the stacks today, Father?"

"This way."

* * *

Eskander, tired of the search for the moment, leaned back to rest. He rubbed his eyes. When his vision cleared, it settled on Joit, happily perusing the books. Eskander watched the old priest. He hummed. He worked with joy written on his face. The dismal work was pleasure for him!

Eskander smiled and said, "What makes you so happy? This job would make other men cry or kill themselves."

Joit looked appraisingly at him, considered the friendship they had been building, and decided to trust him with his most personal disclosure.

"I did not join the priesthood as a young man. I apprenticed as a scribe. Scribes are nearly as celibate as priests, and I was shy. Women interested me as much as they do any other man, but they were unapproachable. I buried myself in the city records without pleasure. Work consumed my life. I became gray in the trade, then my face became lined. I grew long in the tooth.

"Then, so late in life, I met a woman. She was my age, bright, warm, and very attractive. Her first husband had died some time before and they had been childless, so she had little family to demand her time. I still marvel that she chose me over other men. She pursued the relationship more than I, since, hidden in the archives, I'd not become any more comfortable with women. It was a wonder to me. She opened my eyes to a world I'd never known."

"Beer struck me the same way," Eskander said.

"I'm sure." Joit smiled. "In time we married. She brought me out of myself and into society. She taught me to love art, music, good food and theater. We took life into our hands as if we expected to die in our next sleep. And we took in the love of each other much the same way. That was the happiest period of my life.

"For all that she gave me, I taught her only reading and writing, though it is discouraged by society and considered treason among scribes. She showed the same passion for the books I brought her to read that she used in the rest of her life. After she could write, she began making records on cards, putting them in a box kept in the kitchen. I assumed these were formulae for cooking."

"She lived only the span of a cat's age beyond our wedding. When she died, I died. Life meant nothing anymore."

Joit paused and sighed.

"I quit my lifelong vocation. I haunted our home like a lost spirit. Long, suffering sleeps later I woke to find the pain somewhat diminished. Outside the sun still shined. People still walked the street. Finally, I found the strength to sort through her things and dispose of them. When I happened on the recipe box I nearly threw it out thoughtlessly. Instead, I opened the box and began reading. They were not recipes. Each card was a description of a thing she had found to love in me.

"In me!" He looked awed and shook his head.

"One mentioned my eye color. One my laugh. Some were subtle parts of personality, of which I was not even aware. Many were too personal to describe. All were different and they were written right up till her death."

Joit looked out an opened window at the sun, the sky, a tree, a bird.

"If she could find that kind of joy in just me, then I could find happiness in something. This was her living gift. She taught me happiness. I joined the priesthood, trained, took my vows and accepted the position here.

"Now I keep a recipe box. But I don't write about her. My feelings for her are beyond words. I write about something that I find each wake period that makes me love life. The more I write, the more I find in life to love. There is even an entry about you, my son."

Eskander turned away and blinked his eyes. "What about this book over here?" he asked.

* * *

Six sleeps later Joit was reading, "...and His Glory Lunt filed a church indictment upon King Fotane at the unjust..."

"There!" Eskander shouted. "I should have remembered Lunt."

"Shall I continue?"

"No! Just tell me, is Lunt His Glory now?"

"Be serious, sir Sky."

"I am."

"But, he governed Huf's church, let's see," he stared at the ceiling, mumbling and counting on his fingers, "twenty three generations ago."

Eskander fell back against the shelves. Twenty three generations. It couldn't be. But the evidence crashed in upon him. Pinal, the snowman prophet, foresaw the coming of Eskander and the war twenty three generations ago. When Eskander had passed through the snow village with Blute, Loat, and the king's soldiers, headed to his icy burial, he had told Blute, obviously in the hearing of natives, that he would return and a great war would rock the world. It struck him that language must change over time as it does over distance. He, Eskander, was the originator of the prophecy that later sucked him up. He had been buried in the ice, unthinkably, for twenty three generations. And Fotane and Tissa were beyond his reach, dead. The bastards!

Chapter 6

The revelation broke Eskander free of his last ambition. He had driven himself through great hardship with one goal in mind: the eradication of Fotane and Tissa. They were gone. Everyone was gone. The world around him was a world where he did not belong. He was dead and a ghost in it. Nothing remained to engage him. There was no Antu, nor Lunt, nor Loat even, nor Blute, especially Blute. He could really use a rollick with Blute now.

He wandered in a daze from the Church of Huf. Joit called after him, concerned, unheard. The first inn he approached drew him through the door like a vortex, and he ordered a beer. He took little notice of the elbow-by-rib crowd, though his path through them irritated several as he waded to the bar.

He drank with determination. He looked longingly for oblivion at the bottom of every mug. There were many mugs.

He tried to ignore it. If life was that meaningless then it wouldn't matter. What's a full bladder to a dead man, or wet drawers and full boots? But he couldn't do it. He stood and staggered toward the outhouse rather than soil himself.

He navigated roughly on the return trip and fetched up hard against the bowls table, overturning the two standing pegs to the delight of the bowler, who had never before made that particularly difficult shot, but to the horror of the opponent.

"Clumsy ass!," the man shouted. "Get your ugly mug outside or I'll pitch it out!"

Eskander swayed around to find his challenger. The crowd squeezed away to gain space about the men, and Eskander saw the antagonist alone by the bowls table.

"Fuck you," Eskander said, and grabbed the man by the throat, slamming him down on the table. His other hand caught one of the downed bowls pegs and wedged it between the man's teeth, pushing hard. The man struggled, flailed at Eskander ineffectively and gagged.

When it became obvious to the amused crowd that Eskander intended killing his opponent they jumped him and dragged him off.

"None of that in my inn!" the landlord shouted. "Boot him out!"

Eskander, wobbling, picked himself up from the pavement. He brushed off the worst of the dust, stepped back onto the walkway and staggered as far as the next inn, where he rejoined his pursuit of oblivion.

* * *

Atna thought little of it when her tenant, Sky, did not return that sleep. He was just another man. Men, aside from the few regulars, came and went with incredible frequency.

But that man had spent more contiguous time with her than any other outside her own family. By the second sleep, she began to wonder. By the fourth, she began to fidget. She was fuming when she set out to look for him after the fifth sleep. As she went out the inn door a small priest caught her attention.

"Pardon, Miss," he said. "I am looking for a friend whom, I understand, lives here."

She studied him. "You wouldn't happen to be called Joit, would you?"

"Yes!" he said, surprised. "Then you must know the man I seek. You are Atna! What good fortune, thank Huf. He has not come back to the library for several sleeps and I became concerned. The last I saw of him he was very distraught."

"Why? What happened?"

"He found what he'd been looking for and, as frequently happens, it was not what he'd hoped. He left in a daze and I could not stop him."

"You are talking about my Sky, right? Big guy with a scarred face and black beard?" Atna asked.

"Yes, of course. He didn't return here then?"

"No. Did he say anything about where he was headed or what he planned?"

"No," Joit said.

They looked at each other. "That bastard." Atna said. "If I find him I'll kill him."

Joit smiled. "You seem an unlikely murderer, and I think he is a good man. Let me help you."

"All right. But if I find him first he'd better watch out. You search the inns and I'll start with the hospitals. Leave a note here for me if you find him and I will do the same at the church library."

Joit nodded. "Huf be with us, my dear." He turned and walked toward the nearest inn.

Atna checked the two hospitals, the paupers' cemetery, and three jails. He was in the last.

"Sky, what ails you?" she asked through the small slot in the door.

"Eskander," he said.

"What?"

"My name is Eskander."

"I don't like it. Listen, Sky, I can spring you, but you have to behave."

"How so?"

"No more fights. No more hammering the palace gates."

"I don't remember that."

"The palace guards drug you off the gates. You were yelling about some guy coming out to face you. Fotane. The one you thought was king. They got the civils to come pick you up, and here you are."

"Here I am. This cell smells like vomit." He sniffed his shirt front. "*I* smell like vomit. Get me out, Atna."

"No fighting? No treason?"

"No anything. I'm tired. Just get me out, please."

* * *

Atna kept calling him Sky, to which he objected one more time futilely before realizing it was perfectly appropriate that his old name should have died with him. He continued using it at the bar introductions which were his whole social existence beyond the strange relationship with Atna. He dropped in on Joit again to thank him for his help, and regularly visited him afterward. Joit was the only friend he had outside of the bars, and the man he trusted best.

He and Atna kept the rooming arrangement. Their sexual encounters grew better with age, if muted by alcohol, and, though they both felt unsuited to the other, their emotional entanglement rooted deeper. Eskander/Sky marveled that her acting had transformed without a skip to genuine affection. When she told him of the extent to which she had searched while he was jailed, he was embarrassingly pleased. Joit also pointed out to him how deeply Atna obviously felt about Sky. Such attachment was more than he'd expected. Almost as surprised at himself, he invested more heavily in the feelings he already had for her.

Sky spent the time of Atna's work shift drinking at the Boar and Whore, not casually but delving deeply into the bleakest realms of drunkenness. She tried persuading him to ease off with temporary result. His bouts at least had become less antagonistic, so he stayed out of jail.

Two gold eagles buy a lot of beer, bread and bed. He was twelve more sleeps along before the last of it was spent. Atna hoped that this would curb his drinking, but Sky took his armor and sword out and sold them to the first soldier who would bite, for five more eagles.

After the next sleep the tower watch spotted the snowman horde advancing over the horizon. Sky was well pickled when the news hit the Boar and Whore. He broke into hysterical laughter and couldn't stop until he was laid on Atna's bed and passed out. Atna had to cut her shift short for lack of a workbench and was angrier with him than she had ever been in their short liaison.

She retained her room by paying an exorbitant fee to the sleazy innkeeper, which fee stayed the same whether she earned money or not. Other women would jump at the chance to displace her.

When Sky awoke in his usual amorous and still loaded condition, she spurned his advances and finally hit him with her hairbrush when he persisted.

"Hey," he said touching the cut in his brow, "what's wrong?"

"You shortened my work shift by at least two clients! I'm losing money and the last of my patience. Don't you understand? If I can't pay for this room, we'll sleep in the street, and not together either!"

"I'll pay the bastard for the room."

"Not for long at the rate you drink your money. And what was that fit you had before you passed out? What were you laughing at?"

"Laughing? Oh. The snowmen." He chuckled.

"What's to laugh at? Nobody else thinks the snowmen are funny."

"You'd laugh too, if you knew my history better."

"I'm beginning to think I don't want to know you better. Maybe you should leave."

"You're kidding."

That was the wrong thing to say to a woman not in a kidding mood. "I am not!" She shouted. "Get out, get out, get OUT!"

"No. Wait. We need to work this out."

"Get out," she said.

"Please," he said. "I'll compromise."

She looked doubtfully at him and thought hard. "You serious?"

He nodded, with as earnest a look as he could manage in his debilitated state.

"Stop drinking."

His face went slack. "I can't. I'm afraid it'll catch up."

"What?"

"My past. My memories. My nightmares. When I drink hard enough, at least the nightmares are about what I do now instead of what I already did."

"Then you have to go,"

He turned away and swung his legs off the bed. He began dressing slowly and then stopped to turn back to Atna. "Anything else," he said. "I'll do it. You are all I have left. Blute's dead. Everybody is dead. Please, we can get around this."

She dropped her face, hiding behind her loosed hair, then looked up at him and shook her head, not at what he said, but at herself, for she realized that she was going to give in. He looked so pitiful. And she did feel for him. Why? Was it the mystery in him, his dark humor, or just the way he smelled when he wasn't fallen down drunk?

"Can you cut back?" she asked.

"Sure," he said sincerely.

"I'm serious. If you don't, you're out."

He squelched his weak smile. "No, I mean it. I can cut down some."

"Not some, lots."

"Sure." He reached gingerly, cupped her shoulders, leaned in and kissed her.

She put up with it for a moment, then pulled back. "I have to work a long shift to make up the loss. Got to start early."

Atna swung out of bed, and Sky, even so incapacitated, knew better than to reach after her. He'd saved his bacon for now, but he had to muster some will, or he would lose Atna.

Later, musing alone at the bar, he wondered why he had given in so quickly just to keep a woman, and a whore at that. What did it matter, now that his life was so pointless, whether he had Atna or not? Of course, whore or not, she had become part of him, and he also understood that if he kept at the drinking it would slowly kill him. That realization annoyed him because the cowardice it implied, in failing to just slit his throat and have it over, did not fit his self image. He was a soldier, a general who had faced death a thousand times. If he wanted to kill himself, why do it indirectly? No, all that was past. Now he was just another sot. He didn't feel a compelling need to ever see the sun again, yet he did need Atna. And he didn't really want to just fade away, as his past had done. He was even curious to see how the snowman problem turned out. So, by Huf, he would live for his woman, who deserved better than him. And for curiosity. Maybe he could make a new beginning. After all, look at what his friend Joit had done.

He mustered the will and did not drink that wake period, though he knew the hangover could be altogether avoided if he stayed drunk. The following sleep and the next, he did not drink because the pain of that hangover was too fresh in mind. Atna was more than usually affectionate, a welcome reward to the sober Sky.

The beer tasted better than he remembered when it slid down his gullet after the next waking. This time, he only became drunk, not washed away.

He drank moderately for the next several sleeps while the snowmen set up their camp, began building fortifications, a surprise to Sky, and dug in for the long siege. Life claimed him again.

* * *

The snowmen became to Sky like long-lost relatives; life among them was the farthest back his real past went. He sought information about them everywhere. After long, careful persuasion he convinced a guard he'd met at the Boar and Whore to allow him at the wall, where Sky could watch the snow people.

Squatters had packed up and abandoned the houses and sheds when the barbarians first appeared. Some stragglers hung on for a while hoping the Prater army would immediately sweep the snow people back to the land of low sun. When the indecisive Prater commanders activated an alert, wait-and-observe standing, the last squatters bagged their goods and proceeded sunward, with many a shaking fist and rude gesture at the walled city.

"What did they expect, Fazel?" he asked his guard friend.

"Just a bunch of country bums," Fazel replied. "We're better off without 'em."

"Even they should realize they'd have stayed in the walls themselves if they were soldiers. I still can't figure why they even stopped here."

"You say you soldiered some?" Fazel asked, looking at the scars on his friend's face.

"Some."

"You don't talk about it much. What happened? Drummed out?"

"Yes."

"To save some officer's butt, right? I've seen it before."

Sky shrugged. "That's too far back to worry me now." He turned toward the barbarian camp. "Look," he said, "they're mounting pikes in the breastworks. I wonder where they learned that?"

"Oh, they're clever people, the snowmen. My grandfather knew one. Said he copied everything till you could barely tell he was from antisun. Dressed like us. Talked like us. Of course he couldn't hide that pale skin."

"They do learn quickly, don't they?" Sky nodded toward the enemy camp. "But they're making fortifications too long for their number to defend. Stupid."

"Defend from what? I'm not marching out there."

"How long since the last siege?" Sky asked.

"Before my father was born."

"So the commanders have never seen one."

"No."

"Maybe the snowmen have a better chance than I thought." Sky smiled.

"You're a funny guy, Sky."

When it became obvious that the enemy was here to stay, the Prater archers sent fire arrows beyond the wall perimeter road, out among the surrounding buildings. Weather did not cooperate. The fires burned fitfully. Many buildings burned and some grain fields, but patches of both were left to provide cover and resources to the barbarians.

* * *

Atna and Sky sat at the table with their customary shift-end meal and beer.

Sky said, "I wish I knew what Prater is planning. They're too scared to charge out of the gates and too uncertain to just lock down and wait the snowmen out."

"Maybe we do know what they're doing," Atna said with a sideways glance.

"What do you mean?"

"I have a regular client. I know, you don't want to hear about my clients, that's why it hasn't come up. This client is a Prater noble, an officer of the cavalry."

"And?"

"Like all married men, he confides more in me than his own wife. He's worried that the messenger commanding Rendize to send their army will arrive too late."

"I should stop drinking," he said, swigging his beer. "I never thought of Rendize. I could have ridden there ahead of the messenger and riled up the old hatred. They'd have sided with the snowmen."

"Sky," she said looking to see if others had heard, "you promised no treason."

"Do you love Prater?"

"Of course not," she whispered. "If I could get back to Mikkeny, I would. But I live here for now, like it or not, and I don't talk treason. It ain't healthy."

"I lived with the Snowmen, Atna. They saved my life. I returned that favor by leading them to ruin. If I can, I'll help them, even if it means Prater falls."

"That's why you went crazy after hearing they'd come?"

"Yes." He synopsized the tale of his life since awakening in the snow but didn't mention the twenty three generation sleep. He felt she would discount all the story, faced with such an unbelievable fact.

"You sound as though you even liked the Amazons. They didn't save you. Almost killed you."

"I do like them. Not sure why. As a kid, I heard you could tame a squirrel by knocking it out of a tree with a rock, putting it in a pouch, and rubbing it until it came to. I guess I'm just a big squirrel."

"If I'd known that," she smiled, "I could have saved wear and tear on my merchandise. Just hit you with a rock."

"You haven't got me tamed yet, wench. Better get a big stone."

"You're half stoned now. I could use a pebble."

"Hah!" he snorted.

They ate quietly a while.

Eskander brushed a fly away from his plate. "Damn flies. What else did the cavalryman say?" he asked.

"Nothing about the snowmen, a lot about his wife and kids."

"Can you get more out of him?"

"Maybe."

Eight sleeps later Atna's client told her with relief that the messenger had returned from Rendize with assurance that they were marching at his heels.

Eskander cursed.

The next several sleeps, Eskander hung around various city gates, chatting with gatekeepers and guards.

"Atna," he said later in bed, "I'm going outside the city for a while."

"Crap."

"I have to. The snowmen need to be warned. I'll be right back."

"No you won't. Either you'll get caught leaving and jailed, or killed by the snowmen. Or you'll just decide you're tired of me and take off. That's it really, isn't it?"

"No."

"And what am I supposed to do? Wait for the snowmen to take the city and rape me and cut my throat? If you help them, you're killing me."

He sighed and rolled toward her to grasp her slender waist. "No. Unless they changed completely, that wouldn't happen."

"You haven't been with them. You don't know."

"You can come with me."

She looked skeptically at him, then smiled and brushed hair out of his eye. "What a sweet lie."

"Seriously, Atna. We could warn the snowmen."

"How?"

"Somehow. We have time to plan. And then leave Prater, go to Mikkeny or wherever you want. It's all the same to me."

"We don't have a horse or cart."

Eskander laughed. "This soft life has spoiled you. We need all our money for food, clothes and tools. We'll walk."

"Soft life!" she said, taking a swing at him. He caught her hand and held it. She looked him in the eye. "Let me think about this."

He nodded. "Sleep on it," he said.

While Atna considered her options which, unconsidered by Sky, included turning him in to the guard, he extended his contacts among those same guards through his friend Fazel. He collected what travel gear he could afford. He spoke to civilians among Atna's friends, whom she convinced him he could trust.

What finally persuaded Atna to go had almost as much to do with returning to her homeland as her affection for Sky. She had been sold by her paupered father to a dealer in wives, or so he'd said, to go to Prater and wed. The Pratorian purchaser of her contract had not been a husband, but a pimp, who doled her wifely duties out piecemeal to several "husbands" per sleep. A normal marriage so well consummated would have lasted forever. Gradually, out of the pittance she was allowed to keep, she worked up the price of her contract, bought it back and went freelance. Slowly, she had saved toward an eventual return to Mikkeny. Every time she counted the money, she dreamed of the final amount that would be sufficient, and each time she attained that amount she decided it wasn't enough and set the goal higher. At that rate, she would have died or become rich before she returned home. Sky's offered help brought that goal down to equal the money she held.

The snowmen had finished their fortifications by the time Sky and Atna were ready to go. It didn't change Sky's intent.

"Are you ready, Atna?" he asked, picking up a nearly empty, sagging pack.

"I guess."

"Let's go."

He nodded to a friend near the door of the Boar and Whore, who preceded them out.

Sky and Atna sauntered casually through the city, stopping to shop the siege-diminished bazaar, then to a small gate in the wall. The guard, already paid, allowed them into the gate arcade beneath the wall. From different directions, several of Atna's friends arrived over time, each carrying items for the departing pair. Eskander's pack began to fill, and, when Atna's arrived, it too fattened. Anyone approaching the wall with a loaded pack would have been viewed with suspicion now that the snowmen were here. They would not be allowed to leave with hoarded supplies that the city would need during siege. But several people carrying small packages aroused no interest.

The last item to arrive was Sky's bronze-clad walking staff, as tall as himself with a core of straight grained, knot-free hardwood.

He spoke to the gate guard, who stepped inside the city wall and waved a discreet hand in the direction of two watching men.

Atna looked at the staff. "That's it?" she asked. "No sword? No bow?"

"I have a good knife." He patted his coat at the waist.

"A knife?"

"Atna, we couldn't afford a bow. We couldn't afford a sword, but a staff, in trained hands, can defeat a sword. It's not as deadly but can disable a man. And a sword and bow beg trouble. We're safer without. I made a good sling. Have lots of stones. We won't need a bow and sword."

Atna's response was cut off by the pair of Sky's bar friends beginning their mock brawl not far from the gate. All nearby eyes turned toward the fight. The guard ducked into the arcade, opened the outer gate and ushered Sky and Atna outside the city.

The thick, bronze door clanked shut behind them. They headed away from the city, watching the top of the wall. When they could see the guards, they smiled in relief and continued. All the soldiers watched the fight inside the city. That fight might not have been so effective a diversion but the enthusiastic brawlers raised a few bruises and, incited to genuine anger, tore into each other with zeal.

The gate they left through was on the sunleft wall. They had to walk around the city to antisun to reach the crescent shaped barbarian camp. Prater had been built against the antisun side of the river to give them a defensive barrier on their sunward side, forcing any attacking force to work from the opposite side where the sun would glare into their eyes.

"Are you sure they won't just kill us?" Atna asked as they approached the freshly dug ditch in front of the snowman breastworks.

They stopped to breathe.

"No," Sky said.

He looked at the pike studded earthen wall. Eyes peered back between wood barricades.

"But they probably won't. From curiosity if nothing else. We look harmless enough."

"Hah!"

They slid into the ditch and climbed the loose dirt rampart.

Chapter 7

Sky and Atna sat confined in a tent. The guards who had brought them there handled them gently but cautiously and coldly. Pounding rain had begun as they were led into the camp. An interminable period passed.

Sky reassured the fidgeting Atna. "They can't hold us here forever. The news may not go directly to Boda, but when he hears, he'll come."

"If they hold us longer than I can hold my bladder they'll find a puddle when they come. And I'll put it right in the door where they'll step in it." She squirmed some more.

"I'm loaded too," he responded. "The rain doesn't help."

"Hey!" Atna yelled. "I'm floating in here!"

"Shut up," a voice answered.

Before any leakage a snowman unknown to Sky finally entered the tent. "Who are you and what do you want?" he asked.

"My name is Sky, but I'm known to Boda and Grimm as Eskander. This is my woman, Atna. We've come to warn you."

The snowman snorted. "Should I believe that?"

Atna said, "Believe your tent will be knee deep in piss if I can't find the privy right now!"

The man glared at Atna, wiggling where she sat and scowling through an expression of distress. He snorted again, in laughter this time.

He leaned his head back outside the tent door and called a guard. "Take this woman to the latrine."

"Warn us of what?" the snowman asked Sky when Atna had gone.

Sky hesitated briefly, considering demanding an audience with Boda personally, but thought it pointless. "The army of Rendize is marching here to join Prater."

"Anything else?"

"Isn't that enough?"

The snowman didn't answer. He left the tent, and Sky heard him instruct a guard to escort the prisoner to the latrine after the woman had returned. "And get them some food and water."

Much later, as Atna and Sky huddled together for warmth against the rain induced cold, trying to sleep, a head poked through the tent flap, then withdrew. Moments later their furs were thrust through to them. They wrapped up and slept.

* * *

Sky looked around as guards escorted them through the camp. Warriors ditched the mud laden rainwater away from the fortification and bucketed it out of sumps where gravity wouldn't do the job.

"Look all you want," a guard said. "It won't matter." He chuckled without humor and slid a finger suggestively across his throat, ear to ear.

Sky peered at him, reached out and yanked the man's beard.

The guard shouted, pivoted his spear toward Sky and lunged. Sky grabbed the spear behind the head, pulled the man close and clutched him by the throat with his large, bony hand. The other three guards raised their spears. The scene froze.

"Sir," Sky breathed into the face of his captive guard, "we knew the risks of coming here. I've lived too close to death to worry anymore, but my woman is no threat to you and does not deserve to be tormented. Have some respect."

He shoved the man stumbling away. For a moment it seemed the guard would attack him again, but another gestured and the angry man lowered the spear, his pale face reddening.

Within the stillness Atna said, "Sky, you're a maniac."

"Let's move," a guard said, and they walked on.

The boot churned mud lay deepest in front of the tent where they stopped. A snowman pulled the flap aside and told them to enter.

Inside, Sky faced Boda, Grimm, Ryne, several unknown men and, to his astonishment, Tane, taller and even thinner than he remembered.

Sky smiled, raising his hand in greeting.

"Eskander, you bastard." Boda said

"Good to see you, too, Boda. Or should I say, Commander?"

Boda shook his head and chuckled. "You have more luck and nerve than any man I ever met. You survive an impossible trek through the snow lands. You move into the home of the woman I want. Then you drag my people into a war we *don't* want. You run away from the war, leaving us to die. You seem to disappear forever but turn up to battle us with your army of farmers, herders and she-devils. We had to stop for twenty sleeps there, recovering from a fight that should have been like a stroll through tall grass. You escape when I have you in sight. And now, when I expect you to be the last man rooted out of Prater, you walk right into my camp. I'd say that Huf favors you if I didn't believe you're in league with the devil."

Boda glanced toward Atna. "One of your demon women?"

"Not really."

"Still double talk," Boda said. "You haven't changed."

"I changed. But obviously no more than you."

"How?"

"It'll take time to tell."

"We have time," Boda said and sat in some furs. "Let your woman sit." He pointed to a cushion.

Everyone but Sky made themselves comfortable and he took up the tale of his life from the moment he had abandoned the Kendeans at the lost battle.

"Now you come back to warn us." Boda said when Sky had finished. "I believe your shock, finding your vengeance frustrated; you were obsessed. But a new name doesn't make a changed man. If you warn us it's just part of another plan. Another deceit. Another attempt to use us. I suppose you want to be governor of Prater? Won't happen."

"No," Sky said. "Tell him Atna."

Boda interrupted, "She's either joined in your lies or swallowed them."

"Then don't believe us." Sky shrugged. "But will it hurt to prepare for the Rendizi? Even if you doubt me, they're coming."

"Oh, they're coming," Boda said. "That's the interesting part. Whatever your reasons, you thought you were bringing news. I trust the news. The messenger I don't."

Ryne spoke. "Eskander, you left something out of your story."

Sky hesitated, then said, "You wouldn't believe the complete story."

Boda looked from Sky to Ryne. "What is it, Ryne?"

Ryne wiped the corners of his mouth, catlike, with thumb down one side then index finger on the other. His eyes stayed on Sky. "He says his old nemesis is gone, that Prater is changed, but he skips the how and why. I never found evidence of his going to or returning from the shadow land. Since we gathered for this war I've talked to all the shamans. They would have known something. They didn't. Why, Eskander?"

"Because," he said, "I'm from another Prater, another world."

"Oh? And where is your world."

Again, Sky hesitated.

"Well?" Ryne asked.

Sky looked at Atna and said to her, "Back in time--twenty three generations." Her face went slack.

Ryne's eyes lit. "Of course! Pinal predicted your return because he met you, didn't he? Knew your mission. But how did you manage it? Where were you and how did you return after twenty three generations?"

"I don't know. I think about it a lot. My guess is when I was buried in ice--oh, you haven't heard that part. I fell into a crevasse. The last I remember was the snow and ice burying me. Then I woke up on a steaming lava flow. Either I only slept, like a frog in drought, or I was frozen and then thawed to life by the hot stone."

Atna stared. "You're right, Sky. That's hard to buy. No wonder I couldn't get it out of you."

"It's the truth."

Boda laughed. "Truth's the last thing we'll get from you. There must be a better explanation. But it doesn't matter. What is, is. Now you're here. What do I do with you?"

Sky shrugged.

"Grimm," Boda said, "what do you think?"

"Let him go. He can only harm us if we believe him. He can't lie to us if he's gone."

"Ryne?"

"I agree, Boda. He's not a general anymore. No armor. Too much flesh around the middle and too little in the shoulders. By the look of his eyes, too much beer and not enough food. He's harmless."

Boda shook his head. "What if others do believe him? He's seen our camp. We can't let him go."

"Then he'll have to stay," Grimm said.

"We could kill him," Boda murmured.

Sky, jaded as he was, felt the tentative bridge crumble that he'd begun building to this new world. The people he had come to consider his own were rejecting him, wanting him gone or dead. He had hoped the snowmen might not wish him ill, despite the rough history they shared. They might have taken him back. Even that, now, could only be as a pariah, if they let him live. And what about Atna? She took the news of his icy sleep in a way suggesting that her doubts about his sanity now stood confirmed.

"No!" Atna and Tane shouted simultaneously.

Everyone turned toward Tane.

He blushed, some of his mother's shyness finally coming out in him.

"I was not serious, Tane, but why shouldn't we kill him?" Boda asked.

Tane stuttered, "B-because..." He stopped, breathed deeply. "Because you're blaming him for things that aren't his fault. He didn't start the war. He was part of the prophecy. Did he plan to die and come back after twenty three generations? Did he beg us to go to war? The council voted. We wanted to go.

"So he ran away from our war when it was lost! But it wasn't lost, just put off. His leaving put *you* in command, Boda. Is that bad? He fought us with the farmers, but what could he do? They'd have killed him."

"So he says," Boda replied.

"Not everything he says is a lie!"

Silence held for five heartbeats.

Tane wiped his brow and looked down at the sweat in his palm. He had felt betrayed by the general but with time, and unlike Boda, he had forgiven. The more time that passed, the more he remembered only the good parts, the hunting, the treks to map the land. He had stood in deep snow having just brought down a rabbit with a difficult throw, basking in Eskander's praise, the giant's hand resting on his shoulder. Warm pride swelled him. To live forever like this would be all he could ask. The general was more father to Tane than all the Kendee men together. It could never be like that again, but he cherished the memory.

He looked around at the adults. "He's warning us, and you know he's telling the truth. Is he really so evil?"

Ryne, frowning, said, "The boy has a shaman's grasp."

Everyone in the tent awaited Boda's reply. He leaned back in his furs and stared at the tent ceiling, twisting his beard idly in his fingers. Eskander tried to read his face.

He looked down. "Maybe he's no more guilty than any of us. I could have used my influence to turn back to Kendee. But that doesn't mean he's working for our good. It doesn't make anything he's said believable."

"So what do we do?" Grimm asked.

"What you said. Eskander and his woman will live with us. Under close guard. He isn't a soldier anymore, but he's clever. If he helps, he lives."

"How?" Sky asked.

"I'm still new at war. One man can only think of so many possibilities. You point out the ones I miss."

"Sure. Are you ready for one?"

"All right."

"Destroy half your fortification. It's too big to defend with the soldiers you have."

"Ah," Boda smiled. "But remember, I know the Rendizi are coming."

Sky's face lit. "And you need the room for them!"

Boda nodded. "You once told us that the enemies of our enemies would be our friends."

* * *

Sleeps passed awaiting the Rendizi. Snowmen secured the area surrounding the city and kept watch, though non-military traffic was allowed to pass if they weren't carrying supplies into the city. Few people tried passing either direction until word returned to Prater that exit was allowed by the barbarians. Immediately, a flood of women, elders and children poured from Prater. The city expelled them foodless and on foot, while the men of fighting age and health were barred from leaving.

Sky asked Grimm where the snow people had left their own women and children, but the chief said it did not concern him. They were safe.

"Grimm," Sky said. "Letting non-combatants leave Prater gives more food to the fighting men. Is that wise?"

"The Rendizi attache' said the same thing. He also mentioned the women and children would starve first when food got scarce. The war council had a fight about it but decided we don't need to kill the 'non-combatants', as you call them."

"It'll take longer to win."

"We have time. This is fat country. The cattle, goats and pigs taste different from rabbit and bear but they're plentiful. Living is easy."

Sky smiled. That was one of the arguments he'd used to encourage the war at the beginning.

He found himself dealing regularly with the Rendizi attache' during strategy sessions, war council meetings, and camp inspections. Sky trailed a retinue of snowmen dedicated to keeping him in camp, and the attache' went nowhere without a following of assistants, aides, lackeys and boot-licks. Whenever the two met, room was at a premium. Sky was amused by the waltz of dominance that took place between his group and the other's.

The Rendizi was even taller than Sky. Though he didn't have Sky's breadth he was still well muscled, as any field officer must be to face the rigors of battle command. His rounded face contrasted his lean, angular frame. His beard was dark brown, short and patchy on the sides. When, on rare occasion, he removed his helmet, Sky saw that the man still carried only a crescent fringe of hair around his head. His name was Krenk, and Sky hated him.

Sky hated him because he was Rendizi, he was arrogant, rude, smelled of perfume, and worst of all, was always right. The only thing Sky disliked more than a man always wrong was a man always right. There are different types of right; one includes being convinced of your own rightness despite evidence, and the other, worse, being demonstrably right, provably right. Krenk suffered the second, or, rather, Sky suffered. For not only was Krenk right, he was quick. Words that quivered at the tip of Sky's tongue would already have poured from Krenk's lips. Sky wondered if the man was really that clever, or had he, Sky, ruined his own wits during the sloshing sojourn at the Boar and Whore? The snowmen loved Krenk, for which Sky hated him even more. Sky was uncomfortable thinking about it this way, but he remembered when he had been the snow people's darling.

Sky's position allowed little freedom to move against his new nemesis and, when his rational mind kicked in, he knew that the urge to act must be suppressed for the welfare of the snow people. If the bastardly Krenk could help his friends then Sky should encourage him in every way possible, but it was hard.

"You're just jealous," Atna told him.

"Jealous!"

"Yes. You came back wanting to be The General again, didn't you? But they have a new one. Two of them. Boda is a match for either you or Krenk."

"He's good, but green. I could dance all over him given good troops instead of farmers."

"See? Jealous." She shook her head. "Never saw a man so jealous."

"Oh, shut up," he said, trying to ignore her laughter.

* * *

Given the obvious advantage of the secret Rendizi-Snowman alliance, Boda's army put up a good show of agitated, defensive posturing at first sight of the arriving troops, while the Rendizi set up camp at the base of Prater's walls on the blackened perimeter of burned buildings and began barricading the position with found materials. They begged immediate admittance to the city, away from the threatening enemy.

Relieved though Prater was to see them, the ancient animosity dictated caution. All the smiles and good words did not overcome inbred suspicion. Prater's gates stayed closed.

They went to plan number two, wherein the Pratorian army was invited onto the field for a combined assault upon the barbarians. Prater argued that their own troops should be kept in reserve where the Snowmen could not reach, to rescue the Rendizi in the extremely small chance that the magnificent Rendizi warriors should suffer ill luck on the battlefield.

The Rendizi vehemently countered that, rather than deny their brave Pratorian brothers a share of the glory, they would return home without the pleasure of spilling one drop of barbarian blood.

From these opposing poles, similar polite negotiations continued for three sleeps. They agreed eventually that half the Pratorians would remain in the city as reserve, while the other half would, since it was Prater under siege, take the weight of the initial assault, backed up by the Rendizi. Prater reasoned that, if treachery was planned, having their reserve at the backs of the Rendizi would protect the men in the field.

* * *

The Pratorian swords and archers assaulted the Snowman breastworks, holding their cavalry back from the impassible pike wall and warily guarding the back and flanks of the foot soldiers from their idle, supposed allies. The first arrows dropped among the snowmen.

The Rendizi infantry abruptly bunched up and their cavalry drove through their ranks toward the side of the Prater horses.

The Pratorians, cornered and seeing their worst fears unfold, fought like madmen. The commander signaled the city for help. If it had come immediately perhaps he would have returned to safety, or at least have lived, but the same indecisive politicians sat behind the walls who were there three sleeps before. Despite the plan, they hesitated.

The Prater men and horses on the field struggled at every side, retreating where there was room, attacked now by snowmen roaring from the earthworks. They did manage regrouping their cavalry with the infantry, riding down a few Rendizi horses trapped between them.

One of every eight died before reinforcements pounded out of the city gates to engage the Rendizi rear. These soldiers had come out against the orders of their king and nobles, who were still dithering between defending their own goods in the city or saving the lost fighters. The men and commanders could no longer stand idly while their companions died. They stormed their own gates from inside and went without the king's blessing.

Too late, with too little, they hit the Rendizi horsemen. The snowmen, on their lighter, faster horses, swarmed in on both flanks, picking them off with arrows and lightning lance runs.

The dying Pratorians took a share of enemies down with them but not enough. When it became obvious that escape to death would be the only escape left them, they broke desperately and battled a blood-paved path toward the city. Three quarters of the army reached the city alive. The remainder, trapped afield, fought against increasing odds for another, infinite, eighty heartbeats, then threw their weapons and themselves to the ground, begging mercy.

The Rendizi waded into their old enemy, killing now with impunity. The Pratorians rose up panicked and scattered, only to be beaten back by the harvesting Rendizi swords. Eventually they saw their fellows among the Snowmen being quietly rounded up. Those in the killing field crushed toward the Snowmen calling for mercy and protection. The Rendizi tried to cut them off, but when Boda saw the continuing slaughter he sent a wedge of his warriors to collect the surrendered enemy.

Krenk confronted Boda. "You intrude in a private matter."

"Your men go too far," Boda responded. "Prater's lost. Killing these men gains nothing."

"They held our city to tribute for generations. Our people starve to make them fat. It's time to balance the scale."

"That's past. Nothing will change it. Let them live."

Krenk glared down on the stolid Snowman, steaming silently. "So be it, Boda. But, if you can't keep them confined during the siege, we'll finish the job."

Krenk shoved off through the masses, waving his men back from the Pratorians.

Boda shook his head and turned away. The philosophy of these high-sun people baffled him. All their wealth was insufficient. They always wanted more, even more death. Looking out at his snowmen he wondered if living here could infect them with this evil philosophy, and feared that it would--feared that it already had.

At Boda's shoulder, Sky said, "He's right, Boda."

"From you, that doesn't surprise me. He's killing your Pratorians, but then, betrayal comes easy to you."

Sky's face hardened. "It's your people I'm thinking of. If these men live, they'll be a threat while we attack the city."

"Won't they'll feel gratitude for sparing them? Stay pacified?"

"Boda. Let me tell you a story. When I was young the son of a neighboring farmer took it on himself to be my personal demon. He was older and bigger, so there wasn't much I could do. Every time we met I found myself eating dirt, or bugs, or horse shit. I carried bruises in varying shades that kept the score. His favorite greeting was to come up behind and kick me hard. Once, though, I caught sight of his shadow, turned, grabbed his boot and tripped him. He went down on his face. I jumped on his back, grabbed an arm and twisted. Now, I could have made him eat a little dirt or a handy horse biscuit, but I wanted treaty. He struggled and yelled that I had the arm he'd broke before and it hurt. I held him and told him I would let him up if he promised to stop tormenting me. I didn't even have to add any twist to the arm. He swore he'd never lay a hand on me again. So I let him up.

"Then he beat the shit out of me. Made me eat a kilo of dirt and the horse biscuit that could have been his. I almost died from that beating. Vomited bloody mud for two sleeps.

"Gratitude is a myth, nobody keeps a promise made under duress, and a bully is always a bully. Take revenge when you can, and don't let the other man take his. Let Krenk deal with them."

Boda smiled without humor. "Recently, Eskander, I was talked out of that same solution for you. You forget? So I know what you mean. And I had a rough childhood, too. See this face." He touched a cheek. "Do you think I had any friends? But men aren't kids. Those enemies are my friends now. Until you came along, I never felt like revenge."

Sky asked, "Then what about the men you'll waste guarding them?"

"We have men to spare. Krenk says the siege will be mostly waiting."

"You told me you wanted my advice."

"I didn't say I'd take it," Boda replied and walked off.

* * *

Everyone looked after their dead and wounded. Under guard the Pratorians began building a palisade for their own confinement.

Sky and Krenk, both trailing their retinues, stormed into Boda's tent.

"What the devil do you think you're doing?" Krenk shouted at Boda.

Boda puzzled a moment. "Just getting a short rest."

"No," Sky said. "With the prisoners."

"I don't understand."

"Your men are feeding them!"

Boda relaxed. "I knew that."

"For Hufsake, why?" Krenk moaned.

Boda shrugged. "They were hungry."

Krenk and Sky looked at each other.

Krenk turned to Boda and spoke patiently, "You can't feed prisoners. It takes too much effort just to feed your own men."

"Oh, we're not going to keep feeding them. We'll make them feed themselves."

"How? Plant crops in the palisade?"

"They can hunt as well as we can."

"You mean, give them weapons?"

"Of course," Boda smiled.

"Insanity!" Krenk cried.

"Idiocy!" Sky agreed.

"Stop yelling. Get out. I still need that rest."

Boda was good to his word. As soon as the impound was finished he issued spears and bows to a team of Prater soldiers and charged them with feeding their fellows. Oddly, at least to Krenk and Sky, the men all returned with game and reentered the prison. No Rendizi nor Snowman was harmed.

* * *

Tane returned from the women's camp to which he had been banished before the first battle. He sought Sky, carrying the bronze-clad staff the big man had brought out of Prater.

"Teach me to fight," Tane demanded. He hefted his own staff.

"Does Boda know you're doing this?"

"He doesn't care. It's not likely you'd beat two armies with that stick."

"What about Lentie?"

"She thinks I'll be a kid forever."

"All right. Defend yourself!" He swung the staff and tapped Tane on the shoulder.

They sparred until both sweat heavily. Sky instructed as they fought, so Tane improved slowly.

"Stop, stop," Sky puffed. "I spent too long in the tavern. I'm glad you wanted this. I need it more than you. But that's enough. Let's go see how the engineers are doing."

They started toward Prater, stopped momentarily by Sky's guards until he gave up the staff.

"Thanks for standing up for me, Tane. Except for Atna and a small priest you're the only friend I have left."

"It's nothing. Besides, other people take your side, too."

"Like who? Not Lentie."

"Well, she says she hates you, but she's glad you weren't killed."

Sky asked, "How are things with you and Boda?"

"All right, I guess. He's not so bad when you get to know him. And it's good having a step-father commanding the army. The other kids don't peck on me like they did. At least the pecking is different. And Boda takes my side against Mother sometimes."

The Rendizi engineers had cleared several areas in the burned rubble around the city at a distance beyond archery range, where traditional engines of war now began taking shape.

Sky explained the various machines and tools to Tane.

"Lot of fuss," Tane observed.

"Oh?"

"Why take the city anyway? Boda says they already lost."

"They have, if we take the city. If we don't, we can't hold the countryside. Prater would always be hounding our backs, growing strong and, eventually, they'd drive us away. If the snow people really want to live here they'll rule from the city."

The pair, and Sky's entourage, toured the whole city perimeter. At the end of the circuit, they encountered Krenk with his lieutenants admiring the trebuchet.

"Krenk," Sky called, "you better increase the guard here."

Krenk grunted in reply, allowing his own animosity for the ugly Pratorian to overcome his usual good judgment. "They're cowards. They won't leave the walls."

Sky glared at Krenk, shook his head and left. He mentioned the need for increased protection at the trebuchet to Boda, but the snowman sided with Krenk. "He knows what he's doing," he said. I hope, Boda thought to himself.

Tane and Sky practiced fighting every waking. The boy grew proficient and the man regained the strength and balance he'd lost, first at the hands of the Free amazons and later in the clutches of the Boar and Whore.

The trebuchet, finished and ready to test upon Prater, stood silhouetted against the city wall. Sky, though accustomed to the war machine, still found awe for it. That such a mechanism could be conceived and executed by mortal men always amazed him. He and Tane waited with the Rendize and Snowman commanders, anticipating the first demonstration.

The operators sent a man up rungs on the long arm to the top where he hooked a rope loop. The rope fed down to the base, through a block and out to fifty men. They pulled the arm down and latched it. Oldat, the artillery officer, hooked the sling to the arm then gestured his crew forward. They rolled a two hundred kilo stone into the great pouch.

The men cleared the machine. Oldat saluted his commander. That officer glanced about among his fellows, then brought his hand down in a chopping swing. Oldat swung a heavy sledge down on the latch release, the arm groaned, accelerating as it rose, and launched the rock high into the sky at the quiet city.

The stone whooshed through the air, dwindling into the distance, and disappeared beyond the wall. Heartbeats later the roaring crash reverberated over the waiting armies. The men burst into a shouting cheer that abated only when the leftover pendulum motion of the trebuchet ceased.

"Wow!" Tane gaped.

"Wow," Sky agreed.

The demonstration successful, watchers disbanded, returning to their duties.

The trebuchet snagged Tane's imagination. He kept looking back at the machine as he and Sky approached the Snowman fortress. Then he gasped, grabbed Sky's arm and shouted, "Look!"

Sky spun to see a hundred mounted warriors galloping from Prater's main gate. They thundered down on the trebuchet and the handful of men left to guard it. Lancers rode down the disorganized guards, archers shot men running to the defense, and fire bearers stormed the machine. They flung pots of hot oil smashing over the framework. Behind them, men threw torches. The trebuchet exploded flames. Horses reared, turned, and the Pratorians rode, practically unharmed, back to their walls.

Rendizi and Snowmen rushed to the flaming machine with water buckets. The first to arrive nearly torched themselves when the water they threw splashed burning oil back toward them. More wary, those following kept off as they pitched buckets-full onto the machine. Others hurled dirt. When it became obvious that the weapon was lost, all stepped away to watch the huge flames consume their long labor.

Sky, disgusted at the loss, still found pleasure in the discomfiture of his nemesis, Krenk. A look was enough. He didn't say a word.

* * *

"Do you love me, Sky?" Atna asked as they lay in their furs after physical passion subsided.

Do I love her, he asked himself. "What is love?" he said. "Tell me that and maybe I can tell if I love you."

"Wrong answer. The right answer is, 'Yes'. You haven't had much luck with women, have you? But since you ask: No, you're not getting off that easy. You have an idea what love is. I want *your* version."

"Luck with women? I've had lots--all bad. Atna, love is something I know less about the longer I live. I suppose I loved old Blute."

"Blute, always Blute! But he was a man, and ugly. Sure, I understand friendship. Am I just your friend, with handy sex thrown in?"

"Of course not."

"I'm *not* your friend?"

"You're trying to trap me."

"The trap is sprung. Now get out of it."

A wind rustled the tent flap and made a weak but convenient excuse to pull his gaze from her questing eyes. Would she understand why he didn't know, even if he could explain? Even if he knew, for that matter? He found her face again and caressed it. He could try.

"My first love was the wife of a friend. He knew how I felt about her and either trusted my honor, or he trusted her. He wasn't a close friend. We were lieutenants in the same company but she was all we had in common. I'm embarrassed to admit I cultivated him to be with her. She considered us all great friends. I was trapped between my good luck at being near her and my rotten fate that made her somebody else's.

"Then her husband volunteered for a mission to rout a band of highwaymen. He died. I was devastated for her. I comforted her as honestly as I could, but my feelings hadn't changed. I thought I had a chance. Ha! To her, I was a friend, just a friend. I told her how I felt, as if she didn't already know, and she gently rebuffed me.

"A weening later she married again. He was an officer of greater rank, so I never got to speak to her after that. What is this agony? My love went bitter, and I wondered what I really felt. Love? Infatuation? Lust?

"For a long time I couldn't imagine loving another woman. There was infatuation. Lust, sure. But not that intense, soul crushing emotion. Tissa came along. A beautiful noblewoman. Capable, bright, ambitious. And I fell for her. I thought, here is a woman to love. I tried. I tried so hard. And maybe I did love her, but where was that original, deep, all-consuming emotion? Do we just get one chance? Was my heart damaged?"

He paused, uncertain how to finish, then said, "I don't know what to say. If I've ever loved anyone since the first time, I love you."

Atna took her turn looking at the breeze blown tent flap, then she turned to him, eyes afire. "So, men are the only ones who suffered the loss of that one great love! Balladeers, all men, sing about it. Bullshit! Your friend at least let you down easy. I never got that from any man. I've loved and lost. I felt the agony. But I didn't let it poison me. Grow up!"

The vehement response startled him. Here he was, a strong man, or so he considered himself and was considered so by others. But he'd allowed one injury to his heart to deprive him of possible happiness while Atna, of the "weaker" sex, had borne up under worse.

"Do you love me, Atna?"

"Only Huf knows why, but I do."

He sighed. "I don't deserve you. I swear, I'll love you as much as you need."

"Really?" she asked, a touch wistfully.

"Yes," he said, noting the change in her tone. "What's wrong? Something else is bothering you."

She looked up at him almost pleading and said, "I'm pregnant."

"Oh, shit!"

Atna broke into tears, rolled away from him and hid her face.

"No," he said, tugging her back to him. "That's not what I meant. It's just that a war is not a good place for birthing babies. Is it mine?"

"Oh, you *asshole!*" she shouted, hitting him and crying even harder. "You know my period's come since we left the city!"

For an instant, he almost mentioned the propinquity of lustful soldiers; she wasn't with Sky every moment. He clamped his teeth to his tongue until his brain could reclaim its guidance. She was telling the truth. That was obvious. For Hufsake, she really did love him.

"All right. I'm sorry. I'm stupid. But this is the truth: You are carrying our child, and I am proud and pleased."

She sobbed while Sky held her, patting her ineffectually, silently, hoping again that he hadn't botched it completely. Stoically, he kept the creeping trepidation about a coming child out of his manner.

"Really?" she hiccuped.

"Really."

She loosened up, opened to him and they entwined tightly. Her post-cry shudders subsided, her breathing smoothed, and she slept.

Huf help us, Sky thought, and followed her into dreams.

Several sleeps later, when he felt the issue was less sensitive, Sky asked Atna what she had done about pregnancy while plying her trade in Prater.

"I washed out the seed after every client."

"You don't do that now?"

"Left the equipment behind; you said we had to travel light. And besides, I didn't want to wash away your seed. Our children will be magnificent." She grinned.

"Ah," Sky said. "What about when the washing failed?"

"I knew an old sorceress. She'd weigh me and for five sleeps weigh everything I ate, then she mixed up a batch of nasty goop and made me swallow it. Said that it had to be just right for each woman. Too weak and it didn't work, too strong and you died. I believe it. It makes you sick, puking, cramps and the shits, for three sleeps. Then the bud is gone."

"Huf save us," Sky said. "Better to have the kid."

"Not then. Now is all right." She leaned against him and he squeezed her.

* * *

The engineers started a new, larger trebuchet further back from the city. They built a wall around it and posted a permanent guard company.

Even though the reduced fighting force left in Prater was suitable only for defense, certainly not able to mount a serious attack against the combined armies at the gates, the Rendize troops moved into the extra fortification prepared by the Snowmen.

Twenty-five sleeps later, the new trebuchet was finished and tested. The first stone fell short, crushing the corner of a remaining house and digging a horse sized gouge of earth thirty meters from the wall. Oldat added rocks to the counterweight box. The next stone flew into the city, raising a roaring clatter and dust.

Next waking, the bombardment began. A stone flew beyond the wall every thousand heartbeats. Variation in stone weight and sling adjustment placed them at different distances along the line of the aim. They took a break after forty shots to change the azimuth and then began flinging them again.

The attack continued for three sleeps without relief until they ran out of boulders stock-piled during construction. Oldat hustled his crew to the other ammunition—incendiaries—tightly woven balls of dried sticks around a stone, for mass, soaked in black pitch found oozing from the ground a few kilometers away. The smashed houses in Prater would be excellent fuel.

Rain fell lightly, not enough to wet the imperiled city, but urging haste on the attackers for fear that a storm would snuff the planned burning.

The crew ignited a ball. They allowed it to come fully ablaze then rolled it with long pikes into the wetted sling. Oldat tripped the arm. The burning missile scorched through the air, a yellow-orange meteor leaving a black smoke trail. Sky cursed and commented to Boda on its beauty.

"Horrifying," Boda replied. "I had no idea. How Huf tolerates this destruction, I don't understand. The ground should open under that hellish machine and suck it down to Jefit where it belongs."

Sky said, "Men make their own good and evil. That machine is hellish, but it's man made. I don't think the supernaturals take much interest in what we do to ourselves. Until my resurrection from ice I even doubted the existence of Huf. But how else can I explain it?"

"Don't flatter yourself, Eskander. If you're part of any immortal plan, it's a plan of Tevep, king in the underworld."

Sky laughed. "You're probably right, Boda. I don't feel holy. I'm unworthy to be in the same room with Joit, the little priest-librarian of Prater." He stopped at the thought. "I wonder how he's doing."

Boda gave Sky an exasperated look. "Bad if that smoke means anything."

A smoke billow marked the landing of each incendiary. Momentarily, each diminished, then, where the balls found fuel, it thickened.

Thirteen missiles flew. At seven sites, they encountered smashed wood and reeds. Three of these smokes slowly disappeared as fire fighters beat them back. The remaining four grew in size. The smoke rose faster in the center of each conflagration, thinning to hot wavering gases and sparks shooting skyward.

Krenk strode up. "That'll soften 'em." He said, smiling.

Abruptly a huge rock whistled out of the city. It arced over the wall and plunged into the ground among watching soldiers about one hundred meters beyond the trebuchet. The men saw it coming and scattered but flying debris caught one, tumbling him headfirst. He was injured but not killed.

Krenk gaped. "The bastards built their own trebuchet."

"Seems so." Sky said.

"But where did they put it?"

"Probably in the bazaar. Only place big enough."

"Why didn't you warn us--Pratorian?" Krenk snarled at Sky.

"I've been out here with you. How could I know?"

"The towers!" Krenk shouted as he ran toward Rendizi headquarters.

"We should have held stones in reserve," Sky said.

"Obvious now," Boda answered.

Rendizi officers hurried every direction. Drovers hitched their oxen to stone-boats in a panic. It would take time to fetch more ammunition. Even with stones available, destroying the opposing trebuchet would also take time, skill, and luck.

Another missile flew from the city. The inactive Rendize catapult was the obvious target but the second stone fell further away than the first. The ground rumbled like a bass drum.

Sky said, "They'll have the range soon."

"Will the towers stop them?"

"Slow 'em down. And the fires are spreading. That should give them something to think about."

One smoke shrunk as fire crews attacked it, but the other three grew.

Ground leveling laborers had pushed tower paths through the ruined houses and gardens nearly to the city walls. Now they went to finish the job. The five wood and leather armored towers rolled forward behind the covered road builders, rocking dangerously even on smoothed roadbeds. From the top, and slits lower down, archers sent arrows over the wall. Prater men peeked over the ramparts to loose occasional return flights.

A huge stone crashed to earth fifty meters from Boda and Sky. It bounced once, crushing a man running the wrong way.

"Getting closer, Eskander."

"Yes."

The towers crept forward. The crews worked feverishly to complete the last meters to the wall. The first rolling work shield butted into the wall base, its trailing tower rocking close to it. In a burst of dust the ground under the front wheels of the huge tower collapsed. The tower pitched slowly forward, smashed into the city wall, broke mid-point and fell in splinters onto the shield. The added weight drove shield and men through the earth.

Bloodied survivors of the collapse climbed out of the pit through billowing dust to be met by deadly arrows from the wall. Only two ghastly stragglers limped to the Rendizi lines.

One more tower dropped through the ground and crumbled atop the shield before the others could be stopped .

"They mined the perimeter," Sky stated. "That's new. As a field commander I wasn't privy to all the city defenses, but I would have known about that."

Boda looked at him. "Of course," he said flatly.

A rock hurtled from the sky, smashed the new wall, bounded to the trebuchet and stopped, leaning against the base.

"Almost," Sky said.

Men ran forward into the shadow of the city with thick planks above their heads, eight men to the plank, hidden from the falling arrows. They pushed into one of the rolling shields. Enough planks were found to supply only one tower. The engineers spread the planks ahead of the tower. They dug the first five into the ground at lessening depth to provide a shallow ramp the tower could climb without falling. All the soldiers inside the tower moved to the front, providing balance as it crept cautiously onto the plank road. The plank men, over-crowding the shield, entered the tower base in the front and left through the back, running to their lines sheltered from arrows, at least part way, by the bulk of the tower.

A boulder whooshed down from the cloudy sky, burying itself in the fresh earthworks eighty meters beyond the trebuchet.

Oldat's crew rolled the nearly fatal rock, leaning against their weapon, around to the platform and loaded the sling. Their answering shot disappeared over the wall. A hopeful crash rebounded.

The tower moved snail-like toward the wall. It fetched up against the back of the shield, within bridging reach of the defenses. The archers set up a killing volley to drive defenders under cover as the released bridge dropped slowly forward.

Two Prater men began hammering at wedges in the parapet. Arrows dropped them and two others took their place. The wedges crept in. A huge portion of the stone parapet started leaning outward. Those mallet men died and others replaced them. The bridge approached the wall. Soldiers jammed levers in the wedge crack. The stone leaned, scraped, tossing up hot, powdered smoke that smelled of destruction. The bridge touched. The stone screeched out into the air, nudged the bridge, setting the tower to sway, and rushed groundward. It smashed onto the left forward corner of the engineer's shield, crushing wood, men and mined earth. The ground opened, swallowing the shield. Wood cracked, the back of the shield caught the forward lip of the tower, lifted up and up, and tottered it over backward.

The tower squalled, swung out, down, and crushed itself and the men inside against the freshly smoothed road.

Another shot whistled out of the city.

"By Huf!" Sky shouted.

The missile grew rapidly, descended gracefully, and blasted the trebuchet. It struck the arm just above the pivot, snapping it like kindling and blowing splinters fifty meters away. Two men dropped dead, one speared by fragments, the other decapitated.

A desperate cheer rose from the palisade where the captured Pratorians waited.

Krenk took five steps toward the prison compound, drawing his sword. He stopped. He looked defiantly toward Boda, hesitated, then sheathed his sword angrily and strode to his tent.

The rain of stones stopped.

Chapter 8

"I wish we could go hunting like we used to," Tane said.

"Even with guards they won't let me out of camp," Sky answered. "And if they did, the guards would scare off all the game. Been practicing the sling?"

"Yes. Can't hit a thing."

"It'll come. Let's try the staffs."

They sparred until they sweat, taking much more time to arrive there than they had at the beginning. Each nursed a few bruises when they stopped. Tane had become skilled enough to occasionally pass Sky's defense, and Sky couldn't resist retaliating.

The recent rains had greened the grass that survived trampling. Sky and Tane and Sky's followers found a soft hummock, lay down in the sun, and watched the few clouds lazing over. This isle of peace threw the surrounding battlefield, an already horrible aspect, into harsh contrast.

"What next?" Tane asked.

They sat up.

"In the siege? We'll let the pot simmer. The fires still smolder in places and that big smoker there must have been the renderer's. Good news for us. Leaves less oil to pour on our soldiers. The fires will discourage them. They'll worry about what we're up to next.

"I'm worrying some, too. Krenk wants to storm the walls with ladders, backed by archers in the remaining towers, while the rolling shields tunnel the walls and smash the gates. Boda wants to offer them surrender. I want to rebuild the trebuchet. The head engineer says they can build it so big and distant that the Prater machine, constrained by the buildings, would never reach it. We can hammer them till they give up."

"Boda won't listen to you?"

"No," Sky answered. "The good thing is that he's losing confidence in Krenk, too."

"Boda's been talking to the captured Pratorians."

"Yes."

"What is Krenk talking to them about if he wants to attack again?"

"What do you mean?"

"Three times," Tane said, tossing a stone down the slope, "I've seen him go in the stockade."

"You're sure?"

"Nobody else looks like him."

"I haven't seen it." Sky looked toward the penned Pratorians.

"You and Boda are never around when he goes."

Sky grunted. He had never trusted the perfumed Rendizi. Now he had more reason to trust less, though this act alone was not a treasonable offense; the mere act of talking with the prisoners could have an innocent explanation. Something else tickled the back of his mind but would not step forward.

"What's happening with the families?" he asked Tane.

"Nothing new."

"How about you?"

"Nothing."

"No?"

"Well," Tane hedged, "Ryne asked me to be his apprentice."

Sky gripped the boy's arm. "Congratulations! You'll make a good shaman."

Tane frowned and looked down at the grass plucked by his aimless fingers. "But I want to be a warrior and hunter."

Sky said gently, "No, you don't."

"But you are!"

"And now I wish I was a farmer."

"You hate farming."

"I was a boy, like you. Things change. You learn what matters in life. Look at where the power is in Kendee. The chief and the shaman."

"And the elders, and Boda is the commander of all the snowmen."

Sky shook his head. "The elders, except for Resta, are a batch of idiots. Boda was not a leader before the war and won't be after. Even he consults Grimm and Ryne. Be a shaman. You'll live to be old and respected. Be a warrior and you may be like Plint, a great hunter and warrior who died from bad luck."

Tane, who had hoped for support from his friend the general, went silent and pouted at the grass entangled tightly in his fingers. After a time he stood, said, "Have stuff to do," and left.

Sky watched him sulk off toward the snowman fortress and saw beyond it the Rendizi soldiers dug into their encampment, built by the snowmen on their own left flank. He frowned and glanced at Prater. Hmm, he thought, the captured warriors sit on our other flank. He glanced back to Tane. His eye's popped wide. "By Huf!" Sky shouted and, jumping up, ran off down the slope in Tane's track, followed in confusion by his surprised guards.

* * *

"No, Eskander," Boda said. "You're up to your old tricks. Why would Krenk side now with his ancestral enemies? He wanted to exterminate them a few sleeps back."

Sky spread his hands, then touched right fingertips to heart. "I swear. Listen, it all makes sense. He's been talking to the prisoners. The Rendizi moved into the extra defenses despite the mud. Krenk insists that Prater will never open the gates again. Why bother with wet trenches? To be at our exposed flank! He wants a direct attack to distract us when the loyalties turn. Prater at our front and him at our back, just like he did to the Pratorian army. He's like an unfaithful husband. If he screws them, he'll screw us."

"You don't know that."

"And you don't know it's false! For Hufsake, take the safe side on this bet."

Boda thought a moment and said, "Should I ignore the record? Krenk has been true to us. *You* are the betrayer."

"What do I gain by counseling caution? Don't trust me, but keep in mind that a good idea, whatever its source, is still a good idea."

"And Tevep knows Huf's law better than Huf. Arguing with you is like matching wits with the lord of the underworld."

Boda looked at Ryne then Grimm.

"Grimm," Sky said, "remember what I said about the sanctity of the Prater civilization? That I couldn't let barbarians destroy it? You asked if that meant your people. I said it without thought, not meaning you, but who is the outsider here to Krenk? Prater, that he's known since birth, or the snow people?"

Grimm shot a look at Boda. "Boda, he has a point."

Boda looked at Sky, and shook his head. "No," he said. "It can't be." But he thought, it could be true, probably is true. These high-sun people. All liars and back-stabbers. Now what, he thought. Now what? I brought the people here. I could have turned the tribes back. How many have died because I failed to stand against this foolishness? How many more will?

A haunted expression crept onto his face.

"Boda," Ryne said.

I am the destruction of my people, Boda agonized. We'll all die here. And it's my fault. I brought...

"Boda!" Ryne shouted.

He started. "What?"

"You can flay yourself later. Now we save the People. What do we do?"

With his hard-won confidence suddenly cracked, he hesitated, then looked at Sky.

"Eskander, the Rendizi lie to the left, Prater to the front, and the Prater prisoners at right. Behind us retreat is confined by our families. What do we do?"

Sky waited for the thrill of command, that old, heady rush, to sweep his soul. The exhilaration that made soldiering all worthwhile would fill him momentarily. Any time now it would burst over him. Where was it? He looked inside himself. He searched, still in anticipation, for that old feeling. It was nowhere. He really had changed. The fire was gone and in its place was something unidentified. I'll have to study this later, he thought, but now, "Let's think up some options," he said. "First that comes to mind is jump them and fight our way out."

Grimm said, "What if we talk to Prater, make a better offer than Krenk did?"

"Possible. Ryne?"

"It's not likely we can make a better offer in our position. We hold the countryside only where we stand. Rendize has a fiefdom. Should we talk to Krenk? Tell him we're going to withdraw?"

Sky answered, "We can't trust him to allow us out unconditionally. We do hold a lot of booty here that he'd love to have. I imagine there's more cached with the families?" The three snowmen nodded. "Any ideas, Boda?"

He paused, still in the throes of uncertainty. "I think I like Grimm's idea. We could offer the Pratorians some of the spoils to look away when the Rendizi chase us. I have some credit among the prisoners."

"All right. But we can't forget our strength. I doubt Krenk wants to fight us even with Prater's help. He would try to put them in the front again, but they won't fall for that twice. If we put up a good bluff and just move out, what can he do?"

"But," Grimm pointed out, "if we don't have a prior agreement with Prater, they'll see our leaving as opportunity and join Krenk."

"And if we do talk to them," said Ryne, "it'll be warning them of our intent."

The four men thought silently.

"We could sneak away," Boda said.

Grimm laughed. "Sneak an army out? Do you have a spell of invisibility, Boda? How about you, Ryne?"

"Well, we wouldn't get everybody out, but part."

Sky said, "Yes. We could work men away from camp gradually. The remaining warriors will move more quickly when it's time to go, and those already out can set ambush along our retreat."

"Krenk isn't stupid, Eskander," Grimm snorted. "He can count."

"But he's an arrogant, self-satisfied ass. He won't count."

"What about Prater?" Ryne asked.

Grimm said, "Boda, would your contacts among the prisoners try to hold their army back?"

"They might. No guarantee."

"So," Sky said, "if we talk only with them, not the city, we could have a holding action. They delay their people enough, Krenk will hesitate and we'll never be caught."

* * *

Large snowman patrols scoured the countryside, ostensibly to hunt for spies, smugglers and game, carrying such large packs as were possible without raising suspicion. They stayed afield four and five sleeps at a time to justify the heft of the packs, and fewer warriors, lightly laden, returned. As they thinned out, men spent less time abed so that the camp activity remained high. More surreptitious patrols carefully swept the area around the family camp to clear it of any observers. The family guard rounded up women, children, elderly, wounded, and goods, urged them to hasty packing, and started them off antisun. That took three nervous sleeps. Clearing the warrior camp continued slowly. More than a trickle of soldiers from the field would be noticed. The commanders made hard decisions about the items to be taken and those left. Spoils stored in the open, bulkier goods, were a loss.

Krenk maintained dialogue with Boda, urging him to attack the city, and with the Pratorian prisoners, unaware of the spies who now watched him. One of his agents was seen slipping into the city. His pressure on Boda lacked intensity as yet, indication that his agreement with Prater remained unreconciled.

Boda passed quickly from mere acceptance of the possibility that Krenk plotted betrayal to absolute belief. Boda had not approached the prisoners yet. The fewer who knew what was afoot, the less chance of discovery. He kept up his bid for Pratorian surrender.

During the next war council meeting, Boda, Krenk, and Sky each stubbornly held his stance upon the siege. It was to the benefit of all their plans to delay. Krenk gave reluctant permission for his engineers to begin Sky's giant trebuchet, for it made sense to do so while the situation resolved itself. It galled him to waste the resources, but he had no choice if his hidden agenda was to remain covered.

Grimm, as Boda's emissary, entered Prater under a truce flag accompanied by the captured young Pratorian noble, Laket. They passed through the sunright man-gate. Inside the wall they were ushered along a short, canvas passage, put up to block Grimm's view of the city's condition and defenses, into a large tent pavilion. Grimm took this as a good indicator for his survival of the meeting. Guards stood about the room. In the center five chairs stood in an arc, facing a sixth.

An elderly man with a slender, pocked face and thin white beard approached. He stopped, bent himself slightly in an attitude between a deep nod and a shallow bow, smiled obsequiously and said, "Welcome. I am the king's majordomo, Sklat." He looked from Grimm to Laket.

Laket said, "This is Grimm, the pre-eminent snowman chief."

"Ah, Grimm, your military skill is admired by even your opponents."

"It's not my skill. Our military commander waits in camp."

"Yes, naturally. To send your greatest treasure would be foolhardy, and you are certainly not that. Please come, be seated." Sklat gestured toward the single chair.

Grimm sat and Laket stood beside him.

Time passed with no one speaking. Sklat smiled and smiled, looking not quite at Grimm and not quite away. This man, Grimm thought, lacks definition--perhaps a useful trait at court.

Grimm was beginning to believe they were intentionally rude, or placing themselves in the dominant position by making him wait, when there was a light cough at the back of the pavilion and Sklat came to life.

He shuffled quickly to the wall and pulled aside the entrance panel. Five men walked into the tent to the chairs facing Grimm. Grimm was tickled to note that Sklat showed them no more deference than himself.

They stood looking down on Grimm, apparently waiting for something, which he refused to give them. If they would make him wait in the tent, he would not stand for them.

Eventually, frowning and looking at each other, they sat.

"Sir," Sklat said to Grimm, "these are the nobles sitting on the king's advisory council. Blathen," he gestured and the first nodded. "Settel, Weise, Caulder, and Tinn," he went down the line. "My lords, the highest ranking, nonmilitary personage among the snowmen: Grimm." Grimm nodded in turn.

The five ran the gamut of types and attitudes. Caulder was fat and cheerful, Settel tall and aloof like a stork on a chimney. Tinn, vulpine, glared bitterly at Grimm. Weise, sagging, old and arthritic but refusing to show it, affected neutrality. Blathen, a solid, bearish man with a wide beard, seemed to have his thoughts elsewhere and kept glancing at Laket.

"Of course you all know Laket," Sklat said.

"Yes," Blathen responded. "How are you, Laket? You look well enough."

"Fine, Father. We're treated well."

Grimm glanced up at his companion.

Blathen answered, "Good. As it should be among civilized people. Glad to hear it."

Weise, the apparent council head, spoke. "So, Grimm," he said, giving a quick smile which as quickly vanished, "why have you requested this meeting?"

Saving the polite banter for a more respectable foe, Grimm thought. "You're very direct," he said.

"Shall we waste time?"

"Of course not. I offer you the opportunity to surrender."

"Why, you...!" Tinn spat. "The gall," Settel muttered. The others shook their heads.

Grimm raised his eyebrows. "You wanted to be direct."

Weise cleared his throat. "We're a proud people, Grimm." He flashed his brief smile again and spread his hands. "To even suggest that we entertain the notion of surrender is an incredible insult."

"I thought you would appreciate the alternative to complete devastation."

Tinn shouted, "I will not sit here and listen to this! A smelly barbarian threatens us! Guards, drag this filth to the Hole and let him reconsider his offer!"

"Wait," Weise said, raising a gnarled hand though no guard had moved. "Grimm, we feel we are not in a position to discuss surrender terms unless the surrender is yours. This city has undergone many a siege. We're still here. How long will you hold alone?"

"We have allies."

"Yes. Yes, allies. Our subject state, Rendize, makes the same error every few generations. We're still here. Considering your kind behavior to our men, we will allow you to withdraw peacefully now. If you refuse, we will destroy you. Surrender will be impossible then. We must deal harshly with Rendize, a lesson must be taught if we are going to keep them at home a few generations, but you can escape that."

Grimm smiled. "We're at impasse then. My authority extends only to accepting your surrender. I must speak to my fellows."

And that was all. The nobles stood. Grimm followed in a heartbeat. Grimm turned toward the exit opposite that of the nobles' but stopped when Laket didn't follow.

Blathen and Laket stepped toward each other and shook hands firmly.

"You make me proud, Son." Blathen rumbled. "Don't stop."

"Thank you, Father. Give my love to Mother."

"Of course."

Each turned and went his way. Grimm followed Laket back beyond the stone walls of Prater, back to his own people.

* * *

"When do we leave?" Atna asked.

Sky replied, "I wish I could send you now, but you and I have to stay. Krenk thinks all snowmen look alike, but he knows us. If you went he'd be suspicious. He thinks the snow people hold me by keeping you here."

"Supposedly."

"Oh, come on. I stay to help the snowmen, but if you were really their lever, I would stay for you, and you know it."

She smiled. "Touchy," she said. "So when do we leave?"

"When we're down to just under half. Any more would be obvious. Till then, by losing sleep, we keep the same numbers active around the camp. It can't go long or we'll be too tired to move fast."

"And meanwhile everybody keeps play-acting," Atna chuckled. "You check on the pointless catapult..."

"It keeps Krenk's men busy away from us," he interjected.

"...Boda and Grimm try to settle an imaginary surrender. Prater pretends they take the offer seriously. Krenk organizes the next attack that will never happen. Silly!"

"This silly stuff can save us. As long as everybody concentrates on their own deceptions, they won't discover ours."

"Will Prater really throw in with Krenk?"

Sky shook his head. "If they do, they're fools. Knowing him, I think he's running a double deceit. We don't have spies inside his corps that could tell us, but I'll wager he turns on Prater as soon as we're defeated with their help."

He stroked her belly, beginning to round out from her slender frame, and said, "Let's concentrate on something else for a while."

"We keep this up, he'll be born bruised black and blue."

"Might as well get used to it. Life is bruises."

"Still the cheery fellow, ain'tcha?" she said and rolled toward him.

"You don't tell me everything, do you?" Atna asked as she tugged lightly on his beard.

He stayed silent.

"Trying to save me worry. Sometimes you forget I'm not that delicate flower you knew in court so long ago."

"She was far from delicate. Harder than most soldiers."

"But she was never sold into harlotry in a foreign city. Left to live or die alone in the worst slum. I've seen things would turn the rest of your beard white."

"Is it getting that bad?"

"Stop changing the subject, Sir Graybeard," she laughed, shaking his whole head by her grip in the disputed face hair. "I want to know everything that's going on."

"It's just speculation. Why worry about vapors?"

"You do."

He kissed her nose. "You're a pest. Yes, I wonder about some stuff. Like how far can we escape before Krenk attacks? Will our ambush in the foothills turn him back, or will he hound us as far as the families? If he does, how can we fight him with that burden? Will Boda's Pratorian friends really be able to delay their own people? Will they even try?"

"So what do we do about your worries?"

"These are problems without solutions. Only time can say whether they're even problems. If I could solve them, they wouldn't worry me."

"Something else bothers you too. You don't get excited anymore. Used to light up your eyes to talk war. Is it that bad this time?"

"No. I been in worse corners."

"Then what?" Atna asked, beginning to feel concern.

"I'm afraid to tell you."

"Now you're scaring me."

"You'll laugh."

"Laugh? You idiot!" she cried. "What is it?"

He turned his face away. "I think maybe I'm a farmer."

Atna did laugh. She laughed till tears ran. "You poor thing," she gasped. "Poor, poor thing!"

He watched her ruefully.

"It's true," he said. "I find myself thinking about hectares and crops. About a fine team of oxen and a good bronze plow."

"Oh, stop," she coughed. "You're killing me. Ow! My belly."

He considered slapping her.

When she finally controlled the laughter she did her best to console him with passion, heedless of bruises to their unborn child.

* * *

Resta, Darla and Lentie confronted the male elders of the allied tribes. Hundreds of women from all the villages stood at their backs.

"We're going back and there's nothing you can do to stop us," Lentie shouted.

"Be reasonable," Foss replied. "You'll just get in their way."

Resta said, "More of our wounded will survive if the women are there to help. Dragging them all this way is killing half of those who'd live otherwise."

"You'd have women dying too."

"Some of the widows want to die," Darla called. "At least they want to help in avenging their husbands."

"The surviving husbands won't want their wives in danger."

"My husband," Lentie said, "will just have to live with that."

"Foolishness," Foss muttered. "Do as you like. It's obvious nothing I can say will persuade you."

* * *

The banner waved and, as one person, the remaining snowman army turned antisun, shouldering their weapons, and jogged away from camp. The cavalry, in full strength, rode guard at the back.

A number of heartbeats passed before any response came from the Rendizi. One returning Rendizi outrider stopped by the path of the outpouring army, scratching his head. A trotting snowman smiled and raised his spear in salute. The guard returned the gesture. He shrugged and continued toward his company. Soon a shout, "Hey!" brought Rendizi soldiers to their feet. A much scarred sergeant ran to Krenk's tent, bellowing the whole way. Krenk stepped out covering his baldness with his elaborate helmet.

"Murder Huf!" he swore when he saw the already distant army. "Those damn snowmen!"

"Eckba," he commanded the sergeant, "get the cavalry off their butts and after the bastards. Send them all down to Tevep! Fifty gold eagles to any man who brings me the head of Boda or that son-of-dogs Eskander. And get me a horse," he shouted at the departed back of the sergeant.

The prison palisade, in the wild confusion of those first heartbeats, unguarded and opened by the leaving snowmen, spewed forth Pratorian warriors. They dashed straight to a particular set of tents in the abandoned snowman fortification and armed themselves with weapons cached there for them. As the Rendizi hustled in disorganized pursuit antisun, the Pratorians marched toward their city.

Blathen had enough time to dress and make his way to the gate just before Laket entered with his compatriots. They greeted each other warmly but Laket immediately drew his father aside, speaking urgently. The elder man lifted an eyebrow dubiously, but listened. He snatched a passing soldier wearing his livery and issued quick commands.

Tinn was waiting in the council chamber when Blathen and Laket entered, the remaining members were hurrying from home, and Krenk's emissary already lay chained, incommunicado, in Blathen's walled estate.

* * *

Sky said, "Atna, stay near the head of the column. Take care of our kid."

"You don't have to fight this time, you know," she answered.

"Yes, I do."

"Men are so stupid."

"Yup."

He kissed her. She backed away as he picked up his captured weapons. Sky smiled at her and walked off toward the trailing edge of their army to meet his oldest and newest enemy in a long history of enemies.

"You come back alive, you bastard!" she shouted. "You're a farmer now, remember?"

He just nodded and raised his sword without turning. Soon he was lost in the warrior mass and she, alone again, leaned against a tree and vomited. "Damned birth-queasies. Damned man."

Boda greeted Sky as he approached. "What do you think, Eskander?" he asked.

"We're about to get stuffed into a nest of rabid porcupines."

"You and Grimm," Boda grunted.

They engaged in little conversation, marching antisun, and glancing over their shoulders.

Three kilometers along their track they felt the ground rumbling up at them and turned to see the dust cloud, death harbinger, pounded from earth into the sky by the heavy Rendizi cavalry.

"It's time," Boda said.

The snowman horses wheeled to face the Rendizi. They straightened their line and stood nervously. In a few heartbeats the enemy closed to bow range. The snowman cavalry loosed a single flight of arrows, secured their bows, couched lances and stood. Five Rendizi horses went down. Two more snagged their hooves on the fallen and dropped. The rest thundered closer.

The horn blasted. The horsed snowmen broke at the center, rode off to each side. A few enemy swung out to follow them, but the mass rode down upon the infantry and met the bristling pike wall. Arrows rained among them. Horsemen fell now. The pikes brought down twenty animals that reined in too late. Mounted archers and lancers rode back in on the flanks and thinned the Rendizi.

The Rendizi regrouped, turned as a unit to their left flank and rode down the attackers there. This time snowmen tumbled to the ground, no match for the heavier armament. The right flankers harried the Rendizi rear until the heavy cavalry had to turn and regroup again. This time they split their forces to face each side and rode out upon them.

The snow horses turned and ran away, so the Rendizi curved their attack out around and into the snowman infantry flanks. The pikes ran to face them, backed by spearmen and archers. Eight horses broke through at one point and snowmen mobbed them. Five rode back out just to meet arrows from the returning snow horses.

The Rendizi commander sounded retreat and his cavalry beat sunward, raising another dust wall between them and Boda's people.

The snowmen cheered, shook their weapons, and pounded their shields.

"These are good men, Boda," Sky said.

"Yes. Let's get them moving again."

The horn sounded pickup and the uninjured men went forth to help the wounded. They rounded up horses. Fresh riders mounted them.

In eighty heartbeats, only Rendizi wounded and the dead occupied the field while the snowman army marched on antisun.

"Did you see Krenk?" Boda asked.

"No," Sky said. "Was he there?"

"He hung back, but he's here."

"Caught up faster than I'd hoped."

"And he'll be back with the rest of the army," Boda added.

* * *

King Klinden entered the council chamber to find his council deep in their argument. They stopped and stood as he approached his chair.

"Now what is this all about?" Klinden asked as he gestured them into their seats.

Weise, at Klinden's right, said, "Blathen has squirreled away the Rendize emissary. Now he's telling us to let the snowmen go without attacking. In fact, he wants us to assault the Rendizi to let them escape."

"Sire," Blathen injected, "Weise himself offered that very condition to the snowman Grimm."

"But he didn't agree to it," Weise said.

"Weise, you were correct in telling him that the real enemy here is Rendize. If we side with them against the snowmen, they'll think they've got away with this insidious assault. They are the ones we must attack, while their backs are to us. Punish them for their treachery. Drive them back to their city and bring them to their knees."

Tinn shouted, "Let them destroy each other. We've lost too much. Wait till one overcomes the other and smash what remains."

Klinden said, "Tinn is right. We've suffered greatly. Perhaps we should wait."

"We've tried that before, too," Settel reminded. "If we'd confronted the snow people at the beginning, perhaps fewer Pratorians would have died."

"And perhaps they'd have defeated us then," Weise answered.

"What about you?" Klinden nodded toward Caulder.

"I regret we couldn't find some common ground for trade before the snowmen left."

"No, Caulder, now is not the time to be a merchant. Think like the warrior I remember. What about the fight?"

"I've found more profit in trade than plunder, Majesty. A man trying to better you in a deal will not knife you. He knows there'll be more deals if you live."

Weise spoke.   "The snowmen are unaware of that philosophy, Caulder. They hunt. They do not milk cattle, they eat them. I hear they do the same with fat merchants."

Tinn and Settel laughed. Caulder, far from ashamed of his great mass, also chuckled at the allusion to his bovinity.

"No point in regretting what's lost," Caulder said. "Rendize we have always to deal with; the snowmen may never come again. Let Krenk chase off the barbarians. As they near the end of battle, approach Krenk with ultimatum. Offer them normalized trade and their former fiefdom with a minimum of retribution. Crushing them does nobody good."

"But the treachery!" Tinn said. "We must not tolerate it."

"You agree then with me?" Blathen asked.

"Yes. No! As I said, let them crush the barbarians first."

"The snow people will not return in any case," Blathen insisted. "Who tried to massacre our soldiers? Rendize! The snow warriors are more civilized than we pretend to be."

Settel said, "Would the displaced herders and farmers agree with that? And who ever equated civilization and mercy? Our kingdom is unequaled. We make the standards of civilization. Show them no mercy."

"Them?" Klinden asked.

"All," Settel said.

"Now?"

"No. Tinn is right. Let them exhaust each other. We'll clean up what's left."

"So be it," commanded Klinden.

Blathen rose in disgust and marched from the chamber.

"Father," Laket said when Blathen burst out, and asked the question already answered by the look on his face. "How did it go?"

"Badly. They will not hit Krenk's back."

"But, Father, all Boda asked is that we not take Krenk's side."

Blathen stopped. "Son," he said, gripping Laket's shoulder with a huge hand, "You are my heir. You are all that I work for. My life would be meaningless but for your life. Krenk would have killed you. Boda saved you. There must be honor among foes, despite what Settel says. Boda has honor; Krenk does not. I will do all I can to persuade Klinden to attack the Rendizi."

* * *

"Boda, I'm sorry," Sky said.

They strode along together. The subdued sounds of the retreat floated on the air.

Boda glanced up at him. "For what?"

"Dragging you and your people across the world to this."

"So you wished us evil from the beginning, just as I thought."

"No!"

"Then why apologize?"

"I don't know. I guess I'm feeling more human, more fallible. More involved."

"Atna's belly is growing."

"Yup. I'm going be a papa."

"It makes a difference, doesn't it?"

"Yes, and Tane is a son to you."

"Ha!" Boda snorted. "More yours than mine. But Lentie is also pregnant."

"Congratulations!"

"Thanks, but it'll be hard in this mess."

"That's what I told Atna. What does Lentie say?"

"She points at dozens of women who've already birthed kids on the trail. It doesn't comfort me."

"First time jitters. I feel it too. Odd. I probably have children from affairs and other embarrassing tangles that died generations back. My descendants are likely among the soldiers chasing us. But if I had kids, I was never there. This is different."

They marched silently.

Boda looked over his shoulder. "Here they come."

The Rendize army neared. It approached prepared this time. The infantry jogged, paced by the mounted warriors.

"Why does Krenk even bother?" Boda asked.

"Because he's Krenk. He doesn't care that what we have is not worth the effort, or the potential loss. He has more hatred than is good for him."

"You mean we can beat him?"

Sky scratched at his beard. "I always assume I can win. If you don't, you're already lost. And I'm still alive. Battered, but alive."

"No rabid porcupines?"

"You know I'm a sour-puss. I said that to have fun with you. The once I felt I'd lost from the first was against you, when the Free women were all that saved me.

"As for Krenk, we can beat him if we reach our reinforcements before he catches us."

Boda called to the bugler, "Take them to a jog." Turning back to Sky he said, "We've rested long enough."

The burden of wounded slowed the snowmen so the pursuers closed gradually. Sky left Boda, running forward to encourage the wounded and those carrying them. He cut horsemen from the cavalry to take the men who couldn't support themselves. Boda said nothing. Their salvation now lay in speed, not weapons.

For a time the gap held. Krenk exhorted his men to more speed and, despite likewise encouragement among the pursued, the Rendizi grew closer.

"I hope they choke on our dust," Grimm called to Sky. Sky nodded and saved his breath to help along a limping warrior.

Atna stopped to rest. She was a natural runner, but now she carried extra weight in peculiar places. It tired her.

Everyone knew Atna. Passing men called encouragement to her. Several stopped to help her but she put them off. "Just catching my breath. I'll be ahead of you all soon."

She watched Sky hurry past supporting a wounded man and tears came to her eyes. He did not see her. "Stupid tears," she said. "Pregnancy brings out your weakness and your strength." She rubbed away the tears. "So. Time for the strength." She grabbed at the cramping pain in her side and let her long, slim legs loose.

This time Sky saw her as she flew by. He smiled but was concerned at seeing her this far back from the point. She held her side as she ran and he knew she hurt. That's my woman, he thought.

It would not be avoided. Despite the gallant dash, the Rendizi now threatened just beyond bow shot. Boda grabbed the bugler and issued orders that blared out to the troops.

Atna, unacquainted with the horn commands, marveled as the chaotic running mass halted and collapsed in upon itself. She followed the flow until the aimless jostling suddenly acquired a square form bristling outward with weapons. The multitude froze, silence fell over the square and she crazily thought the men had become stone statues forming a massive wall to shield her from the enemy. It was eerie.

Beyond the snowman wall, noise of the advancing army still rattled. The absence of voices made the rumbling, slapping, clanking of the coming menace more sinister.

Boda raised a beckoning arm to Grimm and Sky. Sky looked around the square and saw a bewildered but safe Atna sweeping her gaze across the army, probably seeking him, then walked to Boda.

"What's the worst odds you've beat?" Boda asked Sky.

"Since half the battle is in stacking odds your way, the worst was about two to one, when my spies returned without a needed bit of news."

"We're about four thousand men. Krenk has nine. What do you say now?"

"I say we failed in our preparation. Before we engage Krenk, send runners to our reinforcements. I really didn't think that bastard would catch us before we had cover."

Boda gestured and two horsemen spurred away, shedding weapons as they rode.

The Rendize army stopped.

"What's he doing, Eskander?" Grimm asked.

"Considering. He knows he outnumbers us, but, as I said, he's afraid of us too. He's seen us fight."

"Suppose he'll turn back?"

"No."

Grimm exclaimed, "I swear by Huf's hinder parts, if I get hold of Krenk. He was our ally!"

Sky sighed. "Don't stir your fur, Grimm. That's war."

The Rendizi halt, already nerve-wracking, grew longer and longer. Boda began pacing. "It won't hurt to keep moving while Krenk makes his decision." He signaled the bugler who blew a complicated tonal series. The apparently frozen snowmen rustled into motion, marching slowly antisun without breaking the square.

This was the nudge it took to settle Krenk's decision. His army split into two masses connected by a thin front of soldiers.

Boda's troops, perfectly formed, kept moving.

"Round your corners, Boda," Sky called.

"What?"

"Round your corners. He's attacking the corners where the men have the least side protection."

"You never taught me that one. The bugle commands don't include it and the men wouldn't know how to do it."

"Shit!" Sky gritted. "Send runners. No. If they don't know the move it'll just cause trouble. Get some reinforcement out then. They'll need it. But they have to round up. You take the left corner, I'll go right, and we'll drag them into the maneuver if we have to."

Atna, alone in the center, jumped when the weapons clashed. Wounded and dying began to scream. She covered her ears and hunkered down. For a hundred heartbeats she tried to keep out the sound but then saw the first injured passed back from the front and dropped to the ground. She pulled her hands from ears to cover her eyes, rubbed them, stood up and trotted over to the closest downed warrior. His abdomen lay open. His hands futilely held in the exposed intestines. Blood seeped between fingers and, when he grimaced in pain, the bowels bulged out, escaping his grip. Atna knelt by him.

"What can I do?" she asked.

"Cut my throat."

"No!"

"Then go. I'm dead."

She stood reluctantly, knowing he told her fact. Even if his innards could be replaced and the wound closed, he would sicken and die in agony. No wonder he preferred a cut throat.

"What's your name and tribe?" she asked.

"Fahee of Sprill," he grunted.

"They will hear about you."

Fahee closed his eyes and gritted his teeth. Atna turned away.

More than enough wounded could benefit from attention. She began binding non-fatal, or what she thought to be survivable, injuries. Men died beside her as she helped others.

Sky and Boda each ran to one of the two jeopardized corners. Sky tried shouting instructions from the back. The noise covered his yells. He retrieved a dropped spear, leaving his sword sheathed, and pressed into the mass toward the front. As he passed, he instructed men on what was coming and how to perform it. The maneuver would be clumsy, but they were experienced now as they weren't when they left the snowland.

The pikemen repulsed another cavalry charge. Their diverging points on the corner failed to give complete cover. Three armored monsters crushed through to the spearmen who massed around them, stabbing, leaping. They killed the horses. The horsemen jumped clear, sabers already swinging, and gave up only when dead.

Rendizi infantry swarmed into the gap behind their fallen horsemen. The snowman spears turned on them furiously.

The earthy, sour-metallic smell of fresh gore rose to Sky as he pushed ahead. He hurled his spear through a brief opening then bent to pick up another. He cast again. Each throw took down a Rendizi. Several ranks still stood between him and the enemy. When he could, he grabbed a soldier to instruct in the rounding corner operation. "And pass it on!" he yelled.

Reinforcements swelled forward behind him. The front, weakened, split again under the weight of armored horses. Pikemen, confronted with infantry, unable to retreat between their own packed soldiers, threw down the long poles and snatched up spears where they could, fought bare handed or died where they couldn't.

Sky grabbed the collar of a downed snowman, dragging him back three meters, dropping him for anybody to pass to the interior.

Archers stood on dead bodies or sat on the shoulders of fellows to gain height. Neither provided secure footing, but the enemy closed so tightly that it was difficult to miss. Only shields, armor and chance reduced the mortality from arrows. Unfortunately, the advantage also exposed them to enemy fire. They dropped like ripe fruit.

"The horn call is simple, two long at base tone, one short at third tone," Sky shouted. The man, whose ear he had, glanced over Sky's shoulder and grew big-eyed. Sky looked the same direction and drew his sword.

A probe of Rendizi infantry parted the snowmen almost at a run.

"HOLD NOW!" Sky shouted left and right, then they were there.

No time to analyze. No time to think. Was he still a farmer? Was this thrilling, exciting, his life's desire?

He feels the exhilaration, but this is physical. The body is taking over, doing what it's trained to do. A man comes forward. He dies. Next man, dead.

Eskander glances to the sides. The line is ragged, but firm. He does not advance beyond it nor back behind it. He kills another man.

Boda's horn signaled, and those who'd received instruction did their best to obey. Others followed blindly. Those at the interior moved back quickly, making room. Those to each side of the destroyed corner moved in. Some of the Rendizi failed to escape the pincer and died. Pikes from the side finally swung in ahead of Sky. The archers' whistle shrilled, the front ranks crouched and a death flight plunged among the enemy.

The Rendizi horn sounded retreat.

"Keep the contact line small," Sky yelled. "No sharp corner when they concentrate here. Make a curve. If the square has to move, help your buddy in the curve go the right way."

I hope they get it, Sky thought. He worked back through the men to the interior.

"How you doing?" he asked Atna.

"Better than him," she replied, tying a last knot in the wrapping of the man's leg. She got up and fell toward Sky's chest.

Before she could smear against his bloody front, he grabbed her shoulders, holding her off.

"A kiss'll have to do. I'm a mess."

She raised her arms, blood to the elbows, and said, "So?"

He pulled her in.

The Rendizi horn sounded charge.

"Have to go," Sky moaned.

"No, you don't. But we already talked about that. You're too stubborn."

"Last time it was 'stupid'."

"See? You're getting better." She smiled.

"Can't win," he growled, turning to look for Boda.

* * *

Krenk's infantry came up slowly to the square in a column forty men wide. The barbarian pikemen backed further from the front through the rest of the infantry and the archers returned shots to the enemy. The lines clashed and the slow, wearing fight began.

Boda said, "A battle of attrition. Krenk's using his greater numbers and offensive position to grind us down. He knows we can't break the square to attack his flanks. His column is more easily refreshed than our square."

Sky suggested, "Change the square into a column to match his front."

"That'll only delay the inevitable."

"True. What if we let the cavalry out to attack their flanks?"

"Yes," Boda replied. "They out-maneuver Krenk's horses well enough to keep them off our infantry. Like that," he said pointing.

Rendizi cavalry attacked the front to each side of their infantry column. Rendize foot soldiers pulled back from those corners to leave snow spearmen facing the horses. Pikes tried swinging to intercept the charge.

Boda spoke the signalman and the snow horses spurred out through holes on both flanks of the square. They first rushed in with lances to get the attention of the Rendizi armor, then pulled back and sent arrows among them to keep them distracted.

From then, the battle settled into the grind Boda feared.

Boda chafed. He paced. Grimm wrung his hands and cursed Krenk, luck, and Huf. Sky stood in thought, frustrated at his helplessness.

He looked around at the nearly flat terrain. They hadn't even managed to get off the grain fields. About three kilometers antisun, hills arose where they had hoped to find cover from the terrain and ambush from the troops sent ahead. Would help not arrive before they were worn down? He thought that the two riders should have arrived by now, though he knew his time sense would be distorted by the battle.

Boda's men gave as good as they received, but that was insufficient. Unless they killed at a rate greater than three to one, they were lost.

"Move them Boda," Sky said. "Toward the hills."

"We'll never get there. And it'll increase our losses."

"Anything that shortens the distance between us and our help enhances our survival. I'd move 'em."

"All right. Let's go."

Painfully, slowly the snowmen fought for the hills, each ten steps of the retreat costing a life. It seemed an eternity passed so.

A cheer broke at the antisun rank of the square, and Sky knew their help finally came. Hopefully it arrived soon enough.

When the snowman reinforcements had approached closely enough to see individuals, Boda gaped in horror and cried, "My god! No!"

"What?" Sky asked.

"Our women come with the men."

Grimm cursed one more epithet in his now continuous calumny. "Then our race is finished," he moaned.

Sky said, "Grimm, if we lose this battle, your race is ended anyway. What would the women do without you? Better to die all together, or live all together."

"Easy for you to say, Eskander."

"Don't forget, Grimm, my woman has been here all along."

"You're right. Sorry. But I'm afraid."

"You have plenty company there."

The reinforcements trotted up. Boda's signalman blew and the new army split around each side of the square, breaking in against Krenk's flanks. The Rendizi backed up, bunching to minimize their fronts.

The snow warriors now exceeded the Rendizi numbers and the women further swelled the ranks. For a time the women held back, helping wounded where they fell, taking occasional casualties from arrow flights. Eventually some began working to the front to help men there. One picked up a spear and hurled it into the Rendizi. Another picked up a sword and pushed ahead. Soon many of them battled in the hottest part of the melee. They learned quickly, but this was no time to begin a warrior's apprenticeship. Every time a woman fell the snowmen roared in greater anger and their efforts grew.

The tide turned. Panic entered the eyes of the Rendizi warriors, and was recognized by the snowmen. The fear spread face to face, man to man, back through Krenk's ranks, then down from faces, to hearts, to guts, to legs. And they ran.

Methodically, Boda's people pushed forward, not breaking formation, pursuing slowly.

Now in complete rout, Rendizi stampeded back toward Prater.

Then fate, still unsatisfied, opened the gates of Prater and spewed forth an ordered column of mounted and foot soldiers.

"By Huf's balls," bellowed Grimm. "That's enough! Leave us alone!"

Boda's horn called. The advance stopped, the mass reshuffled until it once more formed a larger, ordered square. They turned and marched quickly antisun. The women were pushed to the interior.

Sky saw Lentie, bleeding badly from her side and her leg, helped along by two others.

Slowly, when he realized pursuit was gone, Krenk stopped and rallied his men. His appeal to Prater must have worked. Seeing the Snowmen getting the upper hand had brought them out. Should he wait for them or go on? For a time he stood undecided, then sounded advance to close on the fleeing snowmen.

Emotion among the snow people, set upon by this latest ill fortune, fell to despair. Boda, however, would not let them slack the pace. He exhorted them, "Come on. We're people of the land. Make your feet and the land kiss lightly. Let the land help push you along. It's kind to its people. It moves us. Go."

"What's this drivel?" Sky asked quietly.

"Shut up, Eskander. I don't know what I'm saying. Just trying to keep them moving."

When Rendize caught them, they turned and fought. Disheartened by the approaching Prater army, they battled their own weariness and hopelessness as much as the enemy. The snowmen crept backward again toward the hills. If they could hold out to there, they stood a chance of surviving.

As Prater's men closed, a hurrah flew up among the Rendizi and the snowmen cringed. But Boda saw a thing which made him smile. Grimm, astonished, fearing for Boda's sanity, followed his gaze, then he too smiled.

Sky caught their expressions and, at a loss, called, "You better let me in on the joke."

"Do you recognize that Prater noble in the lead?" Boda asked.

"No."

"That's my friend Laket. The livery of every man is that of his house. I have reason to hope."

The Prater warriors fell upon the rear of Krenk's army.

* * *

"Mercy, Eskander," Krenk begged, kneeling helmetless before Sky, his sweating bald head glinting.

"Sky! My name is Sky now. And lucky for you. Eskander would have ignored Boda's request, staked you out and personally cut you into small pieces. Very slowly."

"What will happen to me?"

"Since Boda hates torture, we'll settle for beheading."

"Please. I'll return to Rendize and gather tribute. You'll be rich. Or I'll be your slave. Let me live."

Sky mulled this a bit. "Both attractive ideas. How about tribute *and* slavery?"

"Anything. Let me live."

"Krenk, you fought well, but you have no honor. A fighter without honor is not a warrior. Death will be a favor to you. Your family will have at least that small bit of honor. Alive, you'll just keep embarrassing them."

Sky spoke to the clustered soldiers. "Take him and guard him well until his final appointment."

When they were gone, Atna asked, "When will you tell him he's not to die?"

Sky shrugged. "Let it occur to him gradually. The worry will drive some wisdom into him. In future he may be less hasty, more honorable."

"How's Lentie doing?" he asked.

"Bad. They had to tourniquet the leg. She'll lose it if she lives. But the bleeding in her side won't stop. She's getting weak."

"Damn. Let's go see Boda."

They found him kneeling over Lentie. She fluttered her eyes open at their approach and smiled weakly, then closed them. Boda stroked her hand and her hair and her cheek. His hands hovered everywhere, as if they could not find the most precious part of her to touch.

"She shouldn't have come. She's carrying our child," he said.

"We couldn't stop her," Darla whispered.

No one spoke as the pool of blood grew under Lentie. Her breathing diminished. Her face was ghostly. She opened her eyes and whispered, "Boda, I can't see. Boda, love." Her chest fell and did not rise.

Boda wept quietly, and only said, "So little time. We had so little time."

Ryne tugged at Boda. "I must help her to the Other Side now. Let me guide her."

"Huf is not kind," Sky said.

Ryne replied. "But we were warned. Remember her dream? We thought wild Tane would be lost because the Frost Giant told her to love her son. She knew they would have to part, but not that she would be the one to leave."

Grimm said, "What was the rest of her dream? 'Hot bronze will break cold ice.' Yes, the People of ice are broken. By and for bronze."

* * *

Laket, Sky, and Grimm stood watching the disarmed Rendizi army begin the long, hungry march home. Krenk kept looking over his shoulder, expecting a last cruel assault and hurried his step.

"I'm sorry about Boda's wife," Laket said. "We came as quickly as we could. When Father finally realized he couldn't move the king to help you, we gathered all of our men, right down to stable boys. Wish we'd been sooner."

"What about Rendize?" Grimm asked.

"Our council will not hesitate now that the danger is over. We'll send a large armed delegation to extract reparation. This is just part of a cycle that has always existed. We know how to handle it. What about your people?"

"The chiefs and tribal councils all agree. We will go antisun. We won't go back into the snow lands. Living is too hard there. There'll be room somewhere that we can stake before the refugees return. And when they do return, we will approach them as friends. The prophecy was wrong. The snow people want nothing more to do with war, or this deadly cycle you suffer."

"Well, I wish you Huf's blessing. But don't count on avoiding the cycles of life. We did not precipitate this war but what could we have done to avoid it?"

Grimm sighed. "I see what you mean. I ask you to forgive my people."

"Be wary of prophecy, friend." Laket smiled. "Your slavery to the future was no better than our unbreakable tie to the past."

"Yes. And, in the end, all our grand efforts just feed the worms."

Boda walked up to the three. He looked after the Rendizi. "Lentie is gone over. She's with our ancestors."

"She will be a good advocate for you," Grimm said.

Boda remained still. It was too obvious to say that he would rather have her by him than currying favor from the dead.

"Eskander," Boda said without looking at him. "I wish you still lay frozen in the shadows." Then he walked back to his people.

Embarrassment held them silent until Sky finally spoke. "So do I."

Then he turned to the others. "Farewell, Laket," he said. "Thank your father for us. Grimm, you were always right. Little consolation now, I know, but you were right. If it can ever come up without causing too much pain, please apologize to Boda for me."

"Why? Aren't you coming with us? Boda will accept you again in time and the tribes think you're a hero."

"No. I promised Atna we'd go to Mikkeny. It'll be all we can do to get there before she births our child. We're leaving now. Goodbye, Grimm."

Grimm raised a hand and Sky walked off to locate Atna.

Tane found Sky shouldering his assembled pack and helping Atna into hers. "Eskander, where you going?"

"Sunward, Tane."

"But I thought you'd come with us."

"Boda blames me for your mother's death and I have a promise to Atna."

Tears rose in Tane's eyes at mention of his mother and he lowered his face to let them run. He gritted his teeth, wiped his eyes with the back of his hand and looked back up at Sky. "Can I come with you?"

"No, Tane. Boda's your father and will need all your help. Have you decided to apprentice to Ryne?"

"No. Well, maybe. I would learn to help others over as he did for Mother."

"Do it Tane. Your people need you."

"They need you, too."

"Like the plague! I'm going to farm the hills of Mikkeny and raise strong sons, like you. We have to go."

Tane backed off, sadness molding his face, then smiled and said, "You'll look funny behind a plow."

Sky and Atna laughed. "Goodbye, Tane." They hiked away, skirting injured Prater to pick up the main road where the bridge crossed the river.

* * *

"You're really going to Mikkeny?" Atna asked as they strode out of sight of Prater.

"I told you I would."

"I just wasn't sure."

He chuckled. "Thanks for the confidence," he said.

They walked quietly for a time, then Atna began humming. Suddenly she stopped the tune, a frown crossing her face.

"What's wrong," Sky asked.

"I have something to tell you." She stopped walking and he pulled up to turn and face her.

"You've been sleeping with my best friend," he laughed.

"No," she gritted. "Besides, you don't have any friends."

"Except you."

"Except me. And I'm not sure you'll like me after I tell you this."

"I don't think I can be surprised any more. Let's have it."

"Well," she said, "The Mikkeny isles are not large."

"Yes?"

"They're very rocky."

Sky frowned suspiciously. "And?"

She blurted, "All the little bit of farmland is owned by families that go back generations. They never give it up."

"I can't farm?"

She shook her head, nearly beginning to cry.

He looked antisun, imagining the horde of marching snow people. He looked at her moistening eyes. "How do the rest live?" he asked.

"They fish, or herd sheep, or sail for shares on Mikkeny merchant ships." Her tears began to fall at Sky's expression.

Sky shook his head, watched tears drip from her chin, then laughed aloud and shouted, "Then I'll herd damn sheep, or catch damn fish, or sail damn ships." Quieter he said, "Come on, let's go home."

Atna fell into his arms and sobbed, "Thank you."

He rubbed away her tears, kissed her, and they turned sunward together, toward far Mikkeny. In ten paces Atna was humming again.

PART 3

Chapter 1

Sky and Atna continued a full march to the first roadside inn though they had already been awake for an extended time before starting. Considering the distance to Mikkeny and the wish to arrive there before Atna started labor, traveling short on sleep for a few marches would be prudent.

Unfortunately the traveler's inn suffered the same refugee-driven overcrowding that Sky had found on his arrival at Prater and, again, he was surprised that people stayed this long so close to the supposed horror of invading barbarians. The blockheadedness of humanity always entertained him.

Atna saw the congested common room, sighed for her unrelieved weariness and asked Sky, "What now?"

He said, "We won't find a room, but maybe they'll serve us some food. Or we could push on a bit and eat from our packs. Then find a place to camp. We should be able to replace our food later." If the territory hadn't changed much since his earlier life in Prater he knew that they would have to pass through wild lands before more habitation. The optional, faster sea route would have cost more than they could spare and, since the snowman invasion, few ships lay at anchor in Banshod, the deep harbor a few kilometers down river from Prater. This was unfortunate because the prevailing wind blew from antisun, providing a straight sail up the coast.

"I'd like to just sit for a while. Preferably with food. Let's see what they have."

He pushed through the crowd toward the kitchen with Atna trailing in his wake.

He leaned in the doorway and called, "Any chance of a meal?"

A short, blocky woman with fly-away hair, sweating, red face and harried expression stumped over and appraised him.

She said, "If you have the wherewithal and ain't picky."

"How picky?" He asked.

"We're down to salt-pork, weevil bread, shriveled potatoes and rotting apples."

Sky glanced at Atna and she shrugged. "How much for two?" he asked the cook.

She looked at him more studiously, judging how much he could be squeezed. "Four silvers and six coppers."

"For that much I'm pickier than rotten apples, never mind weevils. I'll give you eight coppers and that's twice what it's worth."

"You didn't notice there's a war? See this crowd? Food is short and people just keep getting hungry anyway. Go figure. Three silvers eight."

"So you'll get rich on rotting food at the expense of the helpless. One silver."

She grew even more red-faced. "Insults," she said, "will not lower the price. Three silvers even and that's as good as it gets. I only come down that far because I see your wife is tired and pregnant. Anybody else here would think I've gone mad. They've been paying more."

Sky turned again to Atna. "If we pay as much for every meal we'll arrive at Mikkeny without a copper and starved near death."

Atna asked the cook. "Would you mind if we just use one of your tables and eat our own food?"

The cook frowned, but looked down again at Atna's swelling belly and said, gesturing at the tight-packed room, "Go ahead if you can find a spot.

"And by the way," she continued, turning back to Sky, "if you're looking for a room, you couldn't afford it if we had one."

Sky smiled bleakly at the overworked woman. "Thanks," he said.

They found a couple of spots on a long bench by politely asking if people would slide down a bit. Sky leaned his staff against the wall behind the bench, parked their packs by the staff and started digging out food.

Atna was too tired to make small talk while they set out the simple meal. Sky watched her wearily begin eating. Even he was worn out, used to long marches though he was. He sympathized with Atna who had never been subjected to one before. A quick sprint on her runner's legs was one thing, but long, steady bouncing under a heavy pack was another. But she was young and healthy and the short rest during the meal did great things for her energy. As they wiped crumbs from the table and put away their water bags she said, "We won't make it at at this rate. We'll run out of food soon and have to pay, whatever the price."

Sky said, "I think prices will drop as we get another march or two from Prater. And we don't have to rely on inns or markets. Keep our eyes open for small farms that will be happy to sell without carting it to a bazaar."

Atna agreed. "We have plenty for the next twelve sleeps, as long as we find something before then. Speaking of sleep," she yawned, "where do we bed down? I'm beat."

"Every spare room and horse stall will be packed. We'll walk till we find a thicket by the highway. Toss some brush on the ground and it'll feel like a down mattress."

"I doubt that."

Sky tossed a copper on the table as they left.

Rain had begun while they were at the inn. They sheltered under a weeping willow tree long enough to pull voluminous, hooded cloaks out of their packs. They had originally planned to sit out any extended rainfall in their small canvas tent or a public house. The cloaks would shed water for a while, probably long enough to find a spot to camp.

They adjusted the extended back of each other's cloaks to hang over their packs, parted the hanging willow limbs and stepped out onto the verge of the highway. With their vision blocked by the limbs and confining hoods, they strode out directly into the path of another hooded, equally blinkered man hurrying past.

The man collided solidly with Atna sending her lumbering sideways trying to re-balance the heavy pack. Sky lunged forward to grab her and the stranger, almost as quickly, recovered to get hold of the hem of her flailing cloak. With both men holding a fistful of garment Atna fell softer than she would have, but the mass of her loaded pack bore her down against the ground. Her left arm curled under her. A snap sounded and she gasped out a small shriek.

Sky and the man knelt on each side of her to gently lift her to a sitting position. She held her left arm pulled against her body with the right hand, bowed her head and shook with sobs. Sky pushed her hood back and tilted her face up to the rain. He cradled her chin in his hand, about to reassure her when he stopped, for it was laughter which shook her, not sobs. Granted, her expression was mingled with pain, but it really was laughter.

Sky, when his speech returned, said, "How's the arm?"

"It's broke, you stupid bastard!" she sputtered through grimacing laughs. "What did you think?"

"I think it shouldn't make you laugh."

She gasped through a few more guffaws, slowly calming herself, then said, "It's breaking an arm *now,* after dodging stones, arrows and spears, and otherwise surviving the war without a scratch. *That's* what's funny."

"What about the baby?"

"He's not knocking at the door, if that's what you mean. I think my arm took the shock. Baby's fine."

Sky turned to the man who had toppled Atna and asked, "Is there a physician near here, sir?"

The stranger hesitated, studying Sky's face with a puzzled look, then shook his head. In a pained, hoarse, grating voice that struggled to escape his throat he said. "No, but my aunt and uncle live just up that way. We'll see what help we can give her.

"Very sorry to knock her down. Came from nowhere."

The man was average height and the cloak draped loosely on him as if he were made only of sticks. He was clean shaved, ghostly pale, starved looking and, like Sky, had an empty gap among otherwise healthy teeth. The length of his face and close eyes suggested that, if not fully Mikenny, he surely could claim some ancestry in common with Atna. His eye color, though, was dark brown and the bridge of his nose had the indentation lacking on Atna. More noteworthy, though, than his unhealthy appearance was his harsh, difficult voice.

Sky shook his head. "Not your fault, sir. An accident. Help me get her pack off."

As gently as possible they removed the cloak and slipped the straps of the pack off her shoulders and down her arms. She winced and yipped a couple of times as her left was eased out of the strap.

They stood her up, wrapped her back into the cloak and the stranger shrugged her pack onto his right shoulder. As he and Sky stood facing each other over Atna's head, he grated out, "My name is Berno. Have we met before, sir?"

Sky studied Berno's face. "Not likely," he said. "My name is Sky. This is my wife, Atna."

Berno frowned, trying to place where he'd seen this Sky before. He nodded and said, "We should get her to my aunt's."

Atna turned her head inside the hood as they walked, looking up at Sky with one eye though she could not see his face for his hood. "Sky, that's the first time you've called me 'wife' instead of 'my woman'."

"Oh?"

She smiled to herself in the privacy of her hood.

Chapter 2

They walked about two kilometers along the sunward road, winding between small farms interspersed with patches of woods and fenced pastures, then turned sunright on a narrow track half hidden from the sky by overhanging trees. A kilometer along this the trees stopped at the edge of a meadow inhabited by a cottage, two small outbuildings, a two segment corral and a small brook. Five horses occupied one part of the corral, a milk cow and a pair of oxen the other. Goats stood quietly around the wet meadow nibbling what came to mouth, eying the approaching people, and a dozen chickens clucked and pecked the ground out of the rain under an overhang on one of the outbuildings. A garden plot lay some distance sunward of the cottage surrounded by a tall pale of closely woven sticks to keep out the goats, chickens and wild browsers from the nearby forest. A large stack of wood leaned against the other outbuilding, surrounded by a patch of beaten earth covered thickly in sawdust, bark, twigs and wood chips. A sawbuck stood there and an ax rested against the shed. There was a large, two wheeled cart standing with the tongue blocked up and half loaded with wood. Grass grew everywhere except in the tracks of the road they trod and in a path gouged from the woodlot to the far side of the meadow into the forest. Smoke trickled from the chimney of the cottage and skulked away through the rain.

Atna exclaimed, "It's beautiful!"

"Nice." Sky agreed. "Your uncle's a woodcutter."

"Hunh," Berno grunted.

Two yellow, curly-tailed dogs burst from the interior of the larger outbuilding and came barking wildly down the road.

Berno's aunt, Sepel, was a pear shaped, cheerful woman with braided gray hair coiled and pinned on top of her head. She had apple cheeks and ample laugh lines, and filled any pause in conversation with cheery chat. This more than compensated for Berno's verbal reticence.

"Oh, you poor, poor dear," she dithered while helping Atna out of the wet cloak and seating her at the small dining table. She snatched a towel from the counter, folded it to a thick pad and placed it on the table. "Rest your arm here and wait a heartbeat while I get a splint."

When she returned she tossed the supplies onto the table, pulled up the neighboring chair, gently lifted Atna's arm and carefully examined it with a wrinkled, tanned hand. Atna flinched.

"My, my. I'm not saying it's good (when's a broken bone ever), but it's not bad. The outer bone of the forearm is cracked near the wrist. I'm afraid it'll have to be straightened before splinting to heal properly. Here, put this dowel in your teeth. You," she motioned to Sky, "hold your wife's elbow down firmly on the pad. I'm going to pull the hand and manipulate the bone at the same time, so hold tight.

"Now, dear," she said to Atna, "when I start pulling, I want you to fill your lungs and give a good long, hard scream. It helps."

Atna did indeed scream hard, and nearly passed out. But she remained upright on her own strength, however pale she had become. Sepel placed three sticks, a round one top and bottom and a flat one along the outside of the arm, gestured for Sky to hold them and quickly wrapped the arm with a cloth strip from base of thumb to elbow. Atna took the dowel from her mouth and marveled at the depth of her teeth marks. She placed it on the table, put her good arm by the dowel for a pillow and laid her sweat beaded forehead down.

"Now," Sepel said, patting Atna, "we need to get some food in you and put you to bed."

"No," Atna whispered.

"We just ate, madam," Sky explained. "But if you would let us find a corner in your outbuilding, we'd be grateful. We're behind on sleep."

Sepel scowled at him. "I will not put this poor woman in the shed. We just rose and ate. Harl, my husband, has gone to sell contracts for wood. Atna can have our bed, alone so you don't crush her arm. You're welcome to the shed, or that corner." She gestured across the main room. The small house was approximately square and had two rooms. The larger was "L" shaped with the kitchen in the end of one arm, the fireplace on the internal wall at the corner of the "L", and a sitting room in the other arm. The dining table sat just outside of the kitchen. The bed stood in the separate room. The hearth of the fireplace opened in back to the bedroom to heat it, while a curtain hung in the doorway for privacy and darkness.

Sky glanced at the offered corner. He smiled, but demurred. "I'll take the shed. It'll leave you free to be at your work." He had noticed a simple spinning wheel and the small loom holding unfinished fabric.

"Berno will help you clear a spot while I put your wife to bed."

"Thank you." He looked expectantly at Berno who stood from the chair where he'd waited out of his aunt's way. They left the house.

Sky awoke well rested. He used the pit toilet, found a bowl and pitcher on a stand against the side of the house, filled the pitcher from the stream, and washed. The rain had stopped but the sky remained gray. He noticed an extra horse in the corral. The dogs trailed him around with expressions of interest and wagging tails but he had carefully hung his backpack up beyond their reach and he carried no food with him, to their disappointment. They accompanied him to the house where he knocked on the door.

A burly man with a balding gray head, and bored look on his wide face, opened the door. Sky nodded and offered his hand. "You must be Harl. Thank you for your hospitality."

Harl shook the hand indifferently. "That's the wife for you. Wouldn't turn away a sick polecat," he said. He gestured with his thumb and stepped aside, closing the door behind Sky.

Sky spotted Sepel at her loom and asked, "Atna's still asleep?"

"That's what the body wants when it's healing. She'll get up when she gets hungry or needs to pee."

Sky nodded to Berno seated at the table and joined him there. "Been here all this time, Berno?"

Berno shook his head and Sepel interjected, "Oh no, Berno's been out and come back twice. He had to finish the business he'd been on when he met you."

"Sorry for the delay, Berno. What is it you do?"

"He's a trader," Sepel said. "He was collecting orders, goods and deposits for the next trip sunward."

"You compete with the merchant ships?" Sky asked.

"Of course," Sepel responded, "the ships dominate trade near the coast, but he takes custom orders and trades away from the coast. And he has an advantage in speed on the antisun trip. The ships have to beat against the wind, then their loads have to be transferred to horses and carts to go inland. Goods on ships risk damage from salt water. And pirates, of course. This war was hard, but it'll bring back Berno's fortunes."

"You had losses?" Sky asked.

Berno nodded and his aunt continued, "He was in Prater when the gates were sealed and most of his horses were confiscated, 'requisitioned' the thieving nobles called it, for the war. He had a string of forty eight, but all that's left are the five outside. Then there's his long recovery when his working cash had to be spent for his care."

"You were ill?" Sky asked.

"Ill and injured," Sepel started to say when Berno grunted, frowned at her and shook his head. "Sorry, Sky. Berno doesn't like to talk about it."

Sky didn't notice Berno's sudden look in his direction and the expression of intense interest, nor the way that expression turned to a slit eyed glare. Atna stepped from the bedroom and everyone but Berno turned to her. He continued to study Sky surreptitiously before nodding gently to himself and forcing a neutral expression on his face.

"Atna!" Sepel cried. "How do you feel?"

"My arm woke me, but I feel loads better.

"Hi, Sky," Atna said to her husband. "How'd you sleep?"

"Like a baby. I'm ready to move on. You?"

Her eyes unfocused as she checked internal signs. Then she rose up on the balls of her feet and bounced lightly up and down. She grimaced at the bottom of each bounce. "I think I can," she said. "I'll put the arm in a sling."

Sepel cried, "You're not going anywhere. Sky, what kind of man are you? Your wife needs more rest."

"I wouldn't ask her to," Sky replied, "if we had the time and money. But we're trying to get to Mikkeny before she gives birth."

"Killing her on the highway won't give you a child. You can't take her."

Sky looked appealingly at Atna who smiled and turned to Sepel. "We'll go slow. But we need to keep at it or I'll be a mother in the wilderness."

Frustrated, Sepel addressed her husband. "Harl, do something. Talk some sense into them."

"It's their road, Sepel. We can't walk it for them."

"Oh, you're worthless!" she chided.

Berno growled, "I have an idea." All eyes turned. "I go sunward in two sleeps. But I could wait five, six?" He raised his eyebrows at Sepel.

"Ten," Sepel said.

"Ten sleeps for Atna's arm. Then she and Sky could make up time by riding."

Atna insisted on spending the next sleep in the outbuilding with Sky and they went to bed early to align their schedule with that of their hosts, and to catch up on sleep they'd already missed.

Next wake period Sky accompanied Harl and his ox team down the rutted track to the forest. While Harl drove the team, dragging a small dray and six long ropes, Sky carried two axes and a water bag. The deeper into the woods they passed, the shallower the worn groove they followed became, and more branching paths broke off to wander different ways. Eventually they struck off across undisturbed woodland floor.

Harl said, "I scouted some good deadwood out here."

Harl left the oxen well back from the tree he had selected and asked Sky for an ax. He knocked the lower limbs off and had Sky pitch them out of the way. "Always keep your escape route clear," he told Sky.

"Same as the battlefield," Sky said.

"I thought your scars might have been won at war."

Sky said. "Nobody gets away without some."

Harl set Sky to felling the tree while he went on to a second. Sky had done this as a young man so the ax felt at home in his hand and the familiar rhythm of the job brought peaceful reminiscence to him. His wounded, arrow-pierced, arm began aching before the tree fell, but the pain remained tolerable.

The trees were large enough to provide a load with only three. While Sky finished limbing the third and furthest tree, Harl fetched the oxen. They rolled the butt of the log onto the dray and lashed a rope twice around it. Each downed log was collected as they made their way back toward the woodcutter's homestead. They dropped the logs off near the sawbuck, removed the yoke from the team, herded the oxen into the corral and tossed them some feed.

"Let's eat," Harl said gesturing toward the house, "Then we'll buck 'em up."

Atna spent the time of the men's absence cleaning house, or as much as she could manage one-handed. This included dusting and scrubbing, though not sweeping. She also moved all the kitchen utensils to the table or aside on the counters and scrubbed every surface she could reach. When Atna had neatly replaced the last item Sepel arose from her stool in front of the loom and joined the young woman in the kitchen.

"The men will be along soon. Let's start a meal," Sepel said.

"How do you know?"

"Know what, dear?"

"When Harl will return," Atna said.

"I count the rows I've made in the loom. I know how many it takes for Harl to get home, so I figured about two thirds that many for two men."

"Hmm," Atna said. "But for the meal, you'll have to tell me what you need. I'm worthless with this arm, and mostly worthless in a kitchen even with two good hands."

"You can't cook?"

"I used to help Mother, so I know some basics, but haven't done any for a long, long time."

Sepel cocked her head. "You haven't been married long, I assume. What have you been doing that you can't cook?"

"Ah," Atna hesitated, and blushed. "I, ah, been working at an inn in Prater."

"But not in the kitchen?" Sepel asked.

"No."

"Serving drinks? Cleaning?"

"Occasionally," Atna hedged.

"What else could," Sepel began and then stopped. "Oh!" She said, and, flustered, left quickly through the doorway, calling over her shoulder, "I'll fetch the eggs!"

They both had recovered their equanimity when Sepel returned, and she avoided further questions about Atna's past. Instead she resumed the running narrative that she had kept up since the men left. By the time they heard the jangle of the big bronze ring in the ox yoke, the women nearly had a warm meal ready to set.

After the meal the men used the axes to shorten the logs to pieces they could roll up a ramp into the sawbuck. Then they applied the bronze saw to the logs to produce rounds of about a forearm in length. The saw needed sharpening after each two blocks, when Harl would sit on a bench, place a leather pad on his left thigh and hone the teeth with a small, triangular whetstone. During this Sky split the rounds into smaller pieces with an ax and stacked them neatly in the cart. The three logs more than filled the cart so they stacked the excess split blocks in the overhang of the outbuilding, hitched the oxen to the cart and, after speaking to the ladies, drove down the track toward the highway and customers.

The women went out to the garden. Atna pulled weeds and helped carry buckets of water from the small stream to water plants. Sepel milked the cow and two of the goats, covered the porcelain jars and lowered them into a pool in the stream to cool while Atna took grain to the horses. Sepel climbed a ladder to the loft in the outbuilding to check on cheese they were making from goat milk. There was also some beer fermenting there and sausages hung from the rafters. They collected dried horse dung and dumped it on the midden pile by the garden.

The men returned as the women were pulling baked buckwheat bread from a stone hole under the hearth of the fireplace. Berno had come back earlier and they all crowded around the small dining table for supper.

Atna took Sky aside following the meal and asked him to help Sepel clean the dishes since she, Atna, couldn't, and it was only proper etiquette. Sky frowned but said, "Of course," and began clearing the table over the protests of Sepel.

They relaxed after the meal and Harl broke into his meager supply of beer to share with his guests.

Sky said, "You and Sepel do well for yourselves, Harl. The rest of the kingdom acts like it's the end of the world."

"We have the farm. We still eat when others scrounge. Firewood sales are down, but the wealthy can still pay. It's enough to buy salt, spices and metal and leather goods. I'll barter almost anything with the poor folk."

They all bedded down. Sky and Atna chatted before falling to sleep. Among the few subjects they discussed she asked Sky if he had noticed the odd way that Berno looked at him sometimes. He hadn't.

The next eight wake periods followed a similar pattern. Twice Berno helped the other men in the woods or bucking up logs and loading the cart. He also accompanied them on deliveries, but went about his own business while Harl and Sky unloaded. The help that Atna rendered became greater as the pain diminished and she could use her hand to grasp lightly. Sepel kept up a dialog about her little world, because it was her nature and because she feared asking Atna questions that would touch upon her past in Prater.

Without Berno around to stop her, Sepel told Atna about his recent misfortunes, and as she and Sky settled in the outbuilding for the sixth sleep, Atna passed it to him.

"Apparently Berno was having a drink and minding his own business at a public house when a mad drunk attacked him. The beast picked up a bowls pin and jammed it into Berno's mouth, breaking teeth and shoving it down his throat. Before others could pull the mad man off, the pin had torn the inside of Berno's throat. He bled for three sleeps and it became infected. This happened before the snowman army arrived at Prater, and Berno had only recovered enough to leave the city just as the war ended. He nearly died both from the bleeding and the infection, and then nearly starved to death because he couldn't eat. And it ruined his voice."

"No wonder he looks like death," Sky said. "It's a dangerous world, even in a quiet pub."

"You didn't meet him did you, during your drunken time?" Atna asked. "He still watches you sometimes. It makes me uncomfortable. It wasn't you that hurt him was it?"

Sky shook his head. "He was probably sick then and out of circulation. Not that I'd remember him if we did meet, or much of anything else."

"I wonder that you remember *me*," Atna said.

"Have we met?" Sky laughed.

"Go to sleep, idiot."

Sky did not remember that it was he who, after learning of his displacement in time, had disrupted Berno's bowls game and tried to kill the man in a drunken, vengeful rage. But Berno remembered. And he plotted.

Five horses were not enough to carry much trading stock, even without putting Sky and Atna on two of them. Berno compensated by specifically pursuing new clients willing to forward cash instead of goods. This mated with his plan to rebuild his business by purchasing more horses at the other end for the return trip. It would mean borrowing from a money merchant, but speed was essential if he was to take advantage of the open market created by the war.

The rain, which had plagued them since Sky and Atna left Prater to join the snowmen, gave up, leaving them warm sunshine to load the horses. That and, finally, getting on their way raised the spirits of the travelers, even the sombre Berno. The two pack animals carried impressive loads but bore no more than the riding horses who had to carry food and camping gear as well as the riders. Berno intended to shuffle the horses' duties as they traveled to assure that they all arrived fit in Siklos, the seaport on the mainland nearest to the Mikenny island group.

"Harl and Sepel," Sky said before they mounted their horses, "I can't thank you enough for your kindness and hospitality. Please take these five silvers. It should cover the cost of keeping us."

Harl looked at the money, looked at Sepel who shook her head almost imperceptibly, and he answered Sky. "No, sir. You earned every bit of your keep and then some."

"You and Atna have been a great help around here," Sepel said. "I hate to see you go."

Atna hugged the old woman. "Thank you, Sepel. We'll never forget you."

Sky put the money back in his pouch and shook Harl's calloused hand. The three travelers mounted and rode down the track but turned to wave a last goodbye as they entered the forest. The dogs stopped following them at the edge of the meadow and turned back to Sepel and Harl who already held thoughts only for the next job in their old, familiar routine.

Chapter 3

Atna, Sky and Berno acquired specific duties as they traveled. Berno rode first, followed by the two pack horses, then Atna and finally Sky, keeping an eye on his wife and the integrity of the animals' loads.

For the first three sleeps roadside inns provided shelter and skimpy meals but then began to thin out, occurring two, then three or more wake periods apart. They stopped at farms and occasionally a small village would be found conveniently placed at ride's end. Then, at the eighteenth sleep, though they stretched the travel, they had to camp out.

Chores were divided at camp according to ability which, at first, left Atna little to do because of her broken wing. Atna's arm sling had been removed about ten sleeps out, but the splint remained. Sky had less knowledge of cooking than even Atna so that fell to Berno, who had fed himself well on the trail for much of his adult life. Berno had taught Sky how to unpack the horses at a trip's end and so left him to it while he broke out cooking gear and began their meal. By the time the food was ready to eat Sky would have the horses hobbled, fed and watered, and most of the camp would be set. The first tent up was to protect the trade goods which would remain tarp covered, on the horses, until the tent was ready.

They were still within the boundary of the kingdom of Prater, so they regularly met patrols which kept the road safe for travelers. These encounters provided opportunity to exchange news and barter for goods that Berno kept handy for impromptu trade. The war had pulled most of the road guards back to defend the city, which allowed encroachment by highwaymen at the hinterlands. The freshly returned patrols assured the trio that these were being driven back to the wilds, but would not make promises about safety beyond the border.

Riding away from one of these meetings Sky asked Berno what he did about highwaymen.

Berno growled, "Mostly there are none. The wild lands have a few savages but they don't care about travelers that stay on the road. Near civilization there are robbers but I pay toll and go on. They know traders come back. Ordinary travelers can be in danger. Depends on the mood of the robbers. I know all of them. Some very well." Berno's rough voice gave out there and he cast a shrouded glance at Sky.

Another time Berno explained to them that at his most prosperous he had employed three men to help him with the pack train. Not that those few would discourage the highwaymen from attacking, but one man could not handle so many horses. It would be a long time before Berno would again own a large enough pack string to need help.

The nearer their approach to the frontier, the more Berno seemed to warm to his guests, especially Atna, though his newly acquired smile failed to involve his eyes when interacting with Sky.

At twenty-eight sleeps they encountered the Pratorian patrol posted furthest from the city. The guards were busy re-stacking loose stone pylons on either side of the highway, though that term hardly suited the rough track it had become. They claimed the pylons, which had been knocked apart by outlaws after the guards were withdrawn, marked the official border of Prater. Sky cocked a skeptical eye at the "border" markers, but kept his doubts to himself as to how long they could remain in place if any organized military entity lay in the wilds beyond. According to Berno, no such entity would be found within forty more sleeps of travel.

Berno traded some cheap, skull shaped earrings, that he knew were favored by the patrols, for some food to bolster their supply before stepping into the ungoverned lands.

Two sleeps later, after eating but before crawling into a tent with Atna, Sky left the camp to scour the forest and returned with a freshly dead hardwood sapling. Beginning at the next ride and continuing for three wake periods he let the horse follow the others under its own guidance and spent the time shaping the wood with his knife. When he had a passable bow that spanned nearly the length of his spread arms he fashioned a string for it of catgut and began collecting straight stems for arrows. Before bedding down at each camp he spent time making fletching of quill feathers from a goose he had taken with his sling, then, for want of good work-hardened bronze, he flaked stone arrow heads out of fired chert. He chewed lengths of catgut to soften and split it into fine strips. He used these to bind the heads and fletching to the shafts, carefully allowing them to dry evenly so they would adhere and shrink uniformly. For protection from rain he kept the arrows and the dismounted bow-string rolled in light, oiled leather.

Berno had recognized the first piece as a bow taking shape and asked, "What do you want that for?"

Sky replied, "To vary our fare with bigger game. Keep the larder up."

"You know," Berno pointed out, "it will be useless against a bandit ambush."

"I don't plan to string it if we meet people."

Berno nodded and turned back to his work. Sky continued carving his bow.

Before Sky finished his new weapon, while riding along seven sleeps out from the Prater border, they faced the first highwaymen. Three of them sat on horses and two went afoot. Sky studied the surrounding underbrush, spotting two more with ready bows on either side of the road behind.

Berno pulled up his horse and Sky and Atna rode forward to him.

Berno said, "It's Jama's bunch, but without Jama. Wait here."

Sky asked, "You sure you don't want some backup?"

"Aggression will anger them. And we can't force our way past."

Atna looked at Sky and back to Berno. "Don't be too sure," she said.

Berno glared at Sky. "No," he said. "I have to come this way again. I can't afford the men it would take to defend me. We submit."

"It's your business," Sky said. "Do it your way."

Berno rode to the brigands. They stood far enough away that Atna and Sky could not hear the conversation, though it was obvious they had exchanged greetings and were now dickering about safe passage. The bandits kept assessing the small pack train and one of them gestured repeatedly at himself and then Berno's goods. Berno kept shaking his head and replying with counter offers. Finally Berno shrugged and acquiesced with a nod, turning to wave Sky and Atna forward.

Up close even the leader of the little band looked half starved inside his bagging, ragged clothes. Berno nodded his direction and said, "This is Bilan and his men. Bilan, this is Sky and Atna."

Bilan saluted them in misplaced arrogance with a short, decoratively carved stick that he wielded as his badge of leadership. His men looked with equal hunger at the packed horses and at Atna. Berno, Sky and Atna noticed and each reacted, Sky bristling, Atna shuddering and Berno saying, "We struck a bargain, Bilan."

"Which leaves us poor as bugs. She's a pretty one, too. But we have a bargain, yes. And a promise you'll do better when you come back."

Berno nodded and dismounted, walked to the second packhorse and untied enough of the lashing to part the canvas and dig inside. He withdrew a small keg and a little, wood box. One of the pedestrian bandits stepped ahead reaching out, but Bilan slashed the man's arm with his stick, spurred forward and leaned down to retrieve the keg himself. He slipped it into a bag behind his saddle and, accepting the box from Berno, tossed that to the man he'd struck. "Count them."

The man stopped rubbing his arm, opened the box and dug through it with the point of a knife he'd pulled from his belt, counting silently but mouthing each number. "All here," he said, closing the box and tucking it into the sack slung from his shoulder.

"Good," Bilan said. "Berno. Join us for a meal."

"No, thanks, Bilan. We have a long ride." And, he thought, we don't want to be around when you're all drunk on that beer in your saddlebag.

The ragged band parted, though seeming reluctant, and let Berno's party through.

Beyond earshot of the bandits Sky asked Berno, "Did you find out what happened to Jama?"

"Yes. He took the amnesty that Prater offered to criminals who would fight the snow barbarians. With two of his men. Bilan saw it as a chance to move up. Not much of a move, eh?"

"What was in the box?" Sky asked.

"Arrowheads."

Sky touched his unfinished bow.

"For trade," Berno said. "Only trade."

They traversed a more rugged country three sleeps later—foothills to a chain of mountains that rolled down to the sea. The trail wound down to and in and out of ravines and up to ridge tops. They could sometimes see the ocean far off to sunleft from these heights when the trees did not block their view. The trail wandered into deep forest and crossed exposed granite knobs where stone cairns had been placed at intervals to mark the way, and occasionally it followed a well scoured ravine for several kilometers before climbing out again. Distant thunder rumbled out of the gray, sunright sky as they approached a shelf just before the trail dropped back into a gully.

Berno reined in his horse, turned in the saddle and waited for his fellows to come abreast.

He said, "We camp here," and dismounted.

"But," Sky and Atna chimed together, and Sky continued, "We haven't gone a full march."

"We camp here. You'll see."

As they set camp, tendrils of cloud from the storm to sunright crept over them to loose a few light drops. They were serving steamy stew into their bowls when Berno cocked his head, said, "It's coming," and pointed to the ravine.

The others felt the shuddering earth that had prompted Berno and a grinding, chaotic, watery mass roared into view. Brown foam, muck, boulders, logs, brush and whole trees tore by just below the brow of their platform, to rush off down the gully through which they would have been traveling if they had not stopped. For eighty heartbeats the flood ripped at the walls of the ravine, then abruptly dropped. It fell to an ever lessening flow. The sounds of drips and rivulets trickling back off the banks played a deceitfully peaceful melody in mockery of the roaring torrent they had just seen.

"By Huf and the ancestors and all the spirits," Sky murmured. "I have *never* seen anything like that." He looked at Atna who only stood staring down the ravine with her mouth open.

She finally gulped, "We'd be dead."

Berno grunted, "With many others. You have to know about the floods. We'll sleep and the storm in the mountains will stop. The trip through the trash left by the flood will be hard. Rest."

Challenged and slowed but unharmed they negotiated the stream bed until the trail left it after four kilometers.

Atna suggested at the lunch stop that her arm felt well enough to remove her splint. Sky gently unwrapped it and Atna flexed and swung her arm a few times.

"Great," she smiled.

In four sleeps they were within the first true wilderness. The road was nearly covered by vegetation overhead, and once they glimpsed a large, unidentifiable beast crossing far ahead. Sky strung his bow and rode with it and two arrows in his left hand. Berno claimed the animals were harmless, but Sky remained unconvinced.

Atna exclaimed once and pointed at a hummock among trees to their right, but neither of the men saw anything. "It was a man," she said. "Done up in leather and feathers."

"Smile if you see more." Berno said. "And Sky, put away the arrows. For the next fifty kilometers don't leave the path. We will not hunt their game. We eat what we carry."

Chapter 4

After the tense but uneventful wilderness passage the road became more rutted, turned toward the sea and dropped down to the shoreline. In one more wake period they found a village at the head of a small but well protected harbor.

"This is Piscus," Berno told them. "The citizens are more savage than the wilderness people. Be polite. We pay a toll here."

During the trip Berno's form had filled out to his former healthy shape and even his voice had become less gravelly, though he spoke sparingly and it was evident that it still caused him discomfort. He had grown tanned and more vigorous so there could be no difficulty for the locals, whom he knew, to recognize him, though earlier the bandit Bilan had taken a moment to realize he was Berno, so different had he looked from his old self.

He arranged housing with two families in their hovels, he in one and Sky and Atna in another. He left them there and set off to the shack of the village head man to discuss toll. That business done, he walked to one of the two village bars to discuss other needs with a pair of scabrous, neckless, bent-nosed ruffians.

Sky and Atna sat on stools at the table with their hostess and her three bony children, two barely clad girls and a naked boy just at walking age. The woman, Moteen, had been quizzing them about the war at Prater, the fearsome snowmen, and the trip from Prater. Her interest had dwindled some at the beginning when her guests denied the rumor that the snowmen ate the still beating hearts of their freshly dead victims. She felt better after confirmation that, yes, indeed, the snowmen were so pale as to resemble walking corpses. She gave an appreciative, wide-eyed shudder.

The little boy was arch-backed, pissing on the dirt floor beside Atna while Sky declaimed about the awful devastation wrought with a trebuchet, to the horrified satisfaction of his audience, when Berno rapped at the door and came in.

Berno said, "Come on, Sky. It's going to be a long, dry trek. Join me for a beer."

Sky looked at Atna. "Shoo," she said sweeping her hands toward the door. "Go do your man stuff and I'll relax here with Moteen. Just have some control."

He lifted a brow but patted her knee and stood. "We'll be back soon."

As they entered the low building Berno said, "The local beer is good. They have to import most of the ingredients, but they know what to do with them." He raised two fingers for the barman and patted the rough wood counter.

"They fish for a living?" Sky asked.

"Yes. And hunt. And trade anything they can with anybody they can. Mostly pirates on islands up the coast. This village is beyond laws and won't betray the pirates. And, as I said, most Piscans are just as rough."

The beers arrived and Berno threw down a silver coin. "Keep drawing till that's gone."

"That's a bit much, Berno," Sky protested. "And I'd like to buy my share."

"You're my guest." He gulped down a quarter of his mug.

Sky looked doubtful, shrugged and joined him. "That first swallow always tastes like nectar of the gods," he said.

Berno said, "So, you'll be a fisherman?"

Sky grimaced. "One possibility. Not that I cherish it."

"But you'll do what it takes."

"Yes. I've done nasty chores before and survived. I want to keep my Atna, and it's time I settled to raise some kids. Fishing can do that, or herding a rich idiot's sheep. At least we'll eat."

Berno curled his lips in another smile that his eyes did not join. "You love her?"

Sky shrugged. "I admit it."

"You'd miss her."

"More than my right arm."

Berno said in a flat tone, "I knew that feeling. But she left me for dead in my hardship. It is like losing an arm. Worse."

"Sorry to hear that."

"We'll talk about something else," Berno said.

The barkeep saw their mugs emptied, refilled them and removed the appropriate coins.

Four dubiously human hulks sidled over to the counter and the barman drew a beer for each without asking. Sky noted them and discounted them.

The four talked about a man who's fishing boat had gone down in a recent storm. He had survived the disaster only to be murdered in his house by agents of the money lender who had financed the boat's purchase and who hoped by the example to urge other borrowers to greater care. They laughed heartily.

Sky heard enough of the exchange to justify Berno's opinion of the locals. The four finished their drinks and started toward the exit, passing near to Sky's back. One snaked a cord over Sky's head, yanking it tight around his neck. All hell broke loose as Sky felt the cord stop his breath. But two of the ruffians each grabbed an arm before he could grip the garrote and the fourth pulled a bag over his head and cinched it with a drawstring. Sky flailed like a beached shark, striking out with his feet and head, wrenching to free his arms. The bar splintered as he kicked it and the rebound shoved him and his assailants backward. His heel crushed a foot. The man yelled but held his grip. Though Sky shook them and jarred them and kicked at them, it only burned the little air left in his lungs faster. His sense began to go in thirty heartbeats and at fifty he collapsed limp to the floor.

"Let him breathe!" Berno shouted, wincing at the pain it caused. "Don't kill him!"

The four rolled Sky onto his belly, eased the garrote and, when they saw him take a breath, tied his arms behind him and bound his legs. They knotted the bag cinch to hold it firmly. With practiced skill the men hoisted Sky and hustled him out of the bar. They carried him down to the waterfront, past the indifferent handful of witnesses, and entered a dockside shack. Sky began to struggle again.

Berno followed with a grim, satisfied smile. The men lashed Sky to a wood column. They backed away.

"Good job," Berno said. "I won't be long. Wait outside."

The four left him with Sky in the dim, fishy room. Sky, breathing raggedly through his injured throat, tugged at the bonds.

"Go ahead," Berno said. "But they're sailors. They know knots."

Sky kept working at the ropes but spoke, "Ber..." and broke into coughing. "Why are you doing this?" He finally rasped.

"Ah, your throat feels it. Like mine. Good. Not enough but a start. You don't remember? The inn in Prater just before the snowmen arrived. The bowls game you knocked over. The pin you rammed down my throat."

"You have the wrong guy."

"It was you," Berno insisted. "It took time to be sure, but look at you. You can't be mistaken for another. You're wild; violence is always your first choice." He bent and picked up a meter long board. "And I have good reason to remember your face." He swung the board at Sky's lower ribs.

There was a dull crack and Sky grunted. He could see vague motion through the worn, loose weave of the sack and had tried to deflect the blow with an arm but the ropes allowed too little motion. The board pulled back to swing toward his other side and Sky, turning his whole body around the column, caught the blow just under the right elbow. He yelped and cursed, blood flowed from the cut, and he wrenched mightily at the ropes to get some slack. The board started back again. Sky loosened the bond to the column just enough to slide the rope down it. He squatted to the floor into as small a ball as he could become, pressing his head between his knees. The stick slammed against his back.

Sky tensed for the next blow. Nothing came.

"You rotten bastard," Berno continued. "You ruined my life. Took my wealth, my wife, and left me wrecked." He slammed Sky's back again.

Berno said, "I've had time to plan. A beating won't do. And killing is too quick." The board struck another spot on Sky's back. "You will live to regret your crime. You'll feel penance." He struck again at the lower side, at the cracked rib, and Sky gasped out again. Berno began, "Your Atna..."

"No!" Sky gritted.

"Yes--will die slowly, with your unborn child. Or be sold in slavery. Or become mine, until I'm tired of her. And you will never know her fate, nor she yours. You will struggle to live, fighting for table scraps or a drop of water, and wonder what your wife suffers."

The board cracked against Sky's head and light danced in his covered eyes. "But," Berno said, "I will leave you a personal memory of me. To remind you with every painful breath."

He attacked Sky's knees and shins with the board until blood streamed to the floor, then focused on the elbows and thin flesh just below them. He shifted the blows to the spine and ribs, cracking three more before moving on to the shoulders and finishing with a severe bludgeoning of the head, until the sack tore to tatters and Sky slumped like a rag in the ropes. Berno finally stepped back, breathing hard, to study his work. He stepped in again, bent, ripped the sack away, pulled Sky's face up to gaze at and spit on it. He released the head, reached down, undid Sky's money pouch and tucked it in his shirt as he rose. Then, tossing aside the board, he kicked the unconscious man in the face. The satisfying sound of crunching bone brought a genuine smile as he turned and left the shed.

Outside, Berno doled out two silver coins to each of his thugs. "Take him," he said and walked up the hill.

Chapter 5

Sky suffered the fires of hell. He screamed but bit it off as demons speared his head and eyes and pummeled him everywhere with spiked maces. He tried to open an eye but the pain even that awoke made him struggle to quiet every muscle, hoping to quell the agony. But it would not stop tearing through him. He passed out.

He awoke a lifetime later, vomited and drifted back out of the world.

A voice intruded. "Looks like a good one, if he lives. Get food and water in him. See if you can save him. Extra rations in it for you."

A scorching thirst worked its way to the top of his miseries. Sky tried opening his eyes but only his right one cracked enough to see a hairy, blurred face frowning at him. "Hey, mate," the face said, "you gotta drink this water. You've been out almost three sleeps. You'll die. Drink."

A hand gently, but painfully, lifted Sky's head while a cup presented itself to his lips. He drank the cup empty and croaked, "More."

"In a bit, mate. Slow goes it. Have a spoon of gruel."

Sky lifted a trembling hand and guided the spoon to his mouth.

This began his long, slow return to the living. He had been beaten before, and he had been wounded badly in war, but his whole experience encompassed nothing as painful or lasting as the meticulous pulping that Berno had given him. It was all he could do at first to bite off screams as the pain throbbed harder, and when he carefully explored the damage to his left eye he found a tender, swollen mass. The source of his other pains he left undiscovered for now. He slept for prodigious amounts of time, and when he awoke from the sixth sleep his good eye flew wide and he shouted, "Atna!"

"Atna," he said. "What have I done to you?"

The trauma of his beating had driven its cause out of mind, but it was coming back and his memory had opened the drawer he least wanted exposed. He still had no recall of attacking Berno in Prater, but suspected that he was indeed the culprit. It had been a dark period. He had, after all, awakened in jail with the worst hangover ever, and no idea how or why he was there. In the refugee crowded city his greatest crime had gone undiscovered or he would still be in prison serving time for the near murder of Berno.

These thoughts fired his fears for Atna. If Berno could beat him this savagely then he was capable of honoring his threats against her. And, Sky thought, all I can do is lie here and fret.

His hairy nursemaid, or warder, or whatever he was, appeared. "I heard you yell," he said. "You all right?"

Sky smiled sarcastically and weakly stated the obvious, "No."

"No, I guess not," agreed Hairy. "But you're talking. That's an improvement."

Sky let his good eye wander around the dark, low, wood quarters he occupied. "Where am I?"

"The bowels of *Hell*."

"Well, good. At least I didn't imagine it," Sky grimaced as his cracked ribs grated. "But your company is gentler than I expect from a demon. Which one are you?"

His keeper smiled. "Not a demon. A fellow sufferer. My name is Vindol. And *Hell* is the name of the pirate ship you're berthed in. A good name for this ship."

Sky closed his eye, exhausted. "Thanks, Vindol. I'm Sky." He slept.

Sky awoke disoriented. Then he noticed the gentle roll of the ship and heard the creaking wood and knew where he was, at least very locally. A bowl of gruel and cup of water lay close to hand so he ate and drank. Vindol came down the hatchway at the far end of the empty quarters, crouching to walk over to Sky.

Vindol said, "Sky, if you're up to it, we need to get you cleaned up. I got rid of your bloody clothes while you still couldn't feel it, but that wrap you're in has to go."

Sky for the first time noticed the stench and realized it came from him. "I shit myself," he said.

"Not like you had a choice, but I'll suffer if I don't get the quarters scrubbed down. Give me that old quilt."

Sky shifted, gritted his teeth and more gently pushed back the cover. He worked his way slowly off the portion he'd been lying on and lay on hard, cold boards. Vindol rolled up the filthy quilt distastefully and took it above decks. Moments later he returned with another ratty but more or less clean quilt, two buckets of water and rags.

He set a bucket by Sky. "Can you manage?"

"Or die trying," Sky said, reaching for a rag and dipping it in water.

"Dying is still likely. But I think you'll make it. All your cuts look to be scabbed over and healing. Those bad bruises on your sides must cover broken ribs, but none pierced a lung or you'd already be gone. I don't like the look of that eye. The cheek bone is smashed and we won't know till the swelling drops whether the eyeball is crushed. You could be blind on this side."

Sky grunted in pain at each swab, but managed to wash off the stench.

"The ship's quiet," he said.

"We're in home port. Just a skeleton crew for maintenance. And us two.

"This here is a honey bucket," he said fetching it from one side of the hold. Let me know if you need help using it. And you might as well get used to having it near; as the new man you'll be sleeping by one."

Sky said, "When you have time, I want to ask some questions."

"I'll come back down after I get rid of this mess."

Sky tossed the dirty rag in the wash bucket and dried himself with another, which followed into the bucket. Vindol passed him the quilt and scrubbed down the deck where Sky had lain. Sky wrapped up slowly. Vindol left to throw the dirty wash water over the side.

When Vindol returned he brought a short stool and sat on it. He was hair, skin and bones, wrapped in rags. Not much food had passed through his liver colored lips in a long while. His nose was wide and squished looking. He was bug-eyed, desiccated and looked old except for his long matted hair and beard, which where black. His skin was two shades darker than Sky's but mottled and unhealthy. A thick scar split his right cheek and a freshly scabbed cut ran down his left arm. "What you want to know?" he asked.

"How do I get out of here?"

Vindol cackled. "You don't, even if you wasn't half dead. And I don't and nobody else does, except over the side to the fish."

"Oh?"

"You are now one of the fish-bait gang. What merchant guard would call first boarders. Pirate slaves, drudging for them in home port, and given a dull weapon at sea and sent over the side first, to board ships and die, to soften up a ship's defenders."

Sky said, "You're given weapons, but don't turn on the pirates and free yourselves?"

"With a sword at your back? Half starved? Balanced on the rail between two heaving ships? The sword prodding your kidney isn't the worst. Two ships coming together like a mortar and pestle, and you just a gentle push from becoming grist, that's the worst. I've seen men fall in there, but they don't look like men after the first grind in the barnacles. Your best chance is against the swords at your face. And you can't hang back, or you get the sword in the kidney. And you can't shirk or you'll either be mowed down by the defenders or butchered by the pirates."

Sky thought for a moment. "Why are they feeding me?"

"You're a big, healthy guy, barring recent damage. And they were actually paid to take you. I think they're wagering, too. They want to see if you live and what you do at the next boarding."

"I won't be ready for a fight any time soon," Sky observed.

"You'll be ready when they say. Just hope the last trophy holds them for a while."

"They didn't move me to shore."

"Why bother? If you die it's easier just to pitch you overboard from here. And you're no good as labor."

"Has anybody escaped at port?".

"Nobody. You can run away, but how would you get off the islands? You'd be hunted down before you could build a raft, if you had the strength and if you had the tools. And it's too far to swim for the mainland even without some monster making a meal of you. No, we're all stuck here until we take a blade through the gut. I'm an old-timer; I've taken twelve ships."

"Well," Sky sighed, and closed his eyes. "I need sleep, Vindol."

"Get it while you can, Sky."

* * *

Vindol scrounged him some castoff clothes and the injured Sky carefully dressed. Three sleeps later Sky begged a walking stick and used it to make a clumsy hobble around the cramped slaves' berth.

In four more sleeps longboats bumped against the side of the pirate ship, footsteps thumped overhead and the hoist squawked as slaves began loading and stowing provisions. Sky waited in anxious ignorance for Vindol to appear and explain the activity, but the pirate slave was loading food.

Slaves began climbing down the ladder and kept coming until they were packed so tightly that there was only room for half of them to lie down at once. For the moment they all sat in their favored locations. Like any other group this bunch had their hierarchy; the top men entered the cell last and sat nearest the hatch where, poor as it was, the air was freshest. Vindol did not sit among this elite. He did sit too far away from Sky to speak with him, for Sky sat in the most distant corner which was relegated to the lowest men and the four honey buckets.

Sky reflexively yearned to begin working his way up the rungs of this micro-society, but was not fit for confrontation. I'll be patient, he thought. As ingratiatingly as he could allow himself, he turned to the slave at his left.

"I'm Sky," he said. "What is your name, sir?"

The scruffy fellow looked with curious suspicion at Sky. "Remset."

"Good to meet you, Remset. What's happening?" He gestured at the full quarters.

Remset looked surprised. "Where have you been?"

"Isolated right here in this room since I came to," Sky explained.

"Ah," Remset said. "I heard the rumor."

Sky asked, "Are we heading out to attack a ship?"

"If we find one that isn't protected," Remset replied. "There are two other ships with *Hell*. *Death* and *Bluebird*. If we can cut a merchant ship out of the fleet or catch it with only one guard, we'll run her down."

"Bluebird?"

Remset smiled. "I hear Captain Razak let his daughter name it."

Sky thought. Worry showed on his face.

Remset observed, "You're not fit."

"No. If I get sent over the side, I won't be much good."

"You can hope. We'll be six sleeps just getting to the best hunting, and if we don't take a ship there after ten sleeps we'll move on. If you're lucky it'll be some time."

"Vindol tells me that the best of us don't live long, so maybe the delay won't help anyway."

Remset glowered toward Vindol. "Don't listen to that thump-knuckle. He told you how fruitless it is to hang back?"

"Yes."

"And he's a veteran of twelve bloody battles?"

Sky nodded.

"Well," Remset continued, "Not every boarding is bloody; if the merchant sailors think they don't have a chance, they give up. Vindol was boasting. And he *does* hang back and shirk. Granted, you or I wouldn't get away with it. But he carries tales from the hold to the deck and gets favors for it. He got to nurse you, and extra rations for it."

"He's a traitor?" Sky asked glaring at Vindol.

"That's too strong; he wouldn't rat a man to a killing or flogging offense, but he keeps the ears above decks full of our gossip. Don't trust him."

"Thanks," Sky said. To himself he thought, I might have already said too much.

* * *

Sky's luck held good, if squalid life in the slave hold could be considered good. *Hell* gave up cruising the prime hunting and sailed for eight sleeps to the next target area. Sky stopped hurting and worked as best he could at reconditioning his muscles in the cramped quarters. The swelling in his left eye diminished enough to allow it to open and he cheered to find it would still see. A small gift granted in dire condition is greater than power and riches gained in ease. Unfortunately he saw double and it took time and concentrated effort to force the eye back into alignment. When the swelling completely abated it left his face sunken below the eye at the crushed cheek bone. The lower eyelid drooped open further than the right so it exposed more eye below the iris. His face would be lop-sided for the rest of his life.

His exercises annoyed the closest neighbors but he placated them as best he could and kept at it. Sky considered beginning his climb up the social scale. He studied the activity in the squalor around him. The process of social climbing was not as simple as he had assumed. He knew he could overcome men several tiers above him, but only individually, and the slave quarters was really a conglomeration of many small cliques, each of which worked or fought as a unit to defend its members. To attack a man would bring retaliation from his peers. It was the clique, not lone men, which rose up the scale by recruiting individuals seen as valuable from other cliques through favors and threats. Anybody rejected from a clique as weak or unworthy would move down to a lower group where he might take over the leadership if capable, but more likely settled near bottom. One man, a member of a mid-tier coterie, grew ill and descended in status until he lay in the lowest. The largest group was that of lowest rank, which defended itself from more powerful cliques purely by superior numbers. By default Sky found himself at the bottom of this bunch. For a short while the sick slave fell below Sky in status, but gave back the position when he died and was removed from the hold. Sky could have taken control of his low crowd by beating the leader, but wondered if the small gain in status warranted the energy, not to mention the risk to his barely healed ribs. In the end he contented himself as lowest dog in the pack of most whipped curs. He almost learned to ignore the smell of the honey buckets.

He had expected, given his status, to be the man carrying the slops buckets above decks for dumping. When they filled enough to overflow at the next roll of the ship his clique leader shouted, "Buckets up!" and men passed them carefully through the crowded quarters toward the hatch. The top slave rapped the hatch and called again, "Buckets up!" The hatch would eventually open and the four highest status slaves would each carry a bucket up the ladder.

There, Sky was told by Remset, they would take as much time as they could in the light and the fresh air to dump and scrub the buckets. It could be quite a while if the pirate crew was in a good mood. Sky shook his head in wonder that in this bizarre little society the most menial chore in the world had become a coveted privilege.

The fair division of the little food they had was another surprise to Sky. "Remset, why does the top bunch share instead of grabbing it all?"

"First, there'd be a riot. And second, though we fight down here, when we stand on the ship's rail there is no choice of who'll be at your side. If you starved him, he won't protect you, either because he hates you or is too weak."

Earning respect from these wrecked men was not cause for Sky to join their social game. King of slaves is not a high title. If the food had been withheld he would have become their leader.

Also, his reluctance to attract the pirates' attention overcame the appeal of a few moments in the sun with a honey bucket. An escape plan was forming in his mind, and it would help to be a stranger to the pirates. None of them had checked his recovery and his appearance changed radically after his arrival. He couldn't be mistaken for a gentleman, but being unremarkable might prove useful. He now kept to himself as much as he could in the cramped hold. Sky already had a reputation as the big guy by the slops buckets who wasted energy on exercises, but only the handful of men nearest him, and Vindol, damn him, could describe him.

* * *

The tempo of activity overhead increased, the ship came about with a moan from its timbers and heeled hard.

"Watch yourself, Sky," Remset said as he grabbed one of the nearly full buckets and held it upright. Sky and two others rescued the rest.

Remset suggested, "This could be your test. Sounds like they spotted a ship. Whether we're running or chasing you might have to go over the rail."

Sky twisted and then flexed his upper body side to side. His ribs did not complain so he inventoried the rest of his parts. Everything was in good order, or as good as could be expected. He wondered again at what power kept bringing him back from the brink of and even from beyond death. There must be some purpose in this. But what had his extended life accomplished? Mayhem and destruction followed him everywhere—Kendee uprooted, Free dispersed, Prater cracked like an egg, Atna, poor Atna, lost. If there was a guiding power in his fate then Boda was right that his patron was Tevep and not Huf. Now, he thought, is not the time to resolve this. But if I survive the next trial?

"I'm ready," he said. "I suppose they won't let these damn buckets up first."

"No, but the heel will ease as we get ready to board. After the archers clear their decks they'll get the grappling hooks over. That's when they call us. They want us on the rail just before the ships touch."

"The other ship will have archers." Sky suggested.

"Sure. And we'll lose men when we stand at the side waiting for our weapons."

The ship kept maneuvering while tension grew among the slaves. Finally the shouting from sailors on the target ship could be heard along with the thunk of arrows into the hull outside. A squalling and a big thump on the deck signaled that the gaff was down. The hatch cover slammed open and a voice shouted down, "Up and out, scum! Time to earn your keep!"

The slaves boiled out of the hatch, squinting in the glare, oriented themselves and rushed to the side with the grappled merchant ship. Remset was fortunately mistaken in this case about the archers. The merchantman had a higher rail than *Hell* so the defending archers exposed themselves to pirate arrows if they approached the side close enough to aim. The pirate archers hid behind the huge gaff, boom and the flaked sail and picked off anybody on the other ship who came in view. The slaves got to the rail without injury, hunkered low so the arrows passed above, and reached a hand behind to the pirates who had followed them with weapons.

Sky took in what he could in the instant before the order to attack—the disappointingly poor sword in his hand, scorched spots on the deck where fire arrows had been dowsed, the hook of land a kilometer to leeward against which the pirate ships had cornered their victim, six cumbersome merchant ships fleeing, followed defensively by their two, fleeter escorts. And looking down, the churning sea trapped between ships.

The familiar pre-battle knot lay in Sky's gut as he balanced with one foot on deck and one on the rail, then the order came and he and sixty other bellowing slaves heaved themselves up the side of the merchantman. The sailors and a handful of trained fighters met them with hacking blades and bodies started falling. Sky let the old rhythms possess him and he fought, diminished by his poor condition and knowing that his endurance would soon fail. Even so, he fought defensively, not killing where disabling worked, and not disabling where he could avoid encounter. In the melee he doubted any pirates would be noting his performance. The slaves dropped faster than the better fed, work-hardened merchant sailors.

Sky drove men aside. A pause left him two breaths to assess the battle. A quarter of the slaves sprawled dead over the deck among a much smaller number of defenders. In the middle distance the two merchant guard ships had turned after seeing their charges safely out of reach and were bearing down on *Death* and *Bluebird*. The guard ships' sails lay lashed at their decks and oars brought them straight on.

A sailor lunged his sword at Sky. Sky deflected the blade, ramming his left fist into the man's diaphragm. The man staggered, paled and the sword slipped from his hand. Sky grabbed it and the man stumbled away. Sky followed as the sailor jumped down a forward hatch. He caught the man there at the bottom of the ladder. Sky slammed him against the bulkhead, stunning him, then dragged him deeper into the dark. He threw down the worthless sword the pirates had given him and threatened the man with the weapon he'd captured.

"Give me your clothes," Sky demanded.

The man, recovering sense, took a moment to understand and then disrobed, watching the sword tip.

"The turban, too," Sky said. "Now go off there and stay put."

Sky stripped his slave's rags and put on the sailor's. He tied the turban inexpertly but firmly, bringing a tailing end around to hide his face. A lull in the fight at the hatch allowed him to regain the deck.

Another quick survey showed him a different battle. The pirates had gained the deck of the merchantman and the defending crew were dying by the handful. The slaves, depleted by half, took what rest they could, allowing the fresher pirates to engage the tiring defenders. The oar driven ships had steered past the less maneuverable *Death* and *Bluebird* and were closing quickly, three hundred meters away. The pirates saw the two fast ships and doubled their ferocity.

Sky jumped to the side of a merchant sailor and parried a blow that would have taken his head. The sailor grunted thanks and took the next cut of the pirate's sword on his own. Sky skewered a pirate through the lungs and turned to slash half through the arm of the next. He hacked a third man's thigh and the gush of his blood slicked the deck where he fell and died.

Twenty pirates worked their way back over the side to their own ship anticipating the arrival of, and attempt to board by, the nearest guard ship. This eased the pressure on the beleaguered prize ship and the battle evened out. Sky, worth two warriors at most times, began to tire. He barely parried a series of sword strokes and would have suffered a severe cut but the sailor he'd rescued returned the favor by sliding a knife into the heart of Sky's opponent.

Pirates came flooding back onto the merchant ship. Sky glanced over and saw that the guard ship was not coming alongside but accelerating, oars flashing, directly toward the beam of the pirate ship. A bulge of water swelled above the bronze-sheathed ram.

The din of the fight dropped as combatants directed attention to the hurtling guard ship. Pirates hacked at the lines of the grapples, and renewed their attack. They would have to take the merchantman to have any ship at all. Nothing would stop the ramming, and *Hell* would sink.

Sky worked toward the pirate ship. He stepped over the dead Vindol. "Lucky thirteen," he muttered as he leaned down and took a knife from Vindol's lifeless fingers. The last grappling lines parted and pirates shoved at their ship with poles or swords or anything that came to hand. Sky chopped his way through three men between him and the rail, scrambled to the edge, and leaped. The ramming ship crushed the far side of the pirate craft and drove it back toward Sky just enough for him to catch the railing across his upper chest. He felt another rib crack and the sword flew from his grip. Stunned, he hung on for two quick breaths. The oarsmen were already backing water to extract the ram. Sky swung a leg up, reached out, buried the tip of his knife in the wood for a hand hold, grunting at the pain in his chest, climbed the rail and ran clumsily across the deck to the far side, where he threw himself into space.

The great splash blinded him. Jarring pain shot up Sky's left side from hip to shoulder. In a haze he grasped hold, pushed his hurting leg up and over the ram that had just cleared the hull of the pirate ship, righted himself and clutched at the bow. A line dropped from above. He clung to the rope with his last strength, gritting his teeth against pain, and let the rescuers pull him aboard. The sinking ship behind him gurgled. He thought, now nobody will have to dump the honey buckets.

Chapter 6

"It's making me crazy," Sky, aboard the galley ship, *Gore*, said. "Every heartbeat takes me further from Atna. I can't stand it!"

"Nothing to be done," his new acquaintance, Jobek, replied. "We can't turn the fleet around for one man."

It was five sleeps after the sea battle. The conflict had run itself out quickly after Sky escaped. The pirates had overcome the merchant sailors and turned to shoot fire arrows at the second approaching guard ship. *Death* and *Bluebird* had closed in and would try to burn the guards. With the merchant ship taken, the pirates had the advantage. The guards didn't want to sink it, a natural resistance to destroying what they worked to preserve. But the pirates had no compunction against burning the guards. And six unprotected merchant ships made way over the horizon. The guard ships disengaged, rowed to a safe distance, set sail and pursued their disappearing charges.

"But they won't even set me on shore!" Sky complained.

"Not how it works, Sky. We're on the sea beat. We'll run for fifteen more sleeps before coming about. We don't go closer to shore than to see landmarks. Then swap tacks and beat to sea. Only reason we got close enough to be trapped by the pirates was that a bad storm separated the ships. We had to rendezvous. Resign yourself to seeing Banshod. Make yourself useful and they'll let you ship back sunward."

"But, that'll be a dog's age! My kid will be walking and talking by then, if Atna isn't already dead."

"It's not that bad. Just focus on learning the ship and sailing, and you'll be on Atna's trail before you know."

* * *

Far from boring, life aboard ship kept Sky fully occupied. There was a surprising lot to learn, and maintenance was continuous. Jobek taught him the function of lines and coached him on procedure for coming about to the opposite tack, which was still a great distance off in the mysterious sea. Sky began losing the panic he felt when land had disappeared and the fleet was scattered across rolling water. Once, the wind increased until the order came to shorten sail, a matter of partially dropping the gaff, lashing excess sailcloth to the boom and hauling the gaff to flatten the sail. Waves built quickly. The ships pitched into them, throwing spray over the windward decks, and Sky grew queasy. Jobek had primed Sky with the horrors of seasickness, for he knew the terrible power of suggestion and took it on himself to properly break in the new seaman. It was good for a laugh. All the same, Sky never grew too sick and, when the waves eventually flattened back to long rollers, Jobek confided how lucky Sky should feel for his immunity.

Sky watched with interest as the ship's navigator plied his mysterious trade. It had the appearance of religious ritual more than a practical skill. The obscure actions obviously served some purpose, but Sky couldn't divine it.

Sky asked Jobek about navigation.

Jobek stated, "Navigators have a closed, secret guild. Few are admitted who don't have a father in it. Spies have been killed trying to steal the secrets. So I can't tell you much. We all know that the further we travel sunward, the higher the sun stands in the sky. They measure the height with that funny looking staff. They keep track of our direction of sail and measure ship's speed against their heartbeat. But I don't know how they use it on their maps."

"And what does a map show on barren ocean? Waves and fish?"

"I doubt they show open sea, but they predict where the next tack will bring us to land. Occasionally we approach the other ships and the navigators confer. If we need to land at an exact point on shore, like we did to rendezvous the fleet, we sail sunright with the sun at a given height. Sometimes all the ships meet because they sail the same line, and we don't have to go to shore. They have exquisitely detailed maps of the whole coast that have been drawn and improved over generations, handed down from father to son. Each navigator carries his maps in a locked bronze box which he takes everywhere. If he goes ashore, his maps go. If a ship is at risk of being taken by enemies, the navigator and his assistants stand at the ship's side with the box at their feet and swords drawn. Their last act before death is to the kick the box over and let the sea have it. Stories go 'round of navigators assaulted on shore and robbed of their box, but when opened it's always a stinking, soggy mess."

Sky asked, "What if they get anxious and dump the box overboard before the last gasp and the ship is saved? How do they find themselves?"

"Every navigator memorizes the sun-height of major ports. I even saw one build a crude, new staff, and log, when his were lost overboard (and the assistant flogged), and still get our ship to port."

"Hmm." Sky said. "Say, what if it's cloudy?"

"We steer by the wind."

"Of course. A youngster named Tane showed me that trick once."

* * *

Sky considered navigation and other discoveries for a few sleeps and then asked Jobek, "Do the pirates have navigators?"

"Not trained. The guild bans it. Any taken by pirates die with their secrets. And pirates don't need to leave sight of land. The chance of finding prey is better than open sea. That's our best defense."

"But just defense. I wonder if we could exterminate them."

Jobek shook his head. "It was tried. There's not just one nest. And it's impossible to get the seafaring states to cooperate to get them all. And then the cost makes a merchant faint. Besides, the marauders would spring back."

"But," Sky insisted, "It's an advantage to us if they're spread out. That means we can make up a force just big enough to clobber them one at a time. One small city-state could supply the men and equipment, and a handful of merchants could pay for it."

Jobek scratched his temple with a marlin spike, thinking. "You might have something there, Sky. What about rebound of the pirates, though?"

"Merchants hire fighting men and they still lose ships." (Jobek grimaced and Sky continued,) "So why not use that manpower to sweep the rat holes clean regularly. It costs the same."

"You have a point," Jobek admitted. "But it would be like pulling teeth to break the merchants out of their rut."

"Get me a meeting with your captain. At least we can try."

The captain was dubious, but promised to plant the seed with the merchants' agents on the other ships when the fleet reached Banshod.

Though Sky had used the term "we" in persuading Jobek about eradicating the pirates, he had no conscious intent to involve himself. He planned to find Atna.

Despite Jobek's opinion of the brevity of the trip on to Banshod and back to Siklos, the numbers did not make a happy sum. Atna told Sky she was pregnant just before the attack on Prater began in earnest, probably forty sleeps after conception. They spent forty in battle and rebuilding the trebuchet and jockeying for power. It took about ten sleeps to execute the escape, five to settle affairs after the last battle. They traveled one sleep and stayed with Harl and Sepel for eleven—a total of about eighty-seven to there. It took about fifty-six sleeps to Piscus, forty among the pirates and sixteen since then. That made about two hundred twenty sleeps since conception. The baby would be due in fifty or sixty sleeps.

According to Jobek, the three remaining tacks of the windward voyage would consume fifty-seven sleeps and there were four sleeps left until the first course change. The layover at Banshod would be three, and the straight leeward run to Siklos would take forty-eight sleeps. Sky would be a father at least fifty-two sleeps before he reached Siklos. From there, if Atna lived, who knew how long it would take to find her? At the most optimistic, she would have passed through Siklos heavily pregnant and been remembered for it.

Sky forced his thoughts elsewhere to avoid despair. He pulled the strange knife out. He had taken it from Vindol's dead hand and miraculously kept it throughout his leaping escape and rescue.

The knife had captured his attention when he'd cleaned blood from it and honed a fresh edge. The cleaning failed to expose the color of bronze, instead revealing a strange, gray metal. Some forging imperfections and old scratches were black. Honing produced a silvery shine along the edge and it took much longer than bronze to get the sharpness he wanted. The handle was ivory from the curved tusk of a large boar, carved in scenes and symbols foreign to Sky. It did not have a hilt.

He made a simple canvas sheath to keep the knife securely inside his clothing. The first time he pulled the knife out to admire it he gaped and threw it from him. Cautiously, he retrieved it from the deck and studied it. The new edge, polished to silver a sleep ago, had bled. He touched it gingerly and a brown-red streak came off. He looked for a cut on his finger. His skin was whole. A spirit knife, he thought. This must have been the property of a shaman on the merchant ship, from whom Vindol had wrested it. A pirate would not have handed this to Vindol on the ship's rail. Or maybe he had. Perhaps Vindol had died facing a sword with only this knife.

Superstition made him reluctant to return it to the sheath near his body so he polished the edge again and secreted it in the ship's hold.

Each time he checked it, the edge had bled, so he polished it and put it back. After several polishings, with no harm to him, he returned the knife to its sheath. It continued to scab over with fresh spirit blood each sleep, but Sky remained well. Eventually he became complacent enough to use it without thinking to cut a slab of cheese. He noticed the spirit blood smeared on the cheese but screwed up his courage and ate it. He thought he detected, barely, its flavor on the cheese, like a healing cut lip. The next time he drew it, the knife had not bled.

Now that's curious, he thought. I wonder if the cheese appeased the spirit.

He kept the knife from bleeding by regularly cutting cheese until finding that pork fat worked better, and finally that merely rubbing lard into his sheath prevented the bleeding. The spirit knife held an edge well, so he tested it against a bronze nail and found it could slice shavings from the bronze. He studied the edge. It was dulled but not blunted or rolled.

"This is powerful stuff", he muttered. "What could an army do with swords like this?"

Sky asked Jobek if he had seen anything like it when he showed him the knife. Jobek blanched and urged, "Throw it overboard!"

"Why?"

"They're made by black sorcerers far sunward and inland. A demon is trapped in the knife. Only a magician can control it. I wager you didn't take it off a living man."

"No," Sky chuckled, "but it wasn't a demon that killed him. His neck was half severed by a merchant sailor."

"Demons work in mysterious ways. What guided the hand holding the sword?"

"I won't argue superstition. But I've worn the knife for several sleeps. I sliced food with it."

"Demons are immortal. It can kill you now, or later. It could have a mission for you, maybe finding another magician."

"That reminds me of old questions." Sky remarked. "Immortality, or its kin, and hidden purpose. I told you my story. Why did I live when friends died? Is there a reason? Who's reason? Did the upheaval suit a god?"

"Who knows?"

"If we had more time in Banshod I'd go to Prater and look up Joit. See if he could help. Or maybe I should find your black sorcerers, offer to trade for these knives and ask them."

"Don't joke , Sky. They're cannibals."

Sky laughed. "Everybody thinks far-off men are cannibals. I've met snow barbarians at the antisun end of the world and desert nomads from the sunward end. None of them roasted me up for supper."

Jobek smiled at the scarred, lopsided face. "That doesn't mean a thing. Do you know how unappetizing you look?"

The ship's mate bellowed, "All the watch on deck! Prepare to come about!"

* * *

The rest of the trip to Banshod was uneventful. No pirates appeared and a slight but favorable wind-shift boosted progress on the last leg so they arrived two sleeps earlier than expected. This cheered Sky despite the uselessness of such a small gain.

A delayed shipment from inland meant the fleet would have to linger four sleeps at Banshod instead of the planned three, so Sky decided he would make the trip up river to Prater to find Joit. He could make the hike along the tow path in one, long wake period. That would allow a full period to find Joit and then return to *Gore* with a full period to settle back aboard. The stevedores would handle cargo on the merchant ships while he was absent and he would use the little money, generously given by his ship's captain, to shop for a cheap sword. With his new sailing skills and his old warrior ways he would become a fully fledged, share-owning member of the guard ship for the trip sunward.

* * *

The changes at Prater amazed him. The breastworks thrown up by the Snowmen had disappeared, replaced by ripening grain. Structures that had been haphazardly constructed near the base of the city wall over many lax generations were razed. Nothing to provide cover for attacking soldiers stood within two hundred meters of the wall. The buildings further out that had burned during the siege were rebuilt and bustling with returned residents.

A sense of rebirth energized the city inside the walls. Even buildings which had not suffered in the siege were refurbished to reverse long neglect. Any structure too damaged to repair had been removed and new, grander construction rose in its place. Even in Sky's youth, the city had not been so vital.

This reduced the pangs Sky suffered entering the gates. His part in the near downfall of Prater had been a burden.

He wasn't certain that Joit was still in the city or even alive. Due to urgency and the lack of welcome expected from Prater, he had not taken the time to discover Joit's fate after the war. Now, maybe Prater's citizens would not remember him, and Joit would be well.

Sky did not hurry through the city. New sights that he wanted to savor blossomed at every step, and fear of what he would find at the church mired his feet. He took the snaking, narrow streets toward the Boar and Whore, an obtuse path for finding the church but irresistible. There it stood, coated in new paint with a refreshed sign that made the posed figures more starkly obscene. He paused, the urge to enter almost overpowering, but that period of his life was done. He turned away, sighed and found his proper direction again.

Sky stopped once to gawk at a large edifice under construction, already three stories high, with a machine operating beside it which he had never seen before. A large, hollow wheel, containing five strong workmen, was suspended on an axle between two pyramidal frames. The axle at one side carried a drum wrapped with three turns each of two heavy ropes. The end of one rope was anchored to the framework, while its other end, after the three wraps, suspended a weight made of a small box loaded with rocks. This locked the great wheel in one direction, but allowed it to turn in the other. The tail of the other rope was handled by a man who could haul in slack, release it to slip around the drum, or dally it off on a post. The working end of that rope led from the drum through a series of pulleys to the center of a tower built higher than the building it adjoined. The rope fed to the top of the tower, over another pulley, and out to the end of a heavy boom, where it ran over the last pulley and back toward the ground. It terminated in a large hook with a smaller guide rope tied to it and controlled by a man on the ground.

Sky watched as the tail man threw slack at the drum and the hook man pulled the heavy tackle down. He walked the hook to a bundle of seven timbers and worked its point through a loop of the binding rope. At a shout from the foreman the wheel men climbed up inside the curved surface, rotating the wheel under their weight. The tail man pulled out the slack, the rope gripped the drum and the timbers began to move. As the lifting rope tightened, the boom pivoted around to hang above the bundle. The timbers left the ground and a group of leaning workmen held the bundle to keep it from colliding with nearby structure. Slowly, the timbers rose up the side of the building until they hung well above it. The foreman yelled, "Dog it," and the tail man drew a loop around the post. Then the men at the top pulled a rope which pivoted the boom around until they could handle the timbers. The foreman called to the tail man, "Ease it down," so that fellow unlooped the rope and allowed slack to slip around the drum until the bundle rested on top of the building. The process took a fraction of the time it would have for men to haul the timbers up singly. This marvelous machine not only multiplied the strength of the workmen but also removed them from risk. They did not have to haul from the edge of the structure, they did not have to work under an ascending load, and the built-in brake would not let the wheel spin out of control. Sky scratched his head. He walked on.

The church loomed up, undamaged, with the familiar walkway to the side steps and entrance to the library. Sky hesitated. He climbed the stair slowly, opened and looked through the door to the dim interior. A priest, not Joit, stood at the desk in the small vestibule, copying a document. Sky's heart sank, but he approached.

The priest looked up, frowning annoyance, as Sky entered. "What do you wish?" He asked.

"I'm looking for a friend. Joit."

"He's expecting you?"

Sky smiled. "Probably not," he said, sighing in relief at this confirmation of his friend's well-being.

The priest, a man of no humor, replied. "Well, he is here somewhere among the shelves. If you don't mind hunting...?"

"No, no. And thank you!" Sky gripped the man's ink-stained hand and the priest pulled it away, intensifying his frown.

"Yes yes," the priest said, backing up and shooing Sky away.

The dusty, rawhide covered skylights and narrow windows barely cut the gloom in the large room, but the library was not a popular place, despite the charming host in the vestibule, so when Sky saw a figure down one aisle he knew it was his friend.

"Joit," he called softly.

The little man looked up, squinting. A brilliant smile lit his face and he dropped a book to scuttle toward his big, rough friend, calling, "Sky! You're not dead!"

"Not entirely," Sky laughed.

Joit stopped as if hitting a wall. "By Huf!" he exclaimed. "What happened to your face?"

"A long story. Give me your hand." He stepped forward and grasped the priest's outstretched hand.

Joit smiled again. "Well, it is you. Changed! But still you. You are well, now?"

Sky touched his lopsided face. "Rearranged but recovered. I'm rebuilt and made strong in the guise of a sailor."

"And how did that happen?"

"Let me buy you lunch. We have lots to discuss and I need to be back on my ship in one sleep."

They retired to the nearest eatery and exchanged stories while they dined. Joit was horrified at Atna's unknown fate for he was very fond of her. (They had liked each other immediately during their first efforts together locating the missing Sky.) He in turn assured Sky that the church and he had been in no danger during the siege. The bombardment never threatened them. The fires burned elsewhere. They had a secure water well of their own and enough stored food to eat and share, though dissension flared among the clergy as to whether it was more appropriate for them to hoard the food for themselves, assuring spiritual guidance for the suffering masses, or risk their own starvation to distribute the food and ease that suffering somewhat. The sharing faction pointed out that if the parishioners died of hunger they could not benefit from spiritual aid and the priests would be obsolete. Opponents argued that the eternal salvation of souls was infinitely more important than preserving temporal life. Those wishing to feed the people suggested that any priest worth his salt could minister to the soul simultaneously with dishing out soup, and in fact would give the flock more confidence in Huf's love through practical application. That side prevailed, but barely. Joit remained disillusioned over the narrowness of the vote, though not less fulfilled in his own spirituality. "Even priests are only men," he said. "I will preserve my faith, rather, in Huf."

Conversation stopped at that. Sky beckoned the server who approached to refresh their drinks.

"But," Joit said after a sip, "it's only chance that you're here now. You didn't leave your wife in evil hands and travel all this way just to see me. What now?"

"I hiked from the port to see you. I had to find out if you were alive. And I hope that you can help me with my next steps. I'm going back to pick up Atna's trail. But I need answers before I can be at peace, whatever comes. Tell me, what purpose is there in my existence? Why was I resurrected from the ice? Why has death missed me so close, so many times? Why the destruction around me?"

Joit sadly shook his head. "I know that Huf has a purpose for you but it would take time to figure out what it is. Much study, prayer."

Sky drooped. "So it's hopeless. Too bad you can't come with me."

Joit blinked. His jaw went slack. A smile burst onto his face like a beacon. "But I can!" he shouted, gripping Sky's arm.

"What?"

"I can! And, by Huf, I will!"

"I don't understand."

"All priests have dispensation to take the pilgrimage, the Jefk. Those who return are revered and titled 'Jefko'. I'll travel with you. We'll explore your question. By the time our paths diverge, we might have an answer."

"You mean Kiffej? The holy oasis?" Sky asked. "You expect to see Umanqyt, the mountain where Huf lives?"

"All true! We have three Jefkos here. They have seen it!"

"But..." Sky looked at his friend skeptically.

"Yes," Joit agreed. "I'm old and can't keep up with you on foot. But the first leg of the trip is by sea. When we arrive at Siklos I can hire an animal to ride. A sedate ass would suit me."

Sky spoke dubiously, "I won't balk at providing for you, my friend, but we'll eat poorly on the money I'll earn shipping to Siklos."

"No, no. I'm paid a stipend by the church. Even with the little I keep after helping the less fortunate it has grown to an embarrassing amount. (My needs are small.) Besides, the church will forward me the sum I have coming during the pilgrimage. We will lack nothing!"

Sky began to believe his idle wish could be possible. He looked down at the floor in thought. He sipped wine. He glanced at Joit, then gazed out the door, and sipped more wine. Joit waited patiently with raised brows. No more objections came to Sky. He looked Joit in the eye. "So be it," he said, smiling, and tossed back the last of his wine.

* * *

"This is a war ship. We don't carry passengers," *Gore*'s mate said.

"Not even holy pilgrims?" Sky asked.

"Nope."

Sky turned a hopeless look on Joit.

Joit asked the mate, "How about a chaplain?"

The mate opened his mouth. He closed it with a thoughtful expression. "Stay here. I'll check."

Chapter 7

Joit was assigned to use the navigator's berth off-watch. Sky supposed the captain must have considered the priest's job a type of spiritual navigation and accorded Joit suitable rank. He learned later that this was a customary arrangement on ships carrying a chaplain, for the duties of the priest were flexible enough to never be at odds with those of the navigator. The small space for his personal goods did not discomfit the priest, since all he carried was one change of clothes, a small copy of The Holy Scripture, his money, a bowl, and a journal with pens and ink.

They sailed sunward after an added delay of four more sleeps and Sky saw that the fleet was significantly enlarged. Eight more merchantmen sailed with them and five more battle galleys. Jobek told him that the merchant agents had liked Sky's idea so much that they had approached the Prater merchants, who shipped regularly, and dunned them for the additional ships and funding for a trial eradication of the pirate nest which had held Sky. They had a notion, after consulting the navigators, which island group hid it. Sky's original story of his captivity and the time the pirate ship *Hell* had spent sailing between ambush sites, aided the navigators in narrowing down the location. They would turn aside long enough to send five of the guard ships for the assault.

Sky kicked himself silently and later complained to Joit about his own foolishness. He'd had no suspicion that his plan would be acted on so immediately, or ever.

"Now I'll be caught in one more battle. One more delay. A complete stop if I die. The 'pitcher too many times to the well' comes to mind. Makes me nervous. Especially now that I *have* to live to find Atna."

Joit said, "Not that I suggest you rely on your good luck, or patron god, to sustain you, but there's no reason it should abandon you now."

Sky smiled grimly. "My 'good' luck has taken me so near death that it would have been easier to die. I hope it does abandon me."

"Don't tempt fate, Sky."

They met whenever they were both off watch and eventually Jobek joined their discussions. Jobek absorbed Joit's teachings like a sponge, but Sky was a skeptic. This became apparent at one of the early dialogues when Joit read from the Scripture to support his statement that Huf was interested in the fate of people, and maybe Sky particularly, by the quote, "Huf sees the crawling worm and the flying bird and the swimming fish; surely he sees the heart of humankind."

Sky asked, "Who says so?"

"Why, Huf says so," Joit said, puzzled. "These are Huf's words."

"You mean Huf sat down and wrote this book?"

"No! Of course not. Men put the words to the page, but they are Huf's words, inspired in the minds of the original scribes."

"And," Sky asked, "how do we know that's true? Who says that Huf put the words there and not a demon? Or a deceitful or mad scribe?"

Joit said calmly, "The wisdom and the goodness are self-evident."

"And Huf is good and wise?" Sky asked.

"Yes, that is the character of Huf."

"And men can't be good or wise?"

"Not to that magnitude."

Sky asked, "Enough to recognize that Huf's book is good but not enough to write it? It sounds like you give men both too much and too little credit as needed for your argument."

"Men can be both sublime and base," Joit said. "Consider the Pratorian priests arguing whether or not to share their food."

"But can't Huf do evil? Stories from the Scripture divulge horrible destruction by Huf in a fit of pique."

Joit raised his brows a little. "Huf does not suffer from pique. And the intent of an act by Huf cannot be judged by mortal men. We do not know, nor can we understand, the whole of his plan."

"You're telling me that destroying a city and all its people is not an evil act, but can be good depending on the intent of the destroyer?"

"I'm saying that there will be motives and intentions we can't know which might require what appears to us to be evil, but which are necessary for the long term good. And remember that Huf works at the infinite scale."

Sky said, "You just told me that Huf concerns himself with even low creatures. How does early death enhance the well-being of any creature already confined to a short life?"

"You have your perspective reversed. We live at the behest of, and for the purposes of, Huf—not the other way around. There is no life without him. Our life is his to do with as he sees fit. If he grants life to a creature for a few instants, that is more than would be possible without Huf to call the creature into existence at all. Life is a gift. What could show greater concern than that?"

"I think that 'gift' is not the right word considering the suffering life entails and the demands Huf makes. He wants obedience to rules that contradict the nature he gave us."

"But the reward for obedience is eternal life! That treasure should require struggle."

"Even for worms?"

Joit sputtered, "Don't be flippant, Sky. Worms have no souls."

"Too bad. Their rules are a lot simpler."

"I think it's time to give up our talk for now to let you adjust your attitude."

Duty called in the form of a tearing squall line that heeled them till the lee rail buried itself, despite carrying only a small storm sail. The captain had seen the storm's approach and prepared the ship, so the rowing ports were plugged but leaked. The hatches leaked. The mast collar leaked. Crew hurried below and bucketed water from the bilge, hand to hand and out a reopened hatch. Waves built quickly to great height after the squall line and whenever one swept the deck a man slammed the hatch shut, grabbed a line dangling from it, threw a hitch around a bollard and hung on. He flung it open as the sea sloshed away and threw the next bucket.

This time Sky suffered badly from seasickness, on his knees clinging to the rigging and heaving up his stomach and then some. He wasn't getting the mess over the side and didn't care, but the next breaking wave scrubbed the deck. Below, Joit braced himself between a rib and the bulkhead, likewise bent and spewing his guts into a bucket. The navigator lay wedged in his bunk, back turned to Joit, his distasteful expression toward the booming hull.

Directly behind the squall line the wind blasted in almost on their bow, and the captain turned downwind to run with the waves. It increased abruptly, piling the waves so high that the ship, even running without sail, risked pitch-poling. The crew tossed a sea anchor from the bow, *Gore* drove through two more giant waves and they belayed the line to come about into the seas. The captain timed the maneuver for the trough between smaller waves but the ship still heeled alarmingly so that Sky stared nearly straight down into foaming water and thanked Huf that his suffering would end. But the ship swung around and righted itself before the next wave smashed over the bow.

The wind gradually shifted to starboard until, when it finally diminished, the bow pointed nearly sunright, though the captain had no way of knowing this.

At the fourth sleep, the storm trailed away. The newly scrubbed sunlight on the wet woodwork lured wisps of mist up to be disbursed on the dregs of the breeze.

A scan of the clearing horizon showed *Gore* to be alone on the sea. They turned the bow sunright, toward the invisible shore, and steered for a previously selected rendezvous. During the eighth watch following the course change, they sailed into a debris field. The captain ordered a searching pattern to zig-zag the area, hunting survivors. Once, they doused sail and rowed to a man lying with his upper body lashed to a pair of crossed planks, but as they approached he did not respond to their hails. When they came near they could see that his lower body, trailing in the water from hips down, was gone. Joit said a prayer over the stranger.

Sky shuddered at sight of the halved man, imagining the toothy sea monster capable of severing him, and of the poor fellow's solitary eternity, waiting for those jaws before they struck.

"More likely a thousand small, toothy fishes than one big one," Jobek said of Sky's monster.

Sky's eyes widened envisioning this piecemeal death and he shuddered again. "There is Huf's mercy for you," he muttered. "Give me the sword in the gut."

They left the dead man and searched the rest of the field without finding another soul, nor any sign of which ship it had been.

The debaters picked up their meandering discourse after the ship's damage had all been fixed, Sky beginning by demanding rational proof of Huf's words and Joit maintaining that rational thought is only as good as the knowledge on which it's based. The all-knowing Huf obviously must be more rational than the most educated man.

The watch called out, "Sails! Sails to antisun!"

The crew mustered on the rail to gaze at the distant, white wings. At a command the helm swung the ship over to an intercept course. The fleet flag was run up *Gore*'s short mast and when the strange ships came to visible range it was seen that the newcomers flew the same emblem. Pirate ships were not expected this far from land, but caution was always warranted so the crew armed themselves despite the flag. *Gore* matched course and speed with the nearest ship, a merchantman (as were the other two), and the mate hailed it. It was the *Gold Spice*, of Prater, and it had no news of any other sunken ships. The navigators compared notes. They agreed that they were about eight sleeps from the rendezvous point. The ships, now a fleet of four to the relief of the merchant sailors, proceeded landward.

Six of the original fleet lay at anchor when *Gore* and the ships it escorted arrived at the rendezvous. Over the next five sleeps nine more sailed into the small, hidden bay. After that none appeared for a wait of twelve sleeps and the captains reluctantly assumed the last two were lost. Unfortunately those two were both galleys, and they decided the remaining force would not be able to assail the pirates while protecting the merchantmen. They would assemble a bigger fleet at Siklos and deal with the pirates on the next sweep.

Sky gave a private sigh of relief at the news.

Most storm damage had been repaired by the ships' crews during their individual passages after the storm, so there was no reason to linger when the decision was made. The galleys sailed slowly from the bay in the confined breeze, with the merchantmen following, and the fleet set course sunward of sunleft to make distance from land and pirate hunting grounds.

Sky maintained the role of skeptic during the religious discussions, but they still had their impact. Joit's arguments remained unassailable, not surprising when he could call on an infinitely powerful god on one hand and human ignorance on the other to account for any contradiction. Joit himself was the biggest factor in the persuasion. His positive, loving, and hopeful interpretation of the Holy Scripture made a shining example, and an appealing philosophy. Sky found his own sour outlook taking a beating in Joit's gentle hands.

Chapter 8

The officers and crew of *Gore*, especially Jobek, were disappointed at Sky's leaving them in Siklos, for he was a good hand and easy company, an important trait in close quarters. But they knew his quest and wished him well.

He and Joit strode up the wharf purposefully to the shoreline road, where their purpose ran out of direction. They looked both ways on the road and uphill along the nearest street, seeking any reason to prefer one. Joit, recalling his need for a ride, stopped a man and asked about asses for sale. This was a beginning.

In fact, the mention of the animal Joit needed jogged Sky's thought. "A stable!" he exclaimed. "Berno's horses would need care. He planned to buy more. And we can ask at metal smith shops and farriers. Horses need shoes after a long trip."

"Thanks, Joit. I wondered where to start. Berno's pack train will be easier. If we find him, we could find Atna. If not, he'll tell us what happened or die."

Joit frowned.

Sky saw the expression and said, "You don't approve. But for what he's done..."

"Which," Joit interrupted, "is no more than you did to him first."

"Apparently. But if he hurt Atna, or won't help find her, do I just rely on his better nature?"

"Don't commit before we know the situation," Joit cautioned.

"We'll see."

Siklos provided mainland access for goods from Mikenny (Mikenny's largest harbor could anchor only a half dozen ships at once) as well as acting as a port and resupply point for ships sailing both sunward and antisun. It was a large, commercially dynamic city. Twelve generations ago it had been under the governance of the more warlike Mikenny but when Prater mustered the large, combined naval and ground force and conquered them, Siklos and Mikenny had become separate, semi-autonomous sister-states bound by treaty to build no military and to pay tribute. Their central location in the sea trade gave them such profits that the tribute seemed small by comparison—not worth a rebellion. They had grown out of the ways of war except for the elite mercenaries on Mikenny who upheld the old traditions and fought for the highest bidder.

Siklos was rife with stables and metal smiths. The harbor district itself, catering to freight haulers, had eighteen large stables and six smiths. Joit suggested that Berno would not penetrate this far seeking either, so the best place to search lay on the antisun side of the city. Also, these stables at the harbor dealt in giant horses to pull heavy freight wagons and did not stock donkeys for Joit.

They stopped when the city gave way to rolling, plowed fields with the highway winding away between them. Turning around they surveyed Siklos. A traveler's inn stood nearby, but looked too prosperous and too expensive. They glanced at each other and wordlessly started back into the city. A kilometer along, following a weathered sign, they turned uphill on an uncobbled street and went another half kilometer.

The Oaks Inn needed repairs but was clean. It was operated by a buxom woman, her stoop-shouldered, harried husband and five tattered, stair-step children of indeterminate gender except for the oldest, a girl clumsily blossoming through puberty. An invalid grandmother screeched demands from an upstairs room. The two massive, eponymous trees completely shaded a large courtyard at the front of the inn. Tables and benches sat sheltered there to manage overflow crowds, a rare event, or for fresh-air dining in good weather. The rates were reasonable and rooms available, so Sky and Joit took one at the back just big enough for them both to sleep. It was extravagantly spacious after their ship's berths. Since they didn't know how long their search could take, they arranged to pay on a sleep-by-sleep basis, with first claim on the room in the chance that the inn filled.

They slept, oddly disconcerted by beds that did not roll with the sea, and on rising sat to breakfast rested, but anxious to begin canvassing the stables and smithies.

"We should split up," Sky said through a mouthful of food. "I'll take the sunleft side of the highway and you take sunright. Probably less rough on your side. More farm and less sea scum."

"I agree. You are more adept with the *sea*my side."

Sky barked a laugh, almost choking.

Joit smiled. "We'll find Berno's trail, and follow him."

"When we do, *you* will continue your pilgrimage and *I* will follow him."

Joit shook his head. "I'm in no hurry. Umanqyt will not go missing. I will help find Atna."

Sky frowned. "But if we fail..."

"How do we know we've failed if our only evidence is that we haven't found her? She is well. We just have to locate her."

Sky shook his head, but smiled. "You optimist. No wonder you and Atna hit it off."

"I will buy an ass to cover more ground. It will cost a little more to stay here with an animal in the stable, but we'll save money by moving along sooner."

"Thanks for your help, Joit. And spending your own money on this."

"You would do the same for me."

Sky looked skeptical so Joit continued, laughing, "And if you doubt that, you don't know yourself."

Sky again smilingly shook his head. "Let's go," he said.

The search was ponderous. They wandered the streets asking directions. If the respondent did not use the stable, or live near it, the directions would be wrong. Even if the instructions were correct, they were hard to follow through unfamiliar streets. Half of the directions returned Sky and Joit to stables they had already found.

In the first wake period the only success was Joit's purchase of a quiet little jenny to ride. She carried him patiently back to the inn after that period's search, where Joit uncharacteristically displayed pride in her ownership to a dejected Sky.

"Just be patient, Sky," Joit said cheerily. "We *will* succeed. This was our first attempt."

Late in the second wake period, the third time Sky approached a familiar stable he stopped in frustration and slammed his fist into the slab wall. The boom of his strike startled the horses inside and they stirred, some rearing or kicking.

The owner took an instant to scowl around the corner at Sky before hurrying in to calm the horses. When he saw the apprentices already gentling them he dashed back outside to catch Sky.

"Hey!" he shouted. "Hold up there."

Sky stopped and turned.

The man caught up to him, recognized him. "I remember you. What's your problem?"

"Sorry. But I keep going in circles. What's happening to my wife while I'm stuck sorting out the stables in this damned city?"

"Well, don't spook my horses! They don't... Wait. I thought you said you were looking for a trader."

"I am. My wife was with him and he'll tell me where she is."

The stableman paused, absently scratching his large butt. "What does she look like?"

"You've seen her?"

"I don't know, but there was a woman. Odd, too.."

"Odd how?" Sky asked, grabbing the man by the shoulders.

"Well," the man said, pushing at Sky's arms and trying to back away, "first, she was alone, riding one horse and leading another packed with gear. But she wasn't a trader. Hugely pregnant."

"That's her!" Sky shouted, gripping the man even tighter. "Where is she?!"

"Well, now," the stableman began uneasily, squirming to extract himself. "Let go."

Sky shook him. "Where is she?"

"Look, you got to let me go. I'll tell you what I know. But you got to let me go, first."

Sky's face clouded and he slammed the man against the wall of his stable. The horses kicked again in their stalls and the apprentices called for their master.

Sky moved his right hand to the man's throat. "Tell me now!"

"Yes," he wheezed. "Yes! Please!"

Sky let him breathe.

"She came here. To sell her horses and goods. I said, sure, leave them and come back in a sleep. Well, it was odd, like I said. You can't blame me. It was odd. There's law. What was I supposed to do?"

"What *did* you do?"

Sweat poured from the man. "I---I---I."

Sky pulled, pushed and made the wall thunder again. Horses whinnied in fear.

The man groaned. "I checked the tattoos in the horses' lips. One was on a list of stolen stock. When the woman came back the civils arrested her. She didn't have paper for the animals."

"Is she still in jail?"

"I—I don't know."

Sky's eyes narrowed and his grip closed the man's windpipe. The pinned man flopped and clawed at Sky's wrist. A donkey inside the stable brayed. Sky's face went slack, he looked quickly over his shoulder, backed up and released the stableman to slump against the wall, gasping.

"Where was she taken?"

"Follow the main highway sunward," the stableman rasped. "Turn left at the memorial for lost sailors. Can't miss it."

Sky shoved through the handful of people gathered to see the ruckus, found clear ground and ran.

He did miss it once in his anxiety, but knew as soon as he saw no buildings in front of him large enough to house a jail. He turned back and stopped at the big block building with the now apparent symbol of the crossed clubs and dangling shackles.

Inside, he asked the bored clerk, "Do you have a pregnant woman here?"

"No," he sighed.

"Was a pregnant woman brought in here a while back?"

The clerk picked at his fingernail. "Yes."

"Where was she taken?"

"Nowhere."

A chill shook Sky. "She died?"

"No."

Sky's chill turned to heat. He leaned forward, reaching toward the clerk, but a sane impulse reminded him where he was. Assaulting a civil servant in the civilian guard office would earn him a stint of free housing in this very building.

"What happened to her?" he forced between clenched teeth.

The clerk saw the restrained violence in this large, heavily scarred, dangerous looking man. This clerk was a dull-witted, petty bureaucrat who held enormous power in the lives of unfortunates, and who enjoyed this power as anodyne to the browbeating he got at home from his domineering wife. The clerk had choices. He could rely on the proximity of several club wielding civil officers to restrain the giant. Or he could skip his pleasure this once. To his credit the clerk was struck by the thought that he might not live long enough to savor the torment regardless of what the officers did to the big man afterward.

The clerk, more attentive, said, "She gave birth."

Sky's fingers twitched and the clerk hurriedly continued, "Here in the jail! She's still here in a cell with the child." Then he thought it wise to volunteer, "She's been found guilty of thievery, horse thievery, and murder and will be executed when we find a woman who wants the baby."

This was almost the wrong thing to say. Sky blanched. "Executed!" Then he took a deep breath and demanded, "I will see her."

The clerk shouted at the nearest officer, "This man must be taken to see the woman with the baby on sub-level two!"

The officer looked surprised, but gestured that Sky follow, and walked through the doorway to The Deeps.

Despite occasional light-wells, it took time for Sky's eyes to adjust to level one, and he would have been nearly blind at level two except for a lamp that the officer lit before they climbed down the narrow stone steps.

After a confusing crouch through the turnings of several identical passages, the officer stopped before one particular, thick, oak door and said, "She's here." He must have been a sympathetic man, for he handed the lamp to Sky and retreated down the dim corridor.

Sky crouched, held the lamp to the small hole in the door and looked through beside it, but the light glared more directly into his own eyes than into the chamber. He shielded his eyes with his left hand and saw a bundle in the straw. He had smelled worse than this hole, but it hurt him to think of Atna in that.

"Atna?" he whispered. Why did he whisper? "Atna." he said.

The bundle didn't stir but a resigned voice floated out, "So you found a nursing woman. When will I die?"

"What? No! It's Sky, I'm Sky!"

The bundle moved. The cover flipped back. "Sky's dead. Haven't I already suffered? Why are you doing this?"

"No. Atna. It's really Sky. I found you. Well, me and Joit. And we'll get you out."

"Joit?" she said. "Haven't heard his name in a while. Poor Joit is dead, too, buried under his crumbled church. You can't hurt me. Take my son. Give him a good home. Let me die in peace."

"A son!" Sky said. "I have a son!"

He saw the glint of eyes looking up at the door. "Sky?" she quavered. "Sky," she sighed. "Dalen," she cooed. "Your father is here, back from the dead again."

She rose and came to the door. "Sky, let me see you, let me touch you. Here, touch your son."

The crushed left side of his face stayed hidden by shadow because Sky held the lamp in his right hand. He had not planned it, but it was for the best. He reached his left hand through the hole and she pressed it to her cheek. She stroked it a couple of times and he felt a tear run across his wrist. Then she pulled her cheek away and clasped his big fist around the tiny hand of his son.

"Dalen." Sky said. "That's a good name."

"Atna, I'll get you out. Be patient. I'll go get you something to eat and drink. And anything else. What do you want?"

"A cloth and a basin and water, to wash your son. And a lamp so he can see his mother." She stifled a sob. "But you can't get me out. I'll be hanged as soon as they find a freshened woman who wants Dalen."

"For murder," Sky said. "Preposterous."

"No, I did it."

"Don't talk crazy! They made you believe a lie..."

The jailer walked to Sky and interrupted, "We have to go."

"Wait," Sky said. "Wait. It's a mistake. I have to find out what's going on and fix it."

"Sorry," the officer said. "We can answer your questions upstairs." He held his hand out for the lamp.

* * *

Joit, eyes widening, asked, "They say she killed Berno?"

"And stole two of his horses."

"That's just ridiculous!"

"So I said. I went back with the washbasin and lamp. But they wouldn't let me see her again so soon. They promised to deliver the goods, and I left. What am I going to do?"

"You mean, what are *we* going to do."

"Sorry, Joit. I keep forgetting. You're like old Blute. He would have walked into flames for me. What *will* we do?"

"I adhere to secular law if it doesn't contradict Huf's law. And though I don't recall verse and chapter about this, it must contradict the higher law. Atna, for Huf's sake! It's unbelievable. She's the sweetest, most innocent child..."

"She was a whore," Sky reminded him.

"Exactly! And she came away from that with her innocence, if not her hymen, intact. That's why she's exceptional. Even if she was caught with the man's blood dripping from her hands, I won't believe she deserves death. We must break her out!"

Sky gaped. When he could speak he said, "I'm shocked that you suggest it. But when? And how?"

"Consider the obvious first. Did you see any way take her out with surprise or stealth?"

"Surprise, no." Sky said. "Too many officers. We could watch and count them. Hit them at their lowest number, I suppose. Stealth, maybe. The light wells are big enough to lower a bull, but I wager they have bars. I didn't check. Too obvious, anyway."

"But, we *should* check. People are known to miss the obvious. Anything else?"

"Not for direct action. There's always bribery, but there are lots of men and bribing enough of them would break us."

"But it's an option. Bribing one or two key people might be enough."

Ellet, the innkeeper's pubescent daughter, walked by to halfheartedly clean up after a departed client. Sky and Joit paused to sip their wine until she was beyond hearing.

Sky continued, "Strategic threats might work. The clerk was pliable."

"Last resort. Leave violence alone."

"Joit," Sky grumbled, "she's my wife, with my son. You're a good man. I want to follow your example, but if I have to kill a few people to get her out, I will. If I lose your friendship I'll grieve about that later."

"You would lose your soul, too. If it's not already forfeit. That reminds me. Has Atna accepted salvation with Huf?"

Sky guffawed. "She might be innocent according to you, but she doesn't ignore the way life treated her. No, you're the only thing about the church that she tolerates."

"Oh," Joit said, both pleased and disappointed. "Then we must bring her out at any cost, short of killing. Her soul must be saved. Threat of execution has always been suspect as a condition for accepting salvation. Elucidation is the true basis. Which takes time." He looked pointedly at Sky.

"Fine. How else can we get her?"

They sat in thought, sipping wine.

Joit smiled. "I'm still a scribe."

"And..."

"And you are a skilled man-at-arms. The justice system is light at the top, with judges, and heavy at the bottom with scribes and men-at-arms, doing the real work. Two additions at the bottom would be unnoticeable. How would you like a job with the civil guard?"

Sky smiled, too. "I been looking for steady work since I jumped ship. What's your plan?"

* * *

Sky located another stable and bargained for two strong riding horses. Then he asked the location of the local bazaar, where he bought bags, basic foods, and, with the advice of amused women, supplies for infant care. Near the wharves he found a sail maker who hemmed and sewed cringles into a sheet of canvas for a tent. The sail maker also sold him a hundred meters of fifteen millimeter rope. He found an armorer and bought a solid long-bow with a good supply of arrows, and three knives.

During the two sleeps that it took Sky to prepare their getaway, Joit located the central justice building and applied for and was given a position as scribe. He used the employee orientation to ask questions that, in another context, would have been suspect. Joit found out who hired civil guard officers, who could sign official departmental orders, the form those orders took, and the hierarchy of justice and enforcement personnel. He made notes of these details rather than trusting his aging memory.

Sky visited Atna for the briefly allowed time each wake period, always bringing her good food and drink, fresh supplies for Dalen and clean clothes for her. Despite their promise, the officers had refused to allow Atna the lamp he'd brought, so he could see no more than her face. He reached through the small hole and she held his arm between her and Dalen while they talked. It was a stressful position for Sky, standing half crouched, but the comfort he took in touching his wife and son overcame the pain. It was only later, leaving on stiff legs with an aching back, that he became aware of it. He told her an abridged version of his life since their separation, leaving out the worst of his suffering. In the dark she never saw the ruined left side of his face and he didn't mention it. The jailer accompanying him was different each time and he trusted none, so he never asked to hear her story, and she didn't volunteer it.

At the third wake-period Joit secretly made impressions, in small clay pieces, of the wax seals of every ranking member of the department whose communiques crossed his desk. The fourth period he continued this collection until he had a good representation of the seals of the mighty in justice.

Sky spent every spare moment watching the prison in case Atna's sentence came due. He expected that few guards would escort a helpless woman burdened by a baby, allowing him a chance to take her from them by force. The clubs of two or three civil guard would be ineffectual against his sword.

During Joit's next off-shift he dried the seal copies, carved away the excess clay and coated them with shellac, making a set of small, easily hidden buttons of illegality. They would not make a very clean impression and would not serve for more than one or two sealings, but routine bred complacence and complacence led to indifference; nobody would question their validity.

Joit's first forged order hired Sky into the civil guard and issued him an official club, along with the indigo armband sporting the bronze badge crudely depicting the viceroy as the god of justice. His second ordered the transfer of Atna to a small jail on the sunward side of Siklos, supposedly to ease inspection of the baby by a noblewoman interested in adopting it. The officer named as escort chanced to be the newly hired Sky.

The prison operated on three shifts, like the watch aboard the galley ship, *Gore*. Sky appeared with club, badge and transfer order during the shift before that in which he regularly visited Atna. As intended, he recognized none of the officers and clerks, nor they him. He had warned Atna during his last visit to pretend she did not know him if he appeared in some official capacity, but it had to be communicated cryptically for fear of the nearby listening officer, so she might have misunderstood. He carefully timed Atna's appearance from The Deeps and, just before her arrival, asked the clerk to explain the transfer to her, and excused himself to the toilet.

Sky returned, scanning the room. A full figured woman stood at the clerk's desk with her back toward him. She slouched in a posture of defeat, balancing a bundle on her wide, right hip.

Fear gripped Sky. By Huf, he thought, they brought up the wrong woman. She turned on hearing his step and their eyes locked in mutual amazement. Atna looked at the mangled face of the big, approaching man and thought, he resembles Sky. Then her jaw dropped. Sky looked at her birth-broadened body, the shockingly large breasts, and still doubted her identity for an instant, even though it was Atna's face.

Sky collected himself and brought his club up to rap lightly upon his armband. She saw the gesture and understood. Her face took some effort to erase the astonishment so she turned away from him and settled back into the dejected posture, bowing her head forward to let long, matted hair swing forward to hide her battling expressions.

The clerk, busy preparing the receipt, missed the confusion between the two people at his desk. He finished writing, melted sealing wax onto the bottom of the page and said to Sky, "Here, press your badge."

Sky stripped the band from his arm and pushed the badge into the molten wax. He hadn't paid attention before, but now saw that the badge bore, along with the viceroy, a numeral, reversed, which printed itself legibly mirrored into the wax.

The clerk blew a couple of times on the sealing wax, tossed the document into the proper pile, handed Sky back the order of transfer and said, "She's all yours."

Sky stifled his smile at the ironic statement, nodded his head and took Atna by the arm. She shuffled along beside him out the door, through the reception room, along the entry hall and left the building's oppressive weight looming behind her.

They turned sunward and had just reached the entry of a narrow side street where Joit, his ass, and two horses waited, when an approaching man said, "Hey."

Sky glared with frustration at the clerk whom he had hoped to avoid by missing the man's shift. The fool had come to work early, escaping his wife's latest tirade, and stood puzzling over his recognition of The Dangerous Man—now wearing the badge of a civil—who regularly visited the woman and baby. He glanced at Atna, his eyes bugged, and Sky's club struck his head.

"Oh, Sky," Joit sighed.

The clerk dropped. Sky looked up to see three citizens watching.

"At last!" Sky shouted. "We got the bastard. Been after this notorious criminal for ages." He rolled the clerk onto his face, gathered his wrists and quickly bound them with cord. He hoisted the man onto his shoulder, whispered to Atna, "You and Joit go. Leave my horse."

To the witnesses he said, "Stay here till I get back. I need to ask you about your connection with this criminal."

Sky carried the man to the main entry of the justice building and the witnesses disappeared the instant he stepped through the door.

In the entry hall he paused, pulled his knife and cut the wrist bonds. He strode into the reception room shouting, "One of our clerks has been attacked!" Sky pushed the unconscious man onto the nearest officer. "Quick! Lay him down somewhere and send for a doctor. I have to catch his assailant." And he was gone, ignoring the shouts behind him.

* * *

Joit, on his donkey, and Atna, carrying Dalen in the crook of her left arm, could not ride as fast as Sky so he caught them in less than two kilometers.

He told them, "They won't be confused long. We need to backtrack. Come on." He reined his horse right, leading them uphill.

They crossed the main highway, continuing uphill, and only turned antisun when foothills appeared at the city's edge. Roads here were discontinuous and more wandering than even the confusing city streets. When they found a road worn enough to indicate frequent traffic, winding up a draw into the foothills, they took it.

Jubilation at their escape vied with dread of pursuit. They pushed Joit's mount to its limits and even this moderate speed barred conversation, so they said little. The small ass finally faltered. Joit called, "We have to stop. Poor little Ponder is tired."

They reined up. "Ponder?" Sky asked, smiling to Atna. "Ponder what?"

"My delightful little jenny. Ponder. And she's run enough. We must stop."

"Dalen's hungry, too." Atna added, and the men heard him fussing now that they had stopped.

Sky squinted ahead. "There," he said. "That copse is good. I think we can camp there if we just take a short sleep. But no fires yet."

Joit and Atna nodded and they rode slowly on to the patch of brush and trees while Dalen complained. It had been heavily used by others. They could tell by the sight and smell of previous traveler's feces scattered everywhere. It would have made a good site for an inn. They pressed deep into the growth until tracks and trails and shit ended, and then went further. The land began to rise up on either side so that they found themselves riding up the bottom of a shallow, narrow valley. After a kilometer into it, Sky turned them up the sunright side, angling up and back the way they had come. They found a small flat that allowed a view down into the bottom they had just traversed. They stopped and Atna nursed Dalen.

Sky walked to the edge. Looking down he said, "We can see anybody tracking us."

They made camp. Sky went alone on foot through the trees toward the main road.

He came back and told the others, "The animals can manage the straight route down off the end of this little ridge to the road. If we have to slip away."

They settled in as best they could, but every tiny sound in the silent woods made them jump and study their trail. Sustaining the fear finally became too tiresome and they began to relax. Sky looked meaningfully at Joit and tightened his arm around Atna's shoulders. Joit turned expectantly toward her.

Sky murmured to Atna, "I couldn't let you admit to something you didn't do, with the jailer listening. But now we," he glanced back to Joit, "have to hear your story. What happened after Berno hauled me off?"

* * *

Atna began chafing. Mostly it was because of Moteen's obsequious demands for more tales of sunward lands, and her tiresome kids who clung to Atna while exuding a diseased scent. But the longer Sky stayed away the more she grew annoyed at his reversion to old ways. Finally she had to beg tiredness and asked where she could sleep. Moteen jumped as though pin-pricked, pulled Atna up and led her two steps across the hovel. She presented the only recognizable bed to Atna, who assumed that the family would either join her later or sleep in the dirt while they had guests. Neither prospect appealed.

Atna studied the bug infested nest. She forced a tired smile and said, "I been camping so long, I wouldn't be comfortable. You have space outside?"

Monteen contorted her face in sad happiness at having a paying guest who would not put them out of their bed. They found a flat spot beside the hut and Atna rolled out sleeping gear. The subdued neighborhood noises quickly faded from her sense and she slept.

Berno stood over her saying, "Atna. Where's Sky?"

She threw back her face shade and squinted through her fingers. Her other hand felt the empty space beside her. "He's not with you?"

"Haven't seen him since I left the bar. We had two beers. I was done but he got another one so I left him talking to a fisherman."

Atna sat up in panic. "He never showed. I got to find him."

"Wait, wait." Berno said. "Let's be sensible. We'll eat, then go looking."

She looked up at Berno, rubbed her eyes and said, "Yes, you're right." And sighed, "That stupid bastard."

They asked all over the village and finally found somebody willing to say they'd seen him hauled into a small boat by notorious robbers. The assumption was that they'd assaulted him, taken his purse and drowned him.

Atna tried to control herself but couldn't stop quietly crying.

"Atna," Berno said gently, "We have to let it be, and go on. For the sake of your child."

She shook her head. Then she nodded.

The grief dulled her senses so that she barely noticed the kilometers passing. Many wake periods passed like this, Berno trying with little success to engage her. She went through the motions of living and her belly kept growing, and her breasts.

Berno came to her as they made camp, again speaking gently. "Atna. If we only have to set one tent we'll get to Siklos quicker. Your birth will be easier if we have a midwife."

She shrugged. That sleep they lay in the same tent.

In fifteen sleeps Berno laid his sleeping roll next to Atna, got comfortable and crept his hand over to close on hers.

She pulled away from him as though stung and leaped up. "What are you doing?"

Berno also stood, disarrayed, and spread his hands in entreaty. "Atna, you know by now how I feel about you."

She saw two things. One, Berno was aroused, and two, he wore the old money pouch which Sky had carried so long that the unique beading was half worn away.

She spat, "Get away from me!"

Berno put his hands on her shoulders. "Please," he said, embracing her. "I need you."

Atna scrabbled at her waist until she found the knife that Sky had insisted she carry. She wiggled for space and drove it with all her anger into his belly. Before he could react she rammed it two more times, once just under the sternum and once deep into his inner thigh. Shocked, Berno shoved her away.

"What have you done?" he shrieked. He reached toward her but she slashed his hand and he pulled it back. "I'm bleeding," he said. He swayed, looking at her with dulling, disappointed eyes.

She jumped aside as he fell like a tree.

Atna backed as far as she could in the tent and watched him. He lay prostrate and blood ran from beneath him in two thick streams. She had seen enough wounds to know how much blood a man held but was shocked at the rate of flow. Whether it was chance or knowledge acquired in the war, she had struck two major arteries. Berno died in twenty heartbeats.

* * *

Her story paused. She covered her face in horror at the memory.

Sky was about to tell Atna how proud he was of her when Joit said softly, "Atna, you had no choice. Even ignoring your discovery that he'd murdered your husband, he was going to rape you."

She rubbed her face and looked at him. "That's what I told the court. They said I should have let him. And they didn't believe me about Sky's money pouch. They figured I stole that from Berno along with the horses and other stuff. Sorry, Sky, they kept it."

Sky squeezed her and said, "We know how you got caught. The stableman told me. But what happened before?"

"Not much. Went outside the tent and cried for a while. Finally got mad again, enough to go back in and get my bedroll and your money pouch. Washed the blood off me and everything. Then I loaded up what I figured I needed, turned the other horses loose.

"I didn't know how close I was to Siklos. Three sleeps. The funny thing about the horses I had, and getting caught, was that the stolen one, wasn't. Berno really owned it. That was a mistake in the records." She paused. "If that hadn't happened I'd probably never been grabbed. Anyway, they put me in jail, sent word out and somebody found Berno where I left him. A bit gnawed on, according to court witnesses."

They sat quietly for a while. Sky squeezed her shoulder again and said gruffly, "I love you."

She buried her face against him and cried.

Joit said, "I will take the first watch."

"Get me before you have trouble staying awake," Sky said, stroking his wife's head.

Joit walked to the edge of the flat where he found a comfortable, sheltered spot, sat and gazed into the valley.

Sky watched him disappear into shrubs. He comforted Atna until she had cried out her grief, and her relief. Then they climbed under their covers and made wild, animal love. They rested, tangled in each others' limbs, then began again but as epicures this time instead of gluttons.

Sky muttered to her as they lay sated and drifting toward sleep, "Your cushy new body will take getting used to."

"Don't bother," she breathed. "It won't last. They fed me good in prison, for the baby's sake. I had nothing to do but wait for the hangman. Nursing Dalen and traveling will burn it off."

They woke later to Dalen's crying. He slept on one side of Atna and Sky on the other. Atna fed the infant, and though Sky knew he should relieve Joit, he felt too good to stir, so they lay back when Dalen went to sleep and joined him in slumber.

Sky woke to Joit gently shaking his shoulder. "Shh, quiet," Joit whispered. "Somebody's coming."

Sky whispered back, "Stay with Atna. Get the gear packed. I'll be right back."

"What are you going to do?"

"Scout," Sky breathed.

He quickly pulled on clothes, grabbed his bow and arrows, and jogged lightly to the view point. Joit had spotted them quite a distance down the vale. They were only now reaching the point just below the camp. Three men rode slowly up the track, leading two pack horses, with the first rider leaning forward studying the grass bent by the recent passage of Sky's group.

Sky strung his bow. He jumped as Joit, having crept up behind him, whispered by his shoulder, "You can't just shoot them. We don't know that they are after us."

"Damn it, Joit. If they aren't, they picked a bad place to practice their tracking skills. We can't risk it."

"Why don't you let me meet them and make sure? They don't know that I am with you."

"They followed three sets of tracks. They know."

"No," Joit said. "Three people wouldn't ride one horse, but one person can handle three animals. No way to be sure."

The trackers were nearly beyond bow-shot. "Damn." Sky said. He couldn't take out more than one of them now anyway. Better to work much closer. "We'll try your way. But I'll be ready, and if you can't convince them, I will."

They went back to the camp where Atna had nearly loaded everything onto the animals. Sky explained the situation. "Joit will pretend to be camped here alone. You will take Dalen deep into the brush that way." He pointed uphill. "Go far enough that the bush will deaden any sound Dalen makes. Wait till I come for you, or until one sleep has passed. I'll be ready behind that tree."

Atna looked with trepidation at the husband she had just recovered, then trotted away. Sky said, "Joit, remove your jenny's saddle, and I'll take mine. We'll hide them in the brush along with the extra sleeping rolls."

They finished hiding everything that seemed appropriate in their frantic haste. Joit walked to the campsite where the horses and donkey grazed quietly, and tried to make himself appear comfortable, calm and alone.

Sky had been juggling plans in his head. He headed into the trees after caching the gear, thinking of how far he would have to go to get around behind the trackers and come upon them just before they saw Joit. Would all three come into the clearing? Would one or two hang back? Would they know we camped here?

Sky froze. Of course they would know! As soon as they got to the hairpin turn where Sky's party began their backtrack.

He spun and ran back to Joit. "There's another way," he said, "to find out if they're following us. If they turn on our backtrack and come up the ridge, then they're after us. Get on Atna's horse. Ride out along the escape route. Lead the other animals. I'll stash the rest of the gear. Don't ride any faster than we did before we got here; maybe they'll think we're not aware of them. When you get to the main road turn back the way we came from, turn again into the wayside where we left the road, then turn once more where the grass is most trampled. Get into the trees and hide."

Joit opened his mouth to speak. His brain caught up with the idea, he gathered the leads of the animals, struggled onto Atna's mount and rode away.

Sky collected the goods left behind, ran clumsily to the bushes and stuffed them behind a fallen tree. He ran after Joit, but off the edge of the little shelf and diagonally down toward the valley floor to the point where the riders had been when they first came into Joit's view.

He chose cover where he could see both the valley trail and the lip of the shelf above. Time crawled. Oh, Huf, he thought. If I guessed wrong, they have Atna by now. Did they follow Joit or did they study the mess of tracks at the camp and find one pair running off into the woods with a baby? He wanted to rush back up the slope to her rescue but forced himself to wait. It could be that they really weren't pursuing us, he thought. They went on up the valley where we turned. And if they are after us, it would take them time to creep in and see that we're gone. Then decide what to do. Sky's legs twitched, urging him to action. He had nearly succumbed to the demand when the third rider appeared leading the two pack horses back down the valley trail toward him. So, he thought, they are hunting us.

He grew angry as the man approached. The devils wanted to hang his wife. They must have done as Sky expected and split up when they got to the bend, so that if the two riders above flushed the prey out, the man below could either head them off or spot their path. If the lower rider got to the road quickly enough, they might put the prey in a pinch there.

The lower rider kept looking up, and Sky watched there, too. Motion drew his eye and he saw the upper men creeping on foot through the trees toward the camp. When they found nothing, one walked to the edge and waved the rider down the valley.

Sky thought, they know we're here. They don't shout.

The man above left the edge and the rider heeled his horse into a trot, tugging at the pack horses' lead.

Sky stood hidden in shadow. The rider came closer. Sky drew his bow. At fifteen meters he loosed and the man gasped, clutching at his chest and the arrow. He twisted his face in pain, opened his mouth to yell and the second arrow ripped his throat open. The horse kept trotting until the man swayed, relaxed and rolled off.

Sky looked up to see if the men above were watching. He saw nothing so he dashed out and dragged the corpse back into shadow. The horses had passed him and were stopping fifty meters down the valley.

Content that the dead man was not visible from above, Sky walked slowly toward the horses, murmuring calming noises. They skittered away twice, but finally stood nervously letting him near. He caught the halter of one pack horse, patted the animal and collected the second. He tethered them to a tree and gently walked up to the riding horse. A brief demonstration of his friendliness reassured it. He mounted and kicked the animal into a gallop down the trail.

Joit saw him fly by, began to leave his hiding place, but stopped when he understood that these men were tracking them or Sky would not be riding their horse. And that at least one of them was already dead.

Sky feared that the men above might hear his gallop to the road, but they should assume it was their fellow, hurrying to cut off the fleeing criminals. He wondered where the best ambush could be. They're trackers. They'll follow Joit's trail.

Sky reined in, skidding the horse to a turning stop and jumped off. He yanked at the reins, tugging the horse out of sight. He ran alongside the trail clearly left by Joit's descent from the end of the ridge. The layered shale outcrop looked perfect.

Sky peeked around the sharp stone edge. He saw nothing, withdrew and listened for the step of man or horse. Lichen treed across the cleaved surface of stone beside his face. Three centimeters of growth represented the age of a man, but he didn't care. Rhythmic thumping warned him that they were close. They weren't hurrying, so they thought they had their prey trapped.

Sky heard the quiet squeak of leather. He stepped out, bow drawn. The first man spotted him and reined up, a perfect target. The arrow sprouted from his chest, he grunted, gripped the shaft and slowly slumped off the horse. The second man looked up from his fallen companion, wide eyed, saw Sky and swung to aim the crossbow cradled in his arm. Sky released his arrow and the man fell with the shaft threaded through his left eye and right ear. He hit the ground hard, rolled and began to rise as Sky's sword struck his head off.

Sky strode back to the first man, crawling weakly along on his side and reaching for the crossbow lost when he fell. Sky shoved with his foot, rolling him face up. The man grimaced as the arrow snapped off where it protruded from his back. The shot had not hit his heart so he still lived, barely, drowning in crimson lung blood. "Where's... woman?" the fellow wheezed.

"Safe," Sky replied.

The man took a short bubbling breath. "Now you'll..." He coughed out a spew of blood, gasped another breath. "All hang," he gurgled.

"I doubt it," Sky said. "Would you rather die quickly, or be left to it? You don't have long."

"Fuck you," he said through blood spray.

Sky shrugged. He gathered the crossbows, walked back down the ridge toward the horse he'd left there, stopping once to wipe blood from his sword on a grass hummock.

After Sky had retrieved Atna, he and Joit returned to bury the bodies and sort their goods for useful items. They found that the man had managed to crawl to his horse, grip a stirrup and drag sixty meters down the hill before losing strength. He lay there dead.

Chapter 9

In prison Atna had never asked Sky for anything to groom herself, assuming that her next exposure to public view would only be the brief trip to the scaffold, and not caring about her own comfort. She had used the water and cloth for herself after Dalen's needs were met, but her hair, dirty, uncut and uncombed, was a fright. The next period's travel, when they crossed a stream, she begged time to take care of it. Sky, confident that nobody else followed them since the three pursuers had been eliminated, asked her if she needed help.

"Bring your knife, make sure it's sharp. You can hack away the tangles."

Atna caught a glimpse of Sky's spirit knife as he raised it to begin and she said, "Hey, where'd you get that?" He handed it to her for study and told her what he knew of its history.

Sky said, "In fact, I'm thinking that we should find the place where this was made. We can't live in Mikkeny now, unless you think your family could hide you."

"They sold me before. I doubt they'd welcome me now, with the law chasing me. Father will still be poor. They'd figure I was a threat and another mouth, two mouths to feed. Three counting you. If you think we could settle somewhere else safe, let's go. Just not Prater."

"Not Prater. I only suggest the knife makers because it would be a chance to make our fortune. If I can get them to let me trade these knives, and swords and armor, we'd be rich."

They discussed it while Sky began, under Atna's instruction, to cut her hair.

The uneven result made Sky chuckle, but he kept comments to himself, and she looked so much happier in her short and jagged, but clean, hair that it cheered him up, too. He kissed her. They glanced toward the bank where Joit sat holding Dalen and watching the animals. Then they retreated into nearby brush looking for a smooth, grassy spot.

Atna said as they walked back to Joit, "Tell me about your face."

Sky spun his tale as they mounted and rode off. He told about the bar kidnapping, the fishy warehouse, the sack on his head, the club and Berno's threats toward Atna. He told about the long gap in his memory, followed by slow, painful recovery. He stopped there for she'd already heard about the pirates and the rest.

Atna gritted, "I'm glad I killed him."

Joit looked sorrowfully at her but said nothing. He intended waiting until her anger and grief, and new happiness, had faded.

Six sleeps later they caught up to a trading caravan going the same way and asked permission to join. Sky remembered the lesson Berno had taught about bandits. The caravan had left Siklos before Sky's party and had no news of the prison escape. It would be hard to avoid more searchers if they came upon the caravan, but Sky felt that was the lesser risk.

They encountered two different bands of highwaymen, but nothing much came of either incident, just as Sky had hoped. Sky even offered one of their spare horses, of the five acquired from their stalkers, as part of the toll each time. They didn't need so many animals anyway, and disposing of them among bandits was safer than trying to sell them.

They left the foothills, beginning the steeper climb into the pass through the coastal range toward the interior of the continent, the temperature dropped and Sky realized that their equipment was not adequate to the cold. He shopped around among members of the caravan and soon had proper gear. Light snow fell on them while negotiating the highest reach of the pass.

* * *

A wide alluvial plain spread across the world below. Just beyond the last hills and a strip of green forest, a city geometrically redefined the disorder of nature. They reached it one sleep later. Sky, Atna and Joit thanked their hosts for the protection and went their own way.

This city, Sokov, was another trading partner with Siklos and a hub for distribution to the array of smaller cities and farm towns scattered broadly across the plain. Sky's small party resupplied at the central plaza bazaar and continued to the sunward limit of Sokov where they checked three inns' prices and settled into the cheapest. The speed at which the caravan had traveled was not onerous but one good sleep would fortify them for the continuing trip. They were still fugitives and should not hesitate near Siklos.

Sky knew only that the region he sought lay far sunward and inland from the sea. But he did not ask about it in Sokov for fear that asking would guide pursuers. Two sleeps passage from Sokov they started inquiring about the people who made the knife Sky carried. Most respondents admired the knife, shrugged and shook their heads. A few gestured sunward but had no idea how far it was. Those who recognized the knife usually added warnings like Jobek had made to Sky; the knife makers were sorcerers or cannibals, or both.

The dialect afflicting local speech grew more difficult to understand with each handful of kilometers, and the locals grasped the travelers' alien jabber just as poorly. Atna's better tuned ear and facile tongue elected her their spokesperson. Her place of birth, and the dialect of her youth, lay nearer to this land than did Joit's or, of course, Sky's.

Atna's body regained its sprinter's shape, though her breasts stayed prominent in their duty to Dalen. Sky had tasted her milk and vowed he would stick to beer. "Just as well," Atna laughed. "I can't feed you both."

Joit's morose state over the killing of the three man-hunters was eventually replaced by happy anticipation. The paths they took still ran as one road, sunward toward both the knife makers and the holy oasis. His conversion of both Sky and Atna seemed to be progressing to the point that their salvation would be complete by the time those paths separated.

They had learned the prayer Joit taught them and promised to use it after he was gone. Sky asked about the rambling prayers, filled with requests, that he had heard other priests make, and Joit remarked with asperity, "Huf cannot be petitioned. His purpose can't be turned aside by the ignorant begging of a mere human. Our job is to demonstrate that we accept his will, and are grateful, whatever it means in our petty affairs. So we pray, 'Thank you, Huf. You know best. Thank you Huf. You possess my soul. Thank you Huf. You have my body. Thank you Huf. I am Your's.' And repeat that at least twenty times. More repetitions bring you closer to Him."

Sky found that this chant, sitting with closed eyes, soothed him.

If only Joit could get them to admit contrition and remorse for the deaths at their hands, and accept Huf completely.

Two oddly dressed men rode toward them. One was young, smooth faced and slim, while the other was broadened by a life of ease, lined in face and wearing a close-cropped gray beard. Both were as black as charcoal. The young man carried a crossbow and a scabbarded sword. The elder carried a wood staff capped by a snake head formed of, Sky recognized in delight, the gray metal with which his own knife was made.

At first sight of the trio, the young man had cranked back the bowstring and seated a bolt. He held the crossbow casually but purposefully as they approached and stopped.

Sky sat with his hands flat on his thighs, away from sword and bow. "Tell them how glad we are to meet them," he said to Atna.

She relayed this and continued interpreting.

"Likewise," said the elder man. "You're not from around here. What are you doing in this country?"

"We are looking for a legendary city. A much respected people who are spoken of everywhere. I think that you are of these people."

"What makes you believe that?" the old man asked suspiciously.

Sky said, "The head of your staff, the buttons on your clothes, and the head of that crossbow bolt."

The strange men scowled and the crossbow raised to aim at Sky's chest. He did not move his hands.

The old man said, "Only somebody from far away would consider taking our magic. Those nearby know better."

"No, no," Sky said. "I want to study your magic, not steal it."

The old man smiled grimly. "Among the stories, did you not hear that we are powerful sorcerers and cannibals? What makes you think you won't be butchered for your meat?"

Sky shrugged. "I doubt stories of cannibalism. As for sorcery, I don't expect it will be used on somebody who means no harm."

The two black men looked at each other. The elder said to Sky, "You are either wise--or stupid. Outsiders have come. All intending to rob us. Why should we trust you?"

"I prove it by returning this." Sky said and slowly reached behind him to his sheath, withdrew the knife and offered it flat on his palm.

"Ack!" the old man exclaimed. "Idiot foreigners! You don't know..." He ranted for some time, too fast for Atna to follow, then dug into his pouch, pulled out a cloth, dropped it over the knife on Sky's hand, wrapped it and hid it in his pouch.

The young man tensely watched both his elder and Sky, his hand tight on the crossbow's release. The old man stopped ranting.

He sat scowling at Sky in thought. He gestured for his companion to lower the weapon.

"At least you cared for its physical needs, though it will require spiritual cleansing. Has it spilled human blood?"

"I believe so," Sky said, "but not by me."

"How long have you carried it?"

"A hundred fifty sleeps."

"Hmm," the old man muttered. "You must be protected by Huf. The uninitiated don't live very long."

He studied Sky's group silently, then said, "I am Mombat, second assistant to the Grand Smeltor in Tombak. This is Omto, my apprentice. We were traveling to Wensen on business, but we'll do that another time. Return with us to Tombak, sir..."

"Sky," Atna introduced. "And Joit, and I am Atna, Sky's wife. Our son Dalen." She lifted the boy's face shade.

"Good," Mombat said. "Sky, party of four. We must consult the menu." He smiled with twinkling eyes. "Come." He turned his horse and they rode sunward.

Chapter 10

Tombak was the largest city they had seen since Sokov, in fact probably twice the size of Sokov. Unlike Sokov or other cities they'd found since the escape, it was completely surrounded by a high, stone wall. The circumference of this wall dwarfed the enclosed core of Prater, if not its entire footprint, and Sky shook his head, chagrined at the memory of touting Prater as the world's greatest civilization. He had not even heard of this place before Jobek educated him, yet they had happily survived his ignorance while building a magnificent city. Even before sighting the city, they had seen the dark smoke rising from it and shading the land to sunward.

Sky asked Mombat for the cause of so much smoke, since the climate was too warm to need heat in homes, but Mombat just looked at him with an impenetrable expression.

The gates they passed through were brightly painted with giant, fanciful animals, all ferocious looking. Sky certainly hoped they were fanciful. The buildings were made of daubed mud or clay brick. Forests had thinned as they traveled sunward from Sokov and around this city only sparse umbrella trees and low shrubs grew, bordering the road and the tilled fields that were irrigated by water diverted from a large, brown river flowing past the sunward wall of Tombak.

Black faces on all sides turned in curiosity, following their passage through the city. Sky's party, with skins in various shades of light mahogany, made a novelty in Tombak. Mombat escorted them to his own home, led them to guest rooms, instructed his servants and left to speak of the newcomers with The Grand Smeltor and the First Assistant. He left Omto, as a guard, Sky suspected.

The servants helped them clean off the road grime, set a wonderful table of exotic foods, and fluffed the beds with freshly aired, finely woven bedclothes. Omto told them that after a good sleep Mombat would meet them to discuss the future.

Mombat joined them at breakfast.

After small talk Mombat said, "The Grand Smeltor was impressed by, and grateful for, your return of the spirit knife. And he was surprised that you survived one hundred fifty sleeps with it. As I said, it shows you have favor with Huf. How did you acquire it?"

"From a dead pirate slave."

"That's usual. The only other way ownership transfers is during initiation of a new Smeltor's assistant. Where did the slave get it?"

"I don't know. Either he took it from a merchant sailor or it was handed to him by a pirate just before he died.

"What," Sky asked, "are these knives used for?"

"They are imbued with a spirit and used for ceremonial and religious rites. Of course, we have other knives for common use that are not consecrated.

"I must tell you," he continued, "that, despite the Grand Smeltor's appreciative mood, no foreigner is ever initiated into our magic. Even if they were, you are too old to apprentice. Omto has been immersed in training since his twenty fifth tooth and won't receive his spirit knife for some time yet. I am sorry."

Sky nodded. "I expected that. And I want to be completely honest, so you will know we can be trusted. Atna and I hope to settle here. And I want to increase the wealth of your city..."

"And yourselves?" Mombat interrupted, frowning.

"Yes. Complete honesty. And ourselves. By trading your common knives, and swords and armor of the same metal, with other cities."

Mombat and Omto burst out laughing.

"That," Mombat said, still chortling, "is inconceivable. Why would we make ourselves vulnerable by selling our enemies the very weapons which keep us safe?"

Sky screwed up his face. "Of course," he said. "I was stupid.

"Well," he continued to Joit and Atna, "that end's that. What now?"

Those two looked at each other. Atna said, "Joit will keep on his Jefk. You and I will stay right here and raise Dalen. We'll make a living any way we can. You saw the fields. Here's your chance to farm."

Sky deflated his dream from the riches of a merchant to the humdrum survival of farming, which he already knew too well. He sighed in resignation, smiled ruefully at Atna, and turned to Mombat. "If your people will accept us, we'll live here. And I'll farm."

Mombat said, "We are in your debt for the return of the spirit knife. I will personally sponsor your homestead. You'll have to locate at the fringe of the developed farms, but at least you already have horses. Application for a water right is simple enough, and my support will expedite it. Omto, there are some undeveloped hectares down river, aren't there?"

"I believe so."

"Good," Mombat said. "Atna and Joit are welcome in my home until Sky has located a patch he likes. Not to push you all out, Sky, but I know you have everything you need to live there while you prove the homestead. So, Omto, show Sky the way."

Sky selected a patch larger than he could farm himself, knowing that his son, and future sons, would help him, and remembering that his father had become comfortably moneyed by renting to tenant farmers, though that seemed unlikely in a land where arable hectares remained available for development. It sloped, with the exception of some low rises, gently down toward the river and sunward, providing both good irrigation flow and superior light for crops, though the sun stood nearly overhead here and needed little help. He had to settle for a plot forty kilometers away from the city to get an unclaimed piece which abutted the river, but felt river access would be worth the extra travel. His allotment of water would not come from his own waterfront. To irrigate his upper reach the water had to cross several other properties first. Likewise, settlers downriver would expect him to maintain ditches across his land for their irrigation. He was lucky to find clay on his land that would make a good canal liner to limit water loss. Occasional floods enriched the soil in his lower fields. The higher fields could be fertilized manually and be depended upon to produce crops while the others were under water.

As soon as Sky had a level spot cleared for the tents, Atna and Joit moved onto the land with him. The horses were a problem. They could eat the wild grass growing between the shrubs, but he knew they would grow thin without grain. There was a neighbor to sunright with mature oat fields and Sky found quickly that hobbles were not enough to keep his animals home. He had to tether them to stakes and buy grain from the neighbor to feed them. But Mombat was a man of his word, and money as well as tools came for the asking.

When Sky was not too busy, usually around mealtimes and just before bed, Joit continued his religious education. Joit was sensitive to Sky's moods, so he usually knew how long they could discuss salvation before the big man lost patience. Once Joit pushed too far and Sky exploded, "I know that somebody is trying to tell me something! But Who!? And what is He trying to say!?"

"Your search for purpose is too personal, Sky. Which is natural. But the answer to Who is obvious. Huf. And the answer to what or why is perhaps unknowable, and therefore should be sought without hope of discovery."

Sky glowered. "Then what's the point?"

"Because the journey involves important discoveries that you cannot anticipate."

"If you say," Sky said sourly.

* * *

Atna whispered as they lay together before sleep, "I thought Joit would have gone by now."

"Me, too. I think he worries too much about our souls."

"I think he doesn't want to leave Dalen."

"Could be. He never had kids. He talks about the Jefk, but he thinks about people."

"Well," Atna said, "I love the little priest more than my own father. I won't send him away."

"Same here."

* * *

Sky knew the tents would be good shelter until the sun rotted them away, so he concentrated on transforming the land before worrying about housing. The backbreaking labor of removing brush and rocks reminded him too much of his youth and what he hated about farming, but it was tolerable now. Time didn't weigh as heavily as an adult and he had reasons, a wife and child, to keep him happily at the task. He was delighted with the plow that Mombat gave him. The plowshare was made of the tough, new metal, called iron, that they smelted under the smoke blackened sky of Tombak. The farm took form. The first two hectares were cleared, tilled, ditched and planted.

Atna, when she wasn't adding her strength to field work or animal care, tackled her role as home-keeper by setting up a crude kitchen. Joit helped her. He had made simple meals for himself most of his life, so at least had a clue about cooking. Atna built on the basic skills she remembered from girlhood, learned what Joit had to teach, and soon began experimenting successfully with new dishes. Or at least successful in the opinion of the two men, who might have been too willing to praise her. As they became acquainted with the neighbors, the women in these families taught her more.

Sky knew the value of good neighbors, so he cultivated them even before his crops, offering help with any job that needed another pair of hands. When their initial suspicion of the odd looking and battle-scarred foreigner faded, they gladly accepted his assistance and returned even more. It helped, too, that he was known to be sponsored by the Second Assistant in Tombak.

* * *

Sky stood looking at his ripening oats, barley and potatoes. He had already planted another two hectares to grow while he harvested these first crops. Atna stood beside him as Dalen took experimental steps away from them, fell to his hands, stood again and toddled back. Behind them they heard a weird moan.

They looked querulously at each other and turned back toward the tents. Joit lay by the fire, the tail of his robe beginning to smoke, while he feebly flailed to roll away. They ran to him, pulled him from the fire, smothered the burning robe and laid him softly on the rug they used as the outdoor core of their home.

"Joit!" Sky said. "Joit, what's wrong?"

"I can't, I can't..." He slurred. The left side of his face drooped, he clutched Sky with his right hand but the left lay useless beside him.

"A stroke!" Atna cried.

She and Sky looked at each other. She said, "Take him to his tent."

Sky scooped the small man up like an infant and carried him to the tent, gently placing him on his blankets. Sky gestured Atna back outside, drew her away and whispered, "What can we do?"

"Nothing," she said gloomily. "Keep him comfortable and clean. Feed him. Give him water. He'll live or he'll die."

"We could take him to the city. To a physician."

"No. The trip might kill him, and they can't help unless they know a lot more than the physicians in Prater. My friend's father had a stroke. All they could do was watch him die."

"By Huf," Sky moaned, "I'm tired of losing friends."

"He might live."

"Might."

They undressed Joit, to his embarrassment, wrapped him gently and returned to their routine, each with one ear cocked in Joit's direction. When Joit needed to urinate or empty his bowels, Sky carried him, wrap and all, to the pit latrine, propped him and left him to his business. But by the third sleep Joit toppled over as Sky let him go, so he stayed to hold him upright. Joit could no longer clean himself by then so Sky took care of it and marveled to himself that he could do this personal duty for his friend. But how could he not? Both Sky and Atna came running once when they heard Joit choking. They rolled him on his side and pounded his back. Joit coughed up a wad of phlegm and breathed freely again.

The next time they fed him, he choked on his food. They tried to feed him mush then but that made him cough, too. Eventually they discovered that he could swallow better leaning to his left with his head turned right, but only fluids. His speech became nearly incomprehensible and the few understandable words indicated that he was reliving a delirious version of his distant past. He called frequently for Lespa, his deceased wife. He worked his right arm and leg constantly to the point that Atna had to wrap his heel to prevent a sore from wearing against the blankets, and they finally resorted to tying him down, to his great distress.

Two more sleeps passed. Sky said, "He's going to starve. Or strangle on his food."

"No," Atna said. "There is a way. One good food we have that he can swallow."

"What? All he can take is water."

She looked Sky in the eye. "Dalen is eating more solid food now."

Sky puzzled over this for a moment. "Oh!" He said.

It was not comfortable for Atna, and she demanded that Sky be elsewhere when she fed Joit. He had to lie on his left side with his face turned upward and she nearly smothered him pressing her breast tightly against his left cheek, sealing the slack side of his mouth to allow suction. But he fed. And he lived.

Twenty uncomfortable sleeps passed like this before Joit's words became understandable again. His awareness sharpened intermittently and averaged better overall as time passed. One of his cogent moments struck while nursing at Atna's breast. He looked up into Atna's eyes, screwed his face into a half-faced grimace of embarrassment, and turned away. Atna saw tears squeeze from his tightly closed right eye.

"No, Joit," she soothed. "Don't cry. It's all right." Then tears fell from her own eyes and she stroked the poor man's hair. "Don't," she said. "Don't."

Joit still raved periodically, but his ravings almost made sense. He called Sky "Opet", apparently a cousin remembered from his youth, and he called Atna "Vesta". He offered "Vesta" all his wealth if she would just take him home to his wife, Lespa. He chafed his heel less. At his most calm he was able to eat some mush without aspirating it. Sky hoisted him to his feet, forcing him to take a few weak, half-dragging steps. Soon he could sit upright by himself, though propped with cushions.

Sky's crops came in and he had to leave Joit in Atna's care while he, with the help of his two nearest neighbors, harvested. Then he set aside his seed, collected the next choicest samples of his produce, loaded them into the cart which Mombat had given him, and drove the two sleeps to Tombak. With Omta's help he located a broker who inspected his cartload dubiously.

"Not bad for a first harvest," the broker grudged. "And you have how much?"

"About four thousand kilos of oats, five thousand of barley, and twenty five tonnes of spuds."

They dickered prices for a while and shook hands on a contract in front of a local notary. Sky unloaded his cart and promised to return with the rest over sixty sleeps.

Joit was sitting up on his own, stirring the fire, when Sky returned. He trotted up to the old man jubilantly calling his name. Unfortunately he'd approached from Joit's left side, which no longer had peripheral vision, and Joit keeled over at the surprise. Sky helped him back up, apologized and asked how he felt.

"Well enough, but I do worry about the horses that run through here. Little, ah, ah..." he gestured at Sky's son.

"Dalen," Sky supplied.

"Dalen could be trampled."

Dalen tottered over to his father and gurgled at him. Sky swept him up, stood and threw him into the air. Dalen squealed and Atna did, too. "Sky!" she cried. "You'll break your son!"

Sky set him down and gently boxed him. Dalen grabbed at his father's fists.

"Are these horses wild or our neighbor's?" Sky asked.

"Wild!" Joit said.

Sky looked at Atna for confirmation and she sadly shook her head.

"Well," Sky said. "I'll catch them, tame them and sell them in Tombak."

"Good," Joit agreed.

* * *

Five crop rotations passed, Sky and Atna's fortunes increased, Dalen teethed his twelves, learned to run and giggled at his own jokes, like cuddling Joit and saying, "Daddy!" Sky began teaching the little boy to swim, figuring that with a river so close he'd get into it whether he could swim or not and stood a better chance of getting back out if he could. Dalen and Joit were both weaned to solid food and Atna's breasts shut down. Joit could walk clumsily with Sky's help, but he feared falling and would not try to walk alone with the cane Sky had made for him. Joit's dementia, especially the hallucinations of running horses, never healed completely, but he could be distracted from it by his friends.

Then he began to get worse again.

"He's having more little strokes," Atna told Sky. "From now, he'll just go downhill until he dies."

"And there's nothing we can do about it," Sky sighed.

"There is one thing."

"What?"

Atna clasped Sky's hand. "I never thought I could send you away. But you have to take Joit to finish his Jefk. It won't save his life, but it'll complete it."

Sky studied her face. She was serious. He looked around them at the farm, still needing so much work. A small, brushy corral confined the horses, but only Joit slept in a real house of mud wattle. The two of them and Dalen relied yet on their old, sun-bleached tent.

"How would you manage?" he asked.

"The neighbors are good friends. They like Joit. They'll help. And the land can lie fallow if we store our seed carefully. Me and Dalen will be fine." She did not say that she was pregnant. Surely Sky would return, with or without Joit, in time for the birth, and the knowledge would just add to his worries.

Chapter 11

Poor little Ponder had gone lame. Sky abandoned some of their gear and stowed Joit among the reduced load on the pack horse. Ponder managed better without Joit's weight, but still limped. She was left to recover in care of a friendly farmer with whom they stayed. Joit was barely coherent by then, but cried as they rode off without his beloved Ponder.

Sky practically had to beat a path through the beggars, buskers and hawkers that preyed on the continuous flood of pilgrims in Kiffej. They checked into one of the multitude of inns built up to house the transients. After an expensive meal they slept, or tried to sleep, battling anticipation and the ongoing roar of the milling crowds of Kiffej.

Now they stood at the bottom of Isisiv, the sacred hill on the sunward side of Kiffej, which pilgrims climbed to see the distant mountain, Umanqyt, where Huf lived.

Animals were not allowed on Isisiv so Sky untied the little priest from the padded pack frame. He took Joit in his arms and began the three kilometer climb up the winding stair. The heat here was unbearable without protection from the sun, which stood practically straight overhead. Sweat poured from them. Shaded rest benches were placed at intervals beside the stair and Sky used most of them. He had not thought to bring his water bag and paid the young man, who had been buzzing around them for the last hundred meters, to get a few swallows.

The tight mass of people crowded the mildly sloped hilltop between the trail end and the far side where the mountain was visible. Sky, taller than the others, could see a distant cloud in the sky. He pushed through the people, losing patience until he saw that many others helped invalids, too. No seats were available under the awnings. He hunted until he found a vacant stone far on the sunright end of the hilltop. He placed Joit on this and propped him with cushions rented from the ubiquitous vendors. He rented a large umbrella and jammed the base into the hole in the soil beside the rock where thousands had done the same for generations.

Joit had been delirious through most of the climb and was still unaware of his surroundings. Once Sky had him comfortable, he squatted by his right side and prompted, "Joit, we're there. You can see Umanqyt."

Joit focused at the name of the mountain and stared at Sky. "Umanqyt?" he slurred.

Sky nodded and pointed across the vast desert sunward at the giant mountain standing above the horizon. It's purple base gave way to white and then to the massive cloud which perpetually hid its peak.

Joit turned his head, squinted his good right eye and sighed in awe, "Umanqyt."

"Jefko Joit," Sky said. "You finished the pilgrimage."

* * *

Joit was content to sit with a beatific, uneven smile, gazing at the mountain, so Sky was, too. Sky relaxed. The long sojourn was done, the low, reverent murmur of the crowd was soothing. He sat on the ground in the shade of their umbrella, leaned against the rock by Joit's knees, closed his eyes and slept.

Sky woke, seeing Joit still watched the mountain, as if expecting it to do something more than merely inspire. Sky reached, pulled the loose fabric at Joit's shoulder and used it to sop up a stream of drool on the priest's chin. It must have been a long sleep for, despite the heat, Sky's bladder was full.

He stood. "Come on Joit. It's time to go down." He bent, beginning to collect the man in his arms, but Joit became agitated.

"No. No! Umanqyt!"

Sky let him settle back into the cushions, squatted in front of him and caught his attention. "Joit," he said. "Jefko Joit, you did it, but we have to eat and start home."

"No. No. No." Joit chanted, shaking his head.

Sky thought, then said, "All right. We'll go down, eat, rest and come back up. How's that?"

Joit shook his head.

Sky thought some more. He patted Joit's knee, said, "Fine. Wait here." He stood and went in search of a soup vendor. As he searched he noticed the foul smell of the latrine on the antisun side of the hill, out of view of the holy mountain, and turned aside to use the noisome trench.

Sky found the soup vendor, who also rented bowls, bought some water from a boy and returned to Joit.

Joit's ability to swallow had degraded with his diminishing health. He seemed to manage a few small sips, then choked badly on the soup, struggling to catch his breath, his face purpled with bulging veins. Sky held him and leaned him over to ease his breathing, and his airway cleared. Joit's wheezing breath began to normalize, but then Sky felt the little man's body begin jerking.

"Joit!" he exclaimed, laying him down in the dusty shade. When the seizures continued he sat by him and pulled him into his lap to confine the violence of the convulsions. They slowly calmed and Sky thought he had died, but then felt the weak rise and fall of his ribs. The little man's face was pale and drooped more severely than ever.

"I'll get you to a physician," Sky said.

Joit's eye swiveled toward him. "No," he gasped. "Umanqyt."

Sky studied the poor face. "All right. Umanqyt."

He set Joit aside, steadied him there and rose. He picked Joit up, sat on the rock and propped the priest in front of him between his knees. They were still sitting like that a long, half-sleep later when Sky realized that Joit was gone.

Sky, his body aching from holding one pose so long, pushed the cushions onto the ground, laid his friend gently down on them and covered his face. He stood to relieve his stiffness, and gazed down on Joit's empty shell.

A man who had watched said gently, "Many die on Isisiv. It is a blessing."

Sky looked stonily at the man, and at the distant mountain, picked his friend up and left the hill.

Chapter 12

The scorching heat in this land required that the dead be buried quickly. Sky said his last farewell to Joit at the huge cemetery to sunright of Kiffej only half a sleep after the priest's last breath. With holy men so thick that you could turn any direction and spit on one with your eyes closed, there were many offers to give Joit his last blessing. But it seemed unlikely that the words of these hollow men could ease Joit's passage Beyond, any more than his own deeds had already done. Sky declined their offers. Atna had been right; Joit's seeing the holy mountain had completed his life, but it had also hastened his end. Not that he had much time left, anyway. Another friend was gone. The best friend he'd had since Blute. And in his way Joit was as much a warrior as Blute had been, though serving a different King for a different Cause, and he made as much impact on Sky as Blute had. "It was a good time to die," Sky sighed.

He returned to the expensive inn, exhausted after the ordeal of Joit's death and burial, determined to start home after a reviving sleep.

* * *

Sky sat at breakfast, bleary eyed after an unsatisfying sleep, staring sightlessly at the bright town beyond the shade of the dining veranda. Men and women of all skin shades and every imaginable costume flowed interminably past. Kiffej was the most cosmopolitan town in the world. Sky didn't think about that. He thought about Joit, and Blute, Atna, the Snowpeople, the iron-workers of Tombak, his little son and his future children. He thought about Huf, and fate, and fighting, and faith. He did not, in his grief and weariness, think linearly about any of these things. They all tumbled around in his mind like the roots, rocks and mud of the flash flood he had seen with Atna and Berno. He thought about Berno. That was an evil chain of events—such a stupid first act which resulted finally in the deaths of at least four men, and immeasurable suffering. He had felt at every crossroads in his life that he had weighed options and made his own decisions, but looking back on his history now it all appeared to flow like a continuous, inevitable stream from the highland of his youth to the tangled swamp of his present, and, in future, to the dark ocean of his death—a stream that did not select its course but was turned left or right, slowed or sent crashing over falls, by the uncaring terrain. Was his terrain a random set of barriers, or had they been placed to guide him? Joit had been more interested in saving Sky's soul than in answering this question for him. In fact everything Joit taught indicated that it was likely unanswerable.

Sky looked up at Isisiv and the colorful line of people processing up and down the zigzag stair. He rose, fetched his water bag from his room and walked to the communal artesian well, which kept this oasis alive in the desert, and filled the bag. He went on slowly to the base of Isisiv and wearily climbed the stair.

The rock where Joit had died was vacant. Sky rented an umbrella. He sat and stared at the distant mountain. Much later, hunger and a terrible headache finally drove him stiffly down the hill, where he ate a tasteless meal, slept badly, breakfasted and then returned to the steps.

Pilgrims saw him approaching and one nudged the fellow sitting on Joit's rock. The man stood, gesturing that Sky should sit. He thanked the man mechanically.

After staring silently at the mountain for a time, he began to mutter, " Thank you, Huf. You know best. Thank you Huf. You possess my soul. Thank you Huf. You have my body. Thank you Huf. I am Your's. Thank you, Huf. You know best. Thank you

Huf. You possess my soul. Thank you Huf. You have my body. Thank you Huf. I am Your's..."

The stress of the vigil, though dulled by the endless, mindless repetition of prayer, eventually sent him to the inn again.

The next period people near him took up the prayer when he started. It spread from them to others until the whole mass of hilltop worshipers were motionless, joined as a single voice in the chant. He had a brief vision of singing herder warriors stepping off down hill to meet the snowmen in battle.

Sky's mouth became very dry, and his voice hoarse. Huf cannot be petitioned. Sky stopped chanting. Why not, he thought. If the fate of this world and its people mean anything at all to Huf, why will he not listen to our pleas? Does he truly already know our needs and desires? If so, then everything is predestined and free will nonexistent, and therefore salvation through an act of will is not possible—even the will to submit without conditions. That, too, is a form of petition. Sky saw no path around this paradox.

Huf cannot be petitioned.

Sky went down the stair. He sold his packhorse and packsaddle. He purchased a stout hand cart, bought some longer, lightweight poles and replaced the short ones on the cart. He bought water bags, a bucket, bags of crushed oats, masses of food for himself, and a trio of umbrellas designed to give shade for a horse and his rider during desert travel. Returning to the inn with all of this, he stored it in the stable, fell to his bed and slept a deep, restful sleep.

With a hearty breakfast under his belt, Sky lashed the lengthened poles of his cart to the saddle of his riding horse. Sky rode, looking like a one-man traveling circus with his umbrellas and cart, to the graveyard where he paused a moment looking at the freshly turned soil of Joit's last bed. Then he turned antisun and left Kiffej.

When he could no longer see Kiffej, he turned sunright. He turned sunward after ten kilometers, knowing that nobody would see him as he passed the oasis at this distance on his way to Umanqyt. Even attempting this journey was sacrilege.

"Jasper," Sky said to the horse, "this brings back old times. Of course it wasn't you that came with me out of the snow. And instead of unbearable cold, we've got unbearable hot. But we're still going sunward, and I'm still talking to a horse."

Sky noticed as they rode that the dust stirred by the horse's hooves blew away ahead of them. "We can still steer by the wind," he told Jasper. "And that's good. The sun isn't much of a guide. Too high in the sky."

They stopped at fifteen kilometers to camp. Sky's eyes burned terribly and he felt stupid. He already knew that, without protection, both he and the horse would be blinded by the sunlight reflected off the desert, but he'd been in a distracted state of mind. His desert tent, acquired when he and Joit traveled to Kiffej, had tall poles that held it high enough to shelter the horse, too. The edges came close to the ground to maximize shade while allowing ventilation. He pitched the tent, led the horse in and covered Jasper's eyes with a dark cloth. He poured water into the bucket for Jasper. When the horse had sucked up the last pool and lipped moisture off the bottom, Sky set the bucket outside. It dried in a few heartbeats. Sky allowed some time to let the water pass along the horse's gut and then shook oats from a bag into the bucket and gave it back to Jasper. His diet would need grass before long, but they would likely both die before reaching the mountain, anyway. While Jasper ate, Sky rubbed him down; if he wanted any chance to survive, he would coddle the horse.

Following another restful sleep, he ate, fed Jasper, broke camp, mounted the horse and tied a strip of dark cloth over his own eyes to match that on Jasper. He had distressed the fabric to open the weave a little, so he could get eye protection but still see through it. Man, horse, and cart followed the wind.

The cloud headdress of Umanqyt appeared at about twelve kilometers and rose higher every new kilometer after that.

Sky did not hurry the horse; whatever pace Jasper found comfortable was the one that would get them to the mountain. His lips blistered and his face burned, so he fashioned a turban and wrapped his face, then did the same for Jasper's nose and mouth.

At eleven sleeps they passed out of rocky terrain and sandy hills onto a brilliant white salt flat so broad that its far edge was invisible. Mirages danced on the distant salt. Umanqyt, hugely majestic now, rose out of the illusory water shimmer. Jasper was in good health, but obviously weary of the heat. Their progress had slowed to about ten kilometers each ride.

"At least," Sky said, "It's a straight, flat ride now, for as far as we can see."

The salt began to irritate Jasper's feet after thirty more kilometers, so Sky walked to relieve him. At sixty, Jasper was only reluctantly placing his feet on the hot, painful salt. Then the shimmering mirage gave way to real water. When they reached the poorly defined shoreline, they stopped. It stretched away beyond sight to right and left. The mountain loomed high above them, appearing barely an arm's reach away.

"Jasper, this doesn't look good."

They moved back well away from the moist salt and Sky set camp. He had to think.

Sky was certain of three things. First, there must be a range of hills to left or right that would rise above the salt lake and allow access to the mountain. Second, the lake would get deeper, however shallow it would remain for the next twenty kilometers, and maybe deep enough to drown them before getting to the foothills. Third, they could not camp in water.

So would it be sunleft, or sunright? The coastline to sunleft could have mountains like the range they'd crossed reaching Sokov. But what if the coast did not come this far sunward. Surely Kiffej would not be the goal of Jefk if pilgrims could sail to the mountain. Well, then, sunright it would be. The flat must give way eventually.

Jasper could barely walk when they reached unsalted soil, but Sky urged him on, pulling most of the cart's weight himself. Their fresh water and food were both nearly gone. Sky doubted that Jasper could walk far enough to find either. But even Jasper knew they couldn't stay there. So they followed the low lying ridge toward the mountain. The mountain served as a pointer now; the sun was directly overhead, unhelpful, and unforgiving.

Jasper's every step left a blood print on the hard soil, and he cringed at each contact with the ground, but he kept walking. Then he snorted and his ears perked. He picked up his painful pace and Sky let him set the speed. They topped a small rise and looked down with delight at the pool of fresh water. Sky could barely restrain Jasper long enough to unhitch the cart. He left the saddle and umbrellas.

If a horse could sing, Sky knew that Jasper would be making music now. Jasper stood with his feet in the cooling pool and drank the sweet liquid, a real improvement on the stale stuff he'd been getting from the rotting water bags. Regardless of the horrific heat that beat down on them from the remorseless sun, they camped there for six sleeps to recuperate.

The food was gone on the fourth sleep, but the stunted greenery around the pool had helped sustain Jasper and gave Sky hope of better to be had up along the valley toward Umanqyt. Sky loaded the cart, cinched the saddle, bound the cart poles to it and led a much happier Jasper toward the mountain. That trek they found a stream trickling down a ravine, lined with grass and shrubs. This stream grew larger as they went up hill, at odds with the familiar streams of antisun, for here the dry soil and air sucked the water away more as it ran down to the desert.

Sky was considering Jasper as his next meal when he spotted a small, furry animal ducking down a hole at the side of the ravine. He set a snare and had fresh meat for the first time in too long. They camped here for eight sleeps to let Jasper's feet finish healing and to dry some meat for the trail. Jasper missed his oats but grass was better than nothing.

The mountain dominated the world. Sky could see that they would soon climb into a dry, sparsely vegetated zone, while above that lay a green (though still blue tinted at this distance) forest of mature deciduous trees. He couldn't tell what lay above, but figured he would find out soon enough.

Jasper didn't complain at weight on his back so Sky rode again. They gained elevation with every wake period. Once they crossed a wide plateau of rolling grass fields and saw herds of horses, wild bos and fleet, bounding animals of amazing grace, but ugly appearance. Sky shot one of the bos, dressed it out, cut the meat into thin strips and hung it on shrubs to dry. He had to spend two wake periods guarding it from small dog-like scavengers and carrion birds while it desiccated.

The air became chill. Sky thought this an odd contradiction, for the sun was still dangerously bright. He covered himself with all his few fabric goods to stay warm when he slept, but realized it wouldn't be enough. He extended their stay once more to collect and cure the pelts of some hairy, horned animals who showed no fear of him as he walked within easy bow shot.

The trees gave way to low bunch grass that Jasper would not happily eat. The wind still blew up the mountain. The view across the desert was incredible, and Sky thought he could see Kiffej in the distant haze. Then they found the first rotting dregs of rough snow. Sky harvested as much grass as he could stuff into the empty sacks. This was also where the ground became too rugged to keep the cart, so Sky loaded the food and water onto Jasper and led him.

They struggled through thigh deep snow, Sky taking one step, then resting, panting, and then taking another. He had found that if he didn't slow his pace to this that the darkness would circle his vision and his ears would ring. The last time he'd felt that was on the slippery hill, leading farmers and Amazons in battle against the snowmen, and the arrow in his arm had drained away too much blood. He checked. He wasn't bleeding now. At least the sun couldn't blind him anymore; it was hidden overhead by the everlasting cloud around the peak of Umanqyt.

The cold, too familiar and too frightening, crept into his limbs. The horse hesitated so long at each step that it was a terrible effort to haul on the lead and make him follow.

"All right, Jasper," Sky said. "You've done your part." He unloaded everything from the faithful animal, removed his halter, turned him downslope and slapped his rump. The horse startled, tromped downhill through the snow for a dozen steps, and stopped. He just stood there. Sky struggled down the horse's track and swatted him again. This time Jasper kept walking after the first burst, so Sky went back up to his gear and began sorting through it for what he could carry. It was a woefully small pack that Sky strove to shoulder, but it was far too late to reconsider the quest now. The loss of Jasper, the aloneness, struck him hard in the cold snowscape. Fear crept deeper.

Yes, he remembered this—the numbing feet and hands, the split, frozen lips, the frost encased beard. But the weariness was worse than before. Why did he feel like he was bleeding to death? He thought, at least this will be the last futile search for Huf, and meaning, and purpose. The failure doesn't surprise me. Why did I expect any different, even on Huf's mountain? Well, it's always a good time to die. Huf cannot be petitioned.

* * *

He did not want to give up, but his body refused to obey. If he hadn't been standing hip deep in snow, he would have toppled over. And the thought of lying down and sleeping had an allure that would very soon be impossible to resist. His thoughts were disjointed and feverish. This all feels so familiar, he thought, and then barked out a laugh. "Well, I've made the whole circuit. I woke up from the ice and I will sleep again in ice. This time forever."

"Hello."

Sky jumped, though not far in the deep snow, and saw a man sitting cross-legged on a sheltered rock above and to his left. The stranger had close-cropped, brown hair and beard, and wore a red checked shirt and faded blue pants. His boots were scuffed, brown leather. His oval face was of a color like Sky's, unlined, though maturely structured, with blue eyes that smiled at some private joke.

Sky took several calming breaths and then asked, "Aren't you cold?"

"No, Eskander."

Ah, Sky thought, I'm delirious. Nobody knows my old name.

"True, you're near delirium, but you're not there yet. And though I'm not imagined, neither am I really here."

Sky laughed. "I'm used to talking with myself, so don't think you can embarrass me with an imaginary conversation."

The stranger smiled. He refused to waver and fade away as Sky had both expected and hoped.

When he was bored with silence, Sky said, "All right. Who are you?"

"My name is Michael Huffman."

Sky laughed again, indulging his hallucination. "Well, Michael God-man, what brings you to..." He glowered. "Are you the god Huf?"

"No. I am not Huf, not a god, though I am the source of the myth."

Sky shook his head. "Well," he said, "you could be a god. That's the empty answer a god would give. You're a man?"

"I am the image of a man who died long, long ago."

"You're a ghost," Sky nodded. Or, he thought, I'm insane.

"Bear with me," Michael said. "I'll warm you up while I explain."

Sky noticed that he had already become warmer. This is one of the last signs of freezing to death, he thought.

"True," Michael agreed, "but not this time. You are getting warmer. Note the frost melting from your beard."

It was. Sky thought, well, either I've gone mad, or not. That's a one of two chance. Let's stick with the hopeful side, the Joit side, and play along. "All right. Explain."

"What I'm going to tell you will be hard to accept. But you are here because of your open mind, even if it sometimes has to be pried open.

"Humans did not originate on this world. Yes, there are other worlds."

"Where?" Sky asked.

Michael frowned. "For want of a better term, above your head."

"Up the mountain?"

"No. Higher than the mountain. Higher than the sun."

Sky smiled at the richness of his own imagination. Madness was leading the race.

"And," Michael continued, "Humans first lived on a distant world called Earth. They built machines to leave that world and colonize others. This is one of the colonies."

Sky noticed that he was not only feeling warmer but the snow had melted away from his legs to leave him standing in an expanding pit. He reached up and pinched his sore lip. His attention sharpened. "You're real." he said.

"Yes. Real enough. To continue: This world has a fault. It does not appear to rotate. That is, the sun always stands in one place. This, and the natural human tendency to utilize resources by the lowest energy methods, made colonists forget their ancestry."

Sky said. "What does that mean?"

Michael sighed. "If this world rotated differently, the sun would disappear, approximately every sleep, and it would be dark. And when it became dark you would see lights in the sky. Specks of light that are really the suns of other worlds. You saw one in the twilight land, before you had to turn around."

"Yes." Sky said. "I remember. But," he paused. "How can..." and he stopped, trying to visualize this new version of reality. "How would rotation change anything? The sun is at the center. The disk of the world could spin left or right, if it wasn't too fast and threw us off, and the sun would stay in the center."

Michael asked, "How do you explain the fact that the sun gets higher in the sky as you approach it?"

"The same as approaching a tall apple tree puts the apple more directly overhead."

"An imaginative hypothesis," Michael said, "but wrong. Why does a ship disappear below the horizon when it sails away? Why did this mountain appear to rise out of the ground as you came closer?"

Sky shrugged.

"Because the world is round. The sun is really so far away that if the world was flat it would stand directly overhead anywhere on the world. But as you walk toward the sun around the curved surface of the world, the sun looks higher."

Sky's mind worked better with the rise in body heat. He visualized this odd concept and could see how it explained the behavior of the sun, the ships and the mountain. "You saved my life to teach me geography."

"Yes," Michael said. "And other things. But you needed to know this to understand your mission."

"My mission?"

"You see, your life really has had a purpose and I've had a hand in it."

"Really? You are going to tell me why I've gone through all this hell?"

Michael smiled again, somewhat sheepishly. "Yes, and I do apologize for the inconvenience."

"And that makes it all right, then?" Sky asked bleakly.

"You can judge that when you know more."

"I'm ready," Sky said.

"No. You're ready to collapse. You need some food and rest. Climb into that contraption behind you and we'll go back down to my residence."

Sky looked around and flinched away from the large, gossamer, bird-like machine sitting so close he could touch it. He turned back to Michael. "You mean you don't live at the mountain top?"

Michael glanced up slope. "No. The weather is miserable and the cloud blocks the view. Climb in and I'll meet you at my place."

Sky noticed a barely visible, curved closure standing up from the body of the device ahead of the opening in front of the long wings. He tottered weakly to it, stepped over the side, expecting to crash through the delicate film floor in front of the seat, but it held him. He sat down with a thump. The transparent cover swung down, sealing him in. He nearly panicked when flat webs snaked across his body, confining him. The top layer of snow puffed up in clouds and Sky felt his stomach sink as the machine lifted straight into the air. If he hadn't suspected he was dreaming, he would have truly panicked then. The snow settled back down as the machine rose two hundred meters, and Sky looked back down to see Michael waving reassuringly.

The nose dipped and the machine plummeted, swooping to within fifty meters of the rushing landscape before leveling to the distant horizon and sailing away from the mountain. Sky worried that he might need a change of pants. It turned gracefully to the right and held its distance from the mountain as it descended. The brilliant sun appeared when he sailed out from under the edge of the cloud. The clear cover above his head darkened for shade. Sky watched the face of the mountain roll past his right side and change as he lost height—the snow grew shallower on the exposed rocks, then became patchy, disappeared and left slopes of bunch grass, then needle trees, and at last a wide, nearly flat, grass covered meadow like the one where he had killed the bos. The machine swept gently down to the ground, raised its nose and a down-blast of air flattened the grass beneath. Forward motion stopped, the machine leveled itself and settled lightly as a feather to the meadow.

The top popped open, the webs released him and Sky struggled to climb out, fell back, breathed heavily for a bit and then forced himself up to step over the side. Nothing around him looked like a habitation. A rock outcrop against the mountain side of the meadow swung out, revealing dark, shiny panels. Sky staggered toward them. As he neared, one panel slid aside, so he entered. Michael stood in the small anteroom. Sky looked behind as the panel swished shut and he saw that it was transparent from this side.

"Welcome to my humble home," Michael said.

Sky looked around at the strange, elegant room. "Humble by your standards, maybe."

"Let's get you some food." Michael led Sky down a corridor that lit with a soft yellow light as they entered it. At the end they turned right, entered a small, box-like room which sealed behind them. Sky rested against the wall with closed eyes, felt his stomach drop again and figured they were rising. The wall of the box opened and they passed through to a wonderfully furnished room with more transparent panels that looked out on the lower reaches of the mountain and the world beyond.

"This is my favorite room," Michael said. "Or was before I died."

"Right," Sky said. "You're a ghost."

"I'll explain while you eat. Sit."

Sky dropped into the chair, facing the magnificent view, at a table set with a basic meal of meat, bread, vegetables and a stout beer.

As he picked up a knife and fork, Sky said, "First, what does that other thing you said before mean? About lowest energy and..."

He sawed ineffectually on the meat, threw down the utensils and picked it up in his hand to gnaw off a piece.

Michael said, "The equipment that sustained the colonists on the trip between suns was the largest part of what the ship carried. The plan for colonization is to preserve and disseminate knowledge rather than to bring the machinery of a whole civilization. Naturally they also transported plant seed and selected animals, frozen for the trip like the colonists. Most of the large herbivores here are of Earth origin, but all of the carnivores, like the animals you call bears and wolves, are native to this world and only superficially resemble their namesakes. When the colonists arrived, they spread quickly. They had many children. They used the resources at hand to survive. But you can't spend time smelting metals if it's all you can do just to till the land, hunt, and feed your family. If you need an ax, you won't go to the library and look up the steps between digging ore and finally sharpening a tool, you'll collect a fine-grained stone, flake it to a sharp edge and lash a stick to it. The lowest energy way to make an ax. Over a few generations the library typically comes into use as the population can support skills beyond hunting, gathering and subsistence farming. But in this case, with the libraries far between and the stationary sun hiding the other worlds, the descendants of the colonists forgot their heritage. They even forgot the libraries.

"Another, unforeseen, setback was the effect of uninterrupted sunlight on the crop plants brought from Earth. Because they evolved with dark and light cycles, they needed the dark for proper metabolism. Here they grew poorly or died. It took several human generations replanting the handful of surviving seeds to make the varieties you know today. People barely lived, scrounging the few edible native plants. The animals were too precious to butcher."

Sky asked around a succulent piece of meat, "The libraries are still there?"

"Yes, buried under the rubble of hundreds of generations."

"All right," Sky said. "What about 'before you died'?"

"My job, with three assistants, was to build this facility, using the salvaged ship, as a master copy of the library and to observe the progress of the colonists, stepping in where necessary to guide them back into the highly technological..."

"What?" Sky interrupted.

Michael smiled. "Sorry. Guide them back into a culture with many sophisticated machines.

"Unfortunately, in five generations people forgot what I was here for, and came to think I was a god whenever I dropped in. Soon after that, a couple more generations, I realized that manifesting as a god might hold progress back rather than promote it. The people would do as I suggested, but didn't explore beyond that. They relied on me too much. I tried spreading information while disguised as an ordinary man, but, without the gravitas of a god, they ignored me or, worse, called me heretic for trying to alter the dictates of Huf."

"Wait," Sky said, trying to shake off the unreality of this conversation. "Either you lived a really long time or you skipped something."

"I lived one hundred thirty three years, but stopped traveling after I turned ninety. By contrast, the rigors of colonial life reduced the average lifespan of the population to about thirty years until the crops came back. Average now is forty. To keep up contact with the descendants, I imprinted my knowledge and personality into the computer," Sky opened his mouth to speak, Michael raised his hand, "which is a machine built to think just like you do. And continued my visits in the form you see."

"So..." Sky mulled a bit. "You're not a ghost. And what is a year?"

"A year is the period of time it takes the Earth to revolve once around Sol, about one twentieth of a generation, or three hundred sixty sleeps, or one and a third gestation periods. Ghost is as good a word as any. I'm not substance. I could be, but that would take more energy."

"Ghost."

"Here," Michael said. "Touch me." He leaned forward, reaching out.

Sky took Michael's hand, which he could not feel.

"How can I see you, if I can't touch you?"

Michael half shrugged. "This can get involved. I have four methods to become visible, not including showing you the computer that really *is* me. They all involve our most versatile tool, an actuator so small that it can't be seen without a sophisticated viewing tool. I can, as I said, become substance by building up a set of these tiny motes into my shape, just as I did with the flying machine. Or a set of the motes can be oriented in the air to bend ambient light into a visible image. Or they can be instructed to project light directly into your eyes. But the last, and most efficient, is what I'm using now. Your eyes, and aural nerves, are infused with motes that directly stimulate neurons, creating images and sounds only in your brain."

"What!" Sky shouted, staggering up from the table. "You put these things into me?"

Michael gestured gently. "Calm, Eskander, calm. They won't harm you. In fact they kept you from dying when you froze in the snow lands. They prevented the crystallization of water that would have killed your cells, and managed the orderly shut-down of organs. Then they dismantled all the harmful biota and shut themselves off. Occasionally, over the next twenty three generations, they reactivated to repair damage from cosmic rays. Finally, they restarted your organs when the lava rock thawed you out."

Sky looked at his hands as if they'd become foreign objects. "What else can they do to me?"

"Make you sing like a bird."

Sky studied Michael with trepidation, expecting to begin chirping. Nothing came out.

Michael laughed. "I was joking, Eskander. Relax. The motes can do many things for you, but they can't easily override your own neural instructions. It's not a struggle that would do us any good."

Sky raised an eyebrow at Michael. He scratched his head, then wondered if he had done it or Michael.

"I did not do it, Eskander. If I wanted a machine in human form, I wouldn't start with a human. I need you to be yourself. And you are, to paraphrase a truly ancient document, my only chosen son, in whom I am well pleased. I won't hurt you."

Sky slowly sat back down to finish his meal. "And these little bits of dust in my head allow you to read my thoughts."

"Yes. Finish that bite and I'll show you where to clean up and sleep. We'll continue tomorrow."

"Tomorrow?"

"The next wake period. Come on," Michael said, rising from the table.

* * *

Sky could not sleep despite his exhaustion and the damage his body suffered. His mind burned. This is just too incredible, he thought. I must really be lying in a snowbank, delirious. A god who says that he isn't a god, and that people did not arise on this world. Though, come to think of it, the religious traditions do say that Huf created them elsewhere and brought the First People across the ocean. That is similar.

His cracked lips were real. His frostbitten face was real. But their demands for attention lay subdued under the flood of new concepts.

He rubbed the amazingly comfortable mattress and touched the soft texture of the fine linens. It certainly felt real, if unusual.

He sniffed his forearm. The delicate scent of the soap Michael had instructed him to use lingered there. Sky had never luxuriated like this, even as a general in Prater. And "tomorrow" he would learn the rest of the answer to the question that had dogged him across half the world.

It struck him that he did not yet know his future at Michael's hands. God or not, he had power to do whatever he wanted with Sky. Maybe, he thought with a tinge of fear, Michael's plan for me, the rest of my "mission", does not include ever seeing Atna and Dalen again.

Anger rose out of his determination and his fear, but his thoughts began to dart randomly and fatigue took control. He finally slept.

He broke fast in Michael's favorite room, gazing out on the world. The world that was not *The World*, but one of many worlds scattered through an invisible sky, if Michael was to be believed. Michael had led him back to this chamber, where a hearty meal waited, then disappeared to let him enjoy it without distraction. When Sky put down his fork after the last bite and drank the last of his water, Michael walked in.

"Come sit in this chair by the window," Michael said. "It's more comfortable."

Sky crossed the room, paused to enjoy the view, and sat in the cushioned chair. Michael took its twin.

"Do you have questions or comments, Eskander?" Michael asked.

"Yes. Don't call me Eskander. My name is Sky."

"Sorry."

"That's all right," Sky frowned and shook his head. "There were words I don't understand in the part about my freezing: skells, and cosmic biotus?"

Michael said, "Not important. My intent was to show you there was no magic involved. It might seem magic, but it's just fancy tools. In fact, your freezing and thawing with the help of the motes is the technique the colonists used to cross between suns—a distance so great that it took centuries, pardon me, tens of generations."

"You said I have a mission. Will I be allowed to see my family again?"

"Yes, the mission continues from Tombak. And you've done very well so far. But the job isn't done, and won't be until we again launch ships to other suns. Stars, they're called. That's your purpose. Though you won't live to see it happen; that will take more than a hundred generations if all goes well. But *you* are the catalyst that accelerates the process in these times.

"I waited a long time for the confluence of circumstances. You were ambitious, a rising power, intelligent, fearless, but just another dead end if you had become the king of Prater. This world needed a jolt to get out of its rut, to overcome the stasis of a people that had never seen stars.

"The volcano that brought you back to life had shown signs of pending eruption. I did not know the precise time of its advent, but a few years one way or the other didn't matter. The snow people were ripe for a nicely managed prophecy. I did manifest as Huf to Pinal, to initiate the prophecy.

"You noticed the revival in Prater that followed the war? That's a common effect if a kingdom is left with its wealth intact. The future gets more attention. And now the snowmen are open to peaceful contact from sunward and can guide parties into the snowlands to study stars. The ship's navigators you encountered have the basic mathematics to begin understanding the motion of this world relative to the universe, and the implications of that.

"You are uniquely positioned to tie everything together. You are the only living human who has seen a star. You personally know people in cultures all across the world. The city of Tombak makes iron and the world needs to have it, and you know the trade routes."

"But," Sky said. "Tombak won't trade their iron."

Michael smiled. "They won't trade iron *weapons*. But weapons aren't the only iron trade goods. You haven't considered the impact that iron sewing needles will have, or iron carpenter tools, or loom heddles, or nails, or fishhooks. Go back to Tombak and get rich trading these small things. And watch the world change."

Sky thought for a time. "You mean, everything I've gone through since I was a child was directing me to be the catalyst that will take our people back into the sky?"

Michael shrugged. "Not since childhood, no. Since you became a general. And not everything. That's what I meant by not wanting a human shaped machine. You act by your own will to circumstances that I helped create with small influences. I selected you because the time was right and you were right. My analysis suggested your nature would accomplish what I needed with minimal guidance."

"And that's my purpose in life, my 'mission'." Sky sighed. "Nothing to do with eternity in heaven."

"Again, Sky, I'm sorry. But no, at least not by my efforts. Consider that, despite your hardship, you've already beat the average; you're forty one years old."

"Then what about the things Joit told me? If you're not Huf, who is? Is there one God who will collect the righteous after death and haul them to heaven?"

Michael sat quietly for a moment. "I don't know," he said. "We learned a lot about the universe, but there's always more left to learn. Maybe that 'more' is God. Knowledgeable as we became, we never resolved the God question."

"So Joit could have been right?"

"It's always possible."

"Good," Sky said. Maybe the real search is not done, he thought.

Michael said quietly, "And where will you look?"

Sky, still unused to the mind-reading, smiled grimly back. "At home," he said.

"You won't accept the rest of the mission?"

"I'll go to Mombat with the request to trade in needles and fishhooks. But when I get home I'll stay home. An agent will do the traveling for me. If you expected me to round up navigators and soldiers and snowmen to gaze into the sky of the twilight land, then you'll be disappointed."

"No," Michael said with a sad look, "If you decline, it will follow on its own. It'll just take longer without somebody who has the whole vision. And your mission will leach out through your agents. You will have an effect through them, just as I did through you.

"You look much healthier, Sky. Do you want to rest here longer, or do you feel ready to go home?"

"Home."

Michael nodded.

Sky asked, "What do I tell people about you and my visit here?"

"Use your own discretion. Most people will think you're crazy. Some will believe, but many of those are not desirable company."

"I want Atna to believe."

"All right," Michael said. "I can help there. Say to her that I told you the child she carries now is a girl, and she will have a crescent birthmark on her left ankle."

"She's pregnant?"

"Yes, she wanted to spare you the anguish of leaving her to take Joit on the Jefk."

Sky shook his head. "A girl, you say."

"Yes."

"Well, I'd better round up Jasper, somehow."

Michael's eye's twinkled, amused. "Jasper found the grass plateau and is accepted into a horse herd. He's happy. And I can get you home quicker without him."

"The flying machine?"

Michael nodded.

Sky said, "One last question. Why did you wait till I was nearly frozen before you appeared?"

"I thought I didn't have to. That you would turn back long before. You're just too stubborn for your own good."

* * *

Sky strode across his undeveloped land toward his settlement, stopping once to look back at the flying machine, but it was gone. He scanned the sky and saw nothing. It made sense that if Michael could make things visible which did not exist, then he could make solid things disappear. He topped a rise and stopped, confused. "My developed land is in crops," he puzzled. "Oh," he realized, "the neighbors."

Then he saw Atna pouring out grain for the horses, her rounded belly obvious. He called her name. She looked up. She smiled to outshine the sun.

The End